D1255386

IMMORTAL
OUTLAW

Immortal Brotherhood Novels by Lisa Hendrix

IMMORTAL WARRIOR
IMMORTAL OUTLAW

IMMORTAL OUTLAW

LISA HENDRIX

BERKLEY SENSATION, NEW YORK

THE BERKLEY PUBLISHING GROUP
Published by the Penguin Group
Penguin Group (USA) Inc.
375 Hudson Street, New York, New York 10014, USA
Penguin Group (Canada), 90 Eglinton Avenue East, Suite 700, Toronto, Ontario M4P 2Y3, Canada
(a division of Pearson Penguin Canada Inc.)
Penguin Books Ltd., 80 Strand, London WC2R 0RL, England
Penguin Group Ireland, 25 St. Stephen's Green, Dublin 2, Ireland (a division of Penguin Books Ltd.)
Penguin Group (Australia), 250 Camberwell Road, Camberwell, Victoria 3124, Australia
(a division of Pearson Australia Group Pty. Ltd.)
Penguin Books India Pvt. Ltd., 11 Community Centre, Panchsheel Park, New Delhi—110 017, India
Penguin Group (NZ), 67 Apollo Drive, Rosedale, North Shore 0632, New Zealand
(a division of Pearson New Zealand Ltd.)
Penguin Books (South Africa) (Pty.) Ltd., 24 Sturdee Avenue, Rosebank, Johannesburg 2196,
South Africa

Penguin Books Ltd., Registered Offices: 80 Strand, London WC2R 0RL, England

This is a work of fiction. Names, characters, places, and incidents either are the product of the author's imagination or are used fictitiously, and any resemblance to actual persons, living or dead, business establishments, events, or locales is entirely coincidental. The publisher does not have any control over and does not assume any responsibility for author or third-party websites or their content.

IMMORTAL OUTLAW

A Berkley Sensation Book / published by arrangement with the author

ISBN-13: 978-1-61523-142-3

BERKLEY® SENSATION
Berkley Sensation Books are published by The Berkley Publishing Group,
a division of Penguin Group (USA) Inc.,
375 Hudson Street, New York, New York 10014.
BERKLEY® SENSATION and the "B" design are trademarks of Penguin Group (USA) Inc.

PRINTED IN THE UNITED STATES OF AMERICA

To Kaldi and his goats,
without whom this book
would not have been completed.

The Legend

SENT BY THEIR jarl to capture a great treasure of gold and jewels, the warriors led by Brand Einarsson fell under a spell cast by the powerful sorceress who guarded the hoard and whose son they had killed. The witch Cwen cursed them to spend eternity as shadow beasts, living half as animal, half as man, each taking the form of his fylgja, the spirit companion whose image he wore. After she worked her foul magic, Cwen took their amulets and had them scattered across the land so they would never be found, and she drove the men off into the forest to live their accursed lives.

Some twelve-score years later, Ivar Graycloak, known to the Normans who by then ruled England as Ivo de Vassy, found both his amulet and a woman who loved him even knowing the monster he was, and through their combined magic, Cwen's power over him was broken. The eight remaining warriors found hope in Ivar's victory and began to scour the English countryside for their fylgja amulets. They ransacked ancient ruins and burial mounds, standing stones and wells, graveyards, and even the most venerable buildings of the Christian church, searching for some trace or clue of the amulets. And as they searched, they also watched for signs of Cwen, who had been sore wounded and gone to ground.

Decades passed and neither Cwen nor any of the amulets were found, and the warriors lost hope and once more resigned themselves to their half lives. Slowly, as Ivar had, some began to make their way along the edges of humankind, finding work and friends and even the occasional moment of peace among mortal men and women.

Others could not, their animal forms being too strange to move easily among the beasts of England or too deadly to live near her people. One of these was Steinarr, son of Birgir BentLeg, called Steinarr the Proud, who so terrified the English as the lion he became each night that he was driven from forest to forest without cease and who did such damage to the other warriors that most would not tolerate his company. But even a man who lives in the wilds has need of clothing and food and other things of men, so he learned to find coin where he could, turning to thievery, banditry, and even, when the opportunity presented itself, to hunting men . . .

—from the *Dyrrekkr Saga of Ari Sturlusson*
(E.L. Branson, trans.)

CHAPTER 1

Nottinghamshire, August 1290

HE KNEW BETTER than to try to help an Englishman.

But this one was old and tiny, and the reavers attacking him were young and hale and armed with clubs. And three against one was too many, even when the one wielded a quarterstaff and knew how to use it. Steinarr tossed his packhorse's reins over the nearest branch and quickly fitted an arrow to his bowstring. Before he could take the shot, however, the biggest of the three slipped in behind the old man and brought his club down hard. The crack made Steinarr's stomach clench; he well knew the sound of a deathblow.

His arrow hit the outlaw's shoulder before the old man hit the ground. The reaver bellowed with pain, and his two friends whirled, searching for their attacker. In quick order, two more arrows thudded into the side of the cart between them, and they panicked. Spinning their horses around, they tore away. The injured man trailed after them, weaving perilously in his saddle, the shaft of Steinarr's arrow protruding from his back. Steinarr sent another arrow whizzing past his ear into a tree for good measure, then watched the three disappear up the road.

When they were gone, he galloped over to the old man and leapt off to check him. It was too late; he was gone, his eyes empty and his skull laid open like a gourd, his blood darkening the dust of the road.

Steinarr lifted the old man's flat purse from his belt and emptied it into his palm. All that tumbled out were two silver farthing pieces. Not even a full penny. He shook his head in disgust. Thievery he understood. He practiced it himself when he needed to, waylaying a merchant or nobleman or the occasional churchman when other means of getting money failed. But he chose only those with silver to spare, and he left their skulls intact. These three had set upon a poor man and killed him merely for the sake of killing.

And he, fool that he was, had both failed to save the old man and lost one of his best steel arrowheads in the process. Steinarr considered taking the old man's cart as recompense, but it looked about to fall to pieces, as did the sad little mare, more bones than meat, that stood between the shafts. Even the harness she wore had been patched a dozen times, apparently with more hope than skill. Weighing what little he might gain against the time he would lose taking them to market, he decided to keep the halfpenny and send the mare back down the road for others to find.

First, though, there was the body to deal with. Steinarr dropped the farthings into his purse, and then dragged the old man off the road a little way. He used the edge of his shield to scrape a shallow grave, which he covered over afterward with stones and brush. It wasn't a good grave, but it would serve for the time being, and he could tell the priest in the next village where to find the body to do a better job. Finishing, he took a moment to stand over the grave, silently asking the gods to watch over the old man on his journey.

"His name was John," said a soft voice behind him. "John Little."

Steinarr whirled, hand reaching for sword, but he froze as the voice registered and he saw who stood in the verge. *A woman? Here?* "Where did you come from?"

"There, my lord," she said, pointing to a thick patch of bracken a few yards behind her, still swaying where she had passed. "John heard them coming and bade us hide. He said no one rides that hard in this part of the forest but outlaws or soldiers, and that we wanted to meet neither, since they are so often much the same."

"You are fortunate. If those three had seen you . . ." He knew by the way she blanched that she understood his meaning. "'Tis a shame John Little did not take his own good advice."

"He thought they would not trouble with him. He had nothing of value to steal."

"Only his life," said Steinarr, and her moss green eyes glittered with tears as she nodded. He gave her a moment to collect herself before he asked, "What was John Little to you? Father? Servant?"

"Neither. A kind stranger who offered his aid when our horse went lame."

"You said 'our.' Who is the other?"

"My cousin." Twisting, she spoke over her shoulder to the bracken. "Stand up and let this good man see you, Rob. He means us no harm."

A tall, bony lad wearing a green chape over his reddish hair slowly unfolded from the bracken. He hadn't filled out yet, but by the small, pointed beard that decorated his chin, he must be about the same age as the maid, perhaps eight and ten.

He appraised Steinarr warily. "How do you know? He looks like one of *them*."

"And so I might be."

The maid shook her head. "You drove them off."

"Perhaps I hoped to rob the old man for myself."

"He did empty John's purse," pointed out the boy.

"He would be a fool to bury John's money with him." She turned back to Steinarr. "I am sure he intends to return it to John's family."

"'Tis only a halfpenny," said Steinarr.

"Several days' food for a poor man," she said.

And didn't he know it? Steinarr decided to shift her mind to other matters. "You were foolish to reveal yourselves. What is your name, boy?"

"Rober—"

"Robin," interrupted the woman. "His name is Robin. Mine is Marian. We are pilgrims."

The boy looked flustered, but nodded. "Aye, pilgrims. Bound to Lincoln to pray to Saint Hugh."

But not bound to tell the truth, apparently—not that their

lies or their true purpose made any difference to Steinarr. He pulled the two arrows out of the cart and returned them to his quiver, then swung up on the stallion and started up the road to retrieve the shaft he'd put into the tree. "Well, *Robin*, I hope you take better care of your cousin on the rest of your journey. Fare you well."

"No!" She bolted out onto the road after him. "Surely you will not leave us here alone, my lord."

"You have your saint to protect you," Steinarr said over his shoulder. "I am told that should be enough for a good Christian."

"But those men will be waiting for us."

"Possibly."

"They will kill us!"

"If you are lucky," he said darkly, and once more saw his warning raise a shadow of fear in her eyes. Good. She should be afraid, especially with only Robin for protection. He'd already shown his colors—a lad that size should have been fighting next to the old man, not hiding in the bushes. "Go back to Sheffield and wait for a larger group of travelers. It should only be a day or two."

"He is right," said the boy, flicking a spider off his sleeve as he joined her in the road. "We should have waited to begin with."

"We have no time for waiting," she muttered, then louder, "Why can we not travel with you, my lord?"

"Because I have better things to do than play shepherd to stray pilgrims." Steinarr reached the tree, worked the arrow loose, and jammed it into the quiver with the others. "Make haste, so you are out of the forest by dark. A safe journey to you."

Which would have been a good way to take his leave, except he'd forgotten that his rouncey was still tied where he'd left him, and these supposed pilgrims stood between him and his horse. As he turned the stallion around to go back, hope flared in their eyes. In *her* eyes.

"No." He shook his head firmly. "I only fetch my pack horse. Your path is there." He pointed back the way they should go, then swung his arm around to point south and east. "And I go that way."

She stood there in the road open-mouthed as he retrieved the rouncey, and she was still there when he led the horse back into the road. He could feel her accusing eyes burning into his back as he headed off. He was nearly out of hearing when he heard her call out, "Some help here, Robin, if you please." He glanced back to see her tugging at the mare's harness.

Good. They were going back. Satisfied, he cantered the horses until he'd left the pilgrims well behind, then let the animals settle back into a walk. Keeping one eye alert for the outlaws, he let his mind wander to other things. He was working through his plans for capturing Long Tom when the sound of an approaching horse snapped him back to the present and sent his hand to his bow. He already had an arrow nocked to the string when he realized the sound was behind him, not ahead.

Them. His curse echoed through the forest as he turned. "You go the wrong way, Pilgrims."

"We go the way we must, my lord," the maid called back, as they came bouncing up the road bareback on the old mare.

Then they would go it alone. Making a quick decision, Steinarr reined his horses off the road and headed into the forest.

"I told you," he heard the boy say. "He will not suffer our company."

"I care little for what he will suffer. Go after him." She said something else Steinarr couldn't hear, and they kept coming, the little mare trotting along gamely.

Balls. Perhaps the creature would have been worth taking to sell after all—and if he'd taken her, they wouldn't be following him now. In an effort to discourage them, he sent his horses crashing through a thicket. But the branches slowed his animals, while the mare actually gained ground using the way he'd cleared. Determined to be rid of the pair, Steinarr led them deeper, twisting and turning through the thickest part of the forest in a path as crooked as a ram's horn. They stuck like burrs.

"Stubborn fools," he muttered to himself. They had no idea who—*what*—they were following, nor what trouble they would be in come sundown if they succeeded. Abruptly he wheeled his horse around and drew his short sword. "I will cut that animal's throat if you do not go back."

The boy reined the mare to a halt and backed her up a few steps. "I am sorry, my lord, but my sister . . ."

"Sister?" Steinarr pounced on the word. "I thought she was your cousin."

"I *am* his cousin," said the girl quickly. "He was going to say that his sister is very ill and our pilgrimage is for her sake. He fears that if we go back instead of forward, our prayers will come too late."

"He fears that, does he?" Steinarr nudged his horse closer, glaring at the maid for a long moment before he shifted his frown to the boy. "Do you also fear to speak, that you let your *cousin* put words in your mouth?"

The boy flushed, but raised his hands in a gesture of helplessness. "I find she does whether I speak or not, my lord."

Despite himself, Steinarr snorted back a laugh. "No doubt. And she likely talked you into coming after me as well."

"Aye, my lord, she did that."

"Then you are both fools, putting yourself at the mercy of a stranger, deep in a wild forest, riding an animal that could founder at any moment."

"The mare is stronger than she looks," said the maid, adding, "my lord," as if in afterthought. "She will carry us well enough, so long as you keep your blade from her throat."

Steinarr waggled said blade, sending shafts of light glinting around her head. "Perhaps I should use it on that tongue."

"Perhaps, my lord, but you will not."

Not a whiff of fear in her, when it came to this. Steinarr frowned. "You speak with great sureness, considering you do not even know my name."

"I saw you take the time to bury an old man you did not know. That is enough for me. The name I will learn as we ride together."

His glower deepened. "We will not ride together."

"But you go the same direction we do." She took a long look around her, and a crease formed between her brows. "At least, you did. I am no longer certain . . ."

"And yet you follow me like puppies."

"Only because you force us to it. Please, my lord, let us go on with you. We will be no trouble."

"You are already trouble," he said flatly. He glanced around to get his bearings, then pointed once more. "The road is that way. Go." He turned and rode away.

Behind him the boy began, "If we hurry, we ca—"

"Do not," she snapped. "Do *not*! Ride after him. Go."

Pigheaded little wench. Steinarr pushed the horses a little faster, even as he calculated whether he was going to have to let these dogged pilgrims catch him. He'd lost the entire morning in burying the old man, and now he was losing the afternoon in trying to shake off these two. It had grown too late to send them back; nightfall would catch them still in the woods among the wolves and worse.

The problem was it had grown too late to take them forward as well. If he escorted them on, he was the one who would be caught, changing into the lion too close to where men lived. A cow or sheep—or worse, a man— would be found half-eaten, and frightened, angry peasants would pour into the forest with traps and snares and spears and dogs searching for the beast who had done it. He'd be forced to move on yet again and end up freezing his balls off in Scotland.

"Scotland!" he muttered, and the stallion swiveled his ears around to listen. In four hundreds of years, he'd come to hate Scotland and the Scots even more than he hated England and the English. Every man of them seemed to own a hound the size of a horse, and their weather was as vicious as their dogs. "That's what I get for helping one of these cursed Englishmen. Nothing good ever comes of it. Ever!"

Just then, the maid laughed at something her cousin said, as if to remind Steinarr that she, too, would have died, if those outlaws had found her hiding in the bracken. Now that would have been a shame, he thought, glancing back at her. She was a comely thing, young and fair, with full, red lips and honey-colored braids that peeped from beneath her linen headcloth. She wore a simple gown of dark brown wool, laced to show the curves of her body, in the way Englishwomen tormented their men these days. She caught him looking back at her and leaned against her reedy cousin to murmur something that made the lad grin.

"Cousin!" snorted Steinarr under his breath. "Lover more likely. There's an angry father on their heels, I wager. That's why they don't want to go back the way they came." The lad didn't seem bold enough to lure a quick-tongued creature like that into his bed. Perhaps it was she who did the luring . . . though why, Steinarr couldn't fathom. He assessed the boy out of the corner of his eye: All knees and elbows. Spot-faced. Scarred chin beneath the beard that tried to disguise it. Craven. Unless the lad carried Frey's own pillock inside those breeks, he had little to recommend him.

Well, whatever they were to each other, he'd rather not see the crows picking over their lion-killed bodies come morning. There was only one thing to be done. He reined his horses around in a circle, so he could fall in alongside the mare.

"Steinarr," he said. They both blinked, not comprehending, so he repeated, "I am called Steinarr."

"Oh." The maid found her tongue first, of course. "Does this mean you—?"

"It means I have no stomach for leaving innocents in the forest as wolf bait, even when they have wasted much of my day. We will make camp nearby where you will be safe, and in the morning, I will see you as far as Maltby. After that, you find your own way."

"We are grateful, my lord," said the boy, relief clear on his face.

"Most grateful." The girl battled to keep the smugness out of her smile. "You will not be sorry, my lord."

"Mmm." Steinarr spurred the stallion ahead again before he was tempted to make *her* sorry.

One of his favorite campsites—a shallow cave tucked into the side of a hill—lay nearby, and he led them to it with plenty of daylight to spare. He started unsaddling the stallion, and to the pilgrims' credit, they both set to work without being told. As soon as the mare was secure, the boy hurried over to unload the rouncey, while the girl started casting about for firewood. By the time she returned with her first scant armload of twigs, all three horses were nibbling at the grass nearby and Steinarr was shredding dry bark and leaves into tinder, in preparation for laying a fire.

"Others must have made camp here recently, my lord. There is little wood left on the ground."

"Not others. Me. Last month. There is a fallen tree over that way, about a bowshot. You will find wood enough there." He jerked his head toward the east, then pulled his scramasax from his belt and proffered it hilt first to the boy. "Here. You need something heavier than that plaything at your waist. You'll want four or five good armloads each to keep the wolves at bay all night. See you're done and back here well before sunset."

Steinarr watched until he was certain they were headed in the right direction, then took out his flint and striker and went to work. A tiny flame soon crackled before the shallow cave. He added enough twigs to keep it going until the pilgrims brought real wood, then retrieved his quiver. As the bees buzzed lazily overhead, he pulled out several good, straight reeds he'd been drying for arrows, selected the best, and began to work it smooth with the file he kept for the purpose. The girl and her cousin came and went several times, dumping armloads of wood into a pile nearby, and Steinarr kept working, scraping until the shaft met his satisfaction, then nocking it and working the tip down to a point, which he carefully cured over the fire. Smoke-hardened reed made a poor substitute for good steel, but it would have to do until he could buy more points—that was his penalty for helping an Englishman.

He glanced up as it occurred to him that he hadn't seen his other penalties in a while and that he hadn't heard any chopping either. Even with the long summer afternoon, he would have to leave soon to make certain he was well away by sunset, and he needed to make sure his pilgrims, or lovers, or whatever they were, were safe by the fire before he left. Muttering about their parentage, he slipped the unfletched new arrow into his quiver and pushed to his feet. He'd gone barely a dozen yards when he heard them coming through the woods, laughing and talking.

"What took you so long?" he demanded as they neared.

"It is still well before sunset, my lord." The maid carefully held out a wide curl of bark, piled with brambleberries. I made Robin wait so I could gather some."

He'd forgotten the berries. They hadn't been ripe yet when last he'd been here. "Mmm. Well, I hope you got enough, for they will be your only supper. There was no way to hunt with you two chattering like jays."

"Oh, we have food, my lord," said the boy. "Bread and cheese."

"We would not set out without food," said the maid, adding, "We are not the utter fools you think us."

"We shall see about that." *Cheese.* Steinarr's stomach rumbled at the mere mention of it. *And bread.* His meals had been nothing but wild foods and small game for far too long. "You'd better cut some boughs for your beds, while 'tis still light. I'll take the horses for water."

Steinarr dug through his gear bag for a small leather pail, then led all three horses around the hill to the tiny spring that made this campsite one of the better ones he'd had recently. He filled the pail first, then stood back to let the animals have their fill while he contemplated the possibility of melting some of that cheese over the bread before he had to leave. By the time he led the horses back to camp, imagination had him smelling the toasting bread.

He quickly secured the rouncey. As he bent to hobble the mare, he heard light footsteps coming up behind him. "What?"

"You had no dinner today because of us, my lord. I thought you might be hungry."

He glanced over his shoulder to find her holding out a thick slice of coarse, dark bread. Melted cheese, rich and savory, oozed over the fire-browned edges. The smell alone pulled him to his feet, and he reached out greedily. He took a bite and groaned as the warm cheese hit his tongue.

She accepted the tribute with a nod of her head. "You are welcome."

He made some indistinguishable grunts of thanks and took another huge bite. Stepping past him, she stroked the mare's nose, and he was amused to hear her whisper a few words of thanks to the creature for bearing her and the boy. Next, she went to the stallion, where she murmured a greeting and let him sniff at her palm. Her brow wrinkled in puzzlement, then cleared a bit.

"Ah. He has a raw spot. I think the saddle rubs." She moved around to run her hands over the animal's withers and suddenly stopped. "God's knees. What happened here?"

"He was attacked."

"By what?" She traced the scar lines that raked the stallion's back, spreading her fingers wide to match the breadth of the lion's paw. "They look like claw marks." She lifted her eyes to accuse him. "Or whip marks."

"I would not whip my own horse," growled Steinarr, flushing in fresh shame at what he'd done to his friend so long ago. And not just to Torvald. Nearly every man in the crew had felt those claws, either as man or beast. Steinarr choked down the last of the bread, now gone tasteless, and stepped around to join her. He laid a hand over the scars in apology for the lie he was about to tell to protect them both. "'Twas wolves. One leapt on his back. The wounds are long healed, but I need a new pad to protect the scars better."

In truth, he needed two new pads: the one for the rouncey was just as bad.

She touched the raw spot, and the stallion's flesh rippled as if he shook off a fly. "I have some help, I think." She untied the knot in one long sleeve and fished a tiny wooden pot out of the hem. She twisted the stopper free and dug out a bit of greenish salve on one finger.

"What is that?"

"A balm I carry to ward off blisters on the road." She gently daubed the salve over the wound. "It should bring some ease."

Steinarr had the distinct impression she spoke to the stallion and not him, but he nodded anyway. She finished tending the horse and rubbed the excess into her hands, and as they walked the few yards back to the fire, he admitted, "You may be slightly less trouble than I first thought."

"Thank you, my lord." She picked up another slab of cheese-covered bread from a flat stone that lay at the edge of the coals and handed it to him. "My name is Marian."

He frowned. "I know. You told me earlier."

"You never said it, my lord, not all day," said the boy, coming up to throw a big load of green boughs into the mouth of the cave. "Nor my name. We thought you had forgotten."

"You were mistaken." There had simply been no reason to use names when he'd planned to be rid of them. Steinarr savored another bite as he checked the sun once more. "Well, Marian and Robin, I must leave you now."

Robin started. "Leave? But you said—"

"That you would be safe here, not that I would stay here with you."

"But where will you be?"

"Nearby. Stay near the fire and keep it well stoked and you will be fine. And you will want to . . ." He stumbled to a stop, not sure how to say this to a woman. "Um . . . take care of your needs early." The creases across her brow told him he hadn't been clear, and he tried again. "You can't be going off into the bushes after dark. The wolves." *And the lion.*

Faint pink roses blossomed in her cheeks, but she nodded. "I understand, my lord."

"Good. 'Tis important." He retrieved the roll of clothing that was Torvald's, snagged one more large piece of bread and cheese, and swung up on the stallion bareback, having decided to leave the saddle where it was, secure for once. "I will return a little after sunrise. Be ready."

"We will be, my lord," promised Robin.

"And I will keep some bread and cheese for you," added Marian.

"Do that," called Steinarr as he rode off.

He rode downwind far enough that Torvald's cries of agony during the changing wouldn't be heard, then slid to the ground. He placed the bread and Torvald's clothes on a nearby log for his friend to find when he was a man again, then stripped the bridle from the stallion and hung it in a nearby tree, where it would be safe for the night.

"Guard over them, and we will meet back here, first thing. Cheese or not, I want to be rid of them by midday."

His only answer was the sound of the stallion chewing a mouthful of grass, but it didn't matter; Torvald kept a part of his human-self intact while he was in the stallion's form. He would remember, at least enough, and watch from a distance to see that the lion stayed away. Without bothering to say good-bye, Steinarr set out on foot, trotting away from camp as fast as the terrain would permit. By the time the last of the sun's disk finally slipped below the horizon, he had put enough distance and enough trees between himself and his two pilgrims that the lion's roar should be little more than a whisper on the evening breeze.

CHAPTER 2

IT WAS AMAZING every beast in the forest wasn't ringing their camp, thought Steinarr as he rode back the next morning. The aroma of toasting bread and cheese permeated the still air, and if he could smell it as a man, every creature within a league certainly had the scent. And it did smell wondrous good. By the time he reached the cave, his mouth was watering so much he could barely order young Robin to finish loading up the rouncey.

"And good morning to you, too, my lord," said Marian, handing him some bread and cheese without waiting for him to ask. She stood watching, bemused, as he gobbled it down and took a second piece. As the sharpness of his hunger eased, he looked around. "Are you two ready to go?"

"We will be by the time you finish." She grabbed the pail and dumped water over the dying fire. A cloud of steam boiled up, forcing Steinarr to step back. As it cleared, he saw her heading into the woods.

"Where are you going?" he called.

"The bushes, my lord, now that it is light. Unless you suggest I avoid them all day as well?" She glanced over her shoulder, giving him a bland gaze that made the blood rise in his neck. "Though God's truth, I hope you do not, because I fear I could not manage it."

She sailed off before he could form an answer, and behind him, the boy chuckled. "See? She does have a way of making a man realize he has no wits at all."

A man? This puppy fancied himself a man? Keeping his opinions of Robin and his cousin to himself with difficulty, Steinarr set about saddling the stallion, carefully lining up the thickest parts of the pad to protect the raw place on the animal's withers. Robin finished loading the rouncey and moved on to the mare, and by the time Marian reappeared, all three horses were ready. She grabbed her bundle and put its tie-rope over her shoulder as Robin swung up on the mare. He reached down to help her. "Up you come, Maud."

She gave him a look that would curdle milk. "I think, *Robin*, that I will have better luck if you move her next to the boulder."

"No need." Steinarr stepped around the stallion, laced his fingers together, and stooped down. "Here."

"Thank you, my lord." As she raised her foot, her bundle slipped, pulling her off balance. She reached out to steady herself.

The sudden contact made Steinarr glance up. She was right there, so close he could feel her breath on his face, her hand gripping his shoulder as though she were comforting him. And, oh, how he needed the kind of comfort she could offer. Needed softness and smooth skin and the warmth of another human body. Needed a woman. *This woman. Now.* Her eyes, level with his because of the way he was bent, widened, and suddenly he was floating in their green depths, cool as a woodland pool on a summer's day. All he had to do was drown himself in that pool, in her, and it would all be washed away, all the empty years. As if in a dream, he swayed toward her.

Somewhere far above, Robin cleared his throat. Marian blinked and jerked her hand away, and the connection between them snapped like spider silk. A sudden loneliness welled up at the loss, so thick it made Steinarr's chest ache. He swallowed it back and worked to make his voice sound normal. "Let us try that again."

She nodded, and he handed her up onto the mare without further trouble, though a pang of unreasoned envy twisted through him as she wrapped her arms around the boy's waist. Steinarr let one hand linger on her foot, using that last fragment of contact, of warmth, to steady himself as he turned his attention to Robin, "I intend to move quickly. Keep up."

It took an act of will to move his hand, to force himself away and onto his horse, but soon they were off, the
rouncey trotting along behind on its lead while the mare
brought up the rear. The narrow forest paths forced them to
ride single file, thank the gods. It gave Steinarr the time he
needed to consider what had happened.

It wasn't Marian in particular, he decided, but the simple
fact that she was female and that it had been so long. Too
many months had passed since he'd had a little spare coin
to throw at a whore—better than two years, now that he
thought about it. Two years without human contact beyond
the occasional marketplace handshake. No wonder he'd
reacted so violently to that simple touch. Still reacted—for
he could still feel the weight of her hand on his flesh. He
needed a woman, for certs.

Well, that was something that could be dealt with just as
soon as he collected the bounty on Long Tom. Even with
the saddle pads and arrow points and flour and salt, there
should be a few pence left for him and Torvald each to have
a woman. He would make certain there was.

By the time they reached the great road and could ride
abreast, he would have been fine, except that the breeze
kept wafting the scent of Marian toward him—the intoxi-
cating combination of woman overlain with the aroma of
her simple cooking. And then there was the way she kept
eyeing him, like she wanted to say something.

He finally had enough of it. "What?"

She started at his abrupt demand. "Nothing, my lord."

"Then why are you staring at me?"

"Was I? I was only thinking of how much you enjoyed
the cheese and bread. You must have been in the forest a
long while to take so much pleasure in such simple fare."

"It has been some time," he admitted. "My business
keeps me to the wilds."

"Are you a spy?"

She asked so bluntly, he almost laughed. "Why would
you think that?"

"Because I have never heard speech like yours, my lord,
nor the name *Steinarr*. But I *have* heard that the Welsh and

the Scots and others send spies against England who creep through our countryside looking to know the strength of our armies."

"A spy would gain more knowledge in the cities than in the depths of the forest."

"Perhaps. But your name *is* odd, my lord."

"It is an ancient name, from a time before the Conqueror. It is common enough in the north." All of which was truer than either of them could imagine. "Never fear. I am no spy."

"Are you an outlaw, then?" asked Marian.

He did chuckle this time. "Must a man be a spy or outlaw to pass his days in the woods?"

"Or forester or woodward or charcoal burner. But you are too clean for the last and not furnished for the first. You do not even wear a proper baldric."

"I might yet be a woodward. Or a huntsman for some noble house."

She looked him up and down and said confidently, "No. Your gear is old and worn, but it is a knight's gear. I think you are of noble birth, and that you are outlawed."

His amusement faded. "Then you are mistaken. I *hunt* outlaws—for the bounty. Outlaws hide in the forest, so I follow them to find them."

"You make it sound simple, but surely it is a dangerous way to earn your silver," she said.

"Less so than you might think." He left it at that, not wanting to encourage further prying. He could never explain that he could not be killed.

But Robin suddenly grew a tongue. "Do you go to hunt outlaws after you leave us, my lord?"

"Aye. I would likely have one in hand already if not for those reavers."

"If not for *us*, you mean." Robin twisted to give his cousin a significant look, then turned back to Steinarr. "Forgive us, my lord. We should have done as you said and gone back."

"No, we should not." A breeze whipped a loose strand of hair across Marian's cheek and she brushed it away impatiently. "Our task is equally important. More so."

"But we have kept this man from his living," argued Robin. "And from the king's duty."

"Perhaps. Perhaps not." She glared at Steinarr, challenging him. "If you hunt outlaws, my lord, why did you not ride down the men who killed John Little?"

"You think one man could so easily capture three?"

"You drove them off easily enough."

"Driving off and capturing are two different things. However, if I find there are bounties to be had, I may eventually track them. Otherwise, I spend my time where I will see sure reward . . . unless stray puppies come whining after me and I must do otherwise."

She had nothing to say to that beyond an outraged huff, and her silence influenced Robin, so the peace lasted the rest of the morning. That was both good and bad. Good, in that she wasn't prying anymore, and bad, in that in the process of not prying, she kept those full lips of hers pressed into a thin, stubborn line that taunted Steinarr with the thought of kissing them soft. He contemplated the notion for miles. It was pointless, but it occupied him nonetheless, and by the time they rode out of the trees into the outlying fields of Maltby, he had devised at least a half-dozen ways he might make it happen before they parted, none of which he intended to act on. He wanted to be shed of these two, not further entangled with them.

Marian had apparently been thinking as well, for as they reached the first cottages, she mused aloud, "The bounty on a thief is ten shillings, is it not?"

"Aye," he said warily.

She closed her eyes and took a deep breath. "I will see you receive five shillings if you will escort us on our journey."

"Maud!" exclaimed Robert, then, "Ow!"

Had she just pinched him? Something about that name, Maud, displeased her; Steinarr had noticed her sour look earlier when the boy had used it, but had dismissed it, thinking it was simply an eke name she didn't like. But perhaps not. Perhaps it was her true name, or gave away her true name, for he was as certain as ever that she was not really called Marian, as Robin was not really called Robin. So what was the long form of Maud? He spent so little time among the English that he wasn't certain. It was difficult enough to keep up with their ever-changing language without worrying about their names in all their forms.

No matter. He was about to be rid of both of them, whatever they called themselves. He shook his head. "I would be a fool to take five shillings in place of ten."

"And I would be a fool to offer it," said Marian. "The five are not meant to replace the ten, my lord, but to add to them. You will still be able to hunt your thief and collect your bounty afterward, but you will have five shillings more in your purse, while Robin and I will travel quickly and in safety. It will be a benefit to all of us."

Robin nodded his approval. "A sound idea, Mau—, er, Marian." He clamped his elbows down to protect his sides before she could do more damage.

Steinarr considered the offer for a moment. Odin knew, the additional coin would be welcome. The saddles were nearly as worn as the pads beneath them, and he and Torvald both needed warm new cloaks and gloves for next winter. But . . . He shook his head firmly. "No."

"But why, my lord?" she asked.

"I told you, I am no shepherd." He should have left it at that, but he couldn't resist pointing out, "Besides, your purses are as flat as mine. Where would you get five shillings?"

"You will have it when you deliver us safely at the end, my lord. I give my word."

"I add my word as well, my lord," volunteered Robin, as though his word might mean something. "There will be money at the end for you."

"The answer is still no."

"But my lord . . ." she began.

"No," he repeated in a tone that made it clear he would suffer no further argument. "Now, let us find the priest so I can—"

"Confess your many sins?" she asked tartly

"Have him give you lessons in manners," he snapped back. "And tell him where to find John Little's body."

She had the grace to blush, but her lips clamped shut on whatever apology she might have offered.

They reached the church, a sturdy little stone chapel surrounded by graves and a wall, and found the young priest inside, supervising the filling of the font. Marian and Robin both kept silent as Steinarr explained what had happened. Only when the priest began questioning Steinarr too closely about the circumstances of John's death did they speak up.

"This good man tried to save John Little, Father," said Marian. "And he did save Robin and me."

"It is he who first said we must come to you to see John properly buried," said Robin.

The priest nodded. "Good. Forgive me, my lord, but it is necessary in such cases to be sure the man who carries the news of a violent death is not the one who did the violence. John was a good Christian, I trust?"

"He was at Mass only yesterday morning, Father, before we set out for the day," said Marian.

"Good. Good. Then we can see him buried in our yard. I will go to the manor and ask Sir Matthew to send a cart to fetch the poor man and send for the gravedigger." He led them out into the churchyard. "Will you go with me, my lord, and give your regards to our Sir Matthew?"

"No. I must ride on. But Robin and Marian, here, will stay behind to wait for other travelers to pass through. They are on pilgrimage."

"Where are you bound, my children?"

Robin looked at his feet, clearly uncomfortable, but Marian met the priest's curiosity directly. "In the end, Lincoln, Father, but we would stop first at a certain Lady Well east of Retford to pray. We would be most grateful for your kind aid while we wait for companions."

"You will need very little of my aid, my children. As we speak, a party of charcoal burners makes camp nearby, preparing to leave on the morrow for that very place. Lord Matthew offered them in loan to the abbess of Kirklees, and she has asked for them to be sent to the abbey lands at Headon in Bersetelowe, east of Retford. I think your Lady Well must be very near to there."

"Aye," said Marian, but she looked unhappy. "Charcoal burners?"

"And a grimier lot I have seldom seen, but good men and women nonetheless," said the priest. "They have been in the forest nearby for these past months and have been at Mass every Sunday despite the distance. You will be safe with them. I will take you to meet with them after I see Sir Matthew about the body."

"We need to buy food before we set out, Father," said Robin. "Is there someone with bread and cheese to spare?"

"You can have them at the manor. Come, I will see the steward gives you good value." He held open the gate and waited while Marian pulled a few farthings from her purse.

She pressed them into Robin's hand. "Be certain to strike a good price."

"Are you not coming with us?"

She shook her head. "I must have a word with Sir Steinarr before he rides on. Go on, Robin. I will come anon."

Robin looked to her, then to Steinarr, and back again to her, as if some thought perched on the tip of his tongue and he couldn't decide whether to let it fly. In the end he only nodded and headed off after the priest.

"You may as well go with your *cousin* and see that he doesn't pay too dearly," said Steinarr as he walked out into the lane. "Further argument will do you no good."

She stopped in the archway of the gate. "I do not wish to argue, my lord. I only wish to double my offer. Ten shillings for your aid on our journey."

Steinarr snorted. "You do not have ten shillings."

"Not with me, no."

"Not at all. You pinched those farthings you gave Robin as though you hoped they would give milk."

"We must make what coin we brought last the entire way, but I promise you, my lord, there is money to be had at the end."

"Money or not, my answer is still no." He started for the horses.

"Twice ten."

Startled, he looked back at her, standing there by the churchyard gate. By the gods, she was serious. *Where would a peasant girl get a full pound of silver?* No, curse it. It didn't matter. He wasn't helping her—couldn't help her.

"You grow tiresome, maid. I said no."

He stepped around to check the rouncey's girth, taking his time in the hope she would, for once, remember her place and obey. But when he turned to check the stallion's saddle, he almost tripped over her, she was so close—an arm's length away, perhaps less, one hand resting on each of the horses to let them know she was there and her jaw so stubbornly set it all but shouted that she intended to keep at him until he found it impossible to refuse. He had to find some way to make her stop, lest she follow him right out of Maltby and down the road, still bargaining.

"What would it take, my lord?" She stepped closer still, resolve evident in the determined line of her mouth. "What can I offer that will convince you?"

He found his way in those lips, once more begging to be eased. Softened. Kissed. *Yes.*

"This." His arms went around her before he could think it through; his lips covered hers before she could protest. For a heartbeat she stilled in his arms; her lips went soft and pliant and opened, just enough. The rich, female taste of her flooded his mouth, and the hunger rose in him. *More.* With a growl, he gathered her closer, lifting her, shaping her to his body so her warmth eased the growing ache of arousal. His tongue plunged into her mouth as he showed her what he wanted to do, how he wanted to join with her, how he would like to push her down and make her his, right there on the village green. Right now . . .

Suddenly she stiffened and twisted, wrenching away as if he'd hurt her, though he knew he hadn't. He released her, and she skittered back out of reach. Eyes full of accusation, she pressed the back of her hand to her mouth. "What are you doing?"

"Even a maiden must know the answer to that." He struggled to keep his voice cool when all he could think of was how her lips looked now, all swollen from his mouth. *Why had he kissed her? Ah, yes.* "You asked my price. That is it: a pound of silver . . . and you. I'll take you wherever you wish, so long as I can take you whenever I wish."

"Take—You cannot think I would . . ."

"I will make it pleasant for you." He gave her body a raking gaze—by the gods, she was a ripe thing—and took a step toward her. "Very pleasant. I promise you will enjoy it as much as I." Her eyes widened. He took another step and she turned and fled, pelting toward the manor like the very ghosts of the churchyard were after her.

There. She'd never follow him now.

Somehow, that didn't seem as satisfying as he'd thought. Frowning, he checked the saddles again and fiddled with the baggage while the heaviness in his groin eased. It took a while, what with thoughts of her creeping back every heartbeat or two. When he checked the girth for the third time, the stallion turned and looked back at him.

"Shut up," said Steinarr. He flipped the stirrup down and swung up into the saddle.

She was standing by the manor gate as he passed a few moments later. He dipped his head in acknowledgment. "A safe journey to you and your cousin, Maid Marian."

"The Devil take you, *monsire*," she said quite clearly. The guards at the gate sucked in their breaths at her boldness, then let them out as laughter when Steinarr didn't turn on her. He should, just to remind her of her place, but it mattered little at this point. He was rid of her, her and her cousin who was no cousin and their false names and falser pilgrimage. That was what mattered. He ignored the way her eyes burned into his back and rode on.

What he couldn't ignore, however, was the knowledge of what he'd felt as he kissed her, of what he'd seen as she'd backed away from him, just before she'd turned and run. Fear, yes. But awareness, as well—the same awareness that had been there earlier when he'd almost drowned in the green pools of those eyes.

He could have had her, if he'd cared to woo her, if he'd been willing—able—to spend the time.

He could have had her.

And he had no doubt that the knowledge of that fact was going to ride with him for a very long time.

MATILDA FITZWALTER STOOD at the edge of the charcoal burners' camp and tried to pretend she was happy to be there.

She was not—except that it meant she was well away from *him*.

The Devil take the man. Even now, she could feel him—not just his body, but *him*.

It had begun this morning, in that moment when she'd been about to mount. Their eyes had met and his need had poured into her like water, swamping her, stirring her own desires. It still ached, deep within her. She'd been trying to get rid of him all day.

She could hardly blame him for it, though, when she'd done it, when she was the one with the gift.

It was her benison and her bane. From the time she'd been able to toddle down into the hall, she'd had some strange connection with the animals of the manor: first the cats, then the dogs and horses, the sheep, and even the hens in their coop. She had known their minds—not read their thoughts, precisely, but understood their feelings. No one else saw it as a gift, though, and Father, frightened by the strange pronouncements coming from the mouth of his child, had taken the priests' advice and set out to beat the devil out of her. She'd quickly learned to hide her abilities, even to laugh at them as a childish fancy.

But even as she denied the gift, it had never left her, and as she'd reached womanhood, her skill had stretched to include the beasts beyond the walls of Huntingdon. Practicing in secret, she'd learned to control the power, and even to use it a little. It occasionally proved useful; it was how she'd known that the little white mare was stronger than anyone thought and that the poor beast simply didn't like pulling a cart.

Seldom did her ability include people, however, and

never like this. She could sometimes get a sense of good or evil in another, and it served her well enough. But Sir Steinarr . . . the raw power of all that longing and lust and . . . wildness. She'd only ever felt that kind of wildness in the beasts of the forests, never in any creature tamed by man. The very recollection of it made her tremble, even more than what had just happened.

Take her whenever he wanted . . .

Those words and that kiss were yet more reason she was glad to be away from him. She'd offered him a good wage for a simple task, and he'd refused and then . . . *The Devil take him to Hell.* She wasn't accustomed to people refusing her, especially not someone so clearly of lower rank. And she certainly wasn't accustomed to men kissing her at will and addressing her like a common wench. The lecherous knave shouldn't be speaking so lewdly to any woman, much less to one of noble birth.

Of course, he didn't know she was noble born. She and Robert had gone to great lengths to pass as common folk, and so far, it seemed they had been successful. Even Robert's occasional slips hadn't given them away, and thank the saints she'd been too stunned to rebuke Sir Steinarr for his crude offer—a peasant maid would never dare scold a knight, no matter how poor or rude he was.

Still, she wasn't certain she wanted to appear quite so common as to have to travel with charcoal burners. The colliers who moved their camps through the forest deeps in search of wood to burn had always left her uneasy, what with their soot-blackened skin, rough habits, and unsettled ways, and the word of a priest she didn't know did little to reassure her that she and Robert would be safe.

From the smile that brightened his face, however, Father Albertus clearly didn't share her concern. He'd brought them here to the farthest edge of the village, to the brookside meadow where several wagons of colliers had gathered in preparation before moving on, and was speaking with the leader of the group, a squat, sturdy man who looked to be carved from a piece of coal himself, so deeply was the black embedded in his skin. The man consulted with other men, equally blackened, then nodded, and Father Albertus motioned them near.

Hoping the priest's faith in the colliers wasn't misplaced, Matilda shoved aside thoughts of Sir Steinarr and followed Robert over to meet their new companions. There was the leader, Hamo; his son and right-hand, James; James's wife, Ivetta; and her mother, Edith; a cousin, Osbert; and nearly a score of others, not counting the youngest children. From what Matilda could tell, they were all related to Hamo by either blood or marriage.

Hamo sized up her and Robin as though they were trees to be turned into coal, then nodded. "The priest says you want to travel with us to Headon manor."

"Aye," said Robert. "If you have a place for us."

"Do you bring your own food?"

"Aye, and a bit to put in the pot," said Robert, and Matilda had to bite her tongue to keep from protesting. They'd set out with so little, and to have Robert give any of it away . . .

But Hamo nodded, pleased. "Then you are twice welcome." He put out his hand, so filthy that Matilda expected Robert's palm to come away black when he shook it. "'Tis good you came today. Osbert and his finally turned up, so we'll be leavin' as soon after first light as we can yoke up the oxen."

Father Albertus clapped both men on the shoulder. "Good. Good. Then Robin and Marian here are set, and I will be off. The new water in the font is not yet blessed."

"A blessing here, first, Father, if you will," said Hamo. "Come, everyone. We want a safe journey." The whole tribe gathered quickly and knelt. Robert dropped down next to Hamo, while Matilda took to her knees on the edge of the group. As the priest gave his blessing, first in Latin, then in common English, she opened her mind, reaching out to see if perhaps her gift had changed, grown again. But no, there was only the satisfied boredom of the oxen and the alert curiosity of the horses and the mice in the grass—and nothing at all from Hamo or the priest or any of the others.

So why Sir Steinarr? The question hung unanswered as

she crossed herself to Father Albertus's amen and rose to join the others in wishing him Godspeed.

When the priest had gone, Hamo pointed her and Robert toward Ivetta. "She'll take whatever food you wish to share and see 'tis added to the pot for all. And she'll put you to work as well. Everyone does their part in this camp."

"We expect no less," said Robin. He turned to Marian. "Come, Cousin. Let us give the pot a goodly piece of our ham."

She glanced up sharply. "Ham?"

"Aye. I got it at the hall." When she started to protest the cost, he flashed a crooked grin at her. "Rest easy. Sir Matthew had his steward give it as alms to us poor pilgrims. He gave us *all* the food as alms. I could hardly refuse it—or the two pennies his lady gave. For the sake of their souls, of course. Though I'm not sure about ours, now," he added under his breath.

"We will pray for them at the Lady Well," Matilda assured him. "So you came away with food *and* more money than you set out with?" She laughed delightedly as he nodded and then gave him a quick hug. "Why did you not tell me? Sometimes, you are truly remarkable, Robin."

"Just not often enough to be remarked." He said it lightly, but a flicker of pain passed through his eyes, and Matilda's heart ached for the slights he'd suffered. Father had never been fair to him. Robert quickly shook it off. "The ham is in two pieces. We can share the largest with these good people and still have some for ourselves."

The ham bought them a great deal of goodwill, first from Ivetta, who quickly chopped some to add to the big pot of barley and wild greens, and then from the others as the aroma of the cooking meat wafted throughout the camp. Matilda and Robert did the simple chores they were asked to do—carrying water and wood and seeing to the oxen and such—and by the time the pottage was dished out, they were firmly part of the group and Matilda was past the darkest of her fears. She was, however, silently grateful that, as pilgrims, they carried their own bowls and spoons, especially when she saw how the colliers set their bowls on the ground for the dogs to lick clean afterward.

While the men plotted the next day's journey over a morris board, Matilda sat with the women, playing string games with the little girls and sharing the most recent rumors about King Edward, reminding herself all the while that she was a peasant on pilgrimage with her cousin, and hoping that Robert remembered the same.

As darkness fell, each family group moved off toward its own wagons. Old Edith, matriarch by dint of age and temperament, took charge of Matilda. "You'll bed down beneath my cart, maid, where you'll be safe. Your cousin will sleep with the other lads 'neath the tree."

Matilda nodded, then retrieved her bundle and carried it over to the old woman's wagon. It took some maneuvering and she twice knocked her head against the axle while spreading her blanket smooth, but she soon had a fair bed in the grass. The night was dry and warm enough that she rolled her cloak as a pillow. She lay there, listening to people settle down around her, the older children soothing the younger, the sweet talk between husbands and wives. It wasn't so different from the sounds of the hall at Huntingdon, she realized; these colliers were much like the good people who served her family. The last of her worries drained away, and exhausted, she drifted quickly into sleep.

Some sound woke her late in the night. It took her a moment to recall where she was and why there was a wagon wheel by her head. The sound grew louder, and she listened more closely, then blushed when she heard the whispered soft words and the creaking and moans and realized what it was: James and Ivetta in their wagon, tupping. She rolled away and pulled her cloak around her ears, but it was too late. The sound was in her head.

Then *he* was in her head, Sir Steinarr and his kiss and his words and his lust and the idea of him taking her. It would be bad enough, having touched his mind, but she also knew how his body felt: hard as iron and full of desire. She pulled her cloak more tightly to her ears, but she could still hear the rhythm of James on Ivetta, and even though she didn't want Steinarr, not really, she thought of what it might be like to have him whispering to her in the night, taking her in that rhythm, and her body warmed and softened. Ached.

No. She shouldn't feel this way. She truly did not want him.

But as she told herself that, a tiny voice whispered that even if she didn't, there was no harm in imagining him in that way. He was miles away by now. She would never see him again. Temptation wrapped its warm tendrils around her, made her recall how he felt against her, how his kiss had nearly made her forget herself, how if she'd said a single word, he surely would have tipped her back into the grass. The ache deepened.

Protected by darkness and distance, she set aside her conscience and the echo of every priest who had ever told her that what she was about to do was a sin and let Steinarr slip beneath the blanket with her. She eased her hand down and pressed her fingers to the ache, pretending he was there, on her. In her. She let him take her in imagination just as he'd asked to take her in fact, let the thought of him seduce her, move her, drive her, until she hung on the edge of the pleasure he'd promised. And then abruptly, she was over, arcing as she gave herself to it, her lips pressed together to hold back her moan, keeping yet another secret from the world.

CHAPTER 3

TWO THICK SADDLE pads, a dozen steel arrowheads, some food, and a willing woman.

Steinarr stood at the castle gate, jingling the newly fattened purse at his waist and savoring the sound and smell and delicious tangle of the busy street before him. He had enough money for everything he needed, thanks to Long Tom, who now rested safely in the sheriff's cell, and to a foolishly solitary merchant from whom Steinarr had collected a smaller contribution. All he needed to do now was find everything.

He scanned the row of tradesmen's shops, looking for what he needed, and spotted the last item on his list first. He recognized her easily; she had the look of every whore he'd ever seen, lounging there by her doorway, waiting for a man whose purse would open as easily as her legs. A knowing smile crossed her lips as she recognized him in turn, and she shifted to better show her full breasts, barely contained within a tightly laced gown of some thin stuff. Anticipation tugged at Steinarr's crotch, and he started forward.

"You there! La Roche."

The seldom-heard name almost failed to penetrate the lust, even though he'd just used it to collect his reward. He pulled up short as it finally sank in and turned to glower at the approaching serjeant. "What? Did the clerk miscount?"

"No. Lord Gervase wishes a word with you. This way." The serjeant wheeled around and started off, and Steinarr swallowed back a curse as the prospect of a leisurely tumble faded. He looked at the wench, whose raised eyebrow asked the question he wanted very much to answer yes. Jerking a thumb over his shoulder at the serjeant, he mouthed the word "*Later,*" and turned to follow, tugging his tunic down and raking his fingers through his hair as he went.

Every muscle was tense as he was led to the solar, where two men stood by the window. He knew the one on the left: Gervase de Clifton, recently named lord sheriff of Nottinghamshire, but familiar to Steinarr from encounters in the previous sheriff's company. De Clifton smiled easily in greeting, not angry or overly alert, and Steinarr knew immediately there was no trouble there. He quickly sized up the second man: Rich clothes in brilliant red with matching pointy-toe boots. Figured hose of yellow and black. He looked like a rooster, but for the heavy gold chain around his neck. *Nobleman. And uneasy, by the way he fiddled with that medallion in his hand.* His dark eyes flickered back and forth from Lord Gervase to Steinarr. He wanted something.

Setting aside his immediate distaste for the rooster, Steinarr dipped his head to both men like the common mercenary he was supposed to be for these purposes, then addressed the sheriff. "My lord."

"I am told you've brought another outlaw for the gallows, la Roche. It has been a long time. We thought you might have been killed."

"No, my lord." He'd discovered long ago it was best to speak as little as possible around these people. Tell them as little as possible.

"Sir Guy de Gisburne. La Roche. Pour yourself some wine, la Roche." Lord Gervase waited while Steinarr filled a cup, then said, "Sir Guy came to me seeking aid in a certain matter. When I heard you were among us, I knew fate had sent you. You are the very man he needs."

Balls. He didn't want to work for this coxcomb, but neither could he could afford to defy the sheriff just now. His lordship might begin to suspect his favorite thief-catcher was also one of those lightening the occasional purse on the northern road. "Should I take that as praise, my lord?"

"It is meant as such. I will leave you two to talk." Lord Gervase set his empty cup on a nearby table and left the room, pulling the door firmly shut behind him.

Interesting. The sheriff wanted him to do this Guy's work, but wanted no part in it himself. Something not quite within the bounds of law perhaps? Steinarr nursed his cup as he assessed the situation.

Gisburne assessed Steinarr in turn. He nodded to himself as though satisfied with what he saw. "I need assistance with a thief."

"Your pardon, my lord, but I know nothing of you but your name. Why would I help you?"

"Because I am the new lord of Huntingdon," he boasted, then added with somewhat less haughtiness, "And because I will pay you well. *Very* well."

Perhaps this would prove worthwhile after all. "What has this thief stolen?"

"My cousin, Matilda, for one. Only daughter of Lord David Fitzwalter. He has lured her away from her home." Sir Guy turned once more to stare out the window, hiding whatever emotion passed through his eyes. "My uncle let Matilda fill her head with *gestes* and other such foolishness, and now this knave preys on her fantasies, convincing her that he is on some noble quest and that she should aide him."

"What sort of quest?" asked Steinarr.

"My uncle hid away a portion of his wealth and left a series of hidden riddles meant to lead his heir to a small treasure. To lead *me* to it," he said emphatically, as though Steinarr might not be clear on the subject, then added with a sneer, "I fear he was as enamored of the *gestes* as Matilda. Robert stole the first of those riddles and is now trying to follow it to the others—and the treasure—with Matilda's help."

"Robert?"

"Robert le Chape. The thief. An orphan my uncle brought into his home out of kindness, who now betrays that kindness with treachery."

"Why don't you and your uncle go after him?"

"Sadly, it was my uncle's death at his estate in Loxley a week past that set these events in motion. I was summoned from Gisburne to his sickbed, but arrived too late. My uncle was gone, and Robert had worked his mischief and stolen off with Matilda." Guy took a deep breath, then turned to meet Steinarr's eye. "I will give you ten pounds of silver to stop Robert le Chape and return my cousin to me within the month."

Ten pounds! All the bounties he'd collected for the last five years would not make ten pounds. Either this fellow loved his lady cousin very much or . . . "You don't want this Robert stopped. You want him dead."

The young lordling's tight smile never reached his eyes. "I did not say that. If, however, he never showed his face at my gate again, I would not be saddened."

In other words, yes. Steinarr considered this turn with distaste. He had killed before, of course, both directly, in war or when a murderer with a price on his head fought too hard, and indirectly, when the outlaws he brought in ended up on the gallows. And then there was what the lion did— not murder perhaps, but killing nonetheless. He was used to it. Still, murdering a simple thief outright for the convenience of some minor English lord was a different matter.

But if he didn't take the charge, someone else would. Robert le Chape would wind up just as dead and the coin for it would land in another man's purse. They needed the money. Ten pounds would be enough to buy a new saddle, instead of just a pad, with money left for other necessities. He'd been putting it aside too long, but that foolish girl had drawn his attention to how badly he needed to get the stallion—Torvald—a new saddle. Without saying yea or nay, he asked, "What about the treasure?"

"It is of little concern, unless Robert finds it before you find him." Sir Guy waved off the matter with a flick of his hand. "If he does, he will surely toss my cousin aside like an old cloth, alone in unknown territory and easy prey for whatever man finds her. She was—*is*—to be married in one month. If she is returned in time, her future may yet be secured."

Ah, so that's why the month. Ten pounds in a single month . . . Steinarr made his decision quickly. "Then her future will be secured. I will find her and return her to you."

Relief eased the lines in Sir Guy's face. "And le Chape?"

"Will neither find the treasure he so desires, nor breach your gate again, my lord. For ten pounds."

"Ten pounds," affirmed Sir Guy. They gripped each other's hands in the ancient pledge of agreement. "And as a further show of good faith . . ."

Steinarr felt something hard press into his palm and glanced down to find himself holding the medallion that Guy had been thumbing. No, not a medallion. "A coin of gold?"

Guy nodded. "A new sort, called a florin, for the city in which it is struck. Pure gold, and worth a mark in silver. Take it as surety for your good work. You will have the rest when I have my cousin."

Steinarr tested the coin with his teeth, and satisfied by the metal's softness, dropped the coin into his purse. "'Twill be a pleasure to ride for you, my lord. You say your cousin and this le Chape set out to follow the riddles your uncle left. Do you know which way they went?"

"Only most roughly. A servant followed them some way, out of concern for my cousin. Before they eluded him, he heard them ask about a certain Lady Well."

"A Lady Well?" Steinarr glanced sharply at Guy. "Which one?"

"If I knew that, I would fetch her back myself. I only know they were headed into Nottinghamshire. That is why I came here. They were last rumored to be in the company of an old man in a cart, but all three seem to have vanished."

"Have they?" *No. It couldn't be.* Or could it? "What do these two look like?"

"Robert is thin and red-haired, perhaps a half-a-hand taller than I. He often wears a green hood, thus his byname. His chin bears a scar. Here." Sir Guy touched his chin, drawing a slant down in a place that matched the mark beneath a certain young pilgrim's wisp of a beard. "My cousin stands as much shorter than me as Robert does taller. She is as fair as they come, with a mouth like ripe strawberries and hair the color of spun gold."

An odd way of describing a cousin, Steinarr thought, but such a good portrait of the maid he knew as Marian that he could see her and taste those strawberry red lips. Still . . . "Are either of them called by other names? They, um, may use them to hide their passage."

Guy stroked the underside of his chin with one finger. "I have heard Matilda call the scoundrel Robin. And she is sometimes called Maud by familiars, of course."

Of course. Maud was short for Matilda, like that would-be queen of theirs back a century or two, the mother of the second Henry. He should have remembered that— the incessant battles between Matilda and King Stephen had made it all but impossible to find a quiet patch of forest. That had been one of the times he'd tried Scotland.

And the maid was noble. That explained much.

'Twas all he could do to keep from grinning. He knew exactly where she was, she and the orphan thief who pretended to be her cousin. But did he want to find her, when he'd gone to so much trouble to be rid of her? And what about young Robin? He had little use for the lad—less now that he knew what mischief he was up to—but did he really want to kill him for this popinjay?

But Sir Guy was already at the door, calling for a page to let Lord Gervase know that their business was concluded. He turned back to Steinarr. "A month, la Roche. No more."

Steinarr hesitated. He wanted out of this already, or at least a part of him did. The other part wanted the excuse to track down Marian, to see if he was right about what he thought he'd seen in her eyes when he'd kissed her. Not that either part mattered a whit; he had given his word. Even if he had not already shaken hands and accepted money, his word was enough to bind him to the task. He would find Marian—Matilda—*Maud*—and return her to her home and her true cousin, who would take her father's place in seeing her well wed. And he would deal with the treacherous Robin, who was likely seducing her this very hour. The thought of the puppy between her thighs made the idea of killing him sit much easier.

"A month, my lord." He bowed slightly to his new employer and took his leave.

Lord Gervase was speaking to the steward at the bottom of the stairway. He looked up as Steinarr trotted down. "Is all . . . arranged?"

"It is, my lord."

"Good hunting to you, then."

Steinarr bowed once more and left the hall, crossing directly to the squat building where he had collected his reward earlier. He showed the gold piece to the clerk. "Is this real money?"

"A florin." The clerk peered at the coin, confirming the marks and examining the edges for clipping, then bit it the same way Steinarr had and checked to see how deeply his tooth had marked the metal. "These are yet rare in this part of England, but 'tis real enough. How do you come to have one?"

Steinarr ignored the question. "How much is it worth in silver?"

"Thirteen shillings," said the man without hesitation.

"I was told a full mark."

"Aye. But if you want the silver today . . ."

"Lord Gervase wants his due, eh?" asked Steinarr. The clerk lifted his hands to show his helplessness in the situation, and Steinarr plucked the coin off his palm. "I'll let him steal four pence from me on another day. This is easier to carry."

He sauntered toward the gate, tossing the florin in the air a few times just to watch the flash of gold. It had been an age since he'd had his hands on gold in any form, and the weight and warmth of it conjured up memories of the old days. He would hang on to this bit as long as he could— and with another nine pounds and a third part of a tenth yet to come, that might be a good, long while. He shoved it to the bottom of his purse.

The whore was still there, fingering the ends of her laces as she watched the passing crowd, but next to the possibility of even one afternoon with Marian, she was as appealing as a moldy piece of bread. Steinarr started forward, intending to toss her a farthing to make up for the time she'd spent waiting for him, but as he crossed the road, two men called to her from the seat of a passing cart. The woman looked them up and down and called back, "Three pence for both." The men leapt to the ground, the nearer one reaching for his purse. As they reached the doorway, the whore finally noticed Steinarr. With a grin, she took the coins the men handed her, mouthed *Later*, then turned with a flip of her braids and led the fellows inside.

As the door swung shut, Steinarr burst into laughter. Two men on one woman? He found far more delight in two women on one man, but to each his own vice. *There* was a farthing saved.

He made his purchases quickly, buying some good hunting points and the two thickest, sturdiest saddle pads he could find, and then headed a street over for stores: two loaves of good bread and a week's worth of the common sort, two bags of oats for the horses and for eating, two fat cheeses dipped in wax—one each for him and Torvald— and a small flitch of well-cured bacon. For that last, he spent the coin he'd intended to give to the whore, deciding it would be good not to have to hunt for meat while he was running down Marian and Robin. Pleased with the prices he paid, he toted everything back to where the horses waited patiently in the castle foreyard.

As Steinarr swapped the new pads for the old and reloaded the animals, he considered the pledge he'd made to Sir Guy, reviewing the exact words they had used. No, nothing about returning Marian a virgin—likely because Gisburne suspected she had already given her maidenhead to Robin. Steinarr once more frowned at the thought.

It would take him two days, perhaps three, to find her. He could figure out some way to be rid of the boy, then lure Marian to some woodland bower and spend the rest of the month peeling away her defenses and her clothes. And at the end of it, he would return her to Huntingdon to be married, and any babe he happened to put in her belly would be taken for either Robert le Chape's or her husband's.

If there was a better way to earn ten pounds, he could not imagine it.

There was only one problem—the nights. Torvald would be there to keep her safe from the lion, of course, but Torvald was as much in need of a woman as he, and Marian would be a temptation. Steinarr looked at the stallion thoughtfully. He would have to leave a message anyway, explaining what they were up to and why. He would simply let Torvald know that he had more personal plans for Marian and remind him that there would be plenty of money for women afterward. As for tonight . . .

"Don't worry. I kept back coin enough for you," he said under his breath in Norse as he checked the stallion's girth strap. "We will stop close enough to town for you to come back. There's even some for a jar of ale afterward."

That would hold him. Steinarr flipped the stirrup back down and mounted up. As he rode toward the gate, he saw Sir Guy and the sheriff watching from the window of the solar and gave them a nod. In the street, he turned toward the east gate of the city, riding past the whore, who was now back out on the street looking for business.

He didn't give her another thought.

THE WATERS OF the Well of Wyrd were stirring once more.

Even now, so weak and locked away behind these stone walls, Cwen could sense the dark eddies beneath the movements of the world of man. She had been unsure of them at first, but the currents had grown stronger over the last weeks, and now, with the moon hanging dark in the sky outside her cell, she felt them sweeping her forward.

The time neared.

She sat on the edge of the hard cot and slowly unbraided her hair. Loosed, it rippled around her shoulders in waves, still dark and rich. She raked through it with her fingers, the luxury of a comb being forbidden in this place. Long hair was forbidden as well; her head was shaved clean every few months. But it took such small magic to regrow it that she had worked the simple charm in order to honor the Dark Ones with unbound hair when she supplicated herself to them.

Her hair smoothed, she stood and quickly stripped away the thin kirtle she wore at night, then unwrapped the linen bandage that bound her chest. Her bare skin felt strange, so seldom was she able to undress completely. She examined her body in the light of the single candle.

Still young, of course, but thin. Far too thin. And that scar.

She touched the spot, tentatively probing the angry red lesion. It ached, and her fingertips came away damp, for even after all these years, the wound she'd taken the last time she'd encountered the Northmen still wept, unhealed.

Cwen grimaced at the remembered pain. There had been too much goddess magic with them, much more than she'd expected. She had barely escaped, using every scrap of power in her to vanish into mist. When at last she'd been able to gather her body back into its physical form, she had been wounded and feeble. She'd wandered England, slowly making her way south until she stumbled into a place like this one. There she had taken shelter, but by then the wound had festered, and though shielded from death by the magic she'd worked so long ago, she spent years recovering.

Too many years. By then, they were beyond her reach: the eagle, his lady, and even the girl-child she had so coveted. All gone, except her.

And *them*, of course. The bear, the raven, and the other beasts.

They still hunted her, as they hunted their tokens, and she had too little strength to fight them. So she moved from cell to narrow cell, secreted away where they would never think to look. Generations passed outside the gray stone walls that sheltered and imprisoned her, and still she did not fully heal. But now the waters of Wyrd called to her, and healed or not, it was time to invoke the gods and see if they would deign help her at last.

She found the loose stone in the corner of her cell and wiggled it free so she could remove the items hidden in the space behind it. She fingered each object in turn before laying them out in a circle on the floor. A wand, cut at sunrise from a yearling holly. The feather of a black swan. A knife of purest steel. A cord of flax, never tied. A skull stolen from the crypt. Four stones, white, red, yellow, and black. Twigs of rowan and ash and willow. Root of bryony, harvested on a Monday and wrapped in a piece of a dead man's winding sheet. She had begun to gather these things long ago, even before she'd sensed the coming confluence. It had taken her years to bring together the forbidden items, but she had, to ensure they would be here when she finally needed them.

She reached once more into the wall to pull out the final item, a gold-chased chalice, stolen from the chapel just for tonight. The boy accused of the theft had paid with his skin, taking thirty lashes, but his blood had been an honor to the gods even if he did not know it. She set it in place.

All was in readiness. Smiling, she turned to open the shutter that blocked her window.

Chill night air washed over her bare skin and she sighed with pleasure. It was always so airless within these walls. Even in the garden, she found it hard to breathe. She stood there for a long moment, eyes closed, letting the breeze cleanse her of the taint of this place. She hated it, despite the sanctuary it provided. She hated that she *needed* sanctuary. She was Cwen. Kings had once bowed to her and begged for the honor of her protection, and now she was reduced to this.

But perhaps no longer, if the Old Ones saw she was ready again.

She stepped into the center of the circle, and took up her knife. A quick slice laid her hand open, and she held it out to stream blood into the chalice. When she had enough, she began to weave the spell. Stone, knife, cord, bone, wood, blood, root. They all worked together as she called to the gods. The power rose, dancing over her skin like lightning.

But the gods failed to answer. She spilled more blood,

poured her will into the gathering magic to show them, to prove to them she was worthy. The stars spun in the heavens outside her window, marking the passing hours, and still she worked. The darkness began to fade, and still she conjured.

"A sign, Old Ones," she begged into the vanishing night, her wounded body sagging with the effort of stirring so much magic. "I have been and will be your faithful servant. Help me regain the power I once held in your name. Show me you will aid me."

Finally, as the sky lightened more and still there was no sign, she admitted defeat. There would be no sign, not tonight.

Working swiftly and silently lest the others wake early and hear her, she cleared her tools from the floor and returned them to the hollow in the wall. The stone went back into its place with barely a scrape, and she rebound her chest and slipped back into the discarded kirtle.

She had just finished rebraiding her hair when the bells pealed the approaching dawn. As she had every sunrise for years, she began to dress, drawing on the heavy robes and swathing her head in the wimple that hid her too-long hair. The robes were black, the color of the Old Ones—strange, when the god these Christians worshipped was so new and weak, but she was glad that at least her garments honored her own. She tied the heavy rope around her waist, hung the cross about her neck, and went down with the other nuns to pray.

CHAPTER 4

THE COLLIERS MADE camp outside Retford in a misting rain, but by the time they set out the next morning, the weather had once again cleared. Fortunately for Matilda and Robert, the route to the abbey lands beyond Headon took the little train of oxcarts right past the Lady Well that was their goal.

Unfortunately, Hamo took a liking to the well's sweet water and decided they must empty all their water barrels and refill them. Watching them dumping and filling, bucket by bucket, Matilda began to fear they might decide to make camp right there for the night. Not that she would fault them. The wayside was fair and flat, and the glade a soothing place, with the spring bubbling up at the foot of a bramble-covered hillock.

However, she and Robert couldn't do what they needed to do with a score of colliers watching, so it was a relief when, as Robert helped James hoist the last barrel into his cart, Hamo began bellowing for everyone to load up.

"Are you certain you will not come with us?" asked Hamo, as he mounted the fat little pony that usually trailed behind his wagon. "We can always use the extra hands. And Osbert has taken a fancy to Marian. Stay with us and there'll be a wedding, I wager."

"'Tis tempting to throw our lot in with such good companions," said Robert, his eyes twinkling as he shot Matilda a sidelong glance.

"But no," she added firmly. Widowed Osbert was fat and bald and as coal-blackened as his cousin, and he had a dozen children for which he needed a mother—though even Osbert and his litter would be less insufferable than what awaited her if this adventure did not succeed. "We have our journey to complete, and our pilgrims' pledge to fulfill before all else. Come, Robin. We owe prayers here at this shrine before we find our beds tonight."

Hamo had already recommended they seek shelter in Headon. Now he said, "We go now to the manor to ask the steward where he wishes us to cut. If 'tis close, we will go ahead and may not see you again, but I will tell him you are coming and say you are under Lord Matthew's protection. He will give you bed and board. If you change your minds, come find us. You will always be welcome in my camp."

"As all of you will be welcome in whatever home I have," said Robert. He let Matilda say her good-byes and thanks, then, as she moved off to kneel before the little shrine next to the well, he reached up to shake Hamo's hand. "Our thanks for your kindness and protection, Hamo Collier."

"Travel safely, young pilgrims," said Hamo. He whistled sharply and watched as the oxen plodded off with much creaking of wheels and cracking of whips, then turned his pony after them.

Robert waved them away, and then came over to stand behind Matilda. "What are you doing?"

"Praying, Cousin," she said. "Kneel with me."

"But we aren't—"

"They can still see you. Kneel."

"Sometimes you worry me, Maud. You lie too easily."

"Marian. Blast it, Robin, kneel!"

He did, but he looked uncomfortable. "It feels like a sin, to pretend to pray, and at a Holy well."

"Then do not pretend. We owe a prayer for the benevolence of Lord Matthew and his lady."

"Aye, we do," said Robert, sounding happier. He crossed himself and closed his eyes, and as his lips began to move, Matilda followed suit. The rumbling of the oxcarts slowly faded as they prayed, and by the time Matilda crossed herself and rose, the last cart was disappearing around the bend.

"I never want to travel by oxcart again," she said earnestly.

Robert mumbled a quick "amen," crossed himself, and rose to join her. "You could have ridden behind me."

"It would have been no faster. We would have been here two days ago if we had come ahead on our own."

"If we had, we might not be here at all," Robert pointed out, though they hadn't seen a sign of trouble along the way. "But no matter, for we *are* here. I see no crown. Where do you suppose it is?"

Matilda spun slowly in place, carefully searching the glade around the pool for something that looked like the marker they sought. Nothing.

"Perhaps we should have a look at the riddle again." Robert produced the folded bit of parchment from his pilgrim's scrip and smoothed it across his thigh before he handed it over. "Here. You read it."

"Oh, all right." They'd puzzled over the scrap so many times neither of them really needed to look at it, but Matilda accepted it anyway and worked through her father's bold but difficult hand to be sure. "It says, 'Head on to abbey lands where the Fair One pours forth the season of her day. You will find what you pray for in the crown of the forest king.' The Fair One is Our Lady, of course, and Lady Day is in spring, so it is clear he means that Our Lady pours forth a spring. A Lady Well. That much we're sure of."

"But there are so many Lady Wells, and many on church lands. How are you so sure he meant this one?"

They'd gone over this a hundred times—Papa's support of the nuns at Kirklees, the fact that he'd mentioned Abbess Humberga in almost the same breath that he'd revealed his strange bequest, his odd use of English instead of his usual French to write the riddle so he could play off words like *head on* for Headon—but Robert still doubted. And no wonder, when Matilda doubted it herself. But she couldn't give up, and she couldn't afford to have Robert give up. She slipped her arm around his waist and leaned her head on his bony shoulder. "He did mean it to be found, Robin. He would not have made it impossible."

He sighed forlornly. "Just impossible for me."

"But not for us together."

"You were never meant to be part of it. Why *are* you helping me?" he asked, as if the question had just occurred to him.

"Because I love you, foolish boy." She gave him a quick peck on the cheek. "And because I am helping myself at the same time. Come. We are missing something." She dragged him to the center of the glade. "Look hard. A king with a crown. It must be here somewhere."

But it wasn't. They went over every stone and tree, staring until their eyes crossed, trying to twist each into a face, a head, a crown, or a cap. Robert gave out and sat down by the spring, rubbing his eyes, but Matilda refused. She took up a vantage point in the center of the clearing and began slowly turning in place, searching, all the while muttering. "Papa, you *felon*, where have you hidden it?"

"Sst." Robert's hiss interrupted her. Turning, she started to ask what, but stopped when she saw his raised hand. He pointed.

A handsome red hart stood on the edge of the clearing, barely a dozen yards away, his eyes fixed on Robert. He stood proudly, his mane dark and heavy around his shoulders, and though his new antlers were just beginning to grow, they were thick and sturdy, and she suspected the rack he would carry come fall would be magnificent. They all froze for a long moment, Robert, the stag, and Matilda. Gently, she opened herself to the stag's mind and felt his curiosity as he sniffed the air, but no fear at all. The stag turned and walked away into the forest and she let him go.

"King of the forest," whispered Robert as he vanished.

Matilda started. "King of the forest. Robert, you have solved it! Quick, look for a stag's head."

"No need," he said. He scrambled to his feet and dragged Matilda over to where they had prayed earlier. "Kneel."

"We can give thanks after we have found it."

"Kneel!" He practically pushed her to the ground, then dropped to his knees close behind her. Reaching over her shoulder, he pointed toward the top of the little hill from which the spring flowed. "We will find what we *pray* for. Look."

It took her a moment, but once she saw it, her smile spread wide. There it had been all along: a great stone that gave the brush-covered hillock the rough shape of a huge stag's head. And rising above it, a solitary oak, split and twisted by disease and age into the form of a stag's antlers. "The crown of the forest king."

They scrambled up the hill, leaving scraps of skin and clothing on the brambles as they went. Robert circled the tree, staring up. "In the crown. In the crown."

"There. Look." Matilda pointed. High in the tree, up above the last few living branches, there was a hole the size of a woodpecker's nest.

"Surely not," said Robert.

"There is a faint mark carved next to the hole. See? I think 'tis an *F*, for Fitzwalter."

Robert groaned. "So high. Why would he put it so high? *How* did he put it so high?"

Robert was not a climber. He never had been. When other boys had shinnied up trees, he had hung back, carving little animals in wood. Matilda still kept a clever squirrel he had given her before she went off to her fostering.

"He probably sent a page up," she said. "As to why, well, he would not want someone stumbling on it by chance, would he? Go on. You can do it. You solved his riddle, and you can manage this task as well."

"He never liked me," mumbled Robert, as he prepared to climb.

Which was not strictly true, but this was not the time to argue the point. Matilda wrung her hands as he inched his way awkwardly up the tree, branch by branch. At last he stepped onto the highest living branch and wrapped one arm around the tree so he could reach into the hole with the other.

"Is it there?" called Matilda.

He shook his head. "I cannot reach the bottom. I need to be higher." He hunched around the tree, searching for a place to put his foot. The stumps of two dead branches protruded from the tree, just enough higher that they might work. Robert tested one, then the other, and slowly eased up onto the second, using the first to balance himself.

Matilda moved back to see better. "Be careful."

"I'm fine." He wrapped one arm firmly around the tree and stuck the other back in to grope around. "I think I feel something. If I can just . . ." Straining, he shifted his weight.

With a crack, the dead wood gave way. There was one instant when Matilda thought he'd caught himself, when he hung, safe. And then he yelled and he was falling and all she could do was scream and throw herself out of the way.

He bounced off one of the lower branches and landed in a heap at the foot of the tree. Matilda scrambled forward. "Rob! Robin. Oh, sweet Mother, help him. Robin?"

"Unnh." His agonized moan tore at her, but at least it meant he lived. Thank the saints he had missed the great stone, barely a foot from his skull.

"Lie still. Let me see if you are hurt." Slowly, she sorted him out. Head. Arms. Legs. Oh, God, his leg. The lower part of his right leg lay at an angle so odd it made Matilda's stomach heave.

"My leg," groaned Robert, writhing. "I think 'tis broken."

"It is. Hold still, lest you make it worse."

"Is it bad?"

"Bad enough. Be still. I must get your shoe off before your leg swells." She unfastened the buckles and carefully eased the shoe off, then took out her knife and cut away his hose. "Now, let me find some sticks to brace it."

He tried to rise up on his elbows, but fell back with another groan. "It is no use, Maud. I will never be able to walk."

"You won't have to, boy. Be at ease."

Matilda glanced up, and for half a heartbeat, she thought it was Sir Steinarr coming up the hill. But no, it was only some other tall man with gold hair and a square jaw—though not quite so tall and square as Steinarr after all. "I would ask who you are and where you come from, my lord, but I am too pleased to see you."

"I am Sir Ari. I was below watering my horse and heard the cry." He squatted beside Robert to examine his leg, his fingers moving deftly over the limb. He nodded to himself. "You will mend. Come. Let's get you off this hill, and then we'll put you back together. I will need those sticks you were going to find, maid."

Matilda nodded dumbly, unnerved by the way this unknown knight took command, yet relieved by it and by having something useful to do. She found a pair of straight branches and carried them back to find Sir Ari cutting strips from Robert's discarded hose. Working together, they trimmed the sticks to a good length and bound them to the wounded leg. By the time they finished, Robert was shaking, despite the warm weather.

"The pain is making him chill," the stranger said. "You go on down and gather some boughs to keep him off the damp ground. We'll wrap him in our cloaks. Mine is tied behind the saddle of my horse."

"We carry our own blankets."

"Good. Use both blankets and cloaks."

She nodded. "But how will we get him down without a litter?"

"I'll manage." The stranger flashed a smile, then handed her his heavy knife, much as Sir Steinarr had a few days before. "Go on, woman. We'll be fine. Won't we, boy?"

Robert nodded, pale-faced. "If you so say, my lord. Go on, Maud."

She scrambled back down the hill, leaving yet more skin behind on thorns, and began hacking off the branches of a young maple as though it were responsible for the scream of pain that rose on the hilltop. By the time the stranger came shambling down the slope with Robert slung over his shoulder, she had piled enough boughs to make a thin bed and covered them with one of the doubled blankets and Robert's cloak.

Sir Ari held out a slim gray cylinder. "Here. When I

went to pick him up, I found this under him. He said 'tis his."

"I . . ." She started to deny it, but Rob piped up, "Hold it for me, Maud."

It must be what he'd found in the tree. She took it and quickly slipped it into her scrip. "Thank you, my lord. It would have been a great loss."

"No trouble." Sir Ari shifted around to line Robert up with the makeshift bed. "You ready, boy?"

"Aye," said Robert between gritted teeth.

"Down you go, then. Watch the leg." With Matilda providing a steadying hand, the knight lowered Robert onto his good leg, then down onto the cloaks. Robert paled, but managed not to cry out again. "There's a lad. Good job. Now, let us see to setting this leg." Sir Ari started untying the strips so he could remove the bracing.

"Here?" Matilda quickly covered Robert's torso with the other blanket and both cloaks. "Should we not take him to the village first? I can ride for help."

The stranger shook his head. "Setting the leg will make the trip easier for him. And the sooner 'tis set, the sooner 'twill heal."

"But you . . . Do not take this poorly, my lord, but do you know what you are doing?"

"Maud, he is trying to help." Robert winced as he lifted his head to scold her.

"'Tis a fair enough question, lad, especially when your leg is at stake." He patted Robert on the shoulder, then turned to Matilda. "Maud, is it? I have set many a bone, and even a few of my own." He held up a wrist and waggled it. "They've all healed well enough."

"But—"

"'Tis not as grim as it looks," he reassured her. "The break is clean and the skin is not broken. I can manage as well as any man, and far better than what you are likely to find in that village."

"But—"

"Do it, my lord," said Robert quickly. "I trust you."

The man gave Robert a hard look, then nodded. He cast

about for a sturdy twig, which he wrapped in a corner of his cloak. "Bite down on this when I tell you to. Maud, you are going to hold his shoulders down. Keep him still."

"I will try, my lord."

"Trying is not good enough," said a voice behind them. "I will hold him, Ari."

Matilda didn't even have to turn. She knew that voice. It rippled down her spine to the very pit of her being and sent a flash of heat back up, so fierce it was all she could do not to groan.

But the stranger had turned and was grinning broadly. "Steinarr! What the devil are you doing here?"

Matilda didn't need to hear the answer. She knew precisely why he was here. And she also knew she suddenly had a great deal more trouble than Robert's broken leg.

'TWAS CLEAR SHE cared for the lad. Even now, with him drifting off from a potent mixture of exhaustion and poppy syrup, she fussed over him, straightening blankets and brushing the hair off his forehead.

Steinarr stood off to one side, frowning as Marian leaned over to press a kiss to Robin's cheek, his glee at the boy ruining his own game tempered by the sight of the two of them together.

As he considered what he should do, the reeve of Headon drew Marian aside. He said something that made her eyes widen, then shook his head when she responded. She argued more vigorously, but the reeve shook his head again and walked away, leaving her standing there wearing a look of shock. Steinarr thought he could see the glitter of tears as she turned back to kneel beside Robin.

Ari came up beside him and spoke quietly in Norse. "If you're going to just stand there, I may have a try at her."

"Go away."

"I'm just saying, if a man wanted to bed her, this would be the time to begin the wooing."

Steinarr grinned at him. "Do you never keep that mouth shut?"

"Not when there is something that needs saying. 'Tis clear you want her. Go on. Go to her."

Steinarr glanced to Marian again—he had decided to keep thinking of her by that name so as not to reveal he knew anything more than what she'd told him. "'Tis the wrong time. She is far too upset, and we must leave soon to be away by nightfall."

"'Tis a perfect time."

"But she . . ."

"By the gods, have you been so long in the woods that you've forgotten how these things are done?" Ari thumped Steinarr on the back. "She is holding together in front of the boy, but she is clearly in need of a good, broad shoulder. Comfort her, tell her all will be well, then leave her be for the night. She will think better of you for it and be that much more likely to give you a tumble later."

Think well of him? Little chance of that after what he'd done in Maltby. During the ride out from Nottingham, he had pondered how he might overcome the crude way he'd driven her off, but his ponderings had not included finding her in tears over Robert le Chape's broken leg. He had no idea what to do.

He would have known, once. He would have moved in and won her away from that scrawny puppy without a second thought, but now he stood here, foxed by a bastard thief who was barely more than a boy.

Ari was right; he had been in the forest too long. More to the point, he'd been relying too long on the forthright give-and-take of whores, who needed no wooing beyond the flash of silver—a useful thing for a man who could carve out only a few hours in town once or twice each year, but it had made him lazy. He simply needed to recall what it was to deal with a real woman, albeit one who was pretending to be other than what she was.

Marian suddenly rose and started for the door.

"Now if I were you . . ."

Steinarr clamped his hand down on Ari's shoulder and squeezed. "You are *not*, nor am I you, thank the gods. Stay here."

He gave Marian a moment, then trailed outside in her wake. She veered away from the colliers, who had made a rough camp in the yard with their wagons and their herd of children, and went to stand beside the old mare, where she rested her forehead against the animal's. As he approached, she glanced up. Her eyes went from weary to wary in a blink. "May I help you, my lord?"

"The question should go the other way," said Steinarr, rattled by the mistrust in those narrowed green eyes. "How fares your cousin?"

"Sleeping."

"With good fortune, he will do so until morning."

"Good fortune," she repeated hollowly. "I fear we have run out of that, my lord. The reeve wants a shilling. A shilling!"

"For what?"

"For bed and board while Robin heals. He says he cannot give so much charity without the steward's leave, and the steward left yesterday for Leicester." She blinked furiously, trying to hold back the tears that welled up again. "It will not leave us enough to travel."

Remember who she claims to be, he reminded himself. *Play her game.* "I will speak to the man. Surely you can work for your place, and Robin's leg is not so very bad. A few weeks' rest and he will—"

"We do not *have* a few weeks."

"Of course you do. Your holy shrines will still be there when he is healed."

"But not the—" She cut herself off. "Not Robin's sister. She is frail."

Steinarr bit his cheek to keep from smiling at the near slip, so obvious now that he knew the truth. "Surely your prayers can be heard from here as well as from Lincoln."

She ducked her head, so her headcloth fell and hid her face. "We must finish our journey, my lord. We made a vow."

He nodded as if in understanding, as if he believed her and comprehended why wandering around from cross to cross should bring special boons from the Christian god. "Perhaps you will find a way, then."

She said nothing, just kept staring at the ground.

Steinarr could think of nothing more to say, so he took Ari's advice after all. "All will be well, Marian. You will see. A good night's sleep for both you and Robin will make things look brighter. Ari and I will go now, but we will make camp nearby and come back in the morning to check on you."

She nodded wordlessly, eyes still downcast, and he backed away.

Ari was watching from near the door. As Steinarr approached, he shook his head. "You might have at least got an arm around her. Let her sob on your chest or something."

"That might make sense if she were actually crying. You know, 'tis amazing any woman ever spreads her legs for you," said Steinarr, and headed off to collect his horses. Behind him, Ari laughed and followed.

They rode north and east, hurrying toward the thickest patch of forest in the area. As they entered the edges of the woodlands and had to slow the horses to a walk, Ari unhooked a full wineskin from his saddle horn and passed it across. "I thought you might enjoy this."

Steinarr didn't even bother to answer, but simply pulled the stopper and hoisted the skin to let the wine stream into his mouth.

Ari watched with amusement. "I'm glad I brought another skin for Torvald."

"Me, too," said Steinarr, coming up for air to swipe his mouth on the back of his hand. "What are you doing here anyway? Is there news of . . . ?" He let the witch's name go unsaid.

Ari shook his head. "Brand merely asked me to make a round, to see that everyone is well. 'Twas by chance alone that I happened on those two. I was headed toward the crags."

"We are no longer there. The lion was seen, and I had to move on."

"A shame. Those were good caves."

"Aye. I left a sign for you." Early on, the crew had realized the difficulty of finding each other when circumstances made them move on so often and had set up a way to leave hidden messages pointing toward their next location.

"Well, then I would have found you eventually. I would ask what *you* are doing here, but that is clear from the way you look at Maud."

"Marian," corrected Steinarr. "I rescued her and the boy from outlaws a few days ago and she asked me to help them get to Lincoln. I said no, but I—"

"Changed your mind. I understand. If I had a chance to tumble her, I—"

"You understand nothing." Steinarr jammed the plug into the neck of the wineskin and hung it from his saddle horn. "I have been hired to see to the maid's safety." He proceeded to tell Ari what had happened in Nottingham, leaving out the bit about Guy's intentions for Robert le Chape and his own intentions for Marian. But he did mention the treasure—and the money.

Ari whistled appreciatively. "Ten pounds. A considerable sum for such a simple task." His smile suddenly vanished. "Too considerable. What does this Sir Guy truly want?"

"I told you, the maid delivered and the boy diverted."

"Diverted, or dead? He wants the boy dead, doesn't he?" Ari always had been too quick.

"He never said that."

"Such things are seldom said. Surely you're not planning to kill the boy."

"Only if I must. Oh, stop looking at me that way," Steinarr said as Ari's expression turned sour. "It's not like he's an innocent in this. He is a thief and a seducer."

"So are you. So am I. And Robin is not yet a thief."

"He will be if I do not stop him. Besides, Torvald and I need the coin. Everything is wearing out at once."

Ari shook his head. "If it is only the money, I can provide what you need. In fact, Brand said to ask you if—"

"No."

"But the land—"

"We have been over this, Ari. No."

Long ago, Ivar, living as the Norman lord Ivo de Vassey, had granted manors within Alnwick to Brand and Ari for the benefit of the entire crew. The lands had passed down by subterfuge, each man in turn stepping forth to present himself as heir when the previous owner "died" in some far-off place. To establish the claim, however, that man had to be able to visit the land, to live there for a time. It was an easy enough thing for most of the others; no one noticed an extra dog or bull or stag or even a wolf wandering the fields and forests. Brand had even managed, despite the bear, but only because of Ivar's protection.

But Ivar's time was long past and Alnwick currently lay in the hands of the king—and the lion prowled more widely and far more quickly than any bear. Steinarr couldn't do his share to hold the lands, and he refused to accept his share of their profit. He repeated his reasoning once more. "I take only what I earn."

"But this is no way to earn it, killing this boy," Ari protested. "Let Torvald take a turn in Northumberland. He can say he's Sir Geoffrey's son . . . uh, Theobald, returned from the Holy Land where his father died. A horse will blend in even more easily than the rest of us."

"'Tis not a matter of me letting him, and you know it," said Steinarr. Ari had made the same argument many times, and Brand had made it directly to Torvald the last time he'd come around, what, three-score years ago? But Torvald was the only one able or willing to deal with the lion, to stand between the beast and innocent human prey, and he took that charge seriously, knowing firsthand the pain of the beast's teeth and claws. "He refuses to go. I've told him to, but he will have none of it."

"He is as stubborn as you."

"He is loyal and a good friend. As you are to Brand."

"But I leave Brand to fend for himself on occasion, like now. He manages, just as you would. Torvald—"

"Torvald makes his own decisions, but you are welcome to leave another of your messages for him. Perhaps he will yield this time."

Ari muttered something that Steinarr couldn't hear, but which made the stallion toss his head in irritation. "Does Torvald know what you're about to do to that boy?"

"All I'm about to do is stop him from stealing what is not his. Whether he dies is up to him—though it seems I may only have to wait for him to kill himself."

Frowning, Ari nodded. "What do you suppose he was doing up that tree anyway? I didn't ask."

"Hunting for treasure, I wager, or at least for clues to it."

"Oh." Ari tilted his head, considering. "I think he found it. And I handed it right to her. Sorry."

Steinarr waved off his apology. "You didn't know. But it makes no difference anyway. They're going nowhere for the time being. So, are we the first you harry, or have you seen the others already?"

"I saved you for last this time." As they rode, Ari quickly ran through where the others were and what they were about, and then he came around to Gunnar, who spent his days as a bull, and amusement made his eyes sparkle. "He was up in north Yorkshire by himself for a time, until a crusty old steward spied him on manor lands. He had him caught, then decided he wanted to turn him from bull to ox on the spot. Apparently Gunnar took out three peasants and the side of a barn getting away. He's back with Jaffri now."

"Decided that living with the wolf wasn't so bad after all, eh?"

"Apparently. They found a dene east of Durham that seems to suit them well enough."

"And Brand?"

Ari's grin faded. "Still chasing every hint of magic, light or dark, but as yet to no avail. I left him in Cumberland, tearing down the walls of an abandoned nunnery where it is rumored some treasure was once hidden."

"'Tis a waste of time. One as steeped in the dark ways as Cwen would surely avoid Church lands."

"Perhaps, but remember it was her men who hid our amulets, not she. They may have thought hiding them on

Church lands would protect them. In any case, Brand next wishes to search the chamber where Cwen cursed us once more, to see if we missed anything that might guide us. After I leave you here, I will go to see if there is enough woodland remaining near Odinsbrigga to hide the bear while we do it."

"And if there isn't?"

"He has his mind set. We will find a way." They had reached a thick stand of oaks within the woods, and Ari looked around. "Is this far enough for the lion to hunt safely?"

"Nearly, but I will go deeper on foot." Steinarr dismounted and handed the stallion's reins and the rouncey's lead to Ari. "Ride toward the Lady Well. Go at least—"

"At least a mile. I remember. I will meet you back here in the morning." With a wave, Ari turned the animals west and headed off.

Steinarr watched him go, then set out toward the east and north. He had run only a little way when he spied a patch of moss the exact color of Marian's eyes. He smiled and kept going, his mind full of Marian and the pleasures he might enjoy in the month ahead.

"NO!"

The shout woke Matilda from a sound sleep. For a moment, the odd sights and strange press of the wall against her back confounded her, and then Robert cried out again and it all snapped into place: *Headon Hall. Broken leg.* She scrambled over to the cot where Robert thrashed fitfully with the blanket.

As she knelt beside him, he flinched and flung his arms out.

"Ow," she said as he connected with her jaw. She grabbed at his hands. "Stop it, Robin. Wake up."

"Maud?" He clutched at her, his voice high with pain or fear or both. "Why does my leg ache?"

He sounded feverish, but when she put her hand to his forehead, it was cool. "You fell. Remember?"

"Fell? Yes. I was falling just now." He slurred over the words, thick-tongued from the poppy syrup, and his eyes wandered as if they had come loose in his skull. "I'm sorry. I'm sorry I fell."

"Shh. 'Twas not your fault." It truly was not. The blame lay with Father. He was the one who'd sent Robert up that tree, goading him from the grave as he had goaded him in life. She stroked his cheek, and he turned his head into her hand and pressed a kiss to her palm.

"At least I got it," he muttered. "What'd it say?"

God's knees! He had gotten the riddle, and she'd forgotten all about it. She put her mouth by his ear. "I haven't read it yet. You were hurt."

"Hurt," echoed Robin, mumbling against her palm. He wrapped his fingers around hers and yawned again, hugely. His eyes fluttered shut. "Sorry . . . Cannot . . ."

"Shh. Go back to sleep. I will stay with you." Matilda knelt there holding his hand as the lines marring his face eased and his fingers slowly lost their grip on hers.

When she was sure he slept soundly, she tugged her hand free, quickly found her scrip, and pulled out the little cylinder Sir Ari had handed her. It was dull gray, likely made of tin, and the top was sealed with a drip of heavy red wax. She peeled the wax away with her thumbnail and opened it.

The little curl of parchment that spilled out was dry from its months or years spent sitting in the tree waiting to be found. She exhaled on it, letting the moisture of her breath soften the hide, then slowly eased it open. It crackled slightly, but hung together, and she shifted over by the single candle they'd been given for the night to read it.

"Harworth." That's all it said: just the single word. Cautiously, then with growing agitation, she turned the parchment over, tilted it, looked at it upside down, and held it up to the candle. No trace of any other words or markings could be seen, not even the thin patches that might mark rubbed-out letters. She shook the cylinder over her hand. A fragment of parchment fluttered out, and hopeful, she checked it, too. It turned out to be only an unmarked corner that had fallen off the larger piece.

"Father, you treacherous old fox. What have you done?" she whispered. She'd been ready to work through another riddle, but this must be some different sort of puzzle. Clearly, he intended to make them work for this.

And if she did work it through, then what?

Between outlaws and oxcarts and broken bones, they'd lost so much time. They had—she counted it off on her fingers just to be certain—two days more than thirty left, and from that two-and-thirty they must reserve time enough for Robert to ride to Edward. A week, at the least, since they didn't know where he was—and that with a decent horse. Willing as the little mare was, they must get their hands on a better animal. Perhaps they could borrow one.

But from whom? Not from Headon, surely; the reeve would have no part of it without the steward's leave, and she'd met the stable master earlier, a most unhelpful sort. She ran through anyone she might know within reach, but only one came to mind: Bartholomew of Grantham.

She cheered slightly. Grantham lay in the east of Nottinghamshire, so it must be near, and Bartholomew had been besotted with her the whole time they had fostered together. Surely he would lend her an animal. She could come back for Robert and . . .

And nothing. Even if she could get to Grantham and Bartholomew were there and she could persuade him to help, Robert could no more ride than he could walk, not for a fortnight or more. A fortnight lost would not leave nearly enough time.

There must be some way.

But of course there is a way, a voice whispered in the back of her skull. *A way has been put before you. Use it.*

No. Not that. She turned her mind to other solutions, but it was a fool's effort. Every possibility she lit upon dissolved into naught but shadows, leaving her sitting there in the darkened hall with only the one choice.

She pulled the blanket more tightly around her shoulders and settled back against the wall, trying to ignore the flutter in her belly that had stirred as soon as she admitted even the possibility, the flutter which had already led her to sin in spirit and which now would see that sin fully consummated.

Wherever she wanted, he'd said.

She hoped he was a man of his word.

CHAPTER 5

MATILDA LEFT THE hall shortly after dawn, turning over care of the still-sleeping Robin to the collier woman, Edith, and walked out across the fields in the direction they'd gone the day before.

She soon spotted them riding in. Even from a distance, she knew immediately it was them. The sun set fire to their golden heads, crowning them with light so they looked like angels—especially the new one, Sir Ari, who was as fair a man as ever she'd seen. Give him a pair of wings, she thought as they neared, and he would look at home hovering beside the Virgin.

Sir Steinarr, on the other hand . . . His fall from grace showed in every wight of him, from the confidently lazy way he sat his horse, to the wicked grin that quirked his lips as he met her eyes, to the way his thumb stroked back and forth along his reins in mindless sensuality. If he were allowed anywhere near the Virgin, he would surely invite her into his bed.

The Virgin, of course, would have nothing to do with him, but that was not a choice Matilda could afford to make for herself. The betraying flutter returned, more disturbing for the fact that she was facing its source. Thank the saints she wasn't feeling his mind right now. And thank the saints she hadn't ridden the mare out to meet them. It would be good to have her feet on firm ground when she dealt with him.

"Good day to you, Marian," called Sir Ari, beating his friend to the greeting. "How is young Robin this morning?"

"Easier, I think, my lord, for he slept most peacefully as I left him."

Sir Steinarr swung down off his stallion. "What I do not comprehend is why he was in the top of that tree to begin with."

"I should think that obvious, my lord. He was climbing it."

Chuckling, Sir Ari started to dismount, but Steinarr shot him such a sour look that he settled back into the saddle.

Sir Steinarr turned back to Matilda. "The question is, why?"

"Boys climb," she said lightly.

"He's hardly a boy. And he does not strike me as the climbing sort. But even allowing that he is, why here? And why *that* tree, when there is a whole forest of trees with sturdier branches within a stone's cast?"

"He thought it a challenge. Alas, it proved too much of one." Uncomfortable with the way he was pressing, she gave him a vague smile, then stepped past him to approach Sir Ari on his horse. She sank into a deep courtesy to the knight. "I wish to offer my thanks once more for your aid, *monsire*. I do not know what we would have done if you had not appeared to help us."

" 'Twas nothing," said Sir Ari. "I just happened along."

"As did I," muttered Steinarr behind her.

Only because you want to bed me, she thought as she turned to offer him a courtesy, in turn—polite enough, if not quite so deep. "Yes, my lord, you did. And of course you also have my thanks."

He nodded slightly. "So, what brings you out so early?"

Look at him, wearing that cocky smirk as though he already somehow knew. Bah. She may as well get this over with. "I wish a word with you, my lord. Alone, if you please."

Sir Ari looked from her to Steinarr, and a grin spread across his face. "I will go on ahead then. I will see you at the hall, yes? Um, yes."

He wheeled around and put his spurs to his fine black,

and the animal galloped off toward the hall. As the hoof-beats faded, Steinarr turned to Matilda. "We are alone."

She watched after Sir Ari, her brows drawn together. Perhaps she should call him back to see if he would help instead. Perhaps he . . . But no, she had her help, right here before her, and better the devil she knew at least a little bit. Checking to make sure the wall between her mind and the world was sound, she took a deep breath and squared her shoulders. "You can have me, my lord."

Steinarr froze, just for an instant, then his smile faded. "I am not certain I heard you."

"You heard me quite well, my lord. You can—how did you put it?—take me whenever you want, so long as you will take me wherever I want. And you can have your pound of silver at the end, to boot." She fought to keep her voice level so as to give him no sign of what this was costing her. "I accept your bargain, my lord. All I ask is that you do not hurt me when you . . . that is, when we . . ." She stuttered to a stop as her courage failed in the face of naming the act.

In the face of *him*, with his body so taut it set her in mind of a cat, ready to pounce. *He* would have no trouble naming it.

His face had taken on a dark, hungry look. He took a step toward her. "I can have you? That simply?"

"That simply, my lord, provided you keep to your word, and take me where I wish to go."

"I always keep my word." Another step. "'Tis a strange vow for a holy pilgrim to make."

"My cousin is very ill." She held her ground, despite how he loomed over her, devouring her with those heated blue eyes with their strange golden centers. It was so tempting, to open up just a little and know what he felt, whether his word was good or not, whether her body was enough to bind him to this task. But no, that would not be wise. "I would hear you say it, my lord. If I am to pay such a high price, I wish to know I will reach my goal." She offered her hand in pledge. "Your bond as a knight that you will take me all the way to the end."

"My bond as a *man* that you will go all the way," he promised, the suggestive warmth in his voice telling her precisely what he meant—and it had nothing to do with travel. As her cheeks flamed, he batted her hand aside and snaked his arm around her waist to tug her close. "There are more suitable ways of sealing such bargains, Marian."

She twisted away from his kiss. "There is not yet a bargain to seal, my lord. That was not an honest vow of aid, and I will not be misled by your trickster's words."

He lifted his head a little to look down on her. The faintest smile crinkled the corners of his eyes. "My honest vow, then. I will escort you where you need to go, in exchange for your favors as we travel and a pound of silver from your hand at the end. My bond. And now you, for women have been known to mislead as well."

She flushed under his gaze, but lifted her chin and spoke clearly. "I will lie with you whenever you wish and pay you a pound of silver, in exchange for your aid and escort on the rest of my journey. My bond."

His smile spread, tugging at his mouth. "Then the contract is made to your satisfaction?"

Why did he look so pleased with himself? She reviewed what he had said and what she had said, but found no flaw in the bargain. Slowly, she nodded. "It is."

"Good, for it is most certainly made to mine. A pilgrim's kiss, then, to seal our pact." Again, he bent to her.

She tensed, waiting for the deep plunder of the kiss by the church gate, the ravaging hunger that had stirred similar hunger in her. But it seemed he knew other tricks as well. This kiss was gentle, chaste, very nearly a pilgrim's kiss after all, except no holy pilgrim ever lingered over a kiss the way this man did, drawing it out until it no longer mattered that she didn't really want him, until her body lifted against him of its own accord, searching for more. When he finally released her, she hung there a moment before slowly settling back to her feet.

Something rough touched her cheek, and she opened her eyes to find him frowning down at her as he traced a line along her jaw with one fingertip. "You are hurt. What is this bruise?"

She touched the spot and found it tender. "Mmm." It took her a moment to remember. "'Tis nothing. Robin struck me. He—"

Steinarr's expression went thunderous. "Broken leg or not, I'll teach that puppy not to strike a woman." He whirled toward his horse.

"No!" She grabbed his arm, and for an instant, she felt the power of his anger, surging against the wall she'd thrown up. She pushed back and he faded. "'Twas not like that. He was asleep."

He stopped, every sinew of him vibrating beneath her hands like the strings of a rebec. "Asleep?"

"Aye. He dreamt he fell again. I tried to wake him and he lashed out." She released his arm and stepped back. "Robin would never hurt me, my lord. Never."

"Well. Good, then." He looked away, avoiding her eyes. An awkward silence stretched between them.

Finally, Matilda cleared her throat. "He will be pleased to know that you intend to guard my safety with such zeal."

His expression darkened again. "He knows of this . . . adventure of yours, then? He approves?"

"No. Neither." Her cheeks went hot, and now it was she who looked away. "Please do not speak to him of it, my lord. I will tell him 'tis only silver you ask in exchange for your help. I do not wish him to know what else passes between us."

"Tell him or not, as you will. He is *your* cousin," he said, his voice still rough with the dregs of anger. "When do you wish to set out?"

"Today. As soon as I pay the reeve for his care." The quicker the better, before she lost courage. She turned back to the manor.

He fell in alongside her, leading his horses, and they walked back in silence. She kept up the wall between herself and the world, but even so, her mind spun out all the possible things he might do to her, as though he had somehow tossed the idea of them over the wall to taunt her. Worse, her body responded to each and every thought in ways that both excited and shamed her.

Once more she recalled the warnings the priests had given about the sin of self-pleasure. She had always thought they exaggerated, trying to instill fear in her because of what they knew of her and her childhood strangeness. But perhaps not. Perhaps they had been right all along about the trouble it would bring.

Perhaps they had been right about her.

"YOU WHAT!" ROBERT sat bolt upright, then fell back to his elbows with a groan. "Ow. God's toes, that hurts."

"You must lie still." Matilda hurriedly pushed a cushion behind him, and helped him ease back onto it. She smoothed his hair off his sweat-soaked brow. "Shall I get you more poppy syrup?"

"No." He shoved her hand away angrily. "Are you mad, Matilda?"

She glanced around to see whose attention he'd attracted. She'd waited until the men had headed out to the fields after breakfast, but there were still a few people in the hall. Only a pair of serving girls, scattering fresh reeds over the old, seemed to have noticed, though, and all it took was a quick glare to send them back to their work. Matilda then turned the glare on Robin. "For the thousandth time, 'tis Marian. And keep your voice down."

"You tell me you intend to go hieing off with some stranger and expect me to keep quiet? You *are* mad."

"Sir Steinarr is not a stranger."

"All but!" Robert shook his head in disbelief. "Thank the saints he has no interest in helping us."

She stared at the tapestry on the wall behind him: the Virgin, turning away from the Devil to hold out her hand to a golden-haired angel. She should have asked Sir Ari. "The saints must want me to go."

Robert's eyes widened. "But he said no."

"And now he has said yes. 'Twill cost us a full pound

of silver, but he will take me the rest of way." *I'll see you go all the way,* he'd promised, and at the recollection, heat streamed through her and pooled just where he'd surely intended it to. *The devil take him.* "We can follow the clues and—"

"We? You told him what we're really doing, then?"

"Not yet."

"How can you expect him to help you with the clues when he doesn't even know that you're looking for something?"

"I will tell him."

"When?" he demanded.

"'Tis not something I can simply blurt out when we have lied from the start. I will tell him when I must."

"Bah. And in the meanwhile?"

"In the meanwhile, I will figure out the clues for myself and tell him where to go. He will think the places we visit are part of my pilgrimage. And when I—"

"He is not a fool."

No, he wasn't, but she went on stubbornly, "And when I find it—"

"*If* you find it."

"*When* I find it, we will come back for you. By then you will have healed enough to ride and we can go to Edward."

"*If* we can find him. *If* we have time. *If* Sir Steinarr doesn't simply take the prize for himself."

That thought hadn't even occurred to her, but when she considered it, she shook her head. "Why would he? He is being paid for his work, and the piece is worth little to anyone but you."

"It is worth enough. And then there is Guy. What if *he* catches up to you?"

"Then at least I will be with a strong knight who has already proved he will protect me." She told Robert about the bruise, and as she spoke, her fingers drifted to her jaw.

"I hit you?" Aghast, Robert tugged her hand away to see the mark. "Ah, Maud, forgive me."

She waved off his apology. "'Twas the poppy juice, not

you. I only told you to show you that he is ready to defend me. Even from you."

"Why?" demanded Robin. The question left her stuttering for an answer, and he jumped on her hesitation. "Never mind. I know why. I have seen how he looks at you."

"All men look at women in much the same way. Even you. But I have his vow that he will see me safely through this, and I trust his word as a knight." She cringed at the way she piled one lie on the other. She could offer him one bit of truth, though. "I have to try, Robin. I cannot just sit here and . . . and watch your bones knit!"

"And I cannot watch you go off with that man."

"*That man* will help us, which is what we need just now."

"What I most need is to know you are safe." He blew out a despairing sigh. "You should go home, Maud."

"Marian," she corrected under her breath. "Marian, Marian, Marian."

"You should go back, *Marian*. Ride straight to Lord Baldwin and marry him as you are meant to. At least you will be safe from Guy."

"Safe? Beneath that old whale? He will die atop me and crush me to death." And from what she knew of his habits, that would likely be the best of it.

Safety meant different things to a woman than it did to a man, or so she had concluded in the deep of the night as she'd laid out her choices beside each other: a month of Sir Steinarr or years of foul old Baldwin and the even fouler Guy. Father had thought to protect her by betrothing her to Baldwin, who had once been a powerful friend to Huntingdon. But with Guy waiting in the background for the older man to die, any safety Baldwin could provide would be fleeting. And then there was what Guy would likely do to Robert if they failed. No. They *must* complete this quest, and if that meant giving Sir Steinarr what he demanded, then that's what she would do. Even now, with her body betraying her, she knew it was the right choice.

"No. My best chance lies with your success. And your best chance of success lies with Sir Steinarr."

Robin shook his head. "I will not let you do this."

She folded her arms across her chest. "'Tis not yours to say whether I do or do not, *Cousin*."

"I am *not* your cousin," he grumbled under his breath.

"You are for now," she reminded him gently. "It will be all right, Rob. *I* will be all right. He is an honorable man. He has given me his vow." One of those was truth, at least.

She could see Robert's resolve softening, but she needed to distract him until he got used to the idea. She picked up the tiny corner of parchment he'd knocked aside when he sat up so quickly. "We just need to work out this clue. Harworth. It could be a town or an abbey or . . . or a horse, for all I know."

"'Twould be an odd name for a horse. A place, surely." He stared at the large piece still in his hand, then flipped it back and forth and squinted at it, much the way she had during the night. "I keep thinking if I look hard enough . . ."

"I know. But there is not so much as a scratch or pinprick."

With a sigh, he handed the parchment back to Matilda, who carefully returned it and the scrap to the cylinder. "And what do you propose I do while you follow these clues that are not clues?"

She wiggled the cap into place. "The reeve agreed you could rest here while you heal. I will hold him to it."

"Didn't I hear him say last night that he wants a shilling?"

"That was for both of us. 'Twill be less if I am not here."

"And more because someone will have to care for me with you gone, no doubt. It will leave you little to travel on." He plucked at a loose thread on the edge of his blanket. "Travel," he repeated to himself. "Sir Ari travels a good deal, I think. Perhaps he would know what and where Harworth is."

"That is a good thought. I will ask him."

"*I* will ask him. I will say we need to know for your pilgrimage."

"Then I have your blessing in this?" she asked.

"No, but even a fool can tell when a battle is lost. Go on, fetch him, and bring Sir Steinarr as well. He will need to know where Harworth is, too, to get you there in good time."

She nodded and hurried off, anxious to get on the road. Outside, she spotted Sir Ari by the well and started toward him, calling, "Your pardon, my lord. Where is Sir Steinarr?"

"I am here." Steinarr stepped out from behind Ari. He was naked to the waist and he held a bucket, the contents of which he had apparently just poured over his head, for water ran off him in sunlit rivulets. He plunked the bucket down on the edge of the well and shook himself off, then picked up his chainse and started blotting his chest dry.

"I, um . . ." Her mouth went dry at the sight of all that bare flesh—flesh that she would undoubtedly come to know quite well over the next weeks. Her gaze flickered down to where his worn linen braes draped over the rise at his groin. She'd know *that* soon enough, too . . .

"Are you ready, then, Marian?"

The amusement in his voice jerked her eyes up, but too late. He grinned at her. He knew, curse him.

"No, my lord. I am *not*." Fury and embarrassment lent her voice a steadiness she didn't expect or deserve. She lifted her chin and met his eyes, challenging him to contradict her even as she felt her cheeks blaze her guilt like watchtower fires. "Robin wishes to speak to both of you, *messires*. If you please."

Steinarr's smirk vanished. He shook out his chainse with a snap and pulled it over his head, then snagged his gown from where it hung on the well crank and started for the hall. Ari fell in beside him, and Matilda brought up the rear, where to her consternation she could make out every ripple of muscle beneath Steinarr's damp chainse as he worked his gown over his arms. And if the sigh that escaped her lips as he finally pulled the gown over his head was one of disappointment instead of relief, well . . . she was not going to be the one to admit it.

* * *

THE MAID HAD some steel to her, that was certain, Steinarr thought to himself as he stood aside to let Marian pass through the door, but the steel turned to honey as soon as she knelt beside Robin. Despite his irritation, he understood her concern. The boy looked terrible—better than yesterday, but still terrible. His hair was plastered to his head with the sweat of pain, and the skin around his mouth was taut and as pale as a trout's belly. Even so, he managed a weak grin and a slight bob of the head in acknowledgment. "My lords."

Steinarr nodded back. "How are you doing, boy?"

"Aching, my lord. But in one piece thanks to Sir Ari and you."

"We could hardly let you lie there."

"Some might." Robin's glance alit briefly on the reeve, who had come in through the rear door and was speaking with a serving woman in the far corner. "My cousin says you have agreed to take her to finish the rest of our pilgrimage."

"You have?" Ari gave Steinarr an accusing look. "You didn't tell me that."

Steinarr warned him off with a scowl. "Because it is not your business."

"Apparently it is not mine either, my lord," said Robin to Ari gloomily. Steinarr barely kept the sneer off his face. *Fool, letting his woman go off like this.*

"Do you know where Harworth is?" asked Robin.

Ari nodded. "Near Blyth."

"Closer to Tickhill," said Steinarr.

"Then you know it as well, my lord? That was to be the next stop on our journey."

"'Tis a twisted route you take," said Sir Ari, frowning. "If you came from the west, you would have done better to go there first."

"A pilgrim's path is often long and crooked," said Marian. "How long will it take to get there?"

"Two or three days." Steinarr looked straight at her and grinned. "Depending on how often we stop."

Her eyes widened, then narrowed over reddening cheeks, but she collected herself quickly. "Fine. Then I will pay the reeve his shilling and we can set out."

"There is no need for that, maid." The collier—Hamo, Steinarr thought his name was—had come in behind them, followed by two other men and a pair of women. "Edith told me what the reeve is asking. 'Tis too much for pilgrims to pay. We will keep young Robin with us and care for him. Edith here is good with herbs."

"Would you let me?" asked Robin, cheered by the idea. "Ah, that would be good."

"But they have no beds," said Marian, clearly dismayed. She turned to the old woman, looking for help. "He cannot sleep on the ground, Edith."

"Of course not. And he will not."

"I have a traveling bed," said Hamo proudly. "He can have it. It will not hurt me to sleep on the ground for a few weeks."

"But a charcoal camp is so dirty," protested Marian.

"And this is not?" Robin smacked the pallet beneath him and foul-smelling dust flew up in a cloud around him. "At least their dirt is the dirt of honest labor. They are kind folk, and I am grateful to have their offer."

"As am I, of course," said Marian, "But . . ."

"We will care for him, Marian," said the fatter of the other two men. "He'll eat as well as we do, and have good company while he heals. Ivetta here is a fine cook."

"And I do know my herbs," said Edith. "I know just how to give him ease and make that leg heal fast."

"See, Maud? I know I will be better off there."

With each point made, Marian's expression eased, until she wound up nodding at the end, not even noticing Robin's slip in using her eke name. She took his hand. "Are you certain?"

"I am." Robin brought her hand to his lips for a quick kiss that made Steinarr's shoulders bunch up. Robin looked up at Hamo. "How will you move me?"

"Well, now, we've been thinking on that." The collier scratched his chin. "Our wagons are too full up with gear and food to hang the litter proper, so we'll need to borrow a cart."

"What's that about a cart?" asked the reeve, coming up behind Ari.

"Young Robin here wants to do his healing out at our camp," said Hamo. "We'd be needing something to haul him in."

The reeve shook his head. "I cannot loan a wagon to you lot, not without payment and surety. The steward would have my hide for that, he would."

"Your steward sounds like an unpleasant man," said Steinarr.

The fellow missed the note of mockery. "Aye, he is that. I'll need four pence for it."

"Four pence!" Marian shot to her feet. "For one day's use?"

"Aye, plus a shilling in surety, and the carter's wage."

Ari's lips thinned at the man's avarice. "Tell me, Reeve, would your steward loan a wagon and driver to two noble knights for a day?"

The reeve sucked on his teeth a moment, considering, and finally nodded. "Aye, I could do that without his leave. But there's still a night's board and bed each to pay for. And that poppy juice the maid's been pouring down him."

"He had but one dose, and he has eaten nothing at all but a bit of poor bread this morning," said Marian. "And *I* slept against the wall."

"The boy has taken nothing of value from that filthy bed except a few lice," added Ari. "A penny is more than enough for what you've given, including the wagon and driver. And then you will be done with them."

"With *all* of us," said Steinarr, stepping in next to Ari, ready to back him even if he didn't want to bother with the boy himself. Besides, the reeve was an ass. He let one hand drift to his sword hilt. "It would be to your benefit."

The fellow gave Steinarr a closer look and blanched a little. "Aye, I believe it would."

Marian started to reach for her purse, but Steinarr found his first and flipped a coin to the reeve. The man caught it midair, gave it a quick look, and bobbed his head. He spun and started for the door, calling for men to start loading a wagon.

"Well, then, I'd better see that leg is well braced," said Ari. He bent over Robin and pulled back the blanket to reveal his leg, showing swollen and discolored between the sticks and ties. "This is going to hurt, boy. You'd be happier if you waited three or four days."

"I know, my lord," said Robin. "But 'twill be better in the end."

"I will fetch the litter," said Steinarr, anxious to hurry this along so he could get Marian away from her bastard lover and start working on her himself. He headed outside and, with a little poking around, found the rough litter they'd made yesterday lying against the side of the stable. He had squatted to tighten a loose lashing when Marian came up behind him.

"I came to return your penny, my lord. Here. Take it."

Ari and his stupid knots. He never had learned to tie a proper one. Steinarr gave the loose end an impatient yank. "We will settle later."

There was a short silence, and then something hit him hard, square between the shoulders. He shot to his feet and whirled to find Marian blazing at him. "I may be whoring for your aide, my lord, but I am worth more than a penny."

It took him a moment to think what he'd said. *Ah.* "'Twas not meant that way. I only—"

But by then she was already marching away, back as stiff as a frozen post. Shaking his head, Steinarr scooped up the silver penny and brushed off the stable muck. As she disappeared back into the hall, he tossed the coin once and dropped it into his purse.

By the gods, she truly did have some steel to her. Good. He liked a little steel in a woman—so long as she was soft when he wanted her to be soft.

He pulled out his knife and squatted once more to cut the knot on the bad lashing, smiling as he worked, certain Marian was going to be very soft, indeed.

CHAPTER 6

AS IT TURNED out, Robin possessed a bit of hidden steel himself. Despite refusing to take another dose of poppy syrup out of concern the reeve would demand more money, he handled the swaying and jostling of the wagon with barely a groan. And it wasn't as if Headon's carter tried to ease his journey either; the man couldn't have found more bumps and holes, or taken them any harder, if he'd tried.

After one particularly jaw-rattling drop that took the last bit of color out of Robin's cheeks, Marian pounced on the fellow. "Did your reeve order you to torture my cousin, or do you do it for the sport?"

"Eh? What's that? I drive how I drive. I need no woman telling me how."

"Then I will tell you." Steinarr fell back so he was abreast of the seat. "Find a smoother path for the boy's sake, else I will break *your* leg and drive you back myself. At a full gallop."

The man frowned and muttered something beneath his breath. Steinarr reined the stallion in close and leaned over. "What was that, Carter? I did not hear you."

The driver glanced warily at Steinarr, then at Ari, who had taken a spot on the other side of the wagon and wore an equally stern frown. "Naught, *monsire*. I said only, 'As you will, my lord.' I will take more care."

"See you do." Steinarr gave him a curt nod and fell back so he could keep an eye on how the wagon rode. That it also gave him unfettered leave to watch Marian was merely a boon, as was the look of gratitude she wore as she mouthed a silent *My thanks* behind the man's head.

A little while later, Ari also dropped back a little—to check on Robin, he said, but it didn't escape Steinarr that he took time to coax a smile from Marian while he was at it. No, he got more than a smile—she actually blushed a bit at whatever he said. *By the gods. Did* all *women think Ari's sweet words were for them alone?* Irritated, Steinarr put his spurs to the stallion and rode on ahead. He'd already spent too many years watching Ari beguile women from Kaupang to Kent; he had no interest in yet another demonstration of the moony sigh they all seemed to heave afterward.

The carter did indeed drive more carefully, though, and by midday, Robin had regained some of his color. Not long after that, they followed Hamo's little train down a narrow path that ran between ancient oaks with trunks as thick as the cart was wide. The air immediately cooled, and Marian dragged another blanket over Robin.

A mile or so into the woods, the track suddenly emptied out into a broad grassy lea. Hamo directed the carts where to stop, and within moments, men were unloading gear. Hamo's bed appeared and was set up beneath a broad oak, and men with axes in hand started cutting saplings and branches to make a lean-to near the fire, to shelter Robin in case the weather changed before a proper hut could be built. Children scampered around collecting wood for the fire and dry grass to stuff the mattress, while the women got the cook fire going and started a meal.

Though charcoal burners had more than once driven him from a good camp, Steinarr had to admire the work of this group; by the time four brawny men transferred Robin into the bed a little while later, they had roughed out a decent camp and Hamo had set two men to work with mattocks to clear ground for the first hut, with two more to come later.

"Would you care for some ale, my lords? We brought out two quarters from Retford. We will have better next week, of course, when Ivetta has had the chance to brew, but even poor ale is better than no ale, I always say. Agnes, bring these good knights each a jar," he told one of the passing girls without waiting for an answer.

Brimming ale pots appeared, and Steinarr accepted the one pressed on him, took a deep draught of the sour, weak stuff, and made appropriate noises of thanks. Ari asked a question about charcoal burning, and it set Hamo off. Steinarr tried to follow the conversation, but quickly got lost in talk of flipes and motty pegs and other such nonsense, all of which Ari seemed to understand, and when Hamo bent to show him something about the clay, Steinarr slipped away.

The women had gone off to gather wattling for the lean-to, leaving Marian to watch over the cooking pot and the dozing Robin. Steinarr wandered over to join her. He held out his jar, still half full. "Have some ale?"

She hesitated briefly before accepting it and taking a sip. She grimaced. " 'Twas better yesterday."

"And will be yet worse tomorrow, no doubt. I think 'tis our good fortune that you and I will not be here to have to drink it."

She glanced toward Robin, who snored peacefully on the cot. "Must we leave already?"

"I thought you were eager to be on your way."

"I was. I am. But the journey took so much from him. I would like to see how he fares before I leave."

"It is your journey. Take whatever time you wish. Besides, by the time Ari learns all there is to know about charcoal burning, 'twill be too late to make good progress today. We will start fresh in the morning."

"Does your friend intend to ride with us, then?"

A good question, and one he hadn't really considered. Usually, the *skald* lingered a fortnight or more when he came through, spending the days riding, sharing stories, and hunting. It was Ari who had spent most of one summer early on teaching him to read and write the runes, so he and Torvald could leave messages to each other, and all of another teaching him French after the Normans came. With centuries stretching before them, there was seldom reason to hurry a visit. This time, however . . . "No. I am not certain of his plans, but he will not travel with us."

"Ah."

The disappointment in that one word made Steinarr's jaw tighten. So, she wished Ari to go along, likely in the hopes his presence would shield her from fulfilling her bargain. *Or perhaps because she wanted him instead.* Steinarr reached abruptly for the ale jar, needing to wash the foul taste from his mouth. His fingers grazed Marian's, and for just an instant, less than a heartbeat, he could once again see his want, his need, his anger reflected in her eyes.

Marian gasped and jerked away as if burned. The ale jar dropped to the grass as she skittered backward, out of reach.

"Your pardon, my lord."

It took Steinarr a moment to realize it was the carter who had spoken, not Marian. With a growl, Steinarr rounded on the man. "What do you want?"

The fellow jumped, startled at his vehemence, but recovered quickly. "Naught, my lord. Just to say that I must start back soon, to be home before dark. The other knight said you would ride back with me, at least part of the way."

The idea of riding off now made Steinarr's chest tighten. He scooped up the ale jar, which had miraculously landed unbroken and upright in the meadow grass and was still half-full. He shoved it at the man. "Have some ale. We will be a little longer."

The man's eyebrows went up, but he took the jar. "Yes, my lord. I'm not one to turn down ale."

The carter meandered off, and Steinarr turned his attention back to Marian. She had retreated to the cook fire and was head down over the pot, stirring with great determination. The lines of her back fair shouted *Leave me be*, and beyond her, the sentiment was echoed in Robin's glower— apparently he hadn't been sleeping so soundly after all. It was the first time Steinarr had seen the boy looking anything less than friendly.

By the gods, 'twas only a touch. And barely that. With a grunt, Steinarr turned and stalked off to rejoin Ari and

Hamo, who had moved from charcoal burning to a discussion of how to pick the best trees to burn. Steinarr tried to make some sense of their conversation, but his attention stayed with Marian, watching every sweep of the ladle, every swipe of her hand across her brow . . . and every reassuring smile she gave Robin.

Finally, there was nothing more to say about trees either, and Hamo went off to check on the progress on the lean-to. Ari drained the last of his ale and carried the empty jar over to Marian. Steinarr could hear him talking, but couldn't make out the words. All he knew was that the creases in Robin's face eased, and that Marian once more smiled at Ari.

She hadn't smiled at *him* since Maltby.

"'Tis time we leave," he announced abruptly, out of patience. "Come, Ari. Our carter friend needs to be home before dark."

He threw himself on the stallion, leaving Ari to make their farewells. Marian stayed by the fire, studying the pot like she expected it to bring forth gold and rubies. She barely glanced up when Ari bade her good-bye and then quickly looked down before Steinarr could catch her eye.

It was just as well. If their eyes met again, he wouldn't leave, never mind that her lover lay right there, glaring at him. He was a hair's breadth from carrying her off into the forest right now, burying himself in her whether she wanted him or not. It was as if she'd enchanted him. Enthralled him.

Frowning, Ari untied his horse. "What the devil is wrong with you?"

"Nothing. It grows late and we need to be away."

Ari shook his head, clearly not believing the lie, and mounted up. As they turned to follow the wagon off down the path, Steinarr risked one last glance at Marian.

A maid stirring a pot. That's all she was.

He shook his head at his own foolishness. There was no enchantment. It had been just a touch, just a look, made more potent by the knowledge he would have her soon.

Tomorrow. He could have her tomorrow. The sudden ferocity of his lust made his thighs ache.

She must have sensed him watching her, for the ladle
slowed to a stop and her cheeks went as red as the coals at
her feet. He guided the stallion over so he could look down
on her, as he would tomorrow when he spilled her onto her
back in the grass in some meadow.

"On the morrow, Marian," he said evenly. "Early. Be
ready."

She drew a deep breath and slowly raised her head,
though she didn't meet his eyes. "Yes, my lord. I will be."

HE WAS IN a stew, that was for certs.

Not that Ari hadn't caught glimpses of Steinarr's wroth
before, but usually it took more than a word or two from
some woman to raise the lion's hackles. Interesting that
this woman could, and so easily.

Of course, there wasn't much he could say while the
carter was still around, and by the time they got close
enough to Headon to send the fellow rattling off on his
own, Steinarr seemed to have himself back in hand. Still,
as they turned around to head back toward a night camp a
little closer to the colliers, Ari spied a lingering clench of
jaw and had to ask.

"So . . . what did you do?"

"Do?"

"To Marian. What did you say to her?"

"Nothing."

"It must have been rude," Ari mused aloud. "She was
too embarrassed to look at you. You even made Robin
angry."

"I told her that if she didn't pour me more ale, I'd make
her listen to all of your stories, one after the other." He
glared at Ari. "The prospect fair made her puke."

"Fine. Don't tell me, then." But Ari couldn't leave it
there. "Just tell me how the devil you managed to convince
her to go off with you."

"I didn't. She asked me."

"Why? You're all but a stranger to her. And she's noble."

"And a noblewoman would never associate with someone like me, is that it?"

"No. Pillocks, you take everything badly. I only meant—"

Steinarr cut him off with a slash of the hand. "I don't need your apologies."

"I wasn't apologizing. You're the one being a horse's ass."

Steinarr's mouth opened, then snapped shut. He took a deep breath and blew it out, and when he spoke, some of the anger was gone. "Granted. I just . . . Bah, never mind. You're right, she wouldn't have asked me, but that she is so desperate to find her father's treasure for *him*—although she has not yet told me that, of course. I'm still supposed to think she merely wants to complete their pilgrimage for the sake of Robin's sister." His lip curled. "I doubt he even *has* a sister."

Ari shook his head. "I'm glad I'm not the one who must keep track of this tangle of lies. Between what I know and what I am supposed to know, I barely know what to call her or what to say before her."

"You?" Steinarr jerked as a fly lit on his neck. He smacked at the pest, but missed. "You tell stories that last a sennight and never miss a word."

"I miss scores of words. I just make sure everyone's half gone on ale before I start, so they do not care. She's sober and she's quick. If *you* misspeak . . ."

"I won't," said Steinarr firmly. "Besides, I intend to coax the truth out of her before too many days pass. She will be more forthcoming without *him* around, and then once I 'know,' I will persuade her to return to Huntingdon. The boy's broken leg serves my purposes well."

"A little too well. If I didn't know better, I might think you arranged for him to fall." Ari's eyes narrowed. "Come to think of it, you *were* awfully close by."

"If I'd had a hand in it, he would have broken more than a leg."

"And yet you threatened the carter to make his journey easier. Of course, I suspect that was more for Marian's benefit than his."

"Aye. But there was no reason to torture him. If I do kill him—and I'm not saying I will," he added as Ari started to protest. "But if I must, I will do it quickly."

"It shouldn't come to that. With Marian back home and well wed, the boy will have no reason to badger her again."

"He may not see it that way."

"Then convince him."

"I have a better idea. *You* convince him." Steinarr looked at Ari. "I mean it. Stay here, keep an eye on him while he heals and make sure he doesn't come after us, and get him to tell you the truth. Then convince him that Marian belongs with her cousin and her husband for her own good. When I get back, we can pack him off to someplace where he can make a new life for himself, and then we'll go off and hunt a bit."

"I don't know," said Ari. "I've already been gone a long while. Brand is waiting, and—"

"Ah. Too bad." Steinarr smiled grimly. "Well, I hope *I* can convince him, then. Otherwise—"

"Oh, all right. I'll stay." They rode along a little ways before Ari asked, "What about her? Do you plan to convince *her* of anything?"

Steinarr's smiled changed, softened. "I haven't had to so far."

Very interesting. "Then why was she so upset with you?"

"Why does any woman get upset at a man? They like to pretend they don't know what we want, yet throw a fit when we make it clear."

"You *were* rude, weren't you?" Ari turned his black across the road, so the stallion had to pull up short. "Be careful with her, Steinarr. Do not destroy her affections before you even have them."

"I have no interest in her 'affections,'" he said dryly. "What brings this on? Yesterday you were urging me to seduce her. Now you warn me off."

"I only warn about how you go about it." Ari hesitated,

considering, before he asked, "What if she's the one you need?"

"All I *need* is her quaint." Steinarr chuckled as Ari made a noise of disgust. "You're one to talk. You've tupped women all across England."

"Aye, but I leave each one happy, just in case. Even the whores."

"I'll leave her happy," vowed Steinarr.

"Not if you're crude about it. English noblewomen are not like our village girls back home. You haven't been able to be around them much, but—"

"I know precisely how little I've been around English women, noble or not." Steinarr pointed toward a deer path that angled off into the trees. "This is as close as I want to get to the colliers. Let's turn here."

They rode some way, until they reached a spot where the path forked. Steinarr dismounted and unbuckled his sword belt to hang it on the saddle. "I'll go that way. Meet me back here in the morning."

Ari took the reins of the two animals—the one that was really a horse and the one that wasn't. "Think about what I said."

Steinarr shook his head, chuckling. "How great is the chance that the first woman who stumbles across my path in four hundreds of years who isn't a whore is the one who will break the curse for me? I haven't even found my *fylgja* yet."

"Neither had Ivar when he wed Alaida."

"What happened to Ivar was chance. Even Cwen did not see it. He always had more luck than the rest of us put together."

"Chance or fate, it happened."

"'Twill not happen again."

"Do not presume to know what the gods have planned for you, Steinarr *inn prudhi*," warned Ari. "They have little patience for such arrogance."

"Bah. Have you been having visions again, *Skald*?"

"I need no visions to—"

"Then let go of it." Steinarr started backing down the

path. "Whether I bed her or not, or how I go about it if I do, is no concern of yours or the gods."

He turned and trotted away. Ari shook his head. Stubborn fool. He watched until Steinarr vanished into the trees, then rode off in the opposite direction, knowing Torvald would prefer to be far away when the lion began to prowl, angry, through the night.

THE DAY WAS nearly done when a young novice came to Cwen to say that the Mother Abbess wished to see her in her chamber.

Cwen nodded. "Tell her I will come anon. I must tie this stitch before it ravels."

"Yes, Lady Mother." The girl disappeared back the way she had come, and Cwen went back to her sewing, using the few moments to gather herself.

In her struggle to make the old ones take notice, she had spent her nights calling to the gods, and her days, as she went about the work assigned her, drawing every mote of power she could find in this place. Even as she prostrated herself on the cold stone floor of the chapel with the others, her lips moving in their prayers, she called again and again to the Old Ones in her heart. The effort had left her exhausted and brittle.

But Mother Humberga must not see that. She took a few moments to rid herself of the fatigue, tied off her stitch, then rose and smoothed her robes.

She went to the abbess with downcast eyes, as the nuns were supposed to do. And as the nuns were supposed to do, she knelt and kissed the abbess's ring, though as ever it grated to bow to this weak vessel of a weak god. "Mother Abbess."

"Sister Celestria." The abbess waited for her to rise. "In my prayers this afternoon, it came to me that someone should visit our estate in Nottinghamshire, to see that the charcoal promised us is forthcoming and of good quality."

Cwen tamped down the sudden uprush of hope. "A wise idea, Mother."

"Such worldly business falls to you as prioress, of course, but I have also decided to send Sister Paulina," said the abbess. "Father Renaud has agreed to go as well, for propriety and safety. We need only wait for other travelers going the same direction."

"Of course, Mother. Shall I tell Sister Paulina, or will you?"

"Send her to me. Our younger sister has not left the safety of these walls since she came to us in her eighth year. I fear she may be frightened of the world and I wish to calm her fears as I speak with her."

"Yes, Mother." Cwen genuflected once more and took her leave. Biting her tongue against a crow of joy, she made her way slowly—because the nuns always moved slowly—first to where Sister Paulina worked at her weaving, and then to the herb garden, where old, half-blind Sister Sibilla worked in the far corner, bent over the weeding. There, in the near privacy, Cwen fell to her knees before the holly where she had cut her wand so long ago and raised her clasped hands. If anyone saw her, they would assume she prayed in its shade.

And in truth, so she did both pray and rejoice. This was her sign. There was no more need for someone to see to the charcoal this year than there had been ten years ago. The gods had put the thought into the abbess's head. The Old Ones had heard her and found her worthy at last.

She finished her silent prayer of thanks, then scraped her palm across a holly thorn. The reopened wound bled freely, and she smiled as she smeared the fresh blood on the tree's thick trunk as an offering.

"As always, I am your instrument," she whispered. "So mote it be."

Her prayer finished, she licked her palm clean, relishing the coppery taste of the blood, as surely the gods must, for they rewarded it above all other offerings. How much more she would be able to honor them with a virgin's blood, which she would now have, thanks to Abbess Humberga.

Cwen smiled. A virgin nun and one of their priests.

Surely such potent sacrifices would persuade the gods to fully restore her powers.

Still smiling, she rose and went to prepare for the journey to Headon. It seemed there was, after all, some benefit to being the prioress of Kirklees.

CHAPTER 7

SOMEONE WHO SMELLED of damp grass and willow leaves plopped down next to Matilda. "You said to say when we saw them."

Matilda opened her eyes to a small, dirty-faced girl who stared up at her in the speckled light beneath the tree where she had gone to hide. Goda, this one was. One of Osbert's litter. "So I did. And did you see them?"

She shook her head. "Papa did. Coming down the path."

"Ah."

"Does your head ache? Father said you came over here because your head ached."

"It did a little. Run along and ask one of your brothers to put the bridle on the mare and bring her out."

"Are you really going with them?"

"With Sir Steinarr, yes."

"You should stay and marry Father."

Matilda bit back a smile. Osbert had hinted at the same thing earlier, as they'd broken their fast. Now she told Goda the same thing she'd told Osbert. "I cannot. I must help Robin. And your father deserves a better wife than I would make him. I am far too cosseted and not nearly strong enough to make a collier's woman."

"*I* think you would make a good collier's woman. And a good mother." Goda threw her spindly arms around Matilda's neck in a fierce hug, then scampered off without another word.

Alone once more, Matilda set aside her amusement and closed her eyes again to wait. She had hidden herself away not because her head hurt, but because she had wanted time to prepare herself, to harden her mind against what she knew was coming. *Him*.

She did not want a repeat of yesterday afternoon. She'd thought herself well guarded, but in the innocence of sharing a jar of ale, she must have relaxed a little. No, a lot. Far too much. That moment when he'd touched her hand and she'd found herself suddenly in the midst of all that lust again . . . that moment had frightened her. But what had frightened her more was that she hadn't been able to pull back from it, not until he rode away. He wasn't going to ride away from her for the next month, and so she had come in here to make certain she was ready. She couldn't let herself slip again, or she would be lost.

It would help if she knew why it had happened to begin with, why she could feel this man, of all men, and so clearly. She'd always had to work to read a person, to reach out with deliberate intent, and even then, the rare minds she'd managed to touch had all been blurs, their human emotions a mere shadow of the crystalline clarity of animal urges. This one . . . This one was powerful, raw, his mind brimming with furies and desires and needs as strong as any beast's. And that wildness . . .

Well, she could control when and how she touched beasts, and she would control when and how she touched Sir Steinarr—not at all. She would keep her thoughts close and her walls up. She would block herself off from every creature, including him. For a month. The very thought of it exhausted her already.

She heard horses coming nearer and tested. No, she couldn't feel him at all. Even as Sir Steinarr's voice drifted through the underbrush, she still felt nothing: not man, nor horse, nor oxen, nor even the fox kits that scuffled in the grass nearby. With their minds of purest need—food, sleep, play—young animals had always been among the easiest creatures for her to sense. She watched as one bit the other on the ear, and though the kit yelped, she felt no trace of his pain or anger. Satisfied that her mind was solidly her own and behind the best walls she could mount, she pushed to her feet.

As she stepped out into the meadow, Sir Steinarr turned. Their eyes met, and she checked once more. Nothing. She greeted him with a smile—he needn't know it came from relief and not from any pleasure at seeing him. "A good morn to you, my lord."

"And to you, Marian." His eyes twinkled with mischief. "Are you ready?"

Devil. He was trying to throw her back into the embarrassment of the previous afternoon, but she was prepared this time. Her smile was steady. "Nearly, my lord. A moment to say farewell to my cousin."

Matilda went over to the lean-to and perched on the edge of Robin's cot. "You do look better, now there's enough light to see. You have your color back."

"Edith's willow bark has eased the pain some, and I vow I can feel the knitbone working even as I lie. I told you this was a better place for me." His smile faded. " 'Twould be a better place for you, too."

"Robin . . ."

"I know, I know. You are going no matter what I say."

"For your *sister's* sake." Wearing a wry grin, she winked at him, then leaned over to kiss him on the forehead. "Heal quickly, Rob. You must be ready to ride when we get back."

"I will be." He slipped his hand behind her neck and pulled her down to whisper in her ear. "Tell him. And be wary of him."

"I will do both." She pressed another kiss on him, tugged his hand away, and rose to face Edith and Ivetta. "I could not leave with an easy heart, were he not in such good hands."

"You can be sure he is." Edith stepped past her to hand Robert yet another bowl of pottage—his third this morning, by Matilda's count. "We shall have him healed in a trice, Ivetta and me."

"And he will be fat as Osbert when you come back, no doubt," said Hamo, leaning his mattock against the tree and coming to join the women. "They will do well by him. 'Twas good you let us bring him here."

"I cannot offer thanks enough."

"Then say a prayer or two for us amid those you make for young Robin's sister." He pressed a penny into her hand. "And give this to the priest in Lincoln, to say Mass for us."

"I . . ." Guilt heated her cheeks as Robert frowned at her over the collier's shoulder. No matter what he thought of her skill at lying, she did not enjoy it. "I will see to it."

"And I will remind her," said Steinarr. He came up beside her and plucked the coin off her open palm. "Better yet, I will pay for your Mass, by way of thanks for keeping young Robin. And I will buy you another for putting up with Ari. He has decided to play a little longer at physician. He wishes to linger in the area to watch over Robin and see that his leg heals straight." He tossed the coin back to Hamo, who thanked him. "Come, Marian. We waste good light. You will ride behind me."

Behind him. Touching him. Holding him. Matilda's stomach slid sideways at the idea. She looked to Goda's oldest brother, Much, who had just led out the mare. "But I have—"

"That animal will never complete such a journey." Steinarr held out his hand. "Give me your things."

Unwilling to let either him or Robert see how much this disturbed her, she forced the smile back to her lips and handed over the bundle. But when he stepped around to add it to the pile of gear on the rouncey, she followed him.

"The mare is strong enough, my lord. I would rather ride her."

"If you insist." He pulled the knot tight and wiggled things to make sure the load was secure. "She will slow us down a good deal, but if you think Robin's sister will last long enough, I am willing to try her."

Curse it. He was right, of course, even if for the wrong reason. Robert's wish to join the colliers had cost them yet another day. If the mare slowed them even a little . . . No, she couldn't risk that this whole thing would come to nothing, that she would give her body to this man for naught. "Perhaps you are right. I will ride behind."

She signaled for Much to put the mare back and stepped

around to the stallion's left to mount. It put her out of sight of the others, and her smile fell away.

Before she could get it back, Sir Steinarr ducked beneath the horse's neck to join her. He gave no indication he'd noticed her lack of smile, but as he reached down to check the stallion's girth, he leaned close and dropped his voice. "It is not so terrible, Marian. Think of it as a chance to become accustomed to having your arms around me."

Enough. If she did not regain some of her own, he would make the next weeks entirely miserable. She put on her most innocent expression. "Have others found it so unpleasant, then, my lord, that I must practice to endure it?"

He pulled back to look at her, eyes narrowed, and for an instant she thought she'd exceeded herself as a peasant, or perhaps struck too close to his male pride. Then he chuckled and flipped the stirrup back into place. "You will soon enough discover that for yourself."

He laced his fingers together and leaned down to give her a hand up. She hesitated. This was where it had started, with him helping her mount. This was where she'd first touched him, body and mind. She checked her defenses again, then took hold of the saddle, stepped into his hands, and let him lift her up. A moment later, he settled into the saddle in front of her, and she tentatively slid her hands around his waist.

"See, 'tis not so bad," he murmured.

No, it wasn't bad at all. He was lean and strong, the sort of man she had always liked to ride behind. And more importantly, her mind remained hers. She breathed deeply, perhaps for the first time since she'd made this decision. She truly could do this.

"So you are away, then," said Osbert, coming up beside Hamo. He looked as unhappy as if she really had intended to marry him and was now riding off with another man.

"We are," she said gently. "Farewell, Osbert."

"God speed you back to us. Take care of her, my lord."

Steinarr nodded. More farewells and Godspeeds echoed around the clearing, a few accompanied by childish tears.

Finally, Matilda twisted around to say one more farewell to Robert.

"I will return soon," she said. "You will hardly miss me."

"I already do miss you. Be safe, Maud." He struggled to raise himself up on his hands. "My lord. A word before you go?"

Steinarr reined the stallion around so he could see him more easily, "Be quick about it."

"I fear for my cousin's safety on this journey," said Robert. "Will you see to it with all your might?"

"Of a certs," said Steinarr. "She will come to no harm while I am with her."

"And what of her honor, my lord? Will you guard that as well?"

Matilda gasped. "Robin!"

Steinarr went rigid before her. "What?"

"Will you guard Marian's chastity with as much vigor as you do her safety?" Robin's voice filled the clearing as though he were a priest in a church. "I would have your vow as a man and a knight before I see you ride away with her."

"You little—"

"Of course he will," said Sir Ari quickly, eyes twinkling with amusement. "Won't you, Steinarr?"

Matilda's cheeks burned as though she'd been slapped. "This is not necessary."

"I think it is," said Robin. "Your vow, my lord."

"It seems a fair thing for the lad to ask, my lord," said Osbert, and agreement rippled through the gathered colliers.

"You are taking the maid on pilgrimage, after all." Ari stepped over and grabbed the stallion's bridle. The corners of his mouth, twitching wildly as he fought a grin, betrayed how much he was enjoying the sport. Matilda suddenly understood that he knew what his friend had planned for her, and her cheeks grew hotter yet. It was all she could do not to fling herself from the horse and run away in mortification, but if she got off, she would surely never get back on and all would be lost.

The grin won out, and Ari beamed up at them, nearly laughing. "Surely you don't intend to tup a holy pilgrim."

A growl rumbled up under Matilda's hands and rattled against the edges of her mind. She jerked her hands away. *No, no, no, no, no.*

"Your vow, my lord," repeated Robin. "Or she may not go."

"And who are you to say what she may or may not do?"

Even from behind him and even working to keep her mind away from his, Matilda knew there must surely be murder in Steinarr's eyes. *Please, no.*

"He is her cousin," said Ari, his smile falling away. "And the only man here from her family. It is his right and his duty to protect her. So there it is. You can swear to Robin, or you can leave Marian here and break the oath you made to help her on her journey. 'Tis simple enough. Come, friend, make the vow you surely already intend to keep."

Steinarr's fist bunched and flexed on his thigh. Matilda held her breath. Slowly, almost imperceptibly, he collected himself. The rigidity eased. His back broadened as he drew in a deep breath.

"Of course." The evenness of his voice, untainted by any trace of the anger she knew was there, astonished Matilda almost as much as his agreement. "You shame your cousin, Robin, demanding such a vow before so many when it should have been asked in private, but if you want it, you have it. I will guard your cousin's chastity" —*Did he put some odd weight on that word?*— "with both body and sword. My bond."

Osbert's face fell.

So did Robert's. "Oh. Well. Then. I accept your vow, my lord."

Curse it, Robin had thought to stop her with this humiliating foolishness. He'd thought Sir Steinarr would refuse to make such a promise. But he had made it. He had, and by forcing him to it, Robin had given him good cause to say their earlier bargain was no longer valid. Curse it.

Sir Ari released the bridle and stepped back to give

Steinarr a slight bow. "A good journey to you then. I will see you back here in, what, a month's time?"

"Oh, less than that, my lord," said Matilda. "Little more than a fortnight, I hope."

"Hmpf." Steinarr glowered over his shoulder. "Put your arms around me, maid, or I will tie you on like an infant."

He might have sounded calm speaking to Robert, but he clearly wasn't. Pressing her lips together, Matilda checked her defenses again. His anger was there, but distant. She threaded her arms around him.

Like a lover.

The thought had barely touched her mind when Steinarr put his spurs to the stallion and they galloped out of the clearing, away from Robert and Sir Ari and Osbert.

Away from anyone who had heard his vow.

HE WOULDN'T WANT to be Marian for the next day or two, Ari decided as he watched the stallion and its two unhappy riders disappear down the path. Not that Steinarr would hurt her, but he wasn't going to be pleasant to be around until he figured out that this was for the best.

"To work, everyone," said Hamo, putting his mattock over his shoulder. "Not you, of course, *monsire*, begging your pardon. Nor you, Robin."

Everyone grabbed their tools and headed off to work on the huts, which must be completed before Hamo would let work start on the charcoal pit. Ari waited until they were well away before he went over to squat beside Robin's bed.

"That was a bold thing to do, lad."

Robin flushed. "Maud likely wants my head for it."

"Or something lower." Ari laughed as Robin's color went even darker. "Once she stops to think, she will realize you only did it to protect her. Now, let me see what Edith has done for you."

He flipped back the blankets to expose the injured leg and began to peel away the comfrey root poultice Edith had made.

Robin lifted his head, straining to see. "How does it look?"

"Lie back and let me see." Ari poked around a little and declared, "'Tis better. The swelling is beginning to ease, though, so the splints are loose. I will adjust the bindings so your leg does not move around too much."

He began going through the knots one by one, untying and tightening each just enough to keep the splints in proper position and the leg straight. Robin lay patiently, wincing slightly when Ari had to shift his leg to fix the knots above his knee.

"Sorry."

"'Tis not as bad as yesterday." A cock wren chattered and burbled overhead, and Robin stared up, searching for the bird among the leaves. "Should I have asked for Sir Steinarr's promise in private, my lord? Did I shame Marian with the way I did it?"

Ari shook his head. "Every man here understands why you asked for his vow before all. Even Steinarr."

"He did not look like he understood. For a moment, I feared he would come off that horse and break my other leg, like he threatened the carter he would do."

"I would have stopped him. For you, not the carter," added Ari. "You were shrewd to wait until they were ready to leave. If you had demanded the oath earlier, Steinarr might have ridden off without Marian, and then *she* would be furious. For my own part, I would rather face an angry knight than a raging woman. No, you handled Steinarr rightly enough, lad, even if he did not like it."

"'Struth, he did not." Robin shook his head. "I hope he does not take out his anger on Mau—er, Marian."

"He will be cross, but it will stop there." Ari decided to put the boy out of his misery on the maid's name. He was going to tire of the constant stuttering over it. "Why do you sometimes call her Maud and other times Marian?"

Robin went bright red. "I . . . she . . ." He stopped himself and his brow crinkled with thought. Ari could see the instant he came up with a story. "I had trouble saying her name as a child and shortened it to Maud. She prefers Marian, but 'tis hard to change the habit now."

Not bad, but the boy was not built for guile. His eyes darted around too much. Now the maid—she was practiced. She could lie with the best. If he were a raven during the day instead of at night, he would travel along and watch her and Steinarr spar, just for the sport.

"Well, she is not here," said Ari, turning his mind back to the subject at hand. "Call her what you will, and I will not tell her if you get it wrong."

Robin's mouth twisted in chagrin. "My thanks, my lord, but I should still probably remember to call her Marian."

"And I still will not tell her," said Ari. He pulled the last knot tight and started to put the poultice back in place.

"Hold there, my lord," said Edith, coming up behind him. "I have fresh knitbone."

Ari stepped aside and watched the old woman wrap her cloth, soaked in the paste from boiled comfrey root, around the break. She bound it all loosely, then gently tucked the blankets around Robin's legs and pushed to her feet with the wheeze of someone who had breathed too much heavy smoke. "There you go, lad. Now rest a bit."

"I would rather do some useful work. Prop me up and give me my knife and some wood, and I'll carve you a spoon or a spindle or something."

"In a day or two," said Ari. "For now, stay flat and rest. That leg must stay still lest it heals with a crook. Besides, you had a hard day yesterday."

Robin looked to Edith, but she shook her head. "His lordship's right, lad. Rest. We'll have a spoon from you another day." She took the bowl he'd set aside and carried it over to the fire to dump the uneaten gruel back into the pot to stay hot with the rest.

Ari followed her. "Speaking of useful work, do you have an extra mattock at hand?"

"What do you need dug, my lord? I will set one of the lads on it."

"You mistake me. 'Tis not my work but yours. I want to help Hamo and the others."

"Oh, no, my lord." She watched aghast as he unbuckled his belt and leaned his scabbard and sword against the nearest wagon. "That would not be right. That is work for peasants, not noble knights."

"Knights need strong arms to fight. I can either build them swinging my sword at straw men or swinging a mattock at the turf."

"I don't know . . ."

"I have a month to pass waiting for my friend, and I cannot spend all of it watching Robin mend." Ari peeled off his good gown and tossed it down next to his sword, then tucked his chainse hem into the waist of his braies and started rolling up his sleeves. "Come, woman, where is that mattock?"

THEY KEPT TO the road all day, passing through the scattered villages of northern Nottinghamshire with barely a stop to stretch their legs and let the horses rest. Late in the afternoon, though, Sir Steinarr suddenly wheeled the animals off the road and headed into the woods. "Hold on."

Matilda caught at his waist as they plunged down a short slope. "Where do we go, my lord?"

"'Tis time we stop for the night."

The night. With him. Her body tightened in anticipation or fear or . . . She didn't know, but she did know he hadn't answered her. "That tells me the hour, not our goal."

"A safe place I know. Does that help you?" His voice was crisp. Curt.

She understood his continuing ire; she was still furious with Robert herself. In his zeal to protect her, he had forced Sir Steinarr to renounce the one thing that had persuaded him to agree to this journey in the first place. By all rights, he could claim the bargain he'd made with her was broken. In truth, she was surprised he hadn't, that he'd carried her this far, that he'd brought her along at all. All day, she'd been waiting for him to turn around and take her back, or worse, abandon her in some strange village to find her way back alone.

But here they were, preparing to stop for the night, and she had yet to figure out what he intended to do.

She knew what *she* intended to do—live up to the agreement she'd made. She'd decided that even before they'd reached the Headon road. She had kept it to herself, hoping to find a moment when he wasn't quite so angry, but now the hour was nearly upon her and he still seethed. She was simply going to have to tell him. Show him.

They rode more than a league into the forest, following trails so faint she could barely make them out, although Sir Steinarr seemed to find them easily enough. Finally, one trail led into a clearing at the foot of a slight cliff. Steinarr swung his leg up and over the stallion's neck and hopped off, then reached up to help Matilda down, all without saying a word.

Safely on the ground and out of his hands, Matilda peered at the face of the cliff. "Another cave?"

"A little better." He tipped his head toward the south end of the cliff. "Over there."

It took Matilda a moment to spot it: a tiny, stone wall built into an overhung hollow in the side of the cliff. "A shepherd's hut?"

"A hermit's cell."

"Truly? I have never seen one. Where is the hermit?"

"Long dead."

Curious, Matilda went to explore. It seemed to be an ancient dwelling. Moss encrusted the lower part of the wall and the door had rotted away, leaving only the rust-stained holes where hinges had once hung. The hermit, whoever he had been, had clearly spent some part of his life as a mason, for where the moss didn't grow, the stones fit together so tightly a blade of grass wouldn't fit between them.

She stepped inside and spread her arms wide. She could span the space in one direction, and nearly so in the other. A few cobwebs draped the corners, but for a place that had been abandoned for so long, it was amazingly tidy and free of litter and vermin, as though someone had been there not too many years before.

The light dimmed and she turned to find Steinarr blocking the door, his hands resting against the frame. She steadied herself with a deep breath and plunged in. "Is this where we will sleep?"

He stilled, and anger buzzed at the edges of her awareness. "*We?* Were you not listening to the vow your cousin demanded from me?"

"It was not his place to ask it."

"And yet he did." His hands fell away from the frame and he took a step toward her. "You played it very well, Marian."

"Played it?"

"Having him ask me before Ari and the others."

"I had no hand in that, my lord. I told you I would not tell Robin of our bargain, and I did not."

"You expect me to believe the little *askefise* thought of it on his own?"

"Do *not* call him that," she snapped. *Askefise. Ash-blower—a man who stayed by the fire while others went to war.* Father had wielded the same word like a whip, choosing the English to insult Robin's origins as well as his courage. "Just because a man is gentle, it does not make him a coward."

"*Man.*" Steinarr's lip curled into a sneer. "He hid in the bushes while they killed John Little."

"I told you, John told us to hide. We had no weapons."

"A *man* would have stood by him."

"And died? To leave me to them?"

"Instead, he has left you to *me.*" His gaze raked over her, stripping her naked so quickly, so thoroughly, she had to curl her hands into fists to keep from covering herself.

She raised her chin and glared at him. "Then have me, my lord, as we agreed. I release you from the vow you made to Robin."

His shift from anger to desire and back again hit her like a hammer blow, nearly taking out her knees. "To your fortune, I have more honor than he."

He whirled and stalked out, leaving her shaking amid the cobwebs and the chaos of his emotions. So it wasn't *all* anger after all. That incredible, rutting lust was still there, as strong as ever, but mixed so deeply with the fury she couldn't tell where one left off and the other began.

"Get out here," he bellowed.

Yes, she could: *that* was pure anger. Well, piss on him. It wasn't her fault he'd let himself be outwitted by Robert. She pulled back hard until both his mind and her trembling faded.

When she stepped outside, she found that he was unloading the rouncey, piling the bundles and sacks and kegs neatly under the overhang of the cliff. She stood there, hands on hips, waiting for him to say something, but he kept working. Finally, she stepped into his path, so that he had to swerve around her to toss the rouncey's packsaddle next to the stack. "What did you want, my lord?"

"Firewood," he snapped, turning back to get the stallion's saddle. "Lots of it. These woods are thick with wolves." He tossed the second saddle by the first and dropped both pads on top. "I will water the horses."

He led the horses off, and she began to gather wood. Again. It had been one of her chores with the colliers, too, and she was growing tired of it. She was growing tired, period, and her back ached each time she bent to pick up another stick. She'd thought herself a hard worker; acting as mistress of Huntingdon after her mother's death, seeing to the stores and meals for five-score men and women, and directing all the weaving, spinning, and sewing kept her busy from dawn to dusk. But the sort of labor she'd done in the last week had given her a fresh appreciation of the burden peasant women carried—they did all that she did, plus tended their animals, saw to their children, and worked their own fields beside their husbands, in addition to whatever service they owed the manor.

Of course, they didn't have to hold a man's mind at bay all day either. Some of her exhaustion came from that, and as she moved farther away from Steinarr in search of wood, she realized how much. The greater the distance, the greater the relief, so she wandered far and worked slowly.

By the time she threw the last armload of wood on the pile, Steinarr had returned with the horses, measured out their oats, gotten a good fire going before the hut, and sliced several thick slabs of bacon, which he had hung on sticks over the fire.

Matilda's stomach grumbled aloud as she watched the bacon drip and sizzle. Steinarr looked up. "Hungry?"

"Aye, my lord." She inhaled deeply, savoring the smell. "If there are so many wolves, will not the scent of meat attract them?"

"So will the scent of you." He reached into the food bag and found a cloth-wrapped loaf, which he held out to Matilda. "Food is food to the beasts of the forest, and you would be a tender morsel. Cut some bread."

She cut two thick slices and started to rewrap the loaf.

"More," said Steinarr. He watched her cut another slice. "*More*. I do not want to find myself hungry come midnight. And *you* want it even less."

She eyed him sideways, waiting for an explanation to such a strange statement. When it didn't come, she counted pieces of meat and cut a slice of bread for each. Steinarr seemed satisfied at that, and as soon as the bacon was hot through, they settled back to eat in silence.

Slowly, as they worked their way through the meal, Steinarr's anger began to fade. She knew it without using her ability, just by watching the way the tautness in his face eased. She recalled a similar shift in his mood that first night, when he ate the cheese and bread. It was as though he were starving all the time, and the hunger brought out the anger or made it sharper. Perhaps it was as simple as that. If so, she must try to see that he stayed well fed. It would make her life easier.

When they were done, three pieces each of bacon and bread were left. She started to gather them. "I will set these aside for morning."

"No. Leave them. They will be eaten tonight." He dragged the skin of ale into his lap, removed the plug with a twist, and hoisted it high to take a deep drink. He made a face. "God's knees, this *is* worse than yesterday."

"Why drink it, then? The water in the spring is clear."

"It may look it, but it stinks of sulfur. And as your

collier friend said, even poor ale is better than none." He took another drink and wiped his chin on the back of his hand before he passed the skin to Matilda.

There was no way to sip from a skin, so she steeled herself and hoisted the bag for a large draught. She came up spluttering. "Are you certain the water is worse than this? Why did you even take it?"

He almost smiled. Almost. "Ivetta insisted on filling it for me this morning. I could not find a way to refuse her."

"Likely she wanted to be rid of it, so she can brew her own."

"Likely." He took the skin back and had another draught. "She can hardly do worse."

"In truth, she does far better. We drank the last of what she'd made in Maltby as we traveled. 'Twas so good I would like to hi—" Matilda caught herself just in time. *Hire her for Huntingdon*, she'd almost said. She switched directions and finished without a pause, "Have it every day."

"That good?"

"You can try it when you take me back for Robin."

And his anger was back, that fast. "That may be sooner rather than later."

She sat up straight. "But you swore!"

"I have found myself swearing too many things in the past few days. The vows demanded of me do not agree, one with the next." He stared into the fire, muttering something that ended with the word *English*.

God's knees. She should never have mentioned Robin or even the possibility of him taking her back. Now it was in his mind, and if she didn't do something quickly, it would stay there and all would be lost. 'Twas her misfortune that she knew of only one thing she could do, one thing he truly wanted.

Whenever he wanted. How often would that be?

She scrambled around to kneel beside him. "I meant what I said earlier, my lord. I do not hold you to the oath that was forced on you. You and I made our bargain first, and it takes precedence. I will keep that bargain, on my honor."

"What does a woman know of honor?"

"More than most men." She leaned over and kissed him, quick and hard, and sat back.

He lifted an eyebrow. "Is that all you offer as proof?"

Devil. He wanted proof? She would give him proof. She gathered herself and leaned in again. This time, she poured everything she knew into her kiss, beginning softly, with the merest brush across his mouth. Another brush, slower, then a lingering hesitation in which she ran the tip of her tongue over his bottom lip. As she did, his lips, which had begun stiff and unyielding, slowly softened and parted. Excitement rippled through her, warming her to the task at hand. She deepened the kiss, plunging her tongue into his mouth as he had done to her, then nearly laughed as his tongue lifted to meet and counter her attack. *There.*

Victorious, she sat back and folded her arms across her chest. "Perhaps that is proof enough."

"'Tis proof of something. Of what, we shall see." His hands found her waist and slowly tugged her forward until her face was just inches from his. "You must love this sister of Robin's very much, to risk so much for her sake."

"I do," she assured him.

His gaze drifted down over her breasts, then came back up to meet her eyes with a look of such hunger, she forgot to breathe. That already familiar surge of lust pushed past her defenses, spinning her sense of victory into something else entirely, something that sent heat rushing through her until it found that place at her center where it turned to liquid fire. *Now . . .*

His jaw tightened and the fire turned to ice. With a slight shove, he dumped her on her backside and rose. "It grows late. Use the bushes and get back here."

She sat there in an untidy heap, her heart thumping with anger and confusion as he stalked off toward the horses. *Devil. Pautonnier. Ass.* Biting her tongue to keep from spitting the words after him, she pushed to her feet and stumbled off into the bushes. What had just happened? They had been on the brink; her body still throbbed with it, and she knew he was in an even worse state. She could not conceive why or how he had stopped, and no amount of contemplation or swearing made the sudden shift any clearer.

She returned just in time to see Steinarr swing up onto the stallion bareback, a thin bundle slung over his shoulder with his bow. Alarmed, she flew across the clearing to block him. "Where are you going? You cannot leave me here. Please, my lord, I swear, I will do whatever you—"

"Calm yourself, Marian. A friend of mine will be here shortly after sunset."

"A friend? But—"

"He will stand guard outside for the night, and you will sleep within the hermit's cell." His voice was even but clipped, and he didn't look at her. "Your things are already in there. You will be safe until I return come morning."

"But—"

"My friend is called Torvald." The horse danced away, and Steinarr reined the animal on around, so he could face her again. This time he did meet her eyes, and once again she sensed the passions boiling behind his controlled expression. "I would suggest you not try to practice your sort of 'honor' with him. I trust him with my life and yours, but even the most disciplined man would find it difficult to resist such a kiss."

Yet *he* resisted, when everything about him, every touch, every snap of anger, every lusty desire that hammered against the walls of her mind, said he didn't want to. He wanted her, despite the vow he'd made Robert, and if he did, she still had some hope, some power to bind him to her and make this work.

"Then you will take me the rest of the way as you promised?"

"I have not yet decided." He put his spurs to the horse and galloped away, leaving her alone in a forest full of wolves.

CHAPTER 8

"DEVIL'S SPAWN," MUTTERED Matilda as he vanished down the trail. *Foul scoundrel.* She stormed back to the fire and plunked down on a stone, so disgusted with herself and with him that she shook.

What was she doing here? Here, in the middle of nowhere, offering her body to this strange, wild man? She didn't want him. She didn't even *like* him. This ache . . . this wasn't her. It was all *him*, him and his untamed passions, stirring her body to this fever and her mind to who knew what. Curse him, she wasn't even certain her anger was her own. How would she survive a score of days in his company, much less in his bed?

Wrapping her arms around herself, she stared into the fire, searching for some distraction that would get her thoughts and her body back under her own control. But there was no distraction. There was only Steinarr, his strange blue and gold eyes taunting her from among the dancing flames.

It was a long time later when a distant sound made her glance up. The light had faded, and the high clouds overhead glowed with the pink and gold of sunset. A moment later, the sound wafted through the trees again.

The almost-human agony in the cry sent a chill racing down Matilda's spine. She retreated to the safety of the doorway and stood scanning the darkening forest for any sign of the friend Sir Steinarr had promised would protect her. What if it was him, injured and crying out in pain? A breeze stirred the air, bringing an edge of cold and the scent of coming rain, and Matilda pulled her cloak around her. More time passed, and the sky grew blacker and clouds slowly hid the stars, and he still did not come.

The sudden, nearby crack of a twig made her jump. She darted forward to snatch a burning stick from the fire and then retreated quickly back to the doorway, holding her makeshift weapon before her like a sword.

"You will not need that brand . . . Marian, is it?" He came striding into the firelight, a pale, lean man with long legs and silver-white hair that hung past his shoulders in tangled streamers. "I am Torvald, a friend to Steinarr."

Feeling sheepish, she lowered her stick. "'Twas not for you, my lord. I heard some beast cry out."

"I heard nothing. But I do smell something. Pork?"

"Bacon." She tossed her stick back on the fire and motioned toward the rock where the last of the evening meal lay. "And good bread. And not-so-good ale."

"Better than no ale." Instead of attacking the food like his friend would, Torvald merely nodded his thanks and walked the few paces to where the rouncey stood hobbled. He scratched the animal's nose. "Hello, my friend."

"You know the horse?"

"I have ridden him a few times."

The animal snuffled happily into his hand, and Matilda's opinion of this Torvald swung toward the good. Horses seldom liked evil men—tolerated, but not liked. Then again, she'd had a good opinion of Sir Steinarr at first, too, so perhaps she was mistaken about this friend as well. Perhaps the horse didn't actually like him at all. There was only one way to know, and thankfully, with Steinarr long gone, she could relax her guard for the night and use it. She let the walls fall away and immediately felt the rouncey's pleasure as the man ran his hand over his withers. Yes. A good man.

Then Torvald turned to look at her, and for just an instant . . .

"You seem somehow familiar to me, my lord. Do I know you?"

"I doubt it."

But the strange sensation of familiarity remained. "Have you ever been to Huntingdon? Or perhaps to Loxley?"

"No." Torvald pulled out his knife and bent to lift the horse's front hoof and hold it between his knees. "I spend most of my time in . . ." He paused as a strange, low roar rose up over the forest. "I spend my time in these woods."

"What was that?" Matilda edged as close to the fire as she could without setting her skirts alight. "That was not the same as before."

"Uh, boars fighting, I think." Torvald continued picking at the rouncey's hoof as though nothing were wrong. "You should get some sleep."

"It is yet early, my lord. A little longer." In truth, it was not the hour, but the uneasy feeling that both the sound and Torvald's unlikely explanation had stirred. Why were men like that, so convinced they must protect women from the truth that they made things far worse with a lie? She watched him duck under the rouncey's neck to check the other hooves. "My lord?"

"Yes."

"I have heard boars fighting. That was *not* a boar fight."

"Perhaps not. But whatever it was, it was far away and will not harm you while I am here." He pried a stone from the forefoot and flicked it away, then set the hoof down and moved on.

"My lord."

"What?"

"Does Sir Steinarr intend to keep to his word and take me on the rest of my journey?"

He straightened and, for the space of a long breath, assessed her over the animal's back, and again there was that strange tickle at the edge of her awareness. Then he smiled and it faded away. "He did not say. You should sleep, Marian. You have had a long day."

He looked as wild and fearsome as Sir Steinarr, standing there with his unkempt hair and his threadbare clothes and his deeply carved face, but there was a steadiness to this one that soothed her where his friend did not. She took a deep breath and nodded, then retreated into the hermit's cell.

She found her bundle and a thick sheepskin that Sir Steinarr had thrown down beside it, and she was soon in her simple bed. The stone beneath the skin was hard, but the fatigue that had been dogging her soon had her yawning.

She was about to drift off when another sound lifted over the trees, not a roar but a snarl, fierce and far, far closer. She sat bolt upright. *"Monsire?"*

"Here. Sleep, Marian. It is nothing to concern you."

She leaned forward so she could see him. He sat by the fire, apparently at ease, a piece of bread in his hand and the ale skin in his lap. He certainly didn't seem concerned, and his calm transferred to her.

Wrapping herself more snugly in both cloak and blanket, she settled back down. Slowly, her heart fell back to its rhythm and the exhaustion caught her and she drifted away. It was only as her eyes fluttered open and shut in those final moments before sleep that Torvald rose. The last thing she saw, he was standing just beyond the fire, sword in hand, guarding her from whatever monsters prowled the night.

THE FEMALE.

The lion could sense her, smell her, feel her, distant but present. He tilted his head back and curled his lip, tasting the night air. *Yes. That was her.* He swung his great head, sampling the air until he knew in which direction she lay, and began moving toward her, seeking.

He could smell food, too, mixed together with the scent of her. They were in the same place. Good. He would need food after.

But food was not what drew him. Food could be had anywhere. It was the female that was rare. She was what was important. He didn't have a female of his own, and he wanted one, needed one, beyond any other need. Beyond food or water or sleep or fighting or the hunt.

A female. A mate.

He followed the mingled odors past creatures who would

have been his prey any other night, but they only stood and watched him pass. Even the skittering deer only chewed their cuds, understanding they were safe this night.

Her scent grew stronger, clearer, and he began to huff, in preparation for calling to her. The roar built in his throat. Near. She was near. Then light flickered through the trees and the roar died. *Fire. Human. Him.*

He knew that scent, too. He should have smelled him earlier. He would have, except that the female was so rich in his throat. The scent of her rose up all around, drawing him forward. He crouched down and crept forward toward the light, and when he was close enough, he saw the man who so often stood between him and easy game now stood between him and *her.*

The man had her trapped, there in the den beyond the fire. She shouldn't be by the fire. She shouldn't be with him. He must kill the man, then he could have her. The lion crept closer, but the fire burned bright, and the man watched, and even the promise of her couldn't chase away the memory of the pain this human could deliver. This one wielded fire and sharp sticks with a courage other men seldom had. This man *hurt.*

He backed away until the dark was thick enough to hide him, then he circled, looking for the weakness, the way to her, but the man knew and added wood to the fire, and the flames licked up. He could sense her there, beyond the burning flame, and he snarled. The man lifted his sharp stick and a branch of flame and stepped forward, speaking.

He didn't understand the words, but the intent was clear enough: he couldn't have her.

But the other could. Deep inside, there was the other, the one who walked by day, who also wanted her. *He* didn't fear fire or men. *He* could have her, if he would just take her.

So he settled down, just beyond where the man could see, and watched and waited. And the one who could walk by day watched and waited with him through the night, until the sky lightened and the need to hide became greater even than the drive to reach the female.

It didn't matter. He knew where to find her, and the man would not always be there. He would come back, night after night, until the man grew careless. Then she would be his.

The lion rose and silently padded away.

A MISTING RAIN fell as Steinarr heaved his aching body up off the ground the next morning. Clapping his arms around himself to stay warm, he peered around in the gloom, trying to spot the lightning-struck tree he had picked as a marker.

There.

He stumbled off toward the tree and quickly found the hollow beneath its roots where he'd hidden his clothing. By the time he pulled his cloak around his shoulders, the clouds had lightened to the shade of old pewter and some of the gnawing chill had faded. He again took his bearings, this time by the rise of land to the south, and set off toward the place he would meet Torvald.

It was hard going. The rain made the ground slick, and his head was still thick with the lion's temper. He wasn't sure why, but over the last few days, the beast had clung to him with sharper claws than usual. He could feel it, prowling out of sight, full of killing rage and somehow aware of Marian. How he knew that, he wasn't sure. He simply knew, just as he knew how much more dangerous that awareness made the beast. He would have to travel farther from camp each night to keep her and Torvald safe—another problem to add to the mix.

But his real problem was that he carried the weight of one too many vows to Englishmen.

It wasn't in him to simply pick one to ignore. A man's word was his honor, and he always kept to the letter of what he promised, even to Englishmen—though he sometimes sliced the wording of those promises so finely that the other party might believe he had sworn to something other than what he truly had. He had very carefully balanced what he'd told Marian with what he'd promised Guy; she only assumed that her journey would end with her back in the company of Robin. Robert. Whatever his name was.

And then Robin had thrown that balance all askew. It irked Steinarr to admit the puppy had defeated him on two fronts, demanding precisely the ending Marian expected, plus forcing him to swear off her body. That last was especially galling. He had no interest in spending the next weeks with a hard cock, hauling around a woman he couldn't touch.

But neither had he any interest in choosing between the vow made to a puffed-up coxcomb of an English nobleman and that made to a bastard thief—even if the coxcomb did offer ten pounds of much-needed silver. He was starting to think the best solution to this muddle would be to take Marian back to the colliers' camp and send the gold florin back to Gisburne along with word that his cousin could not be found. That, at least, would put everything back to how it stood before he'd stepped into it.

Unfortunately, it would also put Marian back into the hands of her seducer, and whatever Ari said about his own similar intentions, the idea of Robert le Chape leading Marian off into ruin did not sit well.

Aye, he'd much rather do that himself.

And at least when he was done with her, he would see her safely back home to be wed. But if he did that, it would mean keeping his word to Guy while breaking his vow to—

Bah.

A large animal crashed through the brush ahead. Steinarr whistled. The stallion came trotting out of the mist, looking like a damp ghost, and moments later, Steinarr had collected the bundle of Torvald's clothing and they were headed toward the hermit's cell.

When he rode into the clearing, Marian was standing beneath the overhang, out of the rain. He dismounted and went to join her. "I see you made it through the night without being devoured by wolves."

"Thanks to your friend, though he came so late and left so early, he might well have not come at all. Why did he not stay to greet you this morning?"

"He has other ways to spend his days." He indicated the two pieces of bread and cheese she was holding. "Is one of those for me?"

"Both. I have already broken my fast."

"So are you ready?" He plucked both pieces out of her fingers and took a huge bite from each.

"I am, m'lord." By the way her eyes narrowed, she had caught on to his little jest. "The question is, are *you*?"

By the gods, was he. *Astride his lap.* The image pounded through his skull and set his body throbbing. He could have her that way right now, if not for that cursed puppy. He could have had her already.

"Put out the fire," he said, turning away before his arousal grew too obvious. "I will tend to the gear."

She grabbed the pail and headed off for water, and he gobbled down his meal and reached for the rouncey's bridle.

By the time they were ready to ride, he had himself back under control, and he had decided. He was going to take her back and be done with all of them. Then he would go find himself a wench who would be far less trouble. He helped Marian mount, swung up into the saddle before her, and they headed for the road.

But then came that little slope just before the road, and as the stallion surged up the hill, she had to wrap her arms more tightly around him and lean forward to keep her seat. Her breasts, which had been so temptingly within reach as she'd knelt to kiss him the afternoon before, pressed hard against his back. He'd been aware of them yesterday, but today . . . today, all the cloth between them seemed to burn away, as though they lay in bed and she held him from behind, as though they were lovers.

No. He might have her a thousand times, but they would never truly be lovers. They would never, could never, lie in bed together through the night, no matter how much he might want it. He was ending this. He was taking her back. Today. Right now.

"My lord?"

"What?"

"We are at the road, and I must know. Will you keep to our bargain?"

"I have not yet decided," he said, and turned the horses toward Harworth.

DESPITE THE DRIZZLE that slowly soaked her cloak, Matilda was far happier than she had been the day before. She had rested well and some of Steinarr's anger had waned, so she found it easier to keep her mind away from his. She could still sense him just beyond the edges, though, so she knew the lust was still there. That was just as well. She needed him to want her; it was all the hold she had over him.

The faint peal of bells from some distant monastery had just announced Sext when they topped a knoll. Steinarr pointed to the smoke rising at the far end of the vale below. "There. That is Harworth."

Matilda craned to have a better look. "Already? You said two or three days."

"Depending on how often we stopped. We have not stopped." He swiveled to toss a word over his shoulder. "Yet."

Devil. She kept her eyes firmly on the village. "Then stop, my lord."

"You would like that, wouldn't you?"

"Only in that it would mean you had decided to hold to our bargain."

"Are you certain?" He faced front and started the horses down the hill. "How do you know I won't tup you a time or two and then take you back anyway? Or leave you somewhere without aid?"

Though his words were coarser, he was asking much the same question Robert had, so she ignored the fact that he was trying to rattle her and considered: How *did* she know? "Because you took the time to bury John Little, and because you dare to ask that question. A man who intended to discard me would not want me to even think of it before he had his way with me."

"That may be but—"

"And because you want far more than a tup or two."

He snorted. "You think highly of your wares."

Wares? "Not nearly as highly as you do, my lord," she said tightly, angry at the way he once again called her a whore without even using the word. "Nor nearly so often."

"And how would you know how often I think of it?"

Because I feel it every time you do, she wanted to shout, but she'd already given away too much in her anger.

"You are a man," she said instead. "From what I can tell, men think of swiving every moment they are not doing it."

"There you are mistaken," he said, chuckling. "We think of swiving most especially when we *are* doing it—at least those of us who do it well. Now, where is the shrine you wish to visit?"

Where, indeed? The question of Sir Steinarr's skill—*Did he do it well?* asked that wicked part of her the priests had sought to tame—was forced aside by her real problem: she had yet to solve the riddle from Headon. With no idea where to begin, she made the most obvious guess. "The church."

It was a church much like that in Maltby or in any other village they'd passed through: a simple stone structure at the edge of the village green, with a graveyard off to one side. She stood before the heavy oak door, looking at the carved figures over the lintel: the seven cardinal sins. Appropriately, Lust came first of all, a reminder of her looming downfall.

Steinarr finished tethering the horses and called to her from the lane. "Go ahead. I will see if I can find someone with bread to sell. And some better ale."

"That would be excellent, my lord." She stepped inside, glad to be able to do this without him watching over her shoulder.

A few candles threw dancing shadows over the altar and the tapestries behind it. By habit, she started to dip her fingers in the scented water in the font, but stopped. Her sins were too great; she would have to settle with Heaven when this was all over, but she could not bring herself to play hypocrite now. She stepped off to one side, where she could study the church.

She examined every fixture in the chapel, beginning with the carved stone altar, and ending some while later with the tapestries, which told the story of the Creation in six panels of brilliant stitchery. Squinting in the dim light, she moved from hanging to hanging, studying every inch, every star in the firmament and every creature and plant in Eden, searching for anything that reminded her of her father or of Huntingdon.

Nothing.

Hearing footsteps approaching outside, Matilda hurriedly backed away, so that when the door opened, she looked like she'd just risen from prayer. The priest who entered smiled. "Well, who have we here?"

"A simple traveler, Father." She came to kneel and kiss his ring.

"Ah. I wondered at the strange horses outside."

"They belong to the noble knight I travel with. He is seeking food for our journey, and I thought to take a few moments in the peace of your church."

"A wise use of your time. Go on with your prayers. I have some small duties to attend."

Pretending to pray at a roadside shrine was one thing, but playing false inside a church, before a priest, was a different matter entirely. She felt herself color, and was glad the light at this end of the chapel was so dim. "I am done. Father, are there any shrines or Lady Wells nearby? Any Holy sites at all?"

He thought a moment, and then shook his head. "The nearest is the priory at Tickhill, nearly two leagues, but it is considered theirs, not ours. If the wind was right as you rode in, you may have heard the bells."

"We did. There is nothing on Harworth land?"

"No. Why do you ask?"

"Curiosity. And now 'tis satisfied." She made to leave, but the priest drifted along with her.

"Where are you bound?"

"Here and there." She kept sidling toward the door. "I am sorry, Father, I must go. My lord will want to leave anon."

"Travel safely, my child."

"Yes, Father." She bobbed once more and escaped the church before her sins piled on so thick they crushed her. Outside, she quickly circled the church, hoping something on the outside would give her an idea where to look but, again, found nothing.

She plopped down on a stump not far from the horses, and squeezed her aching head between her palms. She had been so certain that some clear sign would point her in the right direction. Why would Father leave such a poor clue if the answer were not obvious? Perhaps he'd chosen something Robin would know that she didn't, and she once more wished Rob were well and here. Even if the puzzle wasn't designed just for him, it would be good to have a second pair of eyes.

She was about to pull the parchment out again when she spotted Sir Steinarr coming down the road, laden with bags and ale skins.

There is your second pair of eyes, whispered the same ill-advised voice that had set her on this path to lechery. But perhaps it was right. Perhaps it was time she kept her promise to Robin, to tell Sir Steinarr. With a sigh, she pushed to her feet and went to meet him at the horses. "You got more ale, my lord."

"Better ale," he said emphatically as he looped the cords of the two ale skins over the saddle horn and added the bags to the rouncey's load. "I also got three days' worth of maslin bread and a new cheese, so we can save our salted one for the road. Are you done here?"

She stared back at the church and shook her head. "No, my lord, not yet. But there is nothing more I can do today. I will have to come back on the morrow." She made her decision on the spot and blurted out, "I would speak with you, my lord. In private."

He looked her up and down once, and something rippled across the day's calmness, like some unknown beast disturbing the surface of a windless pond. After a long moment, he nodded.

"The man who sold me the cheese told me of an abandoned cottage on the far edge of the demesne woods that travelers often use with no consequence. Will that be private enough?"

Private enough for many things. The ripple spread, caressing her like a too-intimate hand. She tore her eyes away from his and found some dirt on the toe of her shoe that required her attention. "Yes, my lord."

"As you wish, then. We will go."

SHE WANTED PRIVACY, she had it.

Steinarr stood in the doorway watching Marian, who had laid a fire on the open hearth in the center of the floor and now knelt beside it, diligently trying to get it started.

The cottage the man had sent them to was of the old type, partly dug into the earth. It was chill and damp, as such dwellings always were—undoubtedly why Marian was so anxious to get the fire going that she was lighting it herself—but the wattle and daub half walls were sturdy and the thatch roof solid enough to keep the rain out for the night. Sitting in a quiet glade a good league from the village, it was also as private a place as could be found outside an anchorite's cell.

Marian, however, had yet to say one word about whatever matter she supposedly wanted to talk about. Instead, she had busily set about gathering wood and then, while he had seen to the horses, had laid this fire that now consumed her attention—as she consumed Steinarr's. As she struck the flint over and over, her bottom bobbed enticingly beneath her gown. He couldn't tear his eyes away.

She knew it, too. The longer he stared, the more self-consciously she worked and the more she bobbed. Clearly, it was deliberate. And clearly, she had wanted the privacy because she intended to offer herself to him again.

What wasn't clear was whether he was going to let her succeed this time.

He shouldn't. He should take her back, the way he'd planned to. But his senses were already full of her from the ride—the press of her body against his back, the uneven whisper of her breathing at his shoulder, a drift of silken hair against his jaw, the roses in her cheeks as he had helped her off the horse—and he wanted more. He wanted to bury himself in her, inhale her, devour her. What would she taste like? A vision of her spread before him on the furs, ready for his mouth, floated up before him.

She gasped and missed the flint entirely.

"What is it?"

"I . . . Nothing, my lord." She struck again, clumsily, the firesteel stuttering along the flint without drawing a single spark.

"'Twill be a cold night if you keep at it that way."

She sat back on her heels, staring at her hands. "I have never been good with a flint and steel."

"Let me do it." He tore his eyes off her backside long enough to toss the packsaddle on top of the other gear in the corner, then squatted beside her, arranged the char-cloth at the top of the flint, and quickly struck three fat sparks, one of which caught. He tipped it into the tinder, and in moments had a nice little blaze going. "'Tis in the wrist."

"You make it look so easy," she said as she knelt there, feeding sticks to the growing flame. "So does Robin."

Curse it, she was thinking of the bastard in the same breath as she thought of him. Why was he torturing himself over this perverse woman, when what he needed to do was be rid of her? The problem was, he wasn't sure he had it in him to turn her away, and stubborn thing that she was, she would continue coming at him until something made her stop, just like she had in Maltby.

Like in Maltby . . .

Now why hadn't he thought of that earlier? Ari was right. Crudeness would drive her off. He could be crude. *Very* crude.

"'Tis time you learned how to keep warm." Before she had a chance to move, he shifted in behind her, wrapped his arms around her, and pressed the flint and steel into her hands.

"First you settle the steel into the furrow properly." Knees wide, he slid forward so his rapidly hardening cock rested in the groove between her buttocks, took her hands in his, and fitted steel and stone together. "Now, nice strong strokes."

Pretending not to hear her gasp, he guided her through the strike, letting the sparks fly off into nothingness as their bodies rubbed together in similar fashion. She tried to squirm away, but he wrapped his arms around her waist, pulled her back even more firmly, and put his lips by her ear. "Of course, before you begin in earnest, you should always make sure the tinder is properly laid. The sparks need a nice, soft place to land. Make up the bed, Marian. Or would you rather I take you like this?"

CHAPTER 9

LIKE THIS?

Matilda's body tightened and heated all at once, an echo of the confusion in her mind. For the life of her, she wasn't sure if she wanted to go through with this for Robin's sake or for the sake of her own sinful curiosity . . . or if she wanted to go through with it at all.

"Well?" He tugged off her headrail and tossed it aside, then slid his hands down over her thighs and began drawing her gown up. She felt his member pulse against her as though it had a life of its own. Liquid heat pooled between her thighs. Where did she want to be when she took him into her the first time?

"The bed, my lord." She had to wait for him to release her and shift back before she could rise. Her feet felt very far away, as though she'd had too much wine, and she had to think to make them carry her over to find the bedding.

"Use my furs as well as your blanket," he said, unbuckling his belt to lay his sword aside. "You will need a good cushion beneath you. I am known to ride a woman hard."

He was trying to frighten her for some reason, but he did want her. She clung to that certainty as she pulled his roll of furs from the pile and started plucking at the knot. "What I *need* is your assurance that after you . . . ride me, you will keep your word and help me complete my journey."

"You already have that."

"I would like it again."

"Would you now?" He rose and came over to take the furs from her. He opened the knot with a quick yank, then shook the furs out and tossed them down on the earthen floor, near the fire. "Then I would like something as well. I would like to see whether your favors are worth my trouble. Perhaps your body is misshapen and covered with wens beneath that gown."

Wens? She lifted her chin proudly. "That is the chance you take, my lord. Just as I take the chance that your tarse is as crooked as your soul."

His mouth twitched in amusement. "'Tis straight and strong, as you will likely soon learn. However, you bargained only for my arm and my horse, not my tarse. 'Tis *your* body that is in question, and I will see it before I decide whether you are worth breaking my vow to that puppy you call cousin. Bare your breasts."

"What!" She stepped back so quickly, she hit her head against the cruck frame. "Ow."

Steinarr caught her around the waist and steadied her. His expression softened a little as she rubbed at her head. "Are you hurt?"

She probed gently at her scalp. "I don't think so. No."

"Good." The determined glint returned, shunting aside the glimpse of tenderness, and he pushed her back against the wall next to the cruck and leaned into her. "Now where were we? Ah, yes. You were going to show me your teats, so that I may see whether you stir me sufficiently to get good use from you."

"Oh, I stir you well enough, my lord. The proof is at your crotch."

Not that she needed to feel him pressed up against her to know his desire. Despite her efforts to keep well inside herself, away from his heat, it still seeped in, warming her blood until she had to fight down an urge to work her hips against him and see if it would ease the ache.

"That?" He glanced down to where their bodies touched, and he ground against her lewdly, as though he were the one who knew what was in *her* mind. "That is merely the first swelling of interest. What any man would feel with any woman writhing against him."

"I am not writhing," she said between clenched teeth.

"You should be, if you want to excite me." He dragged

his hands up her body, lingering over her breasts to let his thumbs circle the crests. Desire lurched within her. He slowly lowered his mouth to hers, skimming a taunting kiss over her lips. "Writhe, Marian. Show me how you will move as I slide into your quaint."

Crude as they were, his words freed her, gave her leave to do what she so yearned to do anyway. She pushed her hips forward, moving against him, seeking some relief for the incredible need that mounted up in her. Her need or his, it didn't matter. It just *was*, powerful beyond her ability to resist. His lips crushed down over hers with a searing kiss that stole her breath. She lifted to him, and his answering growl only made her move more aggressively, working against him, shifting until she found a way to make his hardness rub perfectly against the place that ached. Not enough. She curled her leg around his and pulled him closer. He began to buck against her, helping her find the relief, and she moaned.

His tongue plunged into her open mouth, matching the rhythm of his body against hers as pleasure and need and burning lust built within her. She knew what he was doing. She wanted what he was doing. She pulled away from his kiss just long enough to say it, and her eyes met his.

"Take me."

The words echoed in Steinnar's skull, driving out all other thought. *Take her. Take her now.* In one motion, he lifted her and spun her down on to the furs. He grappled with her gown, dragging it up, while her hands worked as frantically, shoving his shirt up to reach for the tie to his braies, then dragging them down. Freed, he fell on her. She lifted her hips, searching for him, and suddenly he was pressing into her and she was crying out and there was a moment's resistance that almost, almost, made his mind return.

Then, abruptly, he slipped home, embraced by that welcoming heat he had needed for so very, very long, and the last scrap of reason slipped away. The urgency faded, replaced by the need, not simply to mate but to possess, to pleasure, until she forgot all others and became truly his.

He moved over her, judging how she responded, how she shifted beneath him, instinctively adjusting until he found the rhythm that made her breath come in panting moans. *Mine.*

The need built, stronger. Matilda clung to him, fingers and heels hooked into his buttocks, pulling at him, wanting him deeper. She lifted to him, faster, harder, leading him and following him all at the same time as they searched together for the way to make her his. *His.* He rose up on his hands and looked down at her as he pressed into her, and suddenly she was there, the pleasure on her hard, harder than she'd ever felt by her own hand. She arched back, almost throwing him off as he bore down into her, and then all her defenses collapsed in the quaking wonder of it, and she felt his shock as he abruptly joined her, exploding into her with both body and mind.

And not just with pleasure. The wildness was there, too, animal and terrifying. So was hunger. Cold. Need, deeper than any she'd ever felt. The desolation of true loneliness. It all engulfed her, terrible and dark, mixed up with the golden light of release. A sob of despair welled up and she wasn't sure whether that was hers or his either, but she wrapped her arms even tighter and held on, clinging to him for both their sakes as he poured himself into her.

"'Tis all right," she murmured through tears. "'Tis all right. 'Tis all right." Slowly, some of his agonized pleasure began to fade, and she could close her eyes and little by little begin to gather herself away from him.

It was a long time before Steinarr heard her, longer before his mind returned back from wherever it had been, the shattered pieces slowly coming together so her words made any kind of sense. It was all right. He buried his face in her shoulder, inhaling the scent of her. Their mating had been so frantic that the only bare skin that touched was where they joined. He wanted bare skin. He had to have it.

"I want you naked," he growled into her hair. He began pressing kisses over her face, her neck, her ears, half-incoherent with need as he dragged her garments up. *Bare belly. Yes. More.* "I want you again and again. Your mouth. Your breasts." He hadn't even seen her breasts yet. He shoved at her clothes, willing them gone, frustrated that the yards of cloth didn't simply vanish. "I want you on your knees, from behind, on my lap. I want you in every way, over and over." Astride him, yes. That next. The thought throbbed through his crotch, and he rocked side to side, working to make himself hard again. He felt the stirring and pressed into her.

"Ow." She shrank away from him, pulling back against the earth.

Have to have her. He thrust at her again.

She winced and shoved back. "That hurts. Don't."

"Hurts?" Another piece of his mind came back. He forced his eyes open enough to see the dampness on her cheeks. He tasted his lips, salty where he'd kissed her. *Tears.* "I hurt you."

"No. I mean, yes, but . . . The first time is supposed to hurt, is it not?"

First time? No, surely she didn't mean that. She'd been with at least one man. She knew too well how to move, how to touch him to drive him wild. She'd needed no coaxing, no teaching as a virgin would need; her desire had been every bit as sharp as his. *She knew.* She couldn't be, and yet. Memory of that slight resistance and her cry as he broke through rushed back, slamming another piece of his mind into place.

He pulled away from her, and even that made her wince. With a sense of dread, he sat back on his knees and forced himself to look at the smear of pink that stained the white sheepskin beneath her hips. His head pounded as if *Völund,* the elf smith, were using his skull as an anvil. "You were virgin?"

"Of course I was a virgin." Blushing in shame, she pushed her gown down to cover herself. "Why would I not be?"

"I just thought . . ." Ah, pillocks. What had he done? He was supposed to stop. She was supposed to slap him, make him stop, run away, not wrap her legs around him and pull him in so deep he would drown in her. "I mean, he's only a puppy, but I thought Robin would surely have bedded you by now."

"Robin!" She scrabbled away from him. "You think Robin and I . . . ? My own brother?"

Steinarr grabbed for her, but suddenly froze, hand out, gaping at her. "Brother?"

"Cousin. I mean cousin," said Marian, her face going even brighter red. She scrambled to her feet. "You cannot think I would lie with my cousin."

He shook off the shock, yanking his braies back into place and pulling the ties snug as he rose. "You said 'brother.'"

"You thought I would lie with my *cousin*," she accused as she backed away.

"'Twas clear he was not your cousin. I saw through that lie from the first. I thought you had run away with your lover. And—"

"Robin is *not* my lover." She backed into the wall and slid sideways, but she was too close to the corner and far too slow, and Steinarr trapped her easily, one arm on either side of her.

"Then what is he to you? The truth this time."

He could all but see her wracking her mind for a lie. "He is . . ."

Steinarr grabbed her shoulders and shook her, his fingers digging into her shoulders until she winced. "The *truth*, Marian. What is he to you?"

"My father's bastard by some peasant woman in Kent," she snapped. "My half brother."

The bastard was her *father's* bastard? No. Surely not. "And you are not lovers."

"Of course not! How could you even—" She gagged and clutched at her stomach.

Steinarr stepped back quickly, then glanced around, spotted the bag of oats, and dragged it over by the fire. "Come here. Sit down."

She stumbled forward and sagged onto the rough cushion. Steinarr stood looking down at her for a moment, then picked up the ale skin and held it out. "Drink."

"I cannot." She wrapped her arms around herself.

Well, he could. As she sat trying to hold herself together, he pulled the stopper and drank deeply in an effort to wash away the confusion.

"You truly thought we were lovers?" she asked quietly when he lowered the skin.

He nodded slowly. "I did. He was clearly not your cousin. And you are very . . . tender with him."

"Only as a sister to her brother." She shuddered again. "Even if he were only my cousin . . . How could you imagine we would do anything so vile?"

"I told you, I could tell you were lying about him being your cousin. As for the other . . ." The images tumbled through his mind: Marian leaning against Robin on the mare, murmuring something to make him laugh. Marian bending over Robin in his sick bed, kissing his forehead. A smile here; a gentle hand there. All the tiny things that had played into what Guy had told him. No, he had that backward. What Guy had told him had only played into what he'd decided on his own, ass that he was. He hammered his forehead with his fist. "I read things wrong between you from the start."

"You must have. I never said . . ."

"You never said, but your lies did." He squatted down before her. "And you did lie, didn't you, *Maud*?"

She grimaced and twisted away, trying to avoid his eyes. "I did, my lord."

"Who are you?"

"You already know. I am called Maud. Matilda."

"And who is this bastard-siring father of yours?"

"A smith in—"

"No more lies!" The whipcrack of his voice made her jump. Glowering, he leaned in close, determined to have the truth. "A smith's daughter would not refer to her father's mistress as 'some peasant woman in Kent.' And your speech is too fine to have come out of a smithy. Who is your father? The truth."

Matilda squeezed her eyes shut and sat there a moment.

"My sire is—*was* David Fitzwalter, lord of Huntingdon. I am Matilda, his only daughter."

"And Robin is his bastard?"

"His name is Robert. Robert le Chape." She slowly unwound her arms and straightened. "I think I would like some of that ale after all."

He watched through narrowed eyes as she gulped down the ale. "So. You are a noblewoman, traveling with a bastard brother, lying about who you are, and offering your body to an unknown knight in exchange for his aid. 'Tis a strange pilgrimage you make, Matilda Fitzwalter."

The ale fortified Marian and washed away the bitter taste in her mouth. She squared her shoulders, ready to face him as she should have before it came to this. "I am no more pilgrim than you, my lord."

"None at all, then." He paced back and forth a few times, then stopped in front of her. "What are you? What journey do you make that you are willing to offer up yourself for my aid?"

"A sort of . . . quest. For Robert's title."

"*Robert's* title?" Steinarr frowned down at her. "How is it a bastard stands to gain a title by making a quest?"

"It is a very long tale, *monsire*."

"I have time." He dragged the furs closer to where she sat.

Matilda felt herself pale. "What are you doing?"

"Calm yourself, woman. I only need a place to rest while you spin this very long tale. Unless you would rather have the floor while I sit there?" When she shook her head, he eased himself down on the furs at her feet, as though he were one of the young knights at Huntingdon paying court. "Go on. And you had better not brew up more of your lies."

"No, my lord. I promise you only the truth." Perhaps not *all* of it, but the truth. She chewed her lip as she tried to put her story in order.

"Marian . . ." His voice held warning.

"It is hard to know where to begin, my lord."

"At the beginning," he suggested curtly. "How did your father come to bring Robert to Huntingdon?"

"My lady mother, God rest her, bore no more children after me. She tried, nearly a dozen times in as many years, but all were born too early and dead. When Father realized she would give him no son, he brought his bastard to live with us. He said he would see Robin trained as a gentleman and a knight and acknowledge him as heir."

"Can he do that?"

She looked to see if he was jesting—surely he must know that nearly every great house had at least one bastard in its line—but he seemed serious.

"He can, and he did—and the shame killed Mother, though it took some time," she added bitterly. "Robin was not what Father expected. He is a gentle soul, more fond of carving animals in wood than of hunting them. He is barely fair with a sword, and for all his hours at the quintain, he has never won a single joust. The greater Robert's failures, the harsher Father's words and hand, and the more Robin tried to please him, the less he was able."

"And you pitied him."

"We pitied each other. Father was equally disappointed in me, and no kinder."

"Why?"

So many reasons. She shook her head. "That is not part of the tale, *monsire.* Leave it said that we each stood between the other and Father's anger more than once. It endeared us to him not at all, but it bound us together as brother and sister."

"Fathers can sometimes be hard out of their wish to make their children strong," said Steinarr.

"It was not about making us strong, *monsire.* It was about breaking us. Especially Robin. He called him a coward and a fool." She glared at him. "He called him *askefise.*"

He flushed. "Ah."

"He said the common blood ran too thick in Robin's veins and that he would never be fit to own the title. He vowed he would never acknowledge Robin after all, and said Huntingdon and its lordship would go to my cousin."

"Another one?" He sounded doubtful.

"My *true* cousin," she said. "The only son of my father's only brother, called Guy of Gisburne. An odious wretch, but by rights, the true heir—or so we thought. So *Guy* thought. But Father learned that Guy . . . was not the man he thought, either, noble-born or not. He approached the king with his concern, and Edward offered a solution. A test. One final chance for Robert to prove his worthiness to be lord."

Steinarr frowned. "I have never heard of such a thing."

"Nor I, 'til Father lay dying. He called Robert to him and told him of this test the king and he had devised. He said he had hidden away a certain small treasure and left a trail of riddles to find it. The first was handed to Robert by our steward in the very hour Father was buried. Robin must find the treasure and present it to the king. If he does it in time, he will be acknowledged heir and made lord by the king's fiat."

"And if he fails?"

"Guy becomes lord." Matilda tried to keep the bitterness out of her voice, but even she could hear it. "The weakness in Father's plan is that Guy does not have to produce the treasure. All he must do is—"

"Keep Robin from it," said Steinarr along with her. He pushed to his feet to pace back and forth again, and a new, colder kind of anger pulsed at the edges of Matilda's awareness.

"That is why we travel as peasant pilgrims, and under false names. I am sorry for our lies, *monsire*, but Guy covets Huntingdon beyond all reason. The steward sent word to him at the same time as he gave Robin the first riddle. I fear he is even now on our trail. If he catches us, he will surely kill Robin."

"He does not have the courage for that," growled Steinarr, and that wintry fury sent a frost through Matilda's soul. "He has sent someone else to do it."

The center of her went still and cold as the ice on a lake. *Ah, God.* She knew, but she had to ask anyway. "How is it you know what Guy has done?"

"Because," said Steinarr, "I am the man he sent."

Marian shot off the bag like an arrow off a bow and was half out the door before Steinarr got to her. He caught her around the waist and spun her back into the cottage as he kicked the door shut. "Sit down."

Instead, she scrambled back to put the fire between her and him and whipped out her knife. "Stay away from me."

"Put that thing away before you hurt yourself. If I were going to kill you, you would already be dead. You are safe enough. And so is Robin. Especially now."

"I do not believe you."

"Nonetheless." Steinarr contemplated her a moment, trying to decide how best to approach this. In his arrogance, he had fouled things so thoroughly he might never recover them. "I demanded the truth of you, and now you will have the same from me."

"I have no interest in your version of the truth."

"Interest or not, you will listen." Folding his arms, he leaned back against the door, effectively locking her in. "After I left you in Maltby, I captured the outlaw I sought and took him to Nottingham City." He went on, telling her of meeting Guy, and of what Gisburne had told him about the bastard thief and the maid he had lured away. As he spoke, she paced, agitated, on the far side of the fire.

"And so you agreed to kill Robin because of the word of that *fils a putain*? What did Guy pay you? What is the price of my brother's life?"

Balls. She would ask. Steinarr forced himself to say it aloud. "Ten pounds."

"Less than the price of a good horse," she said bitterly.

"I never told Guy I would kill Robin." Steinarr wanted her to understand. He *needed* her to understand, perhaps even more than he had needed her body. "I said only that I would see that Robin never troubled him again."

"And I am to trust that? That friend of yours is with him." Her voice cracked with a stifled sob. "Robin could be dead even now."

"He is not," Steinarr assured her. "Ari watches over him, to see he does not find more trees to fall out of, and he will stand between him and Guy. I will send a message to ensure it. Was Robin up that tree looking for one of your father's riddles?"

"Why should I tell you anything?"

"You are going to need my aid."

"Your *aid*? I drip with your aid," she spat at him. "Did Guy pay you to debase me as well?"

Her accusation flayed him like a knife. "Ah, pillocks. No, Marian. No. It was not like that. Guy charged me to bring you home to be married."

"And so you decided to tup me along the way?"

"Aye. But if you will recall, I asked you the first time before I met Guy, though I did it to chase you away rather than to bed you. Truly," he said at her doubt-filled snort. "You would not hear me when I said no to helping you. I wished you to go away and so, yes, I was crude. It worked." He held out his palms in surrender, but he couldn't resist pointing out, "When I returned, *you* were the one who bargained to be in my bed."

Her doubtfulness turned to pure poison. "I was desperate. And I did not know you were Guy's man."

He came to his feet, indignant. "I am *not* his man."

"No, only his hireling," she sneered. "God's bones, I cannot believe I was such a fool!"

"No bigger fool than I. I ignored my sense of the man for the sake of a few pounds of silver." Steinarr ventured away from the door a few steps, but let her keep the fire between them. "It may make little difference to you, but when I agreed to this duty, I did not realize that it was you and Robin I would be hunting."

"But once you discovered it, you did not withdraw."

"No. By then, I was convinced Robin was a true scoundrel. Gisburne gave me just enough of the truth that your lies and what I saw for myself only seemed to confirm his words. It seemed that Robin was both thief and seducer."

She curled her lip in disgust. "And you wanted that duty for yourself."

"As any man would." He still wanted it. He craved her worse now than he had before. How had he ever imagined

that driving her away would be a good thing? "I have been
without a woman far too long to say no to one so fair, especially not when she all but insists I take her. And from what
I saw and knew—thought I knew—you were already familiar with men and pleasure."

"A whore, you mean."

"I have never used that word."

"And yet you speak to me like one. You treat me like one."

"I only did it in the hope of driving you away again, as I
did in Maltby." He went on quickly, before the disbelief in
her eyes shamed him to silence. "It is as I said yesterday.
I made too many conflicting vows: to take you to Guy, to
take you to Robin, to bed you, to keep you chaste, to kill
Robin, to help him. I wanted to be rid of all of them and
set things back to how they were before I found you on the
road. I wanted you to demand I take you back to Robin,
but I knew you would insist on going on, on keeping to our
bargain. You are as stubborn as stone."

Her knife wavered a bit, though it remained pointed
straight at his belly. "But why not simply take me back if
you want to be rid of me?"

"I am too weak. I wanted you too much." He offered up
the simple truth in the hope of, what? Forgiveness? Small
chance of that, but at least she would know. "I needed your
strength to set me on the path. I hoped you would have it."

"Clearly I did not."

"Oh, you had strength. Just not the strength I expected."

She looked at the knife as though she wasn't sure how
it had come to be in her hand and carefully put it away.
"What if I were to tell you to take me back to Robin now?"

Please do not. "Then I will take you back."

She pressed her hand to her mouth and chewed a
knuckle, plainly unhappy, her wish to be shed of him so
clear on her face that Steinarr already knew her decision. A
long moment passed in which the only sound he could hear
was the hollow rush of the blood in his ears.

"I cannot go back," she said at last, speaking softly,
almost as if to herself. "I have no time to find another way."

All went silent, even his heart. And then, as it restarted,

his mind grabbed at a single word. "Time. You have said before you do not have time. Why?"

"Robin must present the treasure to Edward within forty days of our father's burial."

"That lying little cockerel!" Steinarr turned and drove his fist into the doorframe. It made a poor substitute for Guy, but it would do until he got his hands on him. Then he would do things to him . . . beginning with shoving that gold florin down his lying throat, then retrieving it with his bare hand to shove up the other end. That would make a good start. He'd decide on the rest later. "Guy said you were to be married within the month, and that's why I must have you back."

When he turned around, her mouth was white with anger of her own. "That, at least, was near truth. I am to marry the day the new lord is installed."

Was that bad or good? His head said one thing and his gut another. He shoved them both aside so he could deal with what was at hand. "How much longer do you have to reach the king?"

"Two and ten days are gone so far. That leaves us eight and twenty, and I have only the one clue we found at the Lady Well."

"How many are there?"

"Father never said. All he told Robert is that all would be found in Nottinghamshire, as would the treasure itself, though why he chose here, I do not comprehend."

"And where is the king?"

"I do not know that either. London. Salisbury. He could even be in France."

Steinarr's mind spun as he calculated how fast they could reach London. "We will seek word along the way."

"We?"

"Aye. I told you, you have my aid. I do not like to be played for a fool, Marian. My vow to Guy was based on lies and is now undone." His eyes went of their own accord to the stain on the sheepskin. "As is my vow to Robin, though the breaking of that one is entirely my own fault. Now there is only what I promised you."

She pressed her hands to her reddening cheeks. "And what I promised you."

Yes. "No. I release you from your part of the bargain, for that was founded upon lies as well. I will keep my own end and help you for nothing more than the satisfaction of stopping Guy."

Outside, the stallion whinnied nervously. Steinarr pulled the door open and was shocked to find the sun already below the tops of the trees. Too much of the afternoon had flown. He made a quick decision.

"I will remove myself for the night, and you can make your decision in peace." He took a risk, but he was going to have to leave her in moments anyway, for the lion was already stirring within him. At least this way, she might think the better of him for it. "You will be safe enough here with the door barred."

"You are going to leave me, just like that?"

"Just like that." Torvald would watch from nearby, just to be sure, but she needn't know that. "You have reason not to trust me, Marian—"

"Matilda."

He dipped his head in acknowledgment. "You have reason not to trust me, Matilda, but I ask that you let me prove myself, earn back some piece of my honor in your eyes. For now, though, I must go."

He grabbed Torvald's clothing and stepped out into the fading light to quickly unhobble the stallion. He mounted, and as the animal adjusted to his weight, he saw Marian standing in the doorway, her face an unreadable mask. "Rest well, my lady."

"You truly are leaving," she said.

"Aye, I truly am. You can tell me what path you have chosen in the morning when I return."

Those angry, mistrustful green eyes bored straight into his soul as she slowly nodded. "I will. In the morning."

He turned the stallion west, toward what he hoped were thick woods. Sunset found him in a clearing by a brook where heavy deer sign told him the lion could find food. By sunrise, the ravening hunger had eased enough that he knew the beast had been successful. On a normal morning, he might find the carcass and cut some venison for his and Torvald's use. Today, he hurried into his clothes and ran to find the stallion.

All was silent as they rode into the clearing before the cottage; not even the welcoming whinny of the rouncey greeted them. The animal might have wandered, Steinarr told himself, but he doubted it. She would have taken it to reach Robin faster. He quickly dismounted and pushed opened the door.

Gone. The weight of centuries of loneliness crushed down on him, nearly taking him to his knees, but he kept his mind on Marian. Whether she intended to go forward or back, she, a woman, couldn't do it alone. He must follow her, keep her safe despite herself. If he was careful, she would never see him and never know.

And then he noticed them: both saddles, still in the corner, and Marian's blankets, neatly rolled beside his furs.

Not gone. He bolted back outside. "Marian. Matilda. Curse it, Maud! Where are you? Answer me."

The woods were silent, but in the distance, the church bells tolled out the hour. More business at the church, she'd said. Would she have gone there?

He threw himself on the stallion and raced toward the village, hoping against hope that he might still have a little time when he was not entirely alone in the world.

CHAPTER 10

"PRAYING WILL NOT make your riddle appear."

Matilda didn't bother to look. She'd felt his intense relief as he'd broached the door. "'Tis more likely than not praying. Why are you here?"

"Someone stole my horse." Steinarr pushed the door shut and came to stand just behind her. "Ah, this is not about prayer at all. You're looking at the tapestries. Do you think your next puzzle is in the stitching?"

"I do not know. I woke with the image in my head this morning and set out to see if it held anything."

"You should have waited," he said. "Did your father like these stories?"

"He often asked the priest to speak of Eve's sin. It confirmed his idea that women are the source of all wickedness."

"I prefer to believe that women are the source of all that is pleasant." His tone was neutral, but even though she could feel him trying to control himself, desire sheeted off him like rain off a roof.

"Do not, *monsire*. We are in a Holy church."

"Where is the priest?"

"His fields. They are turning hay today. I watched him go from the edge of the woods."

"You did not attend the Mass?"

"I did not have the courage. I am not comfortable here, even now, in all my sin, but I thought perhaps kneeling would help me see the answer, as it helped Robin in Headon." She continued to study the garden scene as she told him about the hill and the tree.

"So that *is* why he climbed."

"And why he fell." She stared at the tapestry, willing her eyes to see her father's secret. "There is nothing here."

"Perhaps it is not in the image itself." Before she could rise, he was at the Adam and Eve tapestry, flipping it up to examine the wall behind it, then running the edges between his fingers.

She rushed forward to snatch the tapestry away and smooth it back into place. "These are fine pieces that took years to make, and they are the property of the Church. You cannot . . . paw at them so."

"Do you want to find your riddle or not?" He moved on to the next panel and began fingering his way around the edge. "It could be sewn into a hem."

"I had not thought of that." She bit her tongue and stood back, letting him work his way through the entire set. When he finished, he grunted.

"Nothing. Let me see the clue. Perhaps a fresh eye."

Matilda started to reach into her scrip, but stopped. "Do you truly intend to help me, *monsire*, or do you merely seek more opportunity to bed me?"

"Do not, *ma demoisele*. We are in a Holy church," he said, mimicking her tones so precisely that she found herself smiling despite herself. "Ah, that is better. I do not think you have smiled at me since Maltby. I do truly intend to help you. How can I . . . ? I know."

His sword appeared in his hand so quickly it took her breath away. Heart racing, she shrank back, but he merely laid the blade across his palms and held it out. "Take it."

Hesitantly, she held out both hands. He carefully gave the blade into her care, then knelt to her.

"I am Steinarr the Proud, son of Birgir BentLeg, descended from the line of Harald Glumr, of whom many stories are told before the fires of Vass in my homeland."

"I knew you were not English," she muttered.

"I am not English." A smile touched his lips, then faded into sadness. "I am nothing now, a man with no land, no home, no family, no ties. But in my day, I slew dozens in defense of my *jarl* with that very sword. Now I offer it and myself to you, Matilda of Huntingdon, to use as you will in pursuit of your brother's right to his father's land and title. Will you have me as your man?"

"I do not know. As you said, you have made many vows. Why should I trust this one?"

"Because you and I begin afresh from here with the truth. And because I swear *this* vow on the sword of my grandfather's grandfather."

The blade trembled on her palms. "Then yes, Sir Knight, I will accept your oath."

"Turn the hilt toward me, with the blade beneath your arm." He guided the sword into place, so that the blade lay along her forearm and against her ribs, then curved her fingers around the hilt to hold it—surely some strange custom of his land, for she had never seen a knight swear an oath on his sword except by holding it upright to make the Cross.

He then held his right hand beneath the hilt. "I, Steinarr Birgirsson, make this oath to you, Matilda Fitzwalter: that I am your man for as long as you need me; that I will stand between you and all harm; that I will also defend your brother from harm; that I will do all in my power to see Robert le Chape made lord of Huntingdon; and that at the end, whatever happens, I will return you safely to his charge. So I swear before the Father of All, and may this very blade turn against me if I fail to keep this oath."

Leaning forward, he kissed the hilt then, gently, the back of her hand. Even with the shiver that raced up her arm, she could sense the way he fought to rein his emotions in. "You have my blade and my arm, my lady, but that will be the last kiss I press on you without your leave. Have you heard my oath?"

"I have, *monsire*, as has Heaven, here in this place. And here is my pledge to you. I, Matilda of—"

"No," he said. "I wish no pledge in return. This is my gift to you, in amends for how I have treated you these last days. All I ask is a token to bind me, since you did not present the sword to me."

"I have nothing to . . ." She thought quickly and reached

under her headrail to pull a single ribbon from her plaits. "Only this. It is a poor thing to confirm so fine a pledge. The ends are frayed."

"It is enough."

"Then give me your shield arm, *monsire*." She looped the ribbon around his wrist twice, then knotted it well. Beneath her fingertips, his pulse pounded in rhythm with her own racing heart. "There. You are bound to me."

"I am bound to you." He rose and took his sword to slip it back into its scabbard. "Now, let us see if we can solve this riddle. Show me what you found in Headon."

She pulled the cylinder from her scrip and extracted the parchment. "It gives only the name of the town. Harworth."

He carried the piece over to the fat candles that burned on the altar and went through all the motions she and Robert had done, twisting and turning and peering and flipping.

"You see? Nothing. And yet there *must* be something."

With a grunt, he carried the parchment outside. She followed and together they circled the church, then wandered the graveyard, examining the stones. Each place the word *Harworth* was carved, Steinarr stopped to poke and prod and wiggle. Finally, he ran out of stones to disturb. Frowning, he sat down on the low wall and surveyed the village beyond. "Your father was either cruel or an ass."

"Or both." She sat beside him, spun the cylinder mindlessly between her fingers, end over end. "He would have found it amusing to torture Robert with the possibility and then snatch it away."

"Robin."

She glanced up.

"He must remain Robin," said Steinarr. "And you must remain Marian. Guy may have sent others to hunt you down. I wish no word of Matilda Fitzwalter or Robert le Chape left behind to help them."

"Aye." She sighed. "Thus ends my reign as your lady."

He laid his hand over hers, stopping her fiddling. "You are my lady now, whether I call you that or not."

"But you cannot treat me as such, *monsire*. I think I should be your servant. Or better, the servant of your lady, whom you deliver to her. You would not have leave to beat your lady's servant as you would your own, even if she errs and speaks too boldly before others."

"You will not err. Lies come easily to you."

He said it not as accusation, but as simple truth. Still, it embarrassed her. "Forgive me, my lord. I learned it at my father's knee. He often did not like the truth. It was easier to tell him what he wanted to hear."

"Robin does not have the same skill."

"No. Things might have gone more easily for him if he did."

"Perhaps. But it is not a bad thing to be an honest man. Come, let us put this away and go find something to eat." He plucked the cylinder out of her fingers and laid it across his knees as he rolled the parchment. "We can think on it while we break our . . ."

Matilda had already risen and was shaking out her skirts when he fell silent. She turned to find him staring at the cylinder.

"He is not an ass, after all," he said. He spat on the cylinder and polished it against his sleeve, then held it up. "He is a fox. Look."

His rough cleaning had brought out a pattern of fine lines running down one side of the case, barely visible beneath the tarnish. She snatched it out of his hands and tilted it until the figures became clear. "I know this."

She dashed for the church door and pointed. "There."

Steinarr followed, and together they compared the etchings on the cylinder to the Seven Deadly Sins carved over the lintel.

"One is different," he said. "The rich man has three bags here, but only two in the lintel. Look, the mortar is different as well." He drew his knife and stretched up to scratch at the lighter mortar along one side. It crumbled away in pieces.

Matilda caught a bit as it fell and rubbed it between her fingers. It turned to dust. She touched her tongue to it, then spat. "It is naught but salt and flour with a bit of sand mixed in."

Steinarr carved out what he could reach, then stood on his toes and tried to wriggle the stone free. "There is still enough mortar along the top to hold it in place." He glanced around. "I need something to stand on."

"If you hold me up, I can reach it," said Matilda.

Almost before the words were out, Steinarr bent and scooped her up, settling her on his shoulder. Unprepared, she went dizzy with the yearning that wrapped itself around her with his arms. She grabbed at the lintel to steady herself.

He held the knife up to her. "Quickly, before someone sees us."

She forced her attention to the Sins, now only a hand's breadth above her eyes, gouging at the mortar until the stone wiggled freely, then using the tip of his blade to pry it forward.

"There is a space behind." Balancing the piggish face of Greed on the ledge of the lintel, she gingerly reached into the cranny. Her fingers closed around something soft and leathery—she hoped fervently that it wasn't a dead bat—and she drew it out, breathing a sigh of relief as she opened her hand. "A purse, with something in it."

"Hurry," said Steinarr. "I think I hear someone coming."

She shoved the stone back into place and shifted it to line up properly. "Done."

He dropped her within the circle of his arms and stepped back, and they both turned, so that when the priest and his man rounded the corner, they looked as though they might have just come out the door—except for the knife. Matilda quickly hid it in the folds of her skirts.

"Good morrow, my lord. You must be the knight the maid spoke of yesterday. You missed Mass, my children."

"I found shelter too far away. Your bells failed to wake me," said Steinarr, ignoring the servant with him as a knight would.

"Ah, but you came to pray anyway. Excellent. And now I can give you my blessing before you travel on."

Steinarr frowned. "I fear I must be on my way."

"Oh, please, my lord," said Matilda quickly. Much as she wanted to avoid going inside again, it would look too strange if they refused a blessing. "It will take but a moment."

"You cannot deny your servant a moment's prayer." The priest stepped around them and pulled the door wide. "Come along."

"She is not *my* servant, thank the saints," grumbled Steinarr, turning to follow the priest inside. As he passed, he winked at Matilda and plucked his knife out of her hand to slip it into the sheath at his waist. "I only carry her to my lady. Hurry, girl. Do not waste my time by standing there like a lump of salt."

"Yes, my lord," she said obediently as she dropped the bag into her sleeve. She started forward, but stalled at the threshold. Lust still leered down at her, now joined by Greed, who was just crooked enough to be noticed. God's knees. She had just defaced a church, and now she was going to pray in it, while her body still tingled where Steinarr had held her.

"Go on," said the priest's man behind her.

Matilda forced herself inside, wincing at her own hypocrisy as she sank to her knees. They had better succeed in making Robert lord, she thought as she crossed herself and folded her hands, because this quest was going to cost her a fortune in penance.

Not long later, though, she was listening to Steinarr grumble as they left the village behind. "They always drone on so. Why did you encourage him?"

"We neither of us can afford to refuse a blessing, *monsire*." Matilda reached into her sleeve to pull out the bag. It was made of nut brown leather, thick but soft, a red linen cord wrapped tightly around the neck. She felt the bag to see what might be inside, then began picking at the knot as they rode, finally resorting to her teeth to work it free. "There."

"Open it," urged Steinarr. "See what it says."

She stuck two fingers in and poked around. " 'Tis in bits

and pieces, whatever it is. We had better stop first, lest I lose something."

"Wait 'til we get to the cottage, then. Come on." He put the spurs to the stallion, and the rouncey followed. Thank the saints, she didn't have to wrap her arms around him just now. She was not looking forward to that. Or was she?

They were soon back at the hut, and Steinarr helped her dismount. "You see what it says. I will load the horses."

Matilda carried the little pouch over to a graying stump and tipped it out. A key caught her eye immediately; that, at least, had an obvious use. She set it aside and picked through the rest. It looked like a child's collection of oddments: a chess piece in the shape of a bishop before a gate, a pilgrim's token from some shrine, a chip of black stone, a scrap of cloth embroidered with a bird, and—

"A pointing hand? *Monsire*, what do you make of this?" she held up the bit of carved wood.

Steinarr left the rouncey and came over to take the piece. He squinted at it. "Your hand wears a glove. There are clear seams. Someone put some skill into this."

"It must be broken from some small statue." She examined the chessman. "Not our bishop, here. 'Tis too large, and he is stone."

"The wrist is cut clean, not broken." He showed her. "It may have been carved just for this purpose. What does the rest say?"

"Nothing. I have found no words yet, excepting these." She picked up the pilgrim token and read the Latin. "'*Edburga ad Pontem*.' Eadburgh of the Bridge. Father sometimes spoke of a shrine to Saint Eadburgh he admired." She flipped the disk over. "'*Meridianus puteus*.' South, um, well. South-well. Sudwell."

"There is a big church there," said Steinarr.

"Aye, the Minster. Of course, the Gate." She snatched up the bishop to show him. "The Sudwell *Gate*."

Steinarr only looked confused, so she explained. "Long ago, one of the archbishops demanded support for the Minster at Sudwell. The parishes gather in Nottingham Town each year at Whitsuntide to carry their pence to Sudwell in a grand procession. It is called the Gate." She pointed to the bishop again. "The *gate*."

"It wouldn't be that kind of gate," said Steinarr, frowning. "It would be *gata*. Road."

"Oh. Well, Father enjoyed his plays on words." She quickly explained about Head-on. "Gate or road, Father traveled it as pilgrim one year and took Rob with him as page."

"Robin would know the place then."

"Aye. Now I think of it, he does carry a pilgrim's token for luck. I never looked closely, but I think it is like this one."

"So, Sudwell it is. Come. We will work out the rest of it along the way. We have already wasted too much of the day."

"Hardly wasted, my lord. We have our next riddle half solved, and I have a knight pledged to me, while you have somehow gained a noble lady as servant."

"Perhaps you are right." Grinning, he went back to the packing. Matilda scooped up the items and returned them to the little purse, which she added to her scrip with the other clues. Excited, she hurried to carry out items for Steinarr to add to the rouncey's load.

"I should not have bought so much," he muttered a few moments later as he tied the hide in place over the loaded packsaddle. "I will trade some off along the way. We need to travel more lightly now."

"At least you intended to feed me well as you seduced me," she said with a lightness that was only partly forced.

He leaned forward to eye her around the pile of gear. "Do you forgive me so quickly, then?"

Did she? Or was there anything to forgive? She had taken every bit as much pleasure from their encounter as he, and at least now she knew what it could be. Even if she ended up married to Baldwin, she knew.

"It is not a servant's place to forgive her betters, my lord," she said, an answer that avoided an answer, because she didn't have one. "How far is it to Sudwell?"

He tucked a last strap-end under as he considered. "Two

days, if the weather holds." He laced his fingers and bent for her foot. "Up with you, Marian. We ride."

ON THE MORNING of the third day after Steinarr left, Hamo and Edith came to Ari as he hacked at the turf.

"We must ask a favor, my lord."

Ari laid aside his mattock, and swiped the sweat off his forehead on his sleeve. "What is that?"

"Goda has the squinacy," said Edith. "And now young Robin's throat aches, too."

"I heard the child crying as I rode in this morning." Ari glanced over at Robin, who sat propped up against the tree, whittling a piece of birch into a new ladle for Edith. "But he looks well enough."

"He does now," said Edith. "But he keeps asking for aught to drink. And you see that."

Robin touched his neck and cleared his throat.

"See. It begins to hurt him. He'll be getting the squinacy, too. And I have no myrrh to give them ease, and I've found little yarrow. I need someone to—"

Hamo cut in. "We were wondering if you would do us the great favor of making the ride to Retford to see if you can find some herbs and simples, my lord. It would be a great boon. We have the coin for it and 'tis market day, but my pony is lame and it will be too slow by wagon. I cannot spare a man so long. One of my own men, I mean."

"One who knows what he is doing, you mean," said Ari, laughing. "I will go, and happily before your collier's work breaks my back."

"That will not happen, my lord. You have a strong back and a good arm and a willingness to use them."

"That may be, but I can stand the rest, nonetheless. Tell me what you need, and you will have it by the end of the day."

After several days staked out in the clearing, his horse was as pleased with the ride as Ari, and it wasn't long before they were cantering down the long, gentle slope into Retford. From the height, Ari could see the tents and stands of the market in the square and the bloodred clay in the River Idle that gave the ford its name.

He paid a boy to watch his horse and quickly located a man with dried herbs and medicines displayed in baskets. He rattled off the list Edith had given him, bargained to get what was available at a fair price, and put everything in the pouches the old woman had sent along and rolled them in a bundle to carry.

Cheek by jowl with the herb merchant, a woman sold fat lamb pies heavy with pepper and cinnamon. He laid out a farthing for one, then carried it through the market, looking for the sake of looking.

At the far edge of the square, a simple tavern had taken shape with tables and rough-hewn benches, and next to it, a group of players was in the middle of a mystery play. As saints and demons frolicked across the big wagon that served as the stage, Ari paid for a cup of wine and settled down to eat his pie and cheer and jeer with the townsfolk. The mood grew more somber as the story played out, however, and by the time the Resurrection unfolded, even the drinkers were grave and repentant and ready to disperse.

"More wine, my lord?" the tavern keeper asked, a note of resignation in his voice.

Ari tapped his cup and laid another coin on the table. "Your drinkers have lost their thirst."

"Aye. I should have chased those fool players away when they came along," said the man, motioning a wench over to pour. "They properly belong beside the church, but I thought they would draw more people and I let them stay. Instead, they have driven all away."

"'Tis a shame you do not have a good storyteller to bring them back. Someone who could spin the tale of"—he grabbed at the first names that came to mind—"Robin and Marian."

"Robin and Marian? I do not know the tale."

Neither did Ari, but the pleasure of storytelling lay in the spinning of new thread. "Likely not, because the sheriff does not want it told. Robin was banished from his home by the sheriff himself for suspicion of killing one of the king's deer, though it could not be proved. He lives in the shire wood as an outlaw."

"An outlaw is not the proper hero for a tale."

"But this is no ordinary outlaw. He steals only from the very richest on the road, tax collectors and noblemen and fat abbots and bishops, and lets all others pass." That was Steinarr's way, and Jafri's as well, when he turned to robbery as sometimes he must to live. "In fact, there was a very fat abbot riding to . . . to Saint Mary's Abbey. He wore the finest velvet and silk, ripped from the toil of the peasants who worked the abbey lands."

A man on the next bench turned to listen. "I know the very sort."

"Sadly, too many do. But this abbot, Hugo by name, was of the worst sort, and so full of himself that even as he rode the forest road, he draped himself in velvet and golden chains and rings. When Robin spied the glitter of those riches, he could not resist the lure, and so he rode ahead and climbed into the branches of a great tree to lie in wait for the bishop to pass."

Another man sat down nearby to listen, then a pair of women carrying baskets, then the players themselves, as Ari spun out the tale of Abbot Hugo's humiliation at this Robin's hands. "And so he crawled back home in naught but his braies, and Robin sold his jewels in Lincoln and returned the silver to the men who had truly earned it. And that was the end of that."

"But what about the Marian you spoke of, my lord?" asked the man on the bench.

"Ah, you are right, I forgot to tell of Marian. 'Tis a shame my throat is so dry."

The tavern keeper, who still stood absorbed in the story, suddenly realized he had trade again. He called to the wench, who quickly began circling through the crowd, pouring as quickly as she could dodge the many too-friendly hands. The tavern keeper leaned over with a grin as he refilled Ari's cup with wine. "No charge for you, my lord, so long as you keep talking."

So Ari talked, telling of how Robin rescued a fair maid

from a ne'er-do-well lordling and carried her off to safety in the forest. But when he reached the part where, by all the rules of good storytelling, he should have Robin and Marian fall in love and marry, he thought of Steinarr—who was, after all, the real outlaw—and stopped.

"Did Robin marry her?" asked one of the women, her eyes glittering with excitement.

"Not yet," said Ari, "Though I think he will in the end. And his men do as well."

"What men?" called someone in the crowd.

"Others outlawed by unjust lords, banished for the smallest of crimes. For not paying the lord's due for a daughter's marriage. Or . . . or for getting sick and not being able to do the boon work." That set up a grumble. Every peasant in England had similar complaints and fears, and Ari knew it. The story would ring true to them, little though the local nobles would like him telling it.

"The first of those to join Robin was, um, John. John Little," he added, recalling the name of the man Steinarr had tried to rescue. Perhaps his name could live on, though the old man hadn't. "Robin called him Little John, and here is how they met. One day as Robin Hood was walking through the woods, he came upon a huge rock of a man standing on a narrow bridge, holding a staff . . ."

He kept the crowd entertained, making up more adventures for Robin Hood and his men until his practiced eye told him he had just enough time to get back to the colliers, have a quick meal, and head into the forest for the night. With a stretch, he rose. "I must be away, friends."

"Will you be back, *monsire*?" asked the tavern keeper as the crowd groaned.

"Perhaps."

"I am here each market day, and I will trade you all you can drink for stories whenever you please."

"That will have him back, for certs."

Grinning, Ari turned toward the familiar voice. "What are you doing back? Did she tire of you already?"

"No. I am selling a few things we don't need. What story have you been inflicting on these poor people?"

"Nothing you know." Ari moved off, wanting to get Steinarr away before someone mentioned the names he'd been using.

But the tavern keeper swooped in to grab his cup. "He has been telling us of Robin Hood and Maid Marian, my lord."

Steinarr's face went grim. "What?"

"Of the outlaw, Robin Hood, and his lady love, my lord," said the tavern keeper. "Have you not heard the tale?"

"No. I have not. Come, friend. Tell it to me as we walk." Steinarr clapped Ari on the shoulder like a friend, but his fingers bit into Ari's shoulder as he steered him away from the tavern and toward where the stallion and rouncey stood tethered on the side of the green. "What are you doing?"

"Whiling away an afternoon." Ari jerked out of Steinarr's grip. "So I used their names. 'Twas in sport."

"You'll have Gisburne on us," growled Steinarr.

"But you—" He glanced around to make sure Marian wasn't near. She wasn't, but he switched to Norse anyway. "You're working for him. Aren't you?"

"No. The pig's hole lied to me." Steinarr quickly explained the changed situation. "He's likely hired others to hunt them as well."

Ari groaned as what he'd just done hit him. "And here I am . . . Balls. I'm sorry. But 'twas only a tale told in a village market. Surely it will go no further."

"With good fortune." Steinarr poked Ari in the chest with each word. "But do not repeat it."

"No. No, of course not. What can I do to help?"

"Keep the boy out of sight, and do what you can to get him fit to travel. Once we find the treasure, I'll be back to take him to the king. He must be ready to ride hard."

"I will do what I can, but healing lies in the gods' hands. Where is Marian?"

"Using the garderobe."

"So, with these new plans, are you still keeping your vow to Robin, or are you swiving her?"

Steinarr folded his arms across his chest. "And you call me crude."

"You are swiving her, aren't you? You swore you wouldn't."

"I swore a lot of things."

"You never break your word. You bend it, but you never break it. There *is* something about her, isn't there?"

"There are many things about her, but I'm not going to discuss any of them with you. Now, here she comes." Steinarr grabbed him by the shoulder again, this time to spin him around to face Marian, who was walking toward them across the green. "Keep your mouth shut."

"Never fear." Ari swept off his coif and bowed. "Good day, fair Marian."

Two passing cottagers gave him a puzzled look, and Steinarr growled at Ari's ear, "She's a servant, ass."

"But a fair servant, and worthy of a little fawning from a poor knight."

"You are not a poor anything, my lord." She dropped in courtesy. "I did not expect to see you here. Is all well?"

"I came in to buy a few herbs for Edith. Goda has the quinsy."

"Poor thing." Her brow wrinkled with worry. "Robin will get it, too. He always does. Does Edith have myrrh? It helps."

Ari patted the parcel he carried. "Right here."

"I wish we could take the time to—"

"We cannot," interrupted Steinarr. "But Edith will see to him. Come, we can make another league at least before sundown."

"You already found someone to buy the extra things?"

"Aye. And got more than I paid in Nottingham Town."

"Perhaps you should become a merchant," said Ari, and laughed when Steinarr told him to tup himself in Norse.

"It is not that long. You know," he said, considering as he watched Steinarr help Marian up behind the saddle. "You could take my horse for her. You'd travel faster, and I could make do with the rouncey."

"Servants do not ride fancy palfreys. It would attract too much attention," said Steinarr as he swung up before her. "If it comes to it, I will put her on the rouncey, but for now, she rides behind me. We're moving fast enough. Go on. Get back to camp with those herbs. We need the lad healthy."

"Aye. Travel safely." Ari watched them ride off, and there was something in the way Marian wrapped her arms around his friend's waist . . . Aye, they were swiving all right. And it wasn't all Steinarr's idea.

"Very nice." He muttered a small thanks to Freya for bringing these two together. Even if Marian wasn't the one to break the curse, Steinarr needed a woman of his own for a while, to keep him sane, if nothing else.

Speaking of which . . .

He headed for his horse, taking a path through the tavern just for the sake of catching the passing ale wench around the waist and pulling her close for a quick kiss and a pat on the bottom. "Now for that, I will be back."

"For *that*, you will pay more than a story, my lord," said the woman, and swayed off with a flip of her hips.

"You wound me, fair one." He clapped his hand over his heart and sighed, much to the amusement of the watching men. Joining their laugher, he headed off to find the boy who still watched his horse. He was on the road back toward Headon by the time the bells rang Nones.

CHAPTER 11

"WHY DO YOU leave each night?" asked Matilda as she stirred the coals of the dying fire two mornings later, looking for a last bit of warmth to chase way the night's chill.

Steinarr's knife stopped in the middle of a slice of bread. "Do you not know?"

She kept her eyes on the fire pit, hoping he would blame her rising color on the still-pink morning sky. Two full days now since he had released her from their bargain, and still the effects of his desire kept her body in a constant ache.

Or at least she preferred to blame it on him. In truth, the nights were as bad as the days. They swam with him. No matter that he left, no matter that she did her best to put thoughts of him aside before she slept, she awoke each dawn with the sense he'd been with her, with the remembered weight of his body on hers. If not for his friend's presence each night, she would wonder if he was creeping back to somehow share her bed without waking her. And worse, every time she thought of it during the daylight, of him and what they had done, and what she dreamed of doing again, her blood pulsed with heat. It was a fortunate thing he couldn't sense her mind the same way she sensed his, else she would be lost.

"And what of Sir Torvald?" she asked, directing his attention, and her own, elsewhere. "Why does he not ride along with us?"

"He prefers to travel alone."

She held her hands down to the coals. "Has he taken Holy vows?"

"Torvald?" The chuckle in his voice said he thought the idea daft. "Why would you think that?"

"Because he is so very solitary. He holds himself apart, so that we barely speak of an evening, even when we sit but a few feet from each other. I thought perhaps he was some sort of monk-knight, like a Templar."

"No. He merely keeps to himself, wise man that he is," said Steinarr. "How hungry are you this morning?"

"Not very. That will suffice." She took her bread and nibbled at it as he hacked off three more slabs of the heavy brown loaf for himself. "How does Sir Torvald even know how to find us each night?"

"'Tis a knack he has. Why are you so full of questions this morning?"

"I have had them all along, my lord, I only waited to see if things would change. They do not look to, so I ask to satisfy my curiosity." She watched as he wolfed his bread and washed it down with ale. "You are very different men, the two of you, even to the way you eat."

"How so?"

"He takes his ease. You set upon your food as though you have not seen a good meal in months and fear it will escape."

All trace of good humor faded. Steinarr rose and brushed away the crumbs that clung to his robes. "Do what you must to be ready. I want to be in Sudwell by the time the bells ring Sext."

Matilda stared after him, bewildered by the sudden change in his mood. Such odd things set him off. Robin, and now Guy, she understood; his anger at Rob had been pure jealousy, arisen from his desire and the mistaken belief they were lovers, and he naturally despised Guy's betrayal. But why did her observations on his eating habits sting him so? And why had Sir Ari's teasing courtesy in Retford made him so angry? Shaking her head, she rose and began her preparations.

They reached Sudwell well before Sext, as it turned out. It was barely Terce when they turned onto the southbound road, and not long after that when Marian exclaimed at the tall, pointed towers of the Minster appearing over the trees.

"So close, and you made me sleep in the woods? Why did we not merely ride in? We might have found proper beds."

"We would have been riding in the dark. And besides, I do not rest well within walls."

"*I* do not rest well on bare ground."

"It is safer in the woods."

"So safe a knight must protect me from wolves," she pointed out.

"Wolves will not carry word back to Gisburne of a fair maiden with hair the color of spun gold and lips like ripe strawberries. Nor will they gossip of a servant who scolds her knight as if she were a noblewoman."

"I do not scold."

"You are scolding now."

"Oh. Well, I would hold my tongue before others."

"Nonetheless, we will keep to ourselves as much as we can, for my lady's safety."

"And if your lady should command you otherwise?"

"She will not," he said firmly.

She leaned out so she could see his profile. He didn't seem especially angry, but he wasn't smiling either. "No, I don't suppose she will. Forgive me, my lord. I should not challenge you."

"It is your nature," he said, and now there was a bit of a curve to his mouth. "You have challenged me since the instant you popped up from the bracken."

"I only—" She stopped herself. "Perhaps I have. But I had good reason."

"No doubt. Be ware as we pass this group." He tipped his head toward a grand wagon rolling along just ahead, surrounded by a large contingent of riders. Matilda craned to see the trailing riders past Steinarr's shoulder. Her heart began to race at the sight of parti-colored red and green.

"I know that livery, my lord. 'Tis that of—" She suddenly found herself looking into the eyes of the revoltingly fat old man who lounged beneath the canopy of the wagon, facing to the rear. The streak of self-preservation her father had beat into her made her duck behind Steinarr's back, and the name came in a breath, "Lord Baldwin. Ride, *monsire*!"

"What? Why?"

"He knows me. Go," she urged, just as she heard Baldwin bellow, "*Monsire*, attend!"

Ah, God, too late. An echoing call came from one of the outriders. "*Monsire*, my lord wishes a word with you and your lady."

"Cough," ordered Steinarr under his breath. Then more loudly, "As you will, my lord, though I must warn, this serving woman my lady sent me to fetch has come down with lung fever."

As he spoke, Matilda understood. She coughed obligingly, then let it build to a deep racking, followed by a whooping draw of breath. Not only did her hacking make Baldwin's knight pull up short, it also provided an excellent excuse to drag her headrail across her face to further hide herself in pretense of covering her mouth. Wheezing and shuddering, she risked a peek past Steinarr's shoulder.

"Your lady's servant? I thought—" began Baldwin. He stopped, eyeing her with distaste. "Bah, never mind. Of course Matilda would not be on the road alone with only a single knight. Keep that poisonous creature well away. I have no wish to become ill."

"Wise, my lord. I would leave her by the road to die in peace, but for my lady's certain ire." Steinarr swung back toward the verge. "A good journey to you. Do you know if there is a nunnery in yon town that will care for the wench?"

Baldwin's response was lost beneath yet another paroxysm of coughing that Matilda dragged out until they cantered ahead and left the train well behind.

"Enough," said Steinarr, chuckling.

"I cannot stop. Some ale, my lord. I hurt my throat."

"I'm not surprised." He leaned over to unhook the ale skin from the packhorse and passed it back as she coughed a few more times. "I thought you would bring up a lung."

"So did Baldwin, I hope." She swallowed a mouthful of ale and cleared her throat again. "He fears fevers, especially lung fever. How did you know?"

"Every old man fears lung fever, and fat ones even more than most. So, what is he, a friend of your father?"

"Aye." She took another drink and started to cap the skin. "And the man I am to marry."

"That old *hrosshvalr*?"

His outrage crackled through her like lightning. Startled, Matilda jerked back, nearly dropping the skin. Ale sloshed over her leg, wetting her from knee to foot.

"You are to marry *that*?" he demanded again, noticing neither the ale nor her dismay. "How? Why? What was your father thinking, to give you to that, that . . ." Words failed him and he went back to, "That *hrosshvalr*?"

She shrank away from him and squeezed her eyes shut, which let her pull herself together enough to say, "I do not know that word."

"*Hrosshvalr*, a, uh, a horse-whale. A monstrous seal that sits on the ice of the northern sea."

The act of explaining drew him back from the rage and let Matilda regain her balance. Hesitantly, she opened her eyes. "I have heard tales of such creatures. And I have seen seals in the Thames."

"A horse-whale is far larger. Think of *that*, only half-again longer and with great pointed teeth that hang down." He held up his hands a foot-length apart. "Like so. And a brown hide like old leather, thicker than my thumb. How could your father give you to *that*?"

How, indeed? "He made what he saw as the best match," she said quietly, still working to separate herself from him. "Guy will confirm it, I think." She hoped he would, at least, for it would be better than the alternative. "Robin will see me released."

"No wonder you want him as lord."

There were far more reasons than that for wanting Robin as lord, but Matilda bit her tongue and merely nodded. She risked a look back to where they'd left behind the brilliant red and green of Baldwin's company. "No doubt

Lord Baldwin has heard of my father's death and goes to claim me. But why to Sudwell? That is not along the way."

"Gisburne will have sent a message that you're to be brought to Nottingham. Little good it will do him." Steinarr put the spurs to the stallion and they soon reached the outskirts of Sudwell. However, instead of going into town, he swung right to circle it.

"Do we not go into Sudwell after all?"

"The road from Nottingham comes in from the south and west. We will go in by that way, to see if we can find any sign of your father's riddle."

"Ah, I thought perhaps we would wait. If we cross paths with Baldwin and he spies your lady's servant miraculously healed, she may find herself married before nightfall." She tried to make light of it, but there must have been something in her voice, because Steinarr patted her hands where they linked at his waist.

"I will keep you safe," he assured her. His hand remained over hers, and for once it was comfort she found in his touch instead of merely desire.

A little later, as they reached the southwestern gate, he called to a watchman. "You there, I need someplace to leave two horses for half a day."

"John the Flesher has a pen, my lord. Two streets over, under the sign of the bull and knife." The fellow pointed. "Tell him Tom atte Well sent you."

Steinarr nodded his thanks, and the horses were soon safe in the flesher's pen. "Stay here. I have an idea for our problem with Baldwin."

He vanished toward the flesher's house and returned a few moments later carrying a grease-stained red gown and a black hooded cloak that was nearly as bad. "These should disguise you well enough. Put them on."

She eyed the garments doubtfully. "My lord . . ."

"They were in a chest, and they stink of wormwood and camphor. Whatever beasts might have been on them are surely dead."

Shuddering, she took them between thumb and finger. "I cannot."

"Then stay here out of sight, and hope that I can follow your father's thoughts, for that is the only choice besides these or Baldwin."

She looked around the flesher's yard, well kept but reeking of decaying flesh and curing hides. They'd been here only moments and already the odor was making her ill. She didn't want to stay while he went off. "I will need your aid, my lord."

"Over here." They stepped behind the work shed, and she laid aside her cloak and scrip. As Steinarr helped her tug the red gown over her head, the sharp fragrance of the moth-herbs overpowered the stench of the flesher's shop, giving her nose a moment's respite. Still . . .

" 'Tis huge!" she complained. The narrow sleeves hung past her hands to her knees, and she flapped them like broken wings as Steinarr looked her over.

"Huge, but short," he said. "The brown shows below. Can you pull it up somehow?"

"I think so." She drew her arms inside the red, easy enough, considering how loose it hung, and gathered her gown, tucking the hem into her girdle all the way around so that only her plain wool kirtle showed below. Steinarr shook out the black cloak and pinned it around her shoulders. "Tuck your sleeves in as well."

Matilda did so, rolling them into the red sleeves so that in the end, only a thin stripe of brown showed at her wrists. When she had all arranged, Steinarr stepped back for another look. His mouth worked as he fought a smile.

"What?" she demanded as she pulled the strap of her scrip over her head.

"You look like some fat-hipped butcher's wife. No, 'tis well you do," he said when she spluttered. "Baldwin will never look twice. Just keep your hair covered and that hood well forward. Come." He grabbed her cloak and rolled it, and as they passed the rouncey, he jammed it into the pile of gear.

The flesher stood by the gate, and Steinarr handed him a halfpenny as they left. "Give them both water and a little hay. You'll have the other half of that when we return, plus a farthing for use of your clothing."

"Aye, my lord." The fellow's eyes widened as he took in Matilda in his too-large gown, but he was a wise man and held his tongue.

They made their way back to the gate and started up the wide street toward the Minster. Sudwell was a town for pilgrims, and amid the usual shops and stalls stood others offering various tokens of Saint Eadburgh, from straw-sized vials of liquid reported to be tears shed by her statue to simple parchments scribed with prayers invoking her aid.

"How are we to find anything in all this?" asked Matilda. "And if we do find something, how are we to get it without anyone taking note? This is not a village where every man goes to the fields."

"Perhaps we will not have to ransack a church this time," said Steinarr. "Keep your eyes open. Your father is clever with his riddles. Remember: bird, hand, black stone, and perhaps the bishop at his gate."

"And perhaps the pilgrim's token, although that, I think, was just to get us here."

They found the bird first, at a stall that sold bits of cloth the merchant claimed had been blessed by the Archbishop of York. Among squares stitched with the Cross and Saint Eadburgh's name lay a few that matched the one in the pouch. Matilda snatched one from the pile and held it out. "My lord, look."

Steinarr fingered the square, then motioned the old man over. "What bird is this?"

"'Tis meant to be a linnet, my lord. My wife has been stitching such figures for near a score of years now. Would you or your lady like one? The cloth is blessed by the Archbishop himself, each Whitsun Fair during the Gate. It will cure all your ills merely by laying it on the skin and saying a prayer."

Steinarr snorted and started to move on, but Matilda lingered. "I have seen such a bird before, I think. Might it be carved or painted somewhere in the Minster?"

"Not in it. Beside it," said the man. "The wife took the shape from that statue of the old archbishop that stands in the graveyard. Such birds circle his feet, picking at the ground."

"Ah, of course. No wonder it seemed familiar," said Matilda as if he had confirmed a memory. She turned a servant's pleading face up to Steinarr. "Please, my lord, may I see it again? I would like to offer a prayer for my cousin's sister. She does love linnets."

Steinarr covered a laugh with a cough. "I think we can manage a few moments for a prayer. Come along."

She dropped the square back among the others, nodded a quick thanks to the old man, and hurried after Steinarr, falling in at his heel as a servant would. It was a good place to be: with his size and broad shoulders, he carved a path through the crowds that was easy to follow, just as his big horse had carved an easy way through the briars for the mare. All she had to do was stay close and keep an eye out for other signs of their clues.

As they reached the open center of the town, he suddenly stopped dead and stood staring across the open sward toward the huge Minster before them, his jaw agape. She understood his awe. Combined, the quire and nave stretched a hundred paces or more, and the two square end towers with their silvery caps soared as tall as any church she'd seen, but for the abbey church in London.

"Have you not seen it before, my lord? I thought from what you said that you had been here."

"I have passed nearby, but have never come into town to see it so closely. 'Tis a grand hall, even for one of your . . . Even for a church," he finished.

"The inside must be magnificent. Shall we see it?"

He hesitated, then shook his head. "Baldwin may come to pray. I would not want you caught inside, even looking like that."

"Aye, that would be bad. The priest would be right there to marry us."

His growl was barely audible, but his anger rattled her skull like an earthquake. "Let us find your archbishop with his linnets and see what he has to tell us."

It took little effort to find the handsome statue in the

corner of the yard nearest the minster. To Matilda's surprise, it wasn't like the chess piece at all, but a simple representation of a cleric in a miter holding a shepherd's staff, done in an ancient style. But though it was beginning to show the wear of ages, the graceful linnets around the base stood out clear.

As soon as a group of pilgrims moved aside, Steinarr quickly found the one that matched the figure on their cloth. His forehead creased with puzzlement. "There is an arrow scratched through it."

"How odd." Matilda turned circles, searching for more of their clues. A black marker a stone's throw away caught her eye and she scurried over. "A corner is broken off, my lord."

Steinarr came over as she fished out the black chip and matched it to the piece, a headstone for someone named Petronilla.

"That is Robin's mother's name," exclaimed Matilda.

"I thought she was from Kent."

"She was. Is. This surely is not her, for she still lives, but it is the same name."

"And here is another arrow." He pointed at a few faint lines Matilda had marked as simple scratches, but which now mated with similar lines on the headstone to form a rough arrow. "Now, for the hand."

That took longer. They wandered through the headstones and monuments, searching for an image or statue. It was Matilda who finally spotted the tiny shrine built into the wall, half-hidden by overgrown bushes. In it, a statue of some noblewoman stood with outstretched arms, one gloved hand in the precise position of theirs, except that it held a slender arrow.

"Three arrows. That surely means something. Perhaps . . ." Steinarr backed away, following the line of the lady's arrow. "Sight along the arrow on the black stone."

Matilda hurried to obey. "It meets your track, my lord."

He held out his arm and sighted along it to the archbishop's linnet and kept backing until the three lines converged. "They come together right . . . here."

Here was another headstone, a rich man's stone, nearly shoulder high and heavily carved with leaves and vines. Matilda joined Steinarr before the stone and read out the name.

"Robert fitz Walter!" Stunned, she bent to trace a finger over the next words. "Anno Domini MCXCVII. Year of Our Lord . . . one thousand one hundred ten and . . . no, nine-tens and seven. I think. I have never been good with ciphers."

"An ancestor?"

"If so, one who shares Robin's name. How very strange. I wonder if Father showed this to Rob when they came on pilgrimage." And if he had, whether he had done so with a father's pride or to remind Robert that he would never truly be a Fitzwalter, even if he did share a given name with one. "I have it. A lady—my mother. A bishop who would not let Father annul the marriage for lack of a son. And Petronilla, his mistress. And they all point to this Robert. This must be it."

"Very good, Marian." Steinarr began running his hands over the stone, searching. "The only thing left is the key. There must be something for it to open."

Matilda followed him around to the back of the stone, which was engraved with a quaint figure of a knight wearing mail and an old-style pot-helm. She did a little courtesy. "Good day, Sir Robert. You may be my grandsire's grandsire."

Still searching, Steinarr squatted at the corner of the stone. "Is anyone watching?"

Matilda glanced around. "No. I don't—" A sharp clang at her feet made her jump. She looked down to find Steinarr, his big knife in his fist, hammer-wise. "What are you doing?"

"Hush. Look elsewhere. You draw too much attention."

She bent over, her voice urgent. "You cannot defile a gr—"

Another sharp blow loosened the edge of the stone, revealing a seam. Working swiftly, Steinarr slid the point of his blade in the gap, popped the slab loose, and stuck his hand into the hole. "I think you will find your key fits—"

"You there! What are you doing?"

Matilda glanced up to find a priest charging across the churchyard, a baleful glare in his eye. She stepped out from behind the stone to block him and heard a scuffle of motion behind her.

"Good morrow, Father." She bent a knee and reached for his hand in the hope he would stop and acknowledge her, but he pushed past.

"What are you doing, you . . . oh. My lord."

Steinarr was on his knees, hands reverently folded and eyes closed. His knife was in its scabbard, the stone appeared to be whole, and absolutely nothing gave any indication that he was doing anything besides praying. He opened one eye. "Is there some problem, Father?"

"I, um, no, my lord. That is, I heard a hammer blow and thought it came from here."

"Do I *look* like a carpenter?" asked Steinarr with the kind of disdain reserved for lessers.

The priest flushed. "Of course not, my lord. Is this Robert fitz Walter an ancestor of yours?"

"So I am told. And now, I assume you will let me finish my prayer."

"Yes, of course, my lord. Your pardon. And yours, my lady."

"No lady am I, Father. Only his lady's servant." She strolled away with the priest, moving him along to give Steinarr time to do whatever he must. "He carries me to my lady's service in Newark, but he is a very pious man and we stop at every church along the way. I think he must have ancestors in every churchyard in England."

"The Fitzwalters are a powerful family. The current lord, David, has been a good friend to Sudwell. How is this knight related to him?"

So, word of Father's death hadn't traveled to Sudwell yet. Good. That meant Guy hadn't been here either. Matilda's smile grew more genuine.

"His mother is a distant cousin, I think he said. Forgive me, Father. The blow you heard was my knife. I took it out to trim a thread from my sleeve and dropped it. It hit the stone, and then I bumped it again as I picked it up." She touched the blade at her waist apologetically. "It rang out quite loudly, I fear, though no damage was done."

The priest's pinched expression eased into a relieved smile. "Ah. That is good to know. We had some trouble at that very grave two years past. Some foul spirit disturbed the soil, trying to heave it over, and when I saw you there . . . Please give your knight my apologies."

"Of course, Father. I will explain it to him. But now I must go. He will want to ride as soon as he finishes."

"Will he not go to pray in the church as well?"

"I am not certain. My lady waits, and he has already taken too long getting me to her, with all his prayers. Your pardon, Father, I think he is done." She bobbed neatly and backed away.

Steinarr was on his feet, and he marched off with nothing more than a peremptory flick of his finger. Matilda hurried after, not risking so much as a glance at Lord Robert's grave for fear the priest was watching. *Two years ago.* Father had been with King Edward two years ago. That must be when they devised their cursed test and put it all in place.

They crossed the churchyard and headed down the street and were halfway back to the flesher's before Steinarr slowed enough for her to fall in beside him.

"Did you get it?" she asked, excited. "What is it? I thought the priest was going to—"

A flash of red and green ahead caught her eye, and then vanished as Steinarr tugged the black hood forward over her eyes.

"The *hrosshvalr* comes straight at us." He took her elbow and steered her toward the nearest shop. "Stay here, lest he see us together, and keep your head down, lest he see those lips."

And then he was gone, vanished down the crowded street, leaving her standing there in front of a glover, who took one look at her lumpy, moth-eaten gown and began rearranging his wares, reaching far across the table to pull his finer gloves close in a clear attempt to discourage her from thieving. She glared at him for the insult, but she had no choice but to stay, pretending to examine the few poor pairs he left within reach.

Behind her, Baldwin's outriders called warnings and jostled through the crowd. The wagon creaked closer. Another moment, and he'd be past and she could breathe again.

The creaking stopped. "You there."

The glover looked up. "Yes, my lord?"

"Not you. Her."

Sweet Virgin. Matilda caught at the edge of the table to steady herself. She would fight him, every step. She would never make the vows. She tensed, prepared to run.

"Yes, my lord?" said the woman at the next stall.

"Are those beef or mutton?"

The woman held up a plump pie. "Lamb, my lord, and the best in Sudwell town. Would you have one?"

"Let me see more closely. What spices do you use?"

Matilda's fingers bit into the wood as her heart stuttered and restarted. *Food. Baldwin and food, always food.*

"Buy or move on, woman," growled the glover.

"Your pardon," she muttered, lowering her voice so much, she sounded like the laundress at home. She fought the urge to dash away, knowing Baldwin would take note, and shambled to the next stall, looked a moment, then moved to the next and the next, until she found a corner and could duck off the street into a narrow passage between buildings.

She stood there shaking, furious at Baldwin and his incessant quest for food, at her father for betrothing her to such a man, and at Steinarr for abandoning her on the street, even though she understood why—if Baldwin had recognized Steinarr from the road, he would have taken a second look at any woman with him, fat hips or no. But where was Steinarr now? She flattened against a wall, unwilling to risk sticking so much as a nose around the corner to see if Baldwin was gone, and when a wagon groaned past in the road, she hurried even deeper into the alley and crouched down behind an empty tun of wine.

She was still huddled there, surrounded by the vinegar smell of the barrel, when footsteps approached. She whipped out her knife, ready to fight if need be.

"Marian? Curse it, I saw you come back here. Where are you?"

She unfolded and stood there shaking. "Where were *you*? I thought . . . I thought . . ."

"I know. So did I."

"Lamb pies," she said.

"He bought three."

"You stayed near, then?"

"I would never have let him take you."

The fearsome certainty in his words made tears prick at Matilda's eyes. She nodded, not trusting her voice.

"He has rolled off to gorge himself. I watched to be certain which way he went. Come, my sturdy butcher's wife. Let us return those clothes and get well away from this place and him, and then"—he dropped his voice to a conspiratorial whisper and held out his hand—"I will show you what I found in the graveyard."

Take his hand? Hardly safe, considering how fragile her defenses felt. However, now that the urgency of the moment had faded, she found she needed some strength beyond her own to steady her legs. She drew a bracing breath before she stepped out from behind her tun and laid her hand in his. His fingers closed around hers, bringing with that simple embrace a deep sense of relief that, whether it was his or hers, was most welcome.

"I would like that very much, my lord. The farther away, the better."

STEINARR RODE WEST, carrying Marian into a part of the shire wood he knew well in an effort to get her as far from Baldwin as possible. The thought of her wed to that *hrosshvalr*, at his beck and call, in his bed, drove him to push the horses hard, and before the afternoon was half over, they were deep enough into the forest that he felt she was safe.

As did she, evidently, for as he grew more at ease, so did she, toward the end settling against his back with a sigh that sounded more like a yawn.

"You grow weary."

"A little," she admitted.

"We will stop soon. I know a place."

"Another of your caves or hermit's cells?"

The teasing note in her voice made him smile and respond in kind. "Better. An elf house."

"Truly?" She lifted her head. "My nurse used to tell me tales of elves, until Father caught her at it. He sent her away for filling my head with foolish lies and brought in a cleric to teach me Latin instead."

"To our fortune in this quest. However, elves are as real as you and I," he assured her.

"And they live in this place you take me?"

"I have not seen them there, but it seems the sort of place they would like."

"Gunnora said they live under the ground, in mines and deep caves."

"Only the dark elves. Others live in the waters of springs and in the dark parts of the forest. But still others, the light elves, move between the bright forest glades and the clouds, and slip amongst men and women, disguised as the fairest of the fair. You might be an elf."

"You flatter, my lord. And you surprise me. I did not know you had the tongue of a bard."

"I don't. I only borrow from Ari."

"Ah, well, I am no elf either—light or dark. I do not love the woods enough. I would rather eat in a hall and sleep in a soft bed. You, however, seem to have the greenwood in your blood. Are *you* elvish?"

"You have discovered it at last," he said solemnly. "I am an outlaw elvish woodward."

"I knew it," she said, and her laugh went to his head like strong wine. "Tell me more about your people, my lord elf, to keep my mind from this." She patted the bulk at his waist, the item he'd found in Sudwell.

"You *are* being strangely patient."

"Only because I must. I made up my mind I would not ask to see it until we arrive at our night's camp, so as not to slow us. You were speaking of elves, *monsire*. Do they stay always young as Gunnora said?"

"Young, fair, and full of magic, which sadly, they use for mischief against men. There was once a midwife, who was taken among the elves to deliver a child unto their queen . . ." He told the old tale, one he'd heard from his mother and again from Ari around the fire, drawing on the *skald*'s language as much as he could remember it for the sake of pleasing Marian.

The final mile passed, and at last he spotted the old track, little more than a deer trail. He turned down it, plunging deeper into the forest wilds. There was just enough time to finish the story before they rode into the glade, still strangely open though the trees all around had grown taller and thicker. "And when they realized she'd stolen their queen's magic looking glass to admire herself, they struck her blind in the right eye and left her to live her life as a poor woman."

"I wonder if that is what happened to our cook," mused Marian. "She is blind in the right eye."

"Perhaps she cooked for them and put too much salt in their food. Here we are." He swung off the stallion and helped her down.

"Show me." Her patience vanished the instant her feet touched the ground. She snatched the box from his hand as soon as he produced it and ran her fingertips over the design hammered into the aged green copper. "I know this box! Father used to keep his favorite jewels and rings in it. You never said how you knew it was there in the stone."

"There was a little key scribed on one corner. I saw the seam where a piece had been mortared in. Go on. See what it holds."

She dropped to her knees right there and fished out the little key from the purse in her scrip. But when she fitted

it to the lock, she hesitated, her hand frozen over the key
and her lips pressed into that tempting line. Not for the
first time, Steinarr wished he hadn't sworn off kissing her.
Those lips were so very sweet . . .

As he watched, a wash of pink colored her cheeks.

"Why do you wait?" he asked.

"You solved the puzzle, and you found the casket. It
seems fair that you should open it."

"It is not my quest."

"Nor mine, but we both find ourselves making it, nonetheless." Her fingers tightened on the key, but still didn't
turn. "I keep thinking of what you said at Harworth, that
Father was either cruel or an ass. What if this is a false
trail? What if Father laid it only as an elaborate trick to
hurt Robin one last time?"

"So long as there are clues to follow, you must assume
the game is real." He squatted beside her and curled his
hand over hers, wanting to comfort and offer his strength,
but also grateful for any excuse to touch her. "There is only
one way to find out. Shall we do it together?"

She closed her eyes for a moment, then nodded. Together
they turned the key, and the box opened with a rusty click.
Reluctantly releasing her hand, he flicked the lid open.

"Another parchment." She unfolded it and scanned it
quickly. "'Tis in English. That may mean some play on
words again."

"Can you read it?"

"Aye, but it will take me a little. I am better with French
and Latin."

Three languages. She—a woman—could read in three
languages, and he could barely make out runes in his own
tongue. She was from a different world, newer than his
own, full of books and learning, where a simple lord's hall
was grander than the old king's palace and where soaring
churches reduced even the great hall of Asgard to little
more than a hovel. Ari had been right, even if he'd denied
it: she would never want a man like him. The only way
he'd ever had her at all was by guile, and fool that he was,

he'd done his best to make her despise him. And if she ever found out what he truly was . . .

"*Monsire?*" She looked up, her face pinched with what might be sadness.

"Work out what it says," he said. "I will care for the horses and then you can read it to me."

CHAPTER 12

"WELL?"

Matilda held up the parchment between thumb and finger, much as she had the flesher's gown earlier, and read it out. " 'To prove the worth of your blood, be reborn from its stone beneath the midday sun.' 'Prove the worth of your blood,' he says. Even in this he humiliates Robert."

"What does it mean?" asked Steinarr.

"I do not know." She dropped the parchment back in the box, tossed the purse from Harworth on top, and slammed the lid shut with an angry snap. "I cannot think. I do not *care* to think."

"You are tired. Come, let me show you your elf house."

She looked around the flower-dotted lea with surprise. "I thought this was it. You said the light elves live in the bright glades."

"Move through them, I said. Their houses are hidden away, as places of magic should be."

"The only magic I wish for tonight is a soft bed."

"Then follow me. Perhaps I can make up for some of how I treated you." He led her over to an odd-looking oak, where he pulled aside a low-hanging bough. "My lady Matilda, otherwise known as my lady's maid, Marian, welcome to Elfwood. Go on."

She ducked under the branch and suddenly found herself looking inside the tree. Except it was not one tree, but many—a score or more, she thought—their trunks grown together to form a shadowed chamber a good three yards wide. She slipped through the gap between trunks and the world fell away, its sounds muffled by the enfolding trees and the tapestry of moss that covered the walls in rippling folds of green. Birds chirruped overhead, and enchanted, she stepped to the center of the space to watch them flitter through the soaring space, lit by the beams of afternoon sun that sifted through the high branches. It was like a chapel vault filled with tiny gilded cherubs, and she spun slowly, taking it all in. Beneath her feet, more moss lay thick on the ground, soft as the richest rug. It was less elf house than lover's bower.

He'd brought her to a lover's bower.

"Good. It is much as I remembered."

She turned to find Steinarr standing in the gap, filling the single entrance to the chamber with his broad shoulders. In the green dimness, he was little more than a huge shadow, a shade. The only life came from the glow of his golden hair and the dark glitter of his eyes as he watched her.

"You have . . ." Her voice came out ragged, and she stopped to clear her throat. "You have clearly been here before."

"Long ago." He stepped in and circled around her, tracing the walls of the chamber with his hand. "So long that the trees have grown hoary."

"You are not that old, my lord."

"I am older than you think."

She couldn't take her eyes off his hand, the way he caressed the moss, barely ruffling its surface. If he were that gentle with her the next time . . .

No. She was no longer obligated to lie with him. She didn't have to think of that anymore. And yet she did, all the time. She wanted that strong, gentle hand against her skin. She wanted . . .

"Is your bed soft enough?" he asked, waving a hand to indicate the moss beneath her feet.

She bounced on her toes to test it and was surprised by the give. "It may be softer than my bed at Huntingdon. How is it so flat?"

"The ancient oak that grew here was sawn down, and its sproutlings grew up all around the stump to make the walls. The wood beneath has grown soft as the moss has grown thick."

"No wonder the elves like it so well."

"So you do believe in them."

"Why would I not, when one of their outlaw woodwards is standing before me? Did you live here?"

"For a time. When the weather was foul, I would hang deer hides for a roof. There." He pointed at a branch, and then a second. "And there. But it will be fair tonight. Your only roof will be the stars, and your only light the moon. Once you are in here, you will not even see Torvald's fire."

"Torvald." Disappointment shaded her voice. "You leave me again tonight, then?"

"Yes."

Why? It was on the tip of her tongue when she stopped herself. Had it only been this morning that they'd had this same discussion? It seemed it had happened days ago and in a different world. It was this place, so set apart from everything beyond, so peaceful. Wanting to keep that peace, she let the question drift away like a dust mote on the air. His hand still rested on the moss-covered wall, and she touched her fingers to the ribbon at his wrist. "Only remember that you are bound to me, Sir Knight, and come back at dawn."

"At your will, my lady." He tipped his head and stepped aside to let her reenter the world. "This time, *I* will gather the firewood."

"Then I will water the horses."

She collected the leather pail and the horses and followed the music of water to a stream a bowshot away. The water ran clear and sweet, as it surely should in an elf stream, and as the horses drank their fill, its freshness called to her, reminding her how badly she stank: of the ale she'd spilled and the fumes of sour wine and the flesher's yard and the grime of too many days on the road. Making a quick decision, she tied the horses to a fallen log by the brook, stripped off her headrail, and began working her laces free.

Unaccustomed as she was to undressing herself, it took

a while, but eventually she was able to peel away her gown and the wool kirtle beneath, leaving only her linen chainse. She shook the dust out of her outer garments, then washed them, careful to only wet the muddy hem and those parts that had caught the ale because she didn't want everything sopping wet. When she was done, she wrung them as best she could—she might be able to mimic the laundress's voice, but she didn't have her hands—and spread the dripping garments out across bushes in the sun.

That done, she sat on the bank to take off her shoes and hose. Her right leg and foot had caught the worst of the ale, and she scrubbed that stocking especially hard, making up for the lack of soap with vigor. With her hose well rinsed and wrung and laid out on the log, she waded into the stream knee deep, letting her chainse trail in the water to wash out the last of the ale, hoping there was still enough sun and enough warmth in the day that it would dry before bed.

She washed as best she could without undressing entirely—she was, after all, outdoors, and shouldn't be bathing at all. She would likely catch a chill. There were no towels, no hearth, no warmed bed to be tucked into after—not even any dry clothes to put on. But it felt so wonderful . . .

In truth, her bath amounted to little more than splashing water over the most important bits, but she still felt cleaner than she had in days. She continued scooping water up beneath the chainse, enjoying the coolness, wanting the cleanness . . . *for him*. The thought flashed through her mind and then through her whole body, bringing it singing to awareness.

She wanted to be clean for him, so that if he came to her in that magic place, she would be ready for whatever he wanted to do. As the fever built, she pulled another handful of water up, touching herself intimately as she rinsed the heat away, imagining it was his hand, that gentle hand, that caressed her. Excitement thrummed through her, wild as . . . as *him*.

She whirled to find him standing there, not a dozen feet

away, his eyes full of such heat she wondered the water didn't boil away around her. The stream grabbed at her chainse, wrapping it around her legs like a hobble, and she teetered, nearly falling. In the time it took her to gasp and catch her balance, Steinarr was at the water's edge, his hand out to save her.

"Come out of there."

"I am fine," she said defensively. "Go away."

His voice took on a note of irritation. "Come out before you drown, woman."

"No. You go away, and then I'll come out. 'Tis not proper."

"Neither was what you were doing." His mouth curled into the same wicked leer he'd worn when he was supposedly trying to drive her off. Now that wickedness called to her in the same way the water had. She wanted to immerse herself in it, in him. She wanted him to come into the water and help her wash, to touch her with cool, slick, gentle, knowing hands and show her how he could pleasure her.

No, no, no. That was not her. That was him. If it weren't, she would not be standing in the middle of a stream, half-naked, touching herself as though she were in the privacy of her own bed. It was all him. It had to be. "Be gone."

"I am not leaving until you are safe on dry ground," he said. "You could drown in that ridiculous gown. Come out."

"I am fine," she repeated. To make her point, she untangled the hem of her chainse and pulled up one edge to scrub at her face. "I am merely bathing."

He put his hands on his hips and eyed her closely. "Even the horse knows that's a lie."

She glanced toward the horses. The rouncey cropped at grass, but the stallion watched her with nearly the same intensity as Steinarr did. As she blushed, flustered, the animal reached down and picked up one of her hose, shook it soundly, and flung it aside.

It landed among the reeds, and Steinarr went to retrieve it. He picked it up and examined it. "This is finely made. If

I had seen your hose at the start, I would have known you were no peasant."

"Then 'tis fortunate I do not show my hose to strange men." She could feel every stroke of his fingers on her skin. "Put that down."

"Come out, Marian. I told you, I will not touch you."

No, what he'd said was that he wouldn't touch her without her leave. She could give him leave. She so wanted to give him leave . . .

No, she didn't. She dropped the hem of her chainse and slogged her way toward the bank. She struggled to bring a leg up to step onto the bank, but the linen was a sodden weight that seemed determined keep her in the stream.

"Take my hand."

"No." She plucked at the cloth, trying to pull it away from her legs, but there were yards and yards of linen, and it had wicked the water up so it clung clear up her thighs. Finally, she gave in. "Yes. If you please."

He put out his hand once more. She checked her defenses first, but as his fingers locked with hers, desire shivered through her anyway. She kept her eyes away from his in an effort to avoid that even stronger connection that happened with him sometimes and pulled free as soon as she was firmly on the bank. "My thanks."

Water streamed around her feet and she bent to wring out her chainse so she didn't have to lift it and expose her legs. Steinarr stepped back to give her room.

"What foolishness possessed you to wash this late in the day? You are all wet. Everything you own is wet."

"'Tis warm enough. My things will dry, and if they do not, they are good wool and will be warm no matter what."

"Not that warm. Look, you shiver already." He unfastened his buckle and dropped his belt and sword to the grass so he could strip his gown over his head. "Put this on."

"I do not need it."

He didn't listen, popping the gown over her head and tugging it down like he was dressing a wayward child. There was little she could do but accept his gift and shove her arms into the sleeves. She certainly couldn't tell him her shaking was not from cold but from desire, desire that only increased now that she was surrounded with his scent.

"There. You'll be warm now."

"But *you* will be cold," she said as she rolled up his too-long sleeves. "You cannot go off into the forest for the night in just your chainse."

"I have my cloak, and as you said, it is warm. At least *I* am dry." He untied the horses and led them off. "Get your things. I must be away soon."

Back in the glade, Steinarr helped her hang her clothes from branches where they would catch the earliest sun in the morning, and then he collected the bundle he always carried away with him and headed toward the stallion.

"I was wondering, my lord. Do you think Sir Torvald could help with the clue in the box?"

He frowned at the horse, and sour jealousy bubbled off him. "I suppose you can ask him."

He was jealous of his friend, and yet he let him watch over her every night. She might never understand this man. "I will. God's rest, *monsire*."

"Sleep well, Marian." He mounted and started to ride away, but pulled up short. "Just, um, keep my gown on until your things dry. Torvald does not need to see you in naught but your damp chainse." He leaned over, thumped the stallion on the neck. "Does he, *Horse*?"

And then he put his heels to the animal and was gone.

Matilda stood there, waiting as his mind faded with distance, until even reaching out, she couldn't sense him. Then she ducked beneath the branch and went into the elf house. Its peace enveloped her like a mother's arms, and with a sense of calm she hadn't felt since she'd watched Steinarr put an arrow into that outlaw, she looked within herself.

His face floated up, taut with longing and desire, and her body went all soft and moist, just thinking of him.

With a sigh of resignation, she sank down onto the moss bed to which he'd brought her. It wasn't just him after all. It was her.

And now, knowing that, she had a decision to make.

*   *   *

THE SIGHT OF gowns and hose garlanding the branches
and the faint sound of humming from within the elf house
greeted Steinarr as he rode into camp the next morning.
He sat there on the horse for a long time, just listening, not
because Marian had a sweet voice—she couldn't seem to
stick to the tune, if indeed there was a tune—but simply
because a woman's peaceful humming was such a rare
thing in his life. Tune or not, it spoke of home and hearth
and family, of things he'd long ago set aside as impossible.
It wove through his soul, seducing him even as it made his
chest tighten with longing.

Marian's song trailed away, leaving only the morning
twittering of birds and then a rustling in the branches to
announce she was coming out. "Good morrow, my lord."

"Gmm." His tongue went thick at the sight of her wearing only her linen chainse. She'd taken out her braids so her
hair hung loose in rippling waves of gold, and her bare toes
peeked from beneath her hem, as though she were ready
for bed. For a lover or a husband. *For him.* He swallowed
hard and tried again. "Good morrow."

She held a comb, and as he sat there dumb as wood, she
pulled a thick strand of hair over her shoulder and began
combing. The end curled past her breast, drawing his eyes
to the shadowed pucker of nipple beneath the cloth, and he
choked.

"Are you all right, *monsire*?"

"I, um. Yes." *No.* He swung down off the horse and
looped the reins around the nearest bush, using the time to
pull his brain out of his crotch and think of something to
say, something that would put a safe distance between her
and his desires. "My mother used to do that. Hum as she
combed her hair, I mean."

"You could hear me? How sad for your ears. I have no
voice."

"It was fine." More than fine. Wondrous. Keeping his
eyes off her, he went to the fire and began poking at the
coals, just to be doing something. "You are not ready. I

thought I would find you with your riddle solved, anxious to ride."

"Bloodworth," she said.

"Blood-what? What are you talking about?"

"'Tis the answer to the riddle. 'The worth of your blood.' Bloodworth, or rather, Blidworth. Sir Torvald and I hit on it last evening."

"Blidworth . . ." It took him a moment to remember. "The stone. Of course."

"It has a hole big enough for a man to pass through, by what Sir Torvald said."

"'Be reborn,'"said Steinarr, comprehending. "I should have thought of that myself, with it so close. It even looks a bit like a—" He stopped himself.

"Like a woman's quaint? Sir Torvald said that as well."

"He what?"

"He said there is a great chamber on one side of the stone like a womb, but that the hole on the other side is tighter, like a woman's quaint. He also said that when you turned red and started growling like that, I should remind you that you use the word often enough." Laughing, she came to join him by the fire, still combing at that one lock of hair. Steinarr couldn't keep his eyes from it; it already gleamed like silk, and he tried not to think how it would feel running through his fingers. "Do not be angry with him. He was only trying to help me decipher my father's thoughts."

"He should not be speaking to you so." *Especially not after yesterday.*

"I was pleased to have him speaking to me at all, when he so seldom does," she said, cheerfully unaware that the man who'd spoken of women's quaints by the fire was also the stallion who had watched her by the stream. It was all Steinarr could do not to pitch a stick at him, horse or no.

"He said 'tis only half a league to Blidworth," she went on.

"A little more than that, but from here, the stone is closer than the village. We can be there in moments. Why are you not more anxious to be gone?"

"Father said this rebirth must take place beneath the

midday sun, remember? There is time and plenty to spare."

"True enough." The sun was still barely above the horizon. "I suppose the horses can stand to graze for the morning."

"I thought as much. Our marshal advises one day of rest and good grass for each three days of hard riding."

"You have a good marshal," said Steinarr. "We have not ridden so hard yet that the horses would suffer, but we may have to, and since we have the time now . . ."

"We may as well use it." A smile just lifted the corners of her mouth, giving her an air of mischief that made his blood quicken. "What would you like to do with our time, *monsire?*"

Thread his fingers through that hair and pull her down on the grass. Make her cry out with pleasure. "Break my fast. But you should get dressed first."

"My gown and kirtle are still damp."

"Then put my gown back on. Where is it?"

"In there." She tipped her head toward the elf house, but made no move toward it herself.

"I will fetch it." He ducked under the branches and stepped into the dimness of the tree, where he picked his way past his furs and her blankets, still lying mingled on the moss floor. She'd balled up his gown as a pillow, it seemed, since it still bore the mark of her head. Without intending it, he pictured her sleeping there, one hand flung up over her head as she tended to do. *Now where had that come from? He had no way of knowing how she slept.* He shook his head to clear it, and as he stooped to scoop up the gown, he heard the branches rustle outside.

"I used it as my pillow," she said softly from the entrance. She stepped into the middle of the bedding and brought his hands and the gown up to her nose and inhaled deeply. "It carries your scent."

Did she know what she was doing to him? "Not very sweet, I fear. I have been without a proper bath for far too long."

"It was sweet to me." Eyes closed, she took another deep breath and a blissful smile lit her face. "It was as though you lay with me all night."

She knew. She was torturing him as revenge for how he'd treated her. He deserved it, but he wasn't sure he could bear it. Jaw set, he struggled against the need boiling up within him. He pressed the gown toward her. "Dress yourself. I will go."

"But I want you to stay. I want to lie with you. Properly. With time and care, and in this place."

Not torture, then, but . . . "Marian, you do not have to do this. I will aid you. You have my bounden pledge."

"I know." She shifted one hand to the ribbon at his wrist and traced around the knot. "And I am glad of that pledge and of your faithfulness to it these last days, for it let me come to the truth."

He couldn't tear his eyes off her finger, circling the knot, round and round over the inside of his wrist. "Truth?"

"I thought it was all you and your wanting that pulled us down onto the furs at Harworth."

"It was. I forced you to it. You only did it for Robin's sake."

"No." She laid that same finger over his lips to silence him. "No. You are wrong." Slowly she raised her eyes to meet his.

And suddenly he was lost in those eyes again, adrift in a sea of comfort that seemed to stretch forever. Such solace dwelt in those eyes. A sigh worked its way up from deep in his soul and came out on a soft *ah* that matched hers. In the strangeness of the moment, he fancied he could see their sighs mingling in the air between them. He inhaled deeply, certain that if he could just draw her in, he would find more of that ease he so desperately needed.

A single word, vague, rustled inside his skull like the wind through dry grass. Her voice. *Please.*

"What was that?" he whispered.

"The wanting is not just yours." She tugged his gown away and let it fall, then took his empty hands in hers and pressed kisses into his callused palms. "It is also mine."

He was so still, even in his mind, that Matilda wasn't sure he understood. And then she felt it, the familiar surge of his desire, now recognized as distinct from her own growing need.

"I vowed I would not," he ground out between clenched teeth. "I said I would not so much as kiss you."

"Without my leave. You said you would not kiss me without my leave. I give you leave."

"Marian . . ."

"I give you leave to kiss me. And not just my mouth." She guided his hands to cup her breasts, so he would begin to understand, and she reveled in the sharp intake of his breath. "I give you leave to touch me. I give you leave to take me. I do give you leave, my bounden knight."

"Marian . . ." He squeezed his eyes shut and took two deep breaths before he opened them again. "I cannot ever be a husband to you, if that is what you imagine."

"I imagine only a lover." Her blood pounded in her ears at her own boldness, but she pressed on. "If we fail, I do not want Baldwin and one quick tumble to be all I ever know of a man."

"He will not be. I swear to you, you will never go to him if you do not wish it. But I . . ."

"I want to lie with you. Here. Now. I want to know how it is. With you."

"Are you certain?" he asked even as his thumbs rolled over her breasts, removing any possible trace of doubt with the shock of pleasure that rippled through her.

In answer she slipped her hands beneath his shirt, searching for the tie to his braies.

"No. You first, lest we end like before." He ran his thumbs over her again, then released her and stepped back a half-a-pace. "I still have not seen you naked."

Hands trembling, she reached behind her neck to undo her lacings, tugging the cord free one eyelet at a time. He followed every movement in silence, his gaze skimming over her breasts as they thrust against the thin linen. When all was as loose as she could make it, she lowered her arms.

Her chainse slipped, baring the curve of her breasts, and hung tenuously. He reached to tug it down.

She caught at it just in time. "It hardly seems fair, my lord. I have not seen you naked either."

Without a word, he stripped off his chainse and tossed it aside, smiling as her breath caught and came out in a rough sigh at the sight of all that muscled male flesh. He reached once more for her chainse.

She released her hold, and he drew her chainse down slowly, rewarding her with the same uneven shudder of breath as it fell away and revealed her.

They stood there for what seemed a long time, each of them absorbing the sight of the other. It was Steinarr who moved first, gently tracing the outside curve of her breasts.

"So ripe," he whispered. He splayed his hands over her breasts and slowly pulled his fingers together, plucking at her nipples until they tightened and her breath came out on the faintest moan. His tongue flickered over his lips, and she could feel his struggle for control. With an almost imperceptible shake of his head, he began to explore the rest of her body, his hands wandering freely over her skin, shaping, testing, sending sparks shooting off in every direction until she fell dizzy of it.

Matilda freed her hands from her sleeves and reached for him to steady herself, and as her hands touched his skin, she found herself enthralled. As much as she had held him, her arms wrapped around him over the miles, she quickly discovered that she hadn't touched him at all. The difference between clothed muscle and bare flesh was as great as the difference between ice and steam. His skin glowed with life and heat, the muscles rippling beneath her hand, alive as his heart beneath her palm. She ran her hands over him, mirroring the way he touched her, committing every curve and plane, every ridge and valley and scar, to memory. Absorbed, she barely noticed as he pushed the gown off her hips and cupped her bottom. Only as she followed and her hands met the resistance of his braies did it register.

"We are uneven in our dress again," she complained.

She followed the gathered cloth around to the knot in front.

He caught her hand and stopped her. "If you take them down now, you will hobble me. They will catch on my boots."

"Then be rid of your boots."

"At my lady's command." Balancing himself with a hand on her shoulder, he pried his boots off and kicked them aside so they landed next to the tree-wall. His hose followed, each untied with a quick jerk to the laces and then peeled down and flicked away to lie next to the boots. That left only his braies. "Shall I untie them, or will you?"

She reached once more for the tie. The muscles across his belly tensed, and the cloth jumped. Enchanted, she cupped one hand over him and waited until his body jumped again and pushed against her palm. "It is so strange how it does that."

He groaned. "What is strange is a virgin who knows so much about both torturing and pleasing a man. How did you come to be so wise about things you should not know?"

"I was a wicked child," she said. A tug undid the bow and she slowly loosened the gathers along the cord. "I would hide from my father's wroth in the great barn, in a secret place I found." She pressed a kiss to the center of the patch of gold hair that covered his chest. "I soon discovered that my little nest looked over the loft where the servants and even some of the knights would go to tup."

"You watched," he said, and his tarse jumped again.

"I did not set out to, but once I saw . . . I went back again and again to wait and watch. They never knew I was there. And when I went to fostering, I found a similar place."

"Frey help me," he whispered. "You know all of it, then."

"The good and the bad, and all between."

" 'Tis a wonder you stayed virgin so long," he muttered half to himself as he toyed with her breasts. Suddenly he looked up, comprehension dawning. "You learned to find pleasure on your own."

She blushed for the first time. "Aye. I saw that, too. I learned quickly. The priests tried to beat it out of me with heavy penance."

"You confessed it?" he asked, incredulous.

"We are told so often such things are sin, I thought I must. Father Thomas told me I would burn in Hell. I tried to rid myself of the sin, but even though I stopped visiting the barn, I still could not stop thinking of what I had seen, and when I did, I . . . I did it when I thought of you, too. Even before you found us at the Lady Well."

He made that strange choking sound again. "No wonder I could not frighten you off."

"Oh, you frightened me." She slid her fingers down over his hips, in preparation for sliding his braies down. "But not with your talk. It was what lay beneath. And yet I still found myself thinking of you. Like yesterday in the stream." She pushed and his braies fell away. His tarse sprung forward to brush against her belly. She stroked her fingers down the length and exclaimed with delight, then did it again. "It is both soft and hard at once. Especially here." She ran her palm over the plump head.

He grabbed her hand to still it. "You no longer seem to be frightened."

"I decided last night not to be anymore. It is foolish when I want it as much as you do."

"Ah, sweet Marian," he said. "I do not think that is possible."

He pulled her to him for a kiss that took her mouth the way his body would take hers later, his tongue plunging in to explore and tease. She felt that marvelous soft-hardness against her belly and, without thinking, pressed closer and lifted one leg to catch it and bring it against her more intimately. When she had him trapped, just right, she began to move.

With a groan, he scooped her up, kicked away his braies and her chainse, and laid her down on the furs. He pushed her legs apart and knelt between them, his eyes riveted to her, avid. "Touch yourself."

She had done it so often, but always in private. Now,

with him watching so closely, the shame was too great. "I cannot."

"It will please me," he told her in a husky voice. "And I will learn what pleases you."

She was suddenly frightened again, but instead of retreating into herself, she reached out. She didn't have to go far to find him. His desire filled the air between them, surrounded her, building with every beat of his heart. Need washed over her, incredible craving, so much deeper than her own. She slid her hand down, found the ache, and touched, moving her fingers as she'd learned to do. Embarrassment faded as the pressure built within her.

"Please," she whispered as her back began to arch. "Not this way. I want *you*."

"You saw something. Something you think of whenever you touch yourself. What do you want, Marian? Tell me what you saw that you want me to do."

She knew. She'd known since the first time she'd seen one of the stable boys kneel over one of the village girls that she wanted a man to do that to her. She'd imagined it ten hundreds of times. "Your mouth."

He touched her fingers and made her slide them lower and in a little. "Here?"

"Yes, oh, yes."

"Close your eyes." He pulled her hand away and lifted it. His lips closed around her fingers, and as he sucked them into his mouth, the sensation and the knowledge that he was tasting her drew a low groan from her throat. She opened her legs and lifted, silently pleading with him, but he only pressed the heel of his hand against her and chuckled. "Not yet, sweet. I have barely tasted the rest of you. I am not going to dive straight in, much as I would enjoy it. Keep your eyes closed and let me do what I should have done the first time."

She felt him shift, sensed him hovering above her, and waited for him. The first kisses fell on her eyelids, the next on her cheeks, then forehead, mouth, lips, ear, jaw, mouth again. Not hurried kisses but soft, lingering ones that led from one place to the next, down her neck, across her shoulders, and back across her bosom. Her breasts tightened as he approached, but he veered off to kiss his way down her arm then back up and across to the other arm. Her whole body was trembling by the time he finally skimmed over the upper curve of her breasts then slipped down to take one nipple into his mouth.

She arched off the furs with a gasp, the rasp of his tongue nearly pushing her over the edge. Pleasure hummed through them both, hers purely physical; his, pure delight in hers. He switched to the other breast and she arched again, and he settled in to play, going from one to the other and back again, until he made her so sensitive she cried out for him to stop.

He chuckled, a wicked sound, and went back to scattering kisses over her skin, this time heading lower, over her belly and down, just brushing a kiss through her curls.

"Eyes closed," he whispered again and shifted lower. There was a moment of nothing, then a tender kiss on the inside of her knee. Her other knee. Then a little higher. He went back and forth, working his way up, slowly, so slowly, she thought she would die before he got there. She could feel him looking at her between kisses, feel him getting closer and closer. Molten heat poured through her, as though from a goldsmith's crucible, burning away everything but the touch of his mouth. Closer. He shouldered her legs wider and settled between them. A single fingertip traced down through her moisture, and she heard a sucking sound and knew he tasted her again.

"So sweet." His breath warmed her. "Tell me, my lady. Do you still give me leave to kiss you?"

She could barely form the word. "Yes."

"Where? Where shall I kiss you?'

"There. Ah, there."

A growl rumbled up and he kissed her, the gentlest of kisses, not nearly enough. "Is this the place?"

"Nnn. Yes."

His tongue swirled over the spot. "Here?"

"Nnn."

"Here?" Kiss. "Here?" Tongue. "Here?" Finger, sliding down. "Here?" Slipping in. "Here?"

He asked and kissed and tongued and asked again, circling in on the place. Her answering whimpers went higher, then lower, going animal as he hit the exact spot. His lips closed over her, and he drew that most tender flesh into his mouth and swirled his tongue over her and slid a second finger in, and she was there and fully in his mind all at once.

Increased by his feverish want, her pleasure slammed through her, throwing her hips upward and back down with the force of it. He locked on, sucking and teasing as she shook and arched beneath his mouth. Another finger stretched her and made the spasms stronger, and she pressed against him and pulled back, wanting him to go on and stop and give her more and less all at once.

The need to be in her left Steinarr fighting to stay the course, but only when he had wrung every spasm from her sweet body did he shift up to take her. He moved with deliberation, determined this time to do right by her, to keep his blazing need under control and let her adjust to his size. Incredibly, as their bodies fit together, the extraordinary lust faded, replaced by the deepest peace he'd ever known, growing deeper as he settled in and her warmth enfolded him along with her arms.

"'Tis all right," she murmured as she had before. He wanted it to be. He began to move, to find the rhythm, to take, to possess, and even in that he took his time, enjoying the unrelenting build toward pleasure. She stirred beneath him, matching his pace, meeting him exactly right, touching him as though she knew him, as though they had been lovers for years. Ah, so sweet. So warm. Perfect. And then he was coming and she was coming again, too, gently this time, with him, her body tightening to welcome his seed as he spilled into her.

He stayed with her as long as he could, and then longer, even after his body softened and slipped away from her. He couldn't bear to leave the comfort of her arms, abandon her legs, wrapped around him so tightly. He sprinkled kisses over her face, took deep draughts of her mouth, and savored every sigh and stretch and delighted groan as she came back to herself.

Finally her eyes opened and she smiled up at him. "I could stay like this forever."

Forever. The word yanked him out of the bliss and drove home the truth of his cursed life. Steeling himself, he rolled away from her and sat up.

Marian's smile faded. "What is it that makes you so sad?"

"Only the knowledge that this hour must end." He dragged her blanket over her naked body, pausing just long enough to give himself one last glimpse of her breasts. "The sun is climbing. We need to move on."

He started to rise, but she stopped him. "Are you sorry, *monsire*?"

He couldn't look at her. "Are you?"

"Never."

"Even if all I can give you is this journey?"

"Even if all you can give me is this one morning." She sat up, holding the blanket over herself. "Although if you care to give more, I would most happily take it."

Desire lurched, fresh, within him, driving back a little of the sadness, and his heart skipped a beat. "You are a devil, Matilda Fitzwalter."

"I have often thought the same of you, Steinarr Fitzburger."

"*Birgir*," he corrected, both pleased that she'd remembered his father's name from his oath and amused that she tried to turn him Norman English by changing it. He leaned over and kissed her, satisfied that she was fully happy, at least for the moment. One of them should be. "Now get dressed, before I decide to spend an entire one of Robin's forty days buried in your quaint instead of looking for one of stone."

"Yes, my lord," she said prettily, and reached for her chainse. As she gathered it to pull over her arms, she looked up at him, wearing the half smile that had made his blood run so warm earlier and was just as effective now. Mischief put tiny crinkles at the corner of her eyes. "Is it even possible to spend a whole day at it? None of our servants was ever able to stay in the loft that long."

"Get you dressed, my lady, or you shall find out."

CHAPTER 13

"NOW PASS THROUGH," called Matilda. She was squatting by the stone, peering through the opening at Steinarr. The stone was more arch than tunnel, widely open along one side and through the middle, but narrowing quickly to leave only a small passage through to the far side. Only a man, she suspected, would see it as a womb and a quaint—but her father was a man, and so perhaps Torvald had been right.

It was through the smaller opening that Steinarr was preparing to crawl. He measured it with his eyes. "'Twill be a tight fit."

"As it is for all infants. Hurry. The sun is high."

Steinarr squeezed his shoulders into the narrow space and poked his head out. He peered around carefully. "I see nothing. It may be as simple as where my shadow falls. Mark the place."

Marian used her knife to scribe the outline of his head in the loose gravel, but she was shaking her own head as she did it. "Father has not been so obvious in his other clues. It does not seem like trial enough. And 'tis so close to Sudwell."

"Perhaps he thought it would be more difficult for Robin to decipher where he meant and made finding the clue itself simple."

"Perhaps. Back out, and come help me dig." She started gouging at the ground with her knife.

"No. I should crawl through in case there is something else to be seen." Steinarr snaked one arm out, found purchase, and inched himself forward until he spilled out onto the ground. "Anything?"

"Not to my eye."

"Nor mine. So we dig."

The ground within the outline was nearly as hard as the stone itself, but they hacked at it until their blades hit something even harder. Steinarr scraped away enough of the hardened gravel until he could see. "Solid stone. It is not here."

"Could he have used mortar?" she asked.

He shook his head. "No. You said this was too easy, and you were right. There must be something else. Another shadow to be seen." He rose and circled the stone, searching up and down the face.

As he paced, Matilda studied the hole. " 'To prove the worth of your blood, be reborn from the sorcerer's stone beneath the midday sun.' Be reborn beneath the midday sun."

"Do I need to go through again?"

"You just want to slide into that quaint once more." Shocked at herself, she clapped a hand over her mouth. "Did I say that?"

Steinarr snorted back a laugh. "You did indeed. Torvald is a bad influence on you."

"Not nearly as bad as you, my lord." A shiver of pleasure ran through her as she recalled what they'd just done, and she laid her hand on his chest. "Nor as good."

"He'd better not be. Shall I go again?"

Matilda looked at the sky. The sun was already past its zenith, and if they lost the midday light, they'd have to wait another full day. Much as she would like to pass another night in the elf house, this time with Steinarr, they couldn't afford the time. "Yes, if you please."

He disappeared around the stone and she heard a moment's scraping before his head appeared and he started working his way out.

She mopped his forehead with her sleeve. "You are sweating."

"Being born is hard work."

"Being born," she repeated. There was something . . . "You are the wrong way 'round. When a child comes out, it faces down at first, but as its head comes out, it turns." She rotated her hands. "So, until it faces mostly upward."

"And how do you know this? Did peasants give birth in that loft of yours as well?"

"No, but Lady Amabel bore a child every year while I was fostering and had all of us attend her. She said we might as well see it done by someone who did it easily. Turn yourself."

Steinarr grunted and strained, reminding her very much of Lady Amabel's laboring. "Too tight. Let me back up and come at it the other way."

He vanished like a worm down its hole. A moment later, his arms reappeared, then the top of his head. And then he stopped. "This does not work. I cannot move myself."

"You could if you were not such a large babe," she said as she reached for his hands. She stopped. "You are too large. Robin is thin as a reed, as was Father. Get out of there. 'Tis my turn. Quickly, before we lose the light."

She ran around and slipped into the hole as soon as he was out of the way, wriggling into position quite easily. As she emerged from the hole, however, he wasn't there. She called to him, "What are you doing?"

A hand lifted her skirt and she felt air swirl over her thighs and higher. "Admiring the view."

"Stop that." She kicked out, connecting with something that drew an "oof" of pain. A moment later, he appeared at her head, red-faced, but laughing. "You should not kick at what you cannot see, if you ever hope to enjoy my favors again. Go in and come out slowly, infant. Tell me what you see."

She squirmed back in. Just as her eyes slipped beneath the overhang, she glimpsed a dim flash of crimson. She moved back out. The same flash of light made her freeze.

"There." She pointed. "Something red within that big lump that sticks out."

"I do not see anything." He reached up, feeling for it. "Where?"

"Higher. Near the top."

"I will have to climb." He groped around for hand and foot holds and inched his way up as she guided him.

"Hurry. It grows dim even now. Right. Right. Higher. There. Your hand is on it."

He clung to the face of the rock. "There is no way to loosen it like this. I'm going up. Watch out."

He scrambled up, dragging himself over the edge and out of sight as loose gravel tumbled down the wall. Matilda covered her face with both arms, but she held her position even as pebbles bounced off her head, afraid she'd lose that gleam of red if she moved. The rock fall stopped, and a moment later, Steinarr's head reappeared over the edge. The red vanished as his fingers closed around it. "This lump?"

"Aye. What is it?"

"We shall see. 'Tis fixed in the stone." Steinarr pulled out his knife and began hammering with the hilt. Big chunks flaked away under his blows. "It is mortar, proper mortar, with the pebbles mixed in."

"We have it, then." She scrambled out and stood twisting a sleeve point fretfully as Steinarr pounded at the rock. A moment later, the mass of false stone fell away and the bit of red came away in his hand with something attached. "What is it?"

"I will bring it down so you may see for yourself. Move back a little. I do not want to fall on you." He slipped the object inside his gown, swung around, and gingerly lowered himself over the edge, grappling for toeholds. More gravel and pebbles poured over the face of the rock as he inched his way down.

"Be careful."

She'd no sooner spoken than a clump of rock gave way in his hand. Steinarr fell backward, landing with a thump and a blistering "Shite!"

"Are you hurt?"

He rose and rubbed at his backside. "Only my pride."

"I always thought a man's pride was in front."

Laughing, he caught her around the waist and pulled

her into his arms. "I suddenly find I escort neither lady nor servant, but the king's fool. Is this what a good tup does to you? Gives you a bawdy mouth?"

Her cheeks heated. "I do not know. Strange things just seem to be coming out. They astonish me as much as you. Do you object, my lord?"

"I do not. That you can jest about it tells me you enjoyed yourself."

She pressed a kiss to the wedge of bare skin that showed in the neck of his chainse. "Did you doubt it?

"Not this time, no." He patted her bottom and released her. "Watch that tongue before others, though, my sweet, or I will have to tell them you are my leman rather than my lady's servant."

"I *am* your leman. What did you find me?"

He reached into his gown and handed her another cylinder, similar in size to the one Robin had retrieved from the tree, except this one was wrapped in leather. Matilda carried it out into the sun and sat down in the grass. She polished the large red stone against her sleeve, then held it up against the sun to admire the brilliant red glow. "Is this a ruby, or only a carbuncle?"

Steinarr knelt beside her. "It could be glass, for all that I know of gems."

"You're likely right. Father would surely not have risked burying a precious stone so openly."

"He had built up the mortar over it so there was only a narrow channel to let the light pass through the stone. It could only be seen with good light behind it, which is why it had to be found at midday. Even when I was above it and knew it was there, I could barely spot it."

"Still, what if someone else had found it first?"

"Well, they did not. Go on, open it."

She twisted at the top, but it was firm. She pried at it with the tip of her knife, and it didn't budge.

"Let me see." Steinarr looked it over, then took her knife and cut the stitching that held the leather. Beneath it, copper wire wrapped around top and bottom. Steinarr quickly unwrapped the wire, and as the last twist fell away, the cylinder came apart in four pieces to reveal a rolled-up parchment.

"How did you know?"

"'Tis a sword hilt. The tang fits here, between the two long pieces, with the guard and blade below." He laid his finger in the center channel to demonstrate, then held up the piece with the stone. "This was likely the pommel, and this other bit was purpose made to close the bottom. These grooves held them in. They would not pull free without taking the grip apart."

"I would never have figured that out."

"Robin would have. He has trained with a sword and would recognize a hilt and know how 'tis made. Your father created the puzzle for him. Perhaps Robin would even recognize the stone from a weapon he once used." He picked up the parchment and handed it to her. "Read."

"'Next visit the village where wise men fooled a king and take from it the bird they held in the bush.'" She grinned and started collecting the bits and pieces to put them in her scrip. "He may have created the puzzle for Robin, but this answer, *I* know. We go to Gotham."

He helped her rise and they started toward the horses. "You seem very certain."

"I am. Father told the same story every time the king came through on progress. The wise men of Gotham avoided the burden of hosting King John's court by playing fools of the worst type. Fearing he would catch the madness, the king passed the village by and went elsewhere."

"Wise fools indeed." He bent and linked his fingers. "And the bird?"

"Is the cuckoo," she said as he handed her up. She organized her skirts as he prepared to mount. "One of the foolish things they did before the king was to join hands around a bush. When King John asked what they were doing, they claimed they were keeping the cuckoo trapped, so they could listen to it sing all the year through. You do know where Gotham is?"

"More or less." He settled in before her, and she wrapped her arms around him.

"How far is it?"

"A single day, if we could go by the road, but Nottingham Town lies between here and there. I do not want to take the chance Guy or Baldwin or any of their men will see you. Or me, for that matter. We will keep to the forest and go well around to the west. Two days, perhaps three if those clouds carry rain."

She looked to the west, where a sullen, gray line stretched across the horizon. "Then we will hope they do not."

"PRIORESS CELESTRIA. I was only now told of your coming. Welcome. Welcome to Headon Hall."

The reeve dropped to one knee and waited until Cwen touched the filthy cap he wore on his filthier head. "Heaven's blessings on you, Reeve. Rise, all of you."

The dozen or so men and women who had been in the hall when she'd entered came to their feet along with the reeve.

"We did not expect you, Lady Mother," said the man as she surreptitiously wiped her fingers on her gown. "No one sent word ahead."

"I wished to come upon the manor without the steward's knowledge and see how he truly runs it. Where is he?"

"Leicester, Lady Mother. He went to sell the year's rope. He gets a better price there than in Nottingham."

"Well, then, I will see how *you* run the manor without him. Have fresh horses saddled. I wish to see how the harvest is coming."

"Now? I mean, your pardon, the hour is late, Lady Mother. Would you not rather wait until the morrow?"

"Are you afraid of what I will see?" She waved off the reeve's protests. "I will want supper in the solar when we return. Capon and bitter greens and almond cake."

"Yes, Lady Mother." He snapped a few orders to servants, then followed her outside. He looked around the yard, confused. "Surely you do not travel alone, Lady Mother. Where is the rest of your party?"

"Lost along the way, I fear. Both Father Renaud and Sister Paulina."

"Lost? Dead, you mean?"

She did not want to speak of it, but there would be questions. She might as well tell the story now. "No. But sadly, their souls are lost. They ran off together in violation of their Holy vows."

The reeve's eyes widened in horror. "Worse than dead, then."

"They will be found and punished," said Cwen. And well they should be. She had caught them together on the second night out, swiving like pigs in the woods, spending the girl's virginity before her blood could be spilled for its proper use. They should have been killed on the spot for their blasphemy to both the old gods and their newer one, but others had been near, and fearing discovery, she had let them live. By the morning, they'd fled, leaving her with nothing except the knowledge that she must have been given this journey for some other reason. "Show me the grain first, and then the peas and beans."

They mounted and rode out through the fields, Cwen asking such questions as a landholder might ask of a reeve, and him answering. She paid little heed to the answers, instead turning her attention to trying to find whatever it was the gods wanted for her. "Where are the colliers Lord Matthew sent for our use?"

"In the far part of the eastern woods," said the reeve. "Too far to ride today, Lady Mother, but I will gladly take you on the morrow."

"Have any other strangers passed through?"

"Now that is odd you should ask, Lady Mother. There are two strangers staying at the charcoal camp now. A peasant boy who broke his leg, and a knight who has befriended him. There was another knight, too, and a maid, the boy's cousin, but I am told they rode on a week past."

"Knights?" Palms prickling, she sat up straighter. "What sort of knights would stay at a charcoal camp and not at the manor?"

"Odd ones, with odder names. One called himself Sir Steinarr, and the other, the one still at the camp, is Sir Ari. Tall men, and both fair and golden-haired. They found the boy injured at . . ."

The man's voice faded into nothingness as Cwen smiled to herself. *The lion and the raven. Thank you, Great Ones.* She cut off the reeve's annoying rambling with the flick of a finger. "Why did you not invite them to stay at the manor? It is your duty to serve as good host in the name of Kirklees and the Mother Abbess."

"Oh, I did invite them, Lady Mother, but the boy and his cousin knew the colliers and wanted to stay with them. The knights took them there and did not come back."

"And the boy and the r—this Sir Ari are still there?"

"So far as I know, Lady Mother."

"I want the boy brought to the manor tomorrow. We will care for him while he heals."

"He is only a peasant lad, Lady Mother."

"Peasant or noble, he should have been kept here to begin with. It is our duty to care for the injured and the ill. You will send a wagon for him and prepare a good bed in the solar. I will tend him myself."

"Yes, Lady Mother."

She had no interest in the boy except as a way to draw the raven near. It was him she truly wanted, the Seer-Skald. He had been there at Alnwick when she had confronted the eagle, helping the healer and the stableboy foil a plan years in the making. Now he was here, within reach, given to her by the gods. Perhaps she could draw his power and add it to her own, even as she took her redoubled vengeance.

And then there was the lion and this maid he'd gone off with. That another of the murderers had paired off with a woman made her uneasy; there could be danger there. But there could be opportunity, as well, depending on what the gods had planned. For now, she would simply have to wait, play the prioress, and keep her heart open to whatever the gods offered.

The rest would come to pass when the time was ripe.

*   *   *

THE WEATHER DID indeed hold, so despite a large party of hunters that made Steinarr uneasy and sent them swinging wide into Derbyshire, the journey went quickly. As they reached the edge of tiny Gotham a little after Sext on the second full day, Matilda sat up a little straighter, alert.

"So, where shall we look for this cuckoo first?" asked Steinarr.

She looked around, but could see nothing unusual about the village. "Father has shown a certain fondness for Church property until now. We may as well begin there."

"Begin there, *my lord*," he corrected as he turned toward the church. "Remember that you are my lady's servant once more."

"Yes, my lord. And you, the knight who carries me to her in Leicester from Newstead." They had changed their story over the past days to account for the direction of their travel. "Play a little cross with me, my lord, as you did in Harworth. You were quite convincing."

"Quiet, you foolish creature," he snapped, and she had to bite back a chuckle as he gave her arms a quick squeeze with his elbows.

The days since Blidworth had been a revelation to Matilda. Although they had yet to repeat their lovemaking—their days in the saddle had been so long that Steinarr had insisted on leaving her at night so that, as he put it, they could both rest well rather than spend the hours swiving—the desperate edge to his desire had eased considerably. She no longer had to work so hard to keep her mind away from his, and when she did slip, the contact was not so overwhelming. She could actually be at ease with him, even about matters beyond the enjoyment they'd found with each other. And as an extra boon, the more at ease she became, the easier and more pleasant their conversations. She was beginning to discover that she not only desired her strange knight, she actually liked him a little.

They reached the stone church and dismounted to go inside, but they'd barely taken a dozen steps when Steinarr stopped and pointed at the arch over the gate. "Your cuckoo."

She started forward, then stopped. "Oh, no."

The gate was decorated not with one cuckoo, not with two, but with three and ten—the one at the top Steinarr had spotted, plus six smaller ones carved down each side, sitting in neatly carved bushes. And beyond, in the churchyard, stood a headstone with a bush-and-cuckoo carved on it.

"I fear the people of Gotham have embraced the tale of the wise men too well," said Matilda. "I wonder if there are more."

By the time the bells rang Nones, they knew there were. They'd found cuckoos on the font and on two misericords inside the church; as a sign over a rough tavern in the village proper; and on the gateposts at the manor, looking much like the one at the church, and by its appearance, carved by the same hand.

Dejected, Matilda stood staring at the last. "I should have known when it seemed so easy. How do we tell which one holds the next puzzle?"

Steinarr glanced around to see who was watching, then went over and ran his hand over several of the cuckoos under the pretense of leaning against the gatepost to remove a stone from his boot. "They are solid. There must be something in the puzzle we did not see."

"Aye." She started to open her scrip.

"Not here. We will find a good place to camp and turn our minds to it there."

"Yes, my lord," she said, bobbing like an obedient servant as a group of men came out of the manor yard carrying their scythes. Steinarr strode off toward the horses, ignoring her as a knight would a servant, and she followed as a servant would a knight—mocking him behind his back. The men snorted back laughs and hurried on, heads down, when Steinarr turned to scowl at them.

"What were you doing?" he asked as they prepared to remount.

"You play cross most excellently, *monsire*."

"I have had much experience since I met you." He started to bend to hand her up, but paused. "I could arrange for you to rest in the hall tonight. You would have to sleep with the lady's serving women but . . ."

She tilted her head to look at him, confused by his offer. "We could not speak freely in the hall, *monsire*."

"I know, but you would have at least a pallet to sleep on for one night, and other women to talk to."

"A pallet and other women would not solve the puzzle," she said gently, touched by this kindness. "Besides, I grow used to the ground."

His forehead furrowed, making it appear that, for some reason, he wasn't pleased by her choice. "We will make camp, then. I think I know where to find a good place."

They backtracked north and west, to the river they'd forded earlier that morning, then followed it a little way south until they found some higher ground that lay back far enough to avoid the midges. It took some hunting, but Steinarr finally picked out a spot he liked.

Matilda had to smile at his choice, a place where a fallen tree had taken out part of the slope with its roots and left a small bank. "Even here, where the land is so flat, you manage to find me a cave."

"Hardly a cave, but it will give you something at your back to cut the night breeze and be easier for Torvald to defend." He started undoing the ropes that held the gear on the packsaddle. "You should look at the puzzle again while the light is with us. I will set camp and see to the wood and the horses."

Matilda carried her scrip over to sit on the trunk of the fallen tree. She fished out the parchment and flattened it across her knees. " 'Next visit the village where wise men fooled a king and take from it the bird they held in the bush.' We must be able to carry the cuckoo away."

"It would seem so," said Steinarr.

She examined the parchment as thoroughly as she had the one from the Lady Well. There was a tiny fragment of knotwork across one corner of the scrap that showed it had been reused, but otherwise it seemed to hold no secrets.

She took out the hilt that had held the parchment and started going over it piece by piece, searching for the tiniest marking.

All the while, Steinarr worked, unloading, arranging things for the night, gathering wood, laying a fire. And then he knelt to take out his flint and firesteel, and her mind went straight back to Harworth, as it had every time he'd lighted a fire since. *Take you like this*, he'd said as he'd knelt behind her. She imagined how it might feel to have him enter her that way. She'd seen people do it more than once, and though the priests warned against it, both the man and the woman had always seemed to enjoy it. Steinarr's hands would be free to touch her in the most interesting ways . . .

"We should solve the puzzle first," he said.

"What?" She came out of her reverie to find him watching her with narrow, hungry eyes. He looked the way she felt, and she wondered if it was so clear on her.

"Before we spare the time for what you're thinking of, we must solve the puzzle."

She felt herself blush. "How do you know what I am thinking of?"

"Because I think of it, too, every time I put steel to flint, thanks to my foolishness at Harworth. But if I acted on every thought of you, we would never find Robin's treasure for the swiving."

"It is the same for me."

He froze. His lips pressed together in a thin line and he shut his eyes and took a deep breath that came out on a sigh. "I did not need to hear that just now."

"You said once that it was not a bad thing to be an honest man."

"A little less honesty on your part, *woman*, would help me keep my mind out of your quaint. We must behave ourselves, unless there is truly time free that cannot be spent on our task."

She chewed her lip. "Of course. But—"

"But *now* is a time for the puzzle," he said firmly. "What have you found?"

"*Rien*. Nothing."

"Would it help to tell me the whole tale?"

"You have heard most of it. Father likes . . . *liked* stories, but he was never one to spin one out beyond its barest bones. He only told the story of Gotham because, much as he liked the king, he found Edward's visits burdensome and admired Gotham's cleverness in avoiding them."

Steinarr made a noise of disgust. "Little pig hole."

"My father?" she said, bristling despite the fact that she'd sometimes called him worse in her own head. She didn't want others doing it, though.

"No, Guy. He told me your father was enamored of the *gestes* and let you fill your head with them. He said your love of the *gestes* was why the bastard le Chape was able to lure you from home on this quest. It was part of what made me believe you and Robin . . ."

"Guy lies about many things. If I were a man . . ." Trying to distract herself, she fiddled with the pommel piece, lifting it to her eye to peer through the red carbuncle. "If I were a man, everything would be as upside down as it is through this stone. You stand on the sky, *monsire.*"

She dropped the pommel among the other things on her lap. The stone hit the piece of leather and sent it flying off, and as she bent to pick up the scrap, she glimpsed a few faint lines on the inner surface of the curl. Her heart racing, she carefully flattened the piece. "Look. On the inside of the leather. I think it is a map."

Steinarr came over and together they traced out the lines, most of which were so faint they barely showed against the raw inner surface of the leather. "It is. Well done, Marian."

" 'Twas only chance that let me see it. The light was just so. Is it Gotham?"

"It is. See how the lanes fork, as they do in the village? And that cross is in the right place to mark the church."

"Then that must be our cuckoo." She pointed to a roughly drawn outline of a bird near one arm of the fork. "Is that one we found?"

He touched the map, silently marking the ones they'd seen. "No. We will have to find it tomorrow. The sun will set soon."

"Then we can do no more now?"

"No. Not today."

"Good." She carefully scraped together the bits and pieces of the hilt and put them in her scrip. Setting it aside, she turned and laced her fingers around his neck. "Then we have time to light a flame. Teach me how my flint may be well struck with your steel, my lord."

"A lesson you have already seen demonstrated, no doubt." He kissed her forehead, then carefully pulled her arms away and pressed kisses into her palms before he rose and stepped over to the fire. "Unfortunately, there is no time."

"There is the whole night ahead." She went after him and threaded her arms around his waist. "We had an easy day, and tomorrow we must rest in Gotham at least long enough to find the cuckoo and figure out where it leads us. We can pass the entire night in swiving if we wish." She lifted onto her toes. "And I wish."

She kissed him, but it was like kissing a statue. Determined, she poured her effort into seducing him, sweeping into his mouth with her tongue, nipping at his lip, insisting on a response, until finally he groaned. His tongue plunged into her mouth with that desperate passion she had felt so often, and she moaned encouragement and found his belt buckle and began to work it loose.

His hands went to her wrists as if to pull her away, but he hesitated, and his battle with himself would have been clear to even the most casual watcher. She moved against him, letting him know how very much she wanted him, but something stronger than desire made him pull her hands away.

"No, Marian. Too much of the day is gone. I must go."

"No. Please stay. Even if we don't . . . Please stay."

"I cannot."

"But why? Two nights now, since we lay together at the elf house, and this the third, and I do not understand why."

"I told you—"

"You told me first that I was too annoying, next that you wanted me too much, next that we would be too tired from

swiving to ride. Now we have time and an easy day both
before us and behind us, and still you will not stay. Was I
such poor sport a-bed that you must work so hard to avoid
me?"

"You are delicious sport, a-bed or not," he said and she
felt the lurch of desire that confirmed the truth of that, at
least. "And I do want you again. But not by night."

"Why? The truth."

"I do not rest well at night. I would disturb you."

"Your leaving disturbs me."

"Not as much as if I stayed." His face twisted in agony
and he blurted it out. "I am dangerous at night, Marian."

She laid her hand on his chest to soothe him. "How can
a sleeping man be dangerous?"

"I am . . . possessed by . . ." His jaw clenched, and he
shook his head as though holding back some word too vile
to say. "I have terrible dreams. I grow violent. I have even
harmed others."

"I would wake you," she argued.

"I do not wake from these dreams. Not until dawn."

"Then Torvald could stop you from doing harm. He
protects me from wolves. He could surely protect me from
you."

"No." He jerked away and turned toward the horses so
she couldn't see his eyes, but the bitterness boiling off him
said enough. "He cannot. And do you truly want to tup
while Torvald stands watch nearby?"

She thought of the silent warrior and his vigilance and
blushed. "No. But I would like to sleep in your arms, at
your side, even so."

"And I would like to have you there, very much, but I
cannot stay."

"You could at least pass the evening with us. With me."

His shoulders sagged. "It cannot be. I must have light to
find a place away from you."

His bitterness echoed within her, drawing her frustra-
tion to the fore. "So you wish to tup me when it is conve-
nient and the sun shines, but not share a blanket with me.
This is foul, *monsire*. Truly foul."

"It is, and I am sorry for it. But I would rather have you angry with me than wake to find that I had harmed you in the night." He untied the stallion and swung up. "I cannot discuss this more. I must go."

"And I am to just stay here, and pass another evening staring into the fire with your tight-lipped friend?"

"Aye. For by the fire with Torvald you are safe, and that is what I want above all." He guided the horse over near her. "You have the best of me by day, Marian. Be satisfied with that."

"It seems, my lord, that I have little choice." She turned her back on him, and when she turned around again, he was long gone.

CHAPTER 14

MARIAN WAS STILL angry the next morning, so angry she already had the rouncey loaded and was standing, thin-lipped and arms folded, ready to leave as Steinarr rode into camp. She prickled like a hedgehog when he smiled at her, and his back went up in return. He was just trying to protect her. Why couldn't she see that?

However, though she was in a wroth, she was still willing to feed him: several slices of bread and cheese lay waiting by the fire. Grateful, Steinarr gobbled them down without a word, saddled the stallion, then checked the rouncey to make sure the load was balanced and secure.

It was perfect. He looked at Marian. "You had Torvald do it, didn't you?"

"Of course I had Torvald do it," she snapped. "I am no stable boy. Are you ready, *monsire*?"

He bit back a sharp reply—the entire mess *was* his fault, after all—and helped her mount.

The folk of Gotham were just heading to Mass as they reached the demesne fields. Steinarr lingered in the shadows of the woodland, waiting for the church doors to close behind the last stragglers, then put the spurs to the horse. "If we are fast, we can have your prize and be gone before anyone is the wiser."

They rode straight to where the map was marked. Marian immediately pointed to the well. "There. I never saw it yesterday."

"Neither did I. Stay here." Steinarr stepped off the horse straight onto the edge of the well and reached for the bronze cuckoo that perched atop the well cover. It took all his strength to break it loose, and when it came free, it was with a loud ring of metal on metal. He glanced around to be sure no one had noticed, then dropped it inside his gown. It chimed again, more muted, as it fell. "I think there is something inside."

"Is the bird all?" she asked.

"I see nothing else." He stretched to throw a leg back over the saddle. "Let us be gone before we are accused of theft. We can come back if need be."

He kept an ear cocked as they galloped away, but heard no hue and cry. When they were well out into the woods, he stopped and helped her down, and together, they looked over the cuckoo. It had been cast in two parts. Steinarr borrowed Marian's knife for its finer blade and tried to pry them apart, but the seam was far too precise. As he worked, the bird jangled enticingly.

"There must be some way to get in," fretted Marian.

"There is." Steinarr cast about for a hand-sized cobble, then carried it and the bird over to a large, flat rock nearby. While less brittle than iron, the bronze was still brittle enough. Several sharp blows took the head off cleanly. An egg, also bronze, tumbled out and rolled away. "I should have broken the tail instead."

She ignored his poor jest to snatch up the egg and shake it. "This rattles as well. Look, 'tis in two parts." She twisted, and this time the halves came apart. She spilled the contents out: a peg of wood; a flat, round stone; a scrap of canvas, wrapped around what turned out to be a dozen barleycorns; and a tightly folded bit of parchment.

Marian unfolded it and read it. "Tucker's Ford."

"Tuxford," said Steinarr.

"Tuxford. But we passed by there days ago!" she complained. "Why can he not send us directly from place to place?"

"Because there would be no trial in that. He is being gentle with Robin. If I were out to have a man prove himself, I would have sent him from Headon to here, then to Harworth, then Sudwell and so on. Or set him riding from one end of England to the other and back again."

"Then thank the saints you are not charting our path. The riddles are difficult enough."

"Still, the shorter rides prove your father wanted Robin to have at least a chance at success. That should set you at ease."

"And yet, strangely, it does not."

He would kiss away the dismay that made her frown, if she weren't so soured on him just now. Instead, he rose. "Come. At least we know which way to go."

She refolded the parchment and returned it and the various bits to the egg, put it back together, and dropped it into her scrip. "The bird is too large for my scrip, but I fear leaving anything behind."

"Probably wise, seeing how cleverly your father disguises things." He gathered the pieces of the cuckoo and stowed them in one of the saddle pouches on the rouncey. "We may discover we must have it sawn apart to find some map or riddle scribed inside."

"I hope not," she said as she rose. "I want to have it repaired and sent back."

"Why? Your father clearly had it made and put here just for this purpose."

"I doubt the people of Gotham know that. They likely think it was a gift to the village, and they will miss their cuckoo." She let him help her up and waited while he mounted. "I find I tire of breaking things. The church at Harworth, the gravestone at Sudwell, now this. We even broke the tree and chipped away part of the stone at Blidworth. And there will be more. Father has us laying waste to the entire shire with this foolishness. I want to put some of it right when we are done."

"Then we will."

"We?"

"I am your man for as long as you need me. That was my vow. If you need me in that, too, I will be there."

"You were not there last night." Her voice carried accusation and desire and anger and promise, all at once. "I needed you then."

"No more than I needed you. But it cannot be, Marian.

I cannot share the nights with you, much as I would like. You said that the one morning was enough, if that was all I could give."

"I lied. No, that is not true either. I meant it at the time, but I find myself wanting more than that. And you want it, too. I *know* you do."

"Not at the expense of Robin's title."

"No, of course not. But if not the nights, when? Our days are full of riding and puzzles and this fool's quest of my father's."

"Not every hour. The horses will need rest. *We* will need rest or cover from the weather, or there will be times when we simply can do no more for Robin just then and can steal a moment for ourselves."

"But will we?"

He was grateful she was behind him, so she couldn't see the way he struggled to keep himself off her in that very moment. Knowing how she felt, how she tasted . . . "Yes. Yes, we will. You have my vow on—"

"I need no vow. I can feel the truth in you. Here." She reached around him to flatten one hand over his heart, forgiving him with that simple touch, and something in the center of him seemed to melt.

This woman. He wanted this woman, as his own. And not just for swiving. For laughter and peaceful fires and watching her sew and arguments and all of it. He closed his eyes as the futility of it crushed down on him. *Please, Odin*, he prayed silently. *Let me have her heart for just a little. Let her care for me, even for a day, as much as I already care for her. Give me that one, brief comfort in all these years of torture.*

". . . patience," she said.

He opened his eyes. "Your pardon. My thoughts were elsewhere."

"I said, all I need is a little patience."

"Aye, patience is good." It seemed he'd had nothing but patience for as long as he could remember. He hoped she had enough for both of them now, because he wasn't certain how much more he could manage. *Please, Odin. Please.*

"Here is the road. I think we must risk it, at least for a few miles. We will go east, then take to the woods again to avoid Nottingham and Sudwell."

"Whatever you say, my bounden knight." She wrapped her arms more tightly around his waist and leaned her head against his back with a sigh. "I am in your hands."

And in my heart, he thought to himself. *And in my heart.*

ARI MADE ANOTHER trip into Retford on the very next Saturday, not because Edith or Ivetta needed anything, but because *he* needed something. He found the tavern keeper good to his word and passed some time trading stories for drink before he approached the wench, thoughts of whom had lured him back. He found her good to her word as well: much as she might flirt and jest, she wanted more than a story for her favors. Coin changed hands, a quiet hayloft was found, and some while later Ari headed back to the charcoal camp wearing a smile and bearing the conviction that he had gotten good value for his money.

That sense of gratified well-being faded away as he approached the camp, however, and though he wasn't certain why, by the time he rode into the clearing, his good mood had been replaced by a full measure of disquiet. He swung off the horse and handed the reins to the little boy who ran up to help.

"You can take that to Ivetta," he told the child, pointing to a bag of pears hanging from the saddle horn. "But do not put the horse away, as I will be leaving soon. Where is Hamo?"

"There." The boy pointed toward the ranks of sawn logs that were beginning to fill the first layer of the charcoal pit. "He will want to tell you that they took Robin."

"What?"

"The nun and the reeve and some others came to take Robin back to Headon."

"Pillocks." He started toward the pit, bellowing for Hamo.

"'Twas the prioress herself," said the collier in answer to Ari's demands for an explanation. "She said it was their duty to keep care of the boy, especially seeing as he was hurt on priory lands. Robin said he would rather stay here, but she would not have it, especially once she saw that he still had a bit of the squinacy. And how can a man argue with a prioress? Especially this prioress."

"Why this one?"

"She's a fearsome thing, stiff as a poker and hard as stone, and she has been at Kirklees forever and a day. She blew in here and swept poor Robin up and away like a leaf in a storm. 'Tis good she is of the Church or we would all be the worse for it."

Ari's gut twisted with concern, but the sun was dropping rapidly and he had little time to do anything more than worry and go off into the woods to spend the night hiding from owls. He wouldn't even have time to get close enough to the manor that the raven could fly on to see that Robin was well.

"So will we see you in the morning, then, my lord?"

Ari shook his head. "I think I will visit Headon first. The reeve did not do well by Robin before. I want to see if this lady prioress has a kinder heart."

"*Kind* is not a word I would use about this nun, my lord, but she will do better from obligation if not from her heart."

"That will be enough. I just want to see it for myself."

He took a few moments to down a bowl of pottage he begged off Edith, then prepared to leave.

"You are welcome to sleep here with us, my lord." It had become habit for Hamo to offer, as it had become habit for Ari to say, "Perhaps another time. I will see you all tomorrow with word of Robin."

He rode as far toward Headon as time permitted, passed the night avoiding owls, and went on to the manor as soon as he dressed, arriving at the village just as everyone filed in to Mass. Caught by the priest's eye, he had to attend as well, taking a spot in the very back.

The prioress knelt at the front of the church, where all

that could be seen was her black-clad back, stiff as the statue in the corner. Ari kept his eye on her all through the prayers and the priest's rant about the sanctity of the tithe and never caught a glimpse of more than her hands. At the end of the service, when the others began to file out, he moved forward intending to greet her, but before he'd gone more than a pace or two, she said a few words to the priest, dropped back to her knees, and bowed her head.

"May I help you, my lord?" asked the priest.

"I wish to have a word with the prioress."

"That is not possible, my lord. Mother Celestria said she wishes to spend an extended time in prayer. She will not speak with anyone until she finishes."

"Mmm. Your pardon, then, Father."

The reeve was setting up the next day's work groups in the manor yard. Ari stood off to the side until the other men scattered to their homes, then a little longer as the man spoke with the stable master and smith.

At long last, the reeve turned toward him. "You'll be wanting to see the lad."

"Aye. I was surprised to learn you'd brought him back here."

"'Twas the lady prioress," said the reeve, making it clear in those four words he would never have done it himself. "He is in the solar, set up like a little lord. He will never want to heal, for all the good food she gives him. Go on. He will be pleased to see you, I'm sure."

Ari went upstairs and found Robin sitting propped up in one corner, eating a custard. He was so absorbed in watching a group of maids spinning in the far corner that he didn't notice he had a visitor until Ari put his boot up on the edge of the cot. "I think the reeve is right."

"Sir Ari! Good day, my lord. I hoped you would come. Prioress Celestria carried me away before I could say good-bye." Robin's eyebrows drew together. "Right about what?"

"That you will never want to leave for the good food and care." Ari surveyed his situation and was pleased: this new mattress smelled of fresh hay instead of soured sweat and mold, and Robin's injured leg sported new splints bound with clean bandages. Perhaps this was a good thing for the boy after all. "How are you doing?"

"Well, my lord. The journey back was far more pleasant than the journey out."

"No doubt, as is the vista here." Ari looked pointedly at the spinsters, some of whom were quite fair. "The colliers are good folk, but they have not a maid among them, much less a maid like that sweet one in the red."

Robin laughed. "True enough, but even she could not keep me here if my leg were healed."

"You want to stay, then?"

"In truth, my lord, no. But I feel bad at the colliers'. They are poor folk and every bite I eat comes from one of them."

Ari held his finger up to his lips to shush the boy and dropped his own voice so the spinsters wouldn't hear. "You are poor, too, Robin. Remember that."

After his conversation with Steinarr in Retford, Ari had let Robin know that the truth was out. The lad's relief would have been almost comical, if not for the sudden willingness to talk it had brought on. It had been a trick to keep him from revealing all before the colliers in those first moments.

The risk here would be far greater, what with the nun and her companions, plus whatever travelers passed through—any of whom might be connected with Sir Guy. After checking to make certain the women in the corner were too busy talking to listen, Ari gave Robin some very terse and precise instructions about keeping his identity a secret.

"Most of all, think first. Here." He tapped the side of his head, then pointed to his mouth. "And *then* here. Not the other way around."

"Yes, my lord."

"And your cousin's name?"

"Marian."

"Always, and without fail. This is for her sake, as well as yours. There are too many mouths here, and twice as many ears. You do not want someone carrying tales that would lead Guy to her. Or to you."

Robin's face went somber. "No, my lord. I will be careful."

"Good. I see a morris board. Let us have a game, and you can practice your peasant wiles with me while I wait for your prioress."

"That would be most welcome, my lord. Fair as the view is, just sitting is tiresome. And the prioress doesn't want me carving spoons here in the bed."

"And no wonder," said Ari. "Patience. You will be up and around in a few days."

They played several games, but the prioress never came. Ari finally had to bid the boy farewell and leave him to his dinner—far better than his own, no doubt. As he rode out of Headon, a quick stop at the church found the devout prioress still on her knees, head bowed. Ari cleared his throat, hoping she would say her amen and give him a few moments, but the woman was so lost in her meditations, she never so much as flinched.

Thwarted, Ari left the church and set off. His gut still niggled at him, though, and he hadn't ridden far before he realized it wasn't going to go away. He needed to find out what was beneath this uneasiness, and unfortunately, he only knew one way.

Pillocks. The very idea of calling a vision made his scarred palms sting with remembered knife cuts. It was bad enough when they came on their own, but the blood required to bribe the gods into speaking to him had more than once left him wishing he could die.

"It had better be good," he said to the sky as he turned off the road, headed for a quiet pool he knew. "It had better be good."

AT LAST.

Even for a woman accustomed to spending hours in prayer, this had been a long vigil—so long the priest himself had given up and wandered away to his dinner.

Cwen rose slowly, her knees aching and sore from being on them so long. Unsteady, she made several circuits of the altar, using it to support herself as she worked out the stiffness. The raven had been with the boy far longer than she would have guessed, but she had outwaited him, unwilling to let him see her without magic to disguise her features.

Now, however, he was gone and she had ample time in which to work. She fingered the chased-gold chalice on the altar. If she hadn't brought her stolen one from Kirklees, this would make a proper vessel for her sacrifice. She considered taking it anyway, just for the pleasure of seeing the raven blamed for the theft, but that was not her aim. She had grander plans.

With her legs feeling better, she walked back to the manor and enjoyed her dinner at the high table in the hall. A few words to a servant set things in motion, and a little later she climbed the stairs carrying a cup.

The boy lay sated and dozing after his own meal, but he roused as she entered. "Good day, Lady Mother. I hope your prayers went well."

"They did. How are you, my child."

"Even better than this morning, Lady Mother."

"I think not," she said. "Listen to that throat. It still aches, I think."

"Only a little, Lady Mother. I talked a great deal while Sir Ari was here."

"Still, I think you should be bled," she said thoughtfully. "'Twill clear the foulness from your veins. Neither your throat nor your leg will heal properly 'til that is done."

The boy frowned. "I hate being bled."

"We seldom like what is best for us. We must do it anyway. Here, I have brought you something to make it easier for you. Drink."

He took the cup and sipped at it. Not long after, the door opened on two maidservants, one carrying a basin covered with a cloth, the other, a second basin and a ewer of steaming water. They set their burdens down on the little table beside the cot. The cloth was pulled aside to reveal a sharp blade and the hollow shaft of a feather, which could be used to keep the vein open.

"Close the shutter and pull the screen around the cot to block the draft," directed Cwen. "He must be kept warm so that the blood flows."

When all was arranged to her satisfaction, she sent the women away and barred the door before she carried the basins to the cot.

"It will not take long," she said. Already sleepy, he looked away, and with a quick slash, she opened his arm with two parallel cuts and slipped the basin into place.

"Ow."

"You bleed well," she said as the basin began to fill. Such red blood. He was young and healthy—and a virgin, too, or so she'd decided from watching how he was with the maidservants. No matter. It was his connection to the raven she wanted, and to the cousin who had gone off with the lion. With some careful spell-casting, she could use that blood both to increase her powers and to see why the gods had brought her to Headon.

She bled him until he fainted away, then a little more, so he would stay asleep long enough for her to transfer most of the blood to a ewer she had set aside. She hid that ewer away in the triple-locked chest where her other magical tools rested, then mixed water with the remaining blood so it appeared to be more.

He looked so peaceful lying there, almost as though he were dead.

But not today. Today she only needed his blood.

His death would come later, when the time was ripe to do harm to the raven and the lion. And when it would most honor the gods.

TUXFORD SAT ON the ancient great road that ran from London to York. Every nobleman in England traveled that road at some point in his life, most passing through Tuxford on their way between estates, following the king's court on progress, heading to London, or going off to battle. On any given day, dozens of England's bravest knights and fairest ladies might pass through the town heading north or south.

And every single one of them, Steinarr now realized, was a danger to Marian.

In truth, they were no more dangerous now than they had been a week earlier when he and Marian had ridden south from Harworth, but that was before they'd run into Baldwin. Now he understood how many people could recognize Marian, how many might know her from visits to Huntingdon or Locksley or the great house in which she'd fostered, an understanding reinforced by the near disaster in Sudwell. Now he knew that every eye was a fresh threat. If he was going to carry her into the heart of another town, he was determined to reduce that danger as much as possible.

He left the rouncey in the care of a farmer in an outlying village. They could pick him up later, but a packhorse would slow them if they needed to make a quick escape. From the farmer's wife, he borrowed a saffron-colored wimple that completely covered Marian's hair and a good portion of her face and gave her a sallow, unhealthy look. Just before they rode into town, he had her smudge her lips with a bit of chalk to take away some of the red.

For his own part, Steinarr pulled on his deerskin cap to hide his hair and drew his cloak close around his shoulders. With nearly a sennight's growth of beard, he looked even scruffier than usual, and that was good. Far fewer men knew him than would know Matilda Fitzwalter, but he wanted none of them taking note of his presence. Reports that he'd been seen riding the shire with a woman behind him might get back to Guy and the sheriff. Not only would it put them on his trail, it would draw them too close to Robin; Headon was only a few leagues north of Tuxford, through the woods.

"Keep your head down and your voice low," he reminded Marian as they approached the edge of town. "And English only. No French. You sound too fine when you speak French. And pretend you cannot read."

"Aye, my lord. I will be ware," she said, uncommonly

biddable—a sign, he hoped, that she recognized the danger, too.

What should have taken two days by the main roads had taken almost four by forest paths. The only blessing had been that the extra time in the saddle had given them more opportunity to talk through the riddle. And talk they had, grinding over and over the subject endlessly, sometimes serious, sometimes foolishly tossing ideas about. It had been late the day before that Marian had finally hit on a possible solution.

They had been once more discussing barleycorns and the ale and barrels and taverns they might hint at, when Marian had mused, "I wonder what sort of mill Tuxford has. Water or wind or ox."

"Wind." He remembered the first time he'd seen it, better than a hundred years earlier. He'd thought some fool had dragged a ship to the hilltop. It had turned out he was the fool. "And a small ox mill. The nearest water mill is a league off, on the River Maun."

"What if the barley is not meant for ale? What if it is meant for flour and the other bits for parts of the mill: the stone, the wooden shaft—"

"And the cloth of the sails. I think you may have something."

They'd talked it through further, but hadn't come up with more than her initial vague notion, much less concluded where the actual riddle might be hidden. However, at least they had a place to start. There was only one problem.

"Pillocks. I know why the road is so busy." Steinarr pulled up short a few hundred yards from the first cottage. "'Tis market day. We will have to come back tomorrow."

"No. We cannot afford to wait."

"Yes, we can. I have an idea—we are only two or three leagues from Headon," he said in an effort to distract her from her stubbornness. "I can take you to see Robin and bring you back first thing in the morning when there are fewer people."

"No. Much as I want to see him, I would rather see my

father's next riddle. Our time is already half gone. We must go on."

"But the crowds . . ."

"The crowds will make it easier. All the townsfolk will be at market. Even the miller and his wife, I wager."

"And anyone who does see us will wonder why we are not at the market as well," said Steinarr.

"We are only travelers passing through, and we wish a closer look at the windmill, for we have no such thing in our village."

"A passable excuse," he admitted, unwilling to show her he was once more impressed with the quickness of her lie, for fear it would encourage her. She, however, took his comment as assent and dug her toes into the horse without waiting for him to do it. As they cantered along, he twisted around to eye her over his shoulder. "Do you want the reins as well? I can always ride behind."

She flushed. "Forgive me, my lord. I am too bold."

She was, indeed. When had he come to like a bold woman so well?

They headed straight for the white sails on the far side of town, bypassing the market square notwithstanding Marian's confidence. Despite the brisk wind that raked the rise where Tuxford sat, the blades were still, and as they reached the mill, it appeared they were tied down. Steinarr pushed the door open and called out, "Hallo!"

When there was no answer, Marian hurried over to check the adjoining cottage, which also proved empty. "See, they are at the market."

"So it seems." Steinarr started around the mill. "I will check out here, but it may be inside."

"It is not, my lord."

"And how do you know that?"

"Because it is here."

Steinarr retraced his steps. "Where?"

She started to point, then pulled her hand back and glanced around. "There, my lord. The egg."

He came on around to see. A huge alabaster egg, the size of a grown man, sat on a low pedestal between the cottage and the mill. "God's toes, I do hope Robin appreciates your cleverness."

They examined the stone carefully. The surface was polished as smooth as pond ice, except for a small pattern carved as a band around the middle. Steinarr traced the scrollwork and scratched at it with a fingernail. "It does not seem to be in pieces. Does this pattern have some meaning?"

"Not that I know," she said after studying it a moment. She crouched to examine the base. "The same pattern is here. I think if we . . ." She poked around out of sight, then looked up at him. "Can you move it? I think the pedestal may be hollow beneath."

He squatted, wrapped his arms around the stone, and heaved. It barely wiggled. He set himself better and threw his back into it. The egg slowly tilted sideways.

"Higher." She started to reach beneath.

"No!"

She jerked away just as his grip slipped. The stone fell back with a low thud. "I saw it. I could have had it."

"You could have lost a hand." The sweat of fear mixed with that of effort, and he swiped at his forehead before he stripped off his cloak and tossed it aside. "We need something to wedge it."

They scouted around the yard and found some sturdy wooden blocks stacked by the side of the cottage. Steinarr picked out a pair, one thicker than the other, and handed them to Marian.

"When I lift, wedge the smaller one in. When I lift again, wedge the larger block in on the other side. Make them secure. They need to hold the whole weight of the stone if I cannot. And keep your fingers out of the way."

Only when she'd done as he said and the second wedge was in place did he tell her, "Now."

He strained to hold the stone steady as she scrabbled underneath. Through the pounding of his blood, he heard clanking.

"It will not come," said Marian. "Another inch."

He found an untapped measure of strength and leaned

back with a grunt. The stone slowly rose; Marian leaned in. A moment later, he heard the scrape of metal on stone, then, "I have it."

Steinarr let the stone settle back on the wedges. As the full weight came down, one wedge squirted out. The stone tipped precariously. Steinarr strained to hold it. "Pull the other one. Quickly."

She yanked and fell backward just as the egg slipped from his grip. It landed on the pedestal with a loud thunk and the sound of cracking stone. Steinarr collapsed on the ground, his arms and back burning with exhaustion.

Marian scrambled over to him. "Are you all right?"

"I will be," he groaned. "What is it?"

"A box." She started to hold it out. "It looks like—"

"You, there! What are you two about?" A red-faced, red-haired man wearing a dusty miller's smock came storming through the gate, hands fisted.

Steinarr shot to his feet, putting himself between the man and Marian. "Hold, Miller. We want no trouble. And you do not want to strike a noble knight."

The man skidded to a stop. "A knight?"

Steinarr touched the hilt of his sword. "A knight."

"Your pardon, my lord. I thought you were—never mind that. Is there aught I can do for you, my lord?"

"We were only looking at your windmill. There are none where we come from and my, um, cousin has never seen one. She was curious."

"I was," said Marian, stepping up beside Steinarr. "'Tis big as a ship."

"Aye, it is that," the miller said proudly. "God's truth, I thought you were meddling with the egg."

"A stone egg is a strange sign for a mill," said Marian. "How did you chose it?"

"It chose me, my lady, or rather was chosen for me. 'Twas set here at behest of the king. I get a pound each year for keeping it, though I do not know why. That is why I worried you were doing something to it."

"I must admit to it. We were." She batted her eyes at the man in a sweetly apologetic way that made Steinarr's heart

race. "I challenged my cousin to test his strength by moving it. 'Twas foolish, I know, but fortunately his strength
matches his boastfulness. We can go now, cousin. My curiosity on both counts is satisfied."

The miller's face cleared even though Marian's explanation was nearly as odd as the truth. "If you wish, my lady, I
can show you the inside of the mill."

"No need," said Steinarr. "I am sure it works much as
our water mill. Come, Marian."

"Marian." The man looked from Marian to Steinarr,
took in the deerskin cap and the ugly wimple, and grinned
broadly. "*That* Marian?"

"Um. What Marian would that be?" she asked.

"I understand. 'Twould not do to have it known. Would
you care for a sack of flour, my lord? I have more than
enough to spare a bit."

The fellow had clearly breathed too much rye dust.
Steinarr shook his head carefully. "I think not. We travel
quickly and must keep our load light. Perhaps another
time."

"'Twill be here for you when you need it, my lord."
Beaming with a sudden outbreak of goodwill, the miller
stood aside. "A safe journey to you both."

As they headed for the horse, Marian seemed to be
walking oddly. Steinarr slowed to help her. "What is wrong
with you? Where is it?"

"Between my knees," she said under her breath. "Slow
down."

"Pillocks. Don't let it fall." They reached the stallion.
"Now what?"

"Is he watching?" she asked.

He tipped his head to look past her. "Aye. Like a hawk."

"Bah. Er, bend as though to help me up." She checked
the lane then, lifting her gown as if to step up, hoisted the
hem 'til he could just see a fat little copper box pressed
tightly between her legs just above her knees. "Take it, then
hand it to me and help me up."

He grabbed the box, and in one fluid movement, she
took it and stepped up into his relinked hands. She was

seated, with the box tucked out of sight in her skirts, before even the closest observer could have caught more than a glimpse. The miller's smiling face gave no sign he'd seen anything at all.

Moments later they were riding out of town, and Steinarr's laughter broke free. "Between your legs?"

"I had nowhere else. My gown is too tightly laced—your fault, my lord—and the box is too fat for my sleeve or my scrip. I could only think to slip it beneath my gown as I rose. 'Twas good you were between us."

"Still . . . How did you know you could walk with it?"

"I did not. I only hoped."

"He might have let us simply take it. From what he said, Edward put the egg on his land just for this purpose."

"I do hope so. The pedestal cracked in three when you dropped the egg. His stone will soon fall over and he will lose his pound from the king."

"I wager he would lose it anyway when the quest is complete. And I did not drop the egg. Your wedge failed because you did not seat it well. You are fortunate you did not lose an arm. It weighed a ton. I could barely tilt it."

"Robin could never have done."

"He would have needed help, for certs. Perhaps that was the test—to see if he could gather men to him. Do you want to stop and open the box?"

"Not until we land someplace safe. And not until I am rid of this foul wimple."

"It does make you look yellow."

"It makes me *feel* yellow. Hurry, *monsire*, before it actually gives me the jaundice."

They retrieved the horse and gear, returned the wimple, and rode off a little way into the woods where no one would see as Marian opened the box.

"Empty."

"The miller," growled Steinarr. "He moved the egg and stole what was in the box. I will go back tomorrow and learn what he did with it. I will carve it out of him if need be."

"Perhaps that will not be necessary," she said, chewing her lip. "Father was many things, but he was no fool.

He would have known the temptation might be too great. Perhaps . . .'"

She felt around the inside of the box, then took out her knife and cut away the leather lining. Slipping the blade along the edge of the underlying metal, she gently pried away a false bottom to show a compartment beneath, from which she pulled a folded sheet of parchment. "You see? He is a fox."

"And you have a bit of the vixen in you, I think. But how do we know that is all? The miller still may have taken something. Some key piece."

"The leather bears no mark of anything laying on it." She unfolded the parchment. "'Tis in English again." Her lips worked in and out as she struggled through the script. "It says, 'In the Vale of the Leen, regard the lady of Torcard at work. The way to travel will be clear.' Did we not cross the River Leen on the way to Gotham?"

"We did. I do not know the name *Torcard*."

"Nor I. We will have to ask when we come to the vale. But you see, my lord. We must go south again. We are nearly a full day ahead because we did not go to Headon."

He pulled her into his arms. "And you will likely not let me forget it."

"Never," she said, nestling up against him, her forgiveness complete. "If Father keeps to the same pattern, we will be back this way in another sennight or so, and Robin will be healed enough to ride with us."

"With luck." With real luck, they would have the treasure by then, and he could leave her safely with Ari and the colliers and take only Robin on the final race to the king. That was when Guy would be truly dangerous. If he were Guy, he would have men on the roads, ready to do murder if need be, especially as Robin got closer to Edward. He did not want to take Marian into that.

He wrapped his arms more tightly around her and kissed her forehead. "Come. We can make another few miles today. Perhaps even to Edwinstowe. 'Tis a pleasant little village, and I think I know where you can have a bed for the night."

CHAPTER 15

"**WE COULD USE** one of your caves, *monsire*." Two days later, the weather had changed for the worse, and Matilda found herself huddling against Steinarr's back for protection from the rain-laden wind. "Surely there is one in these hills."

"The ones I know are no nearer than where we are going. Can you press on?"

"Of course."

The rains had begun as they rode south from Mansfield, torrents of rain that had drenched Matilda and Steinarr to the skin and quickly turned the road into an impassable bog that left the horses slipping and sliding and weighed down with mud. They'd had no choice but to take to the woodland paths, where the footing was easier but the tracks so overgrown that Steinarr had resorted to hacking the branches back with his scramasax. It made for exhausting, slow, unpleasant travel, especially as they crossed over the hills, and it left Matilda wishing her father were alive just so she could kill him herself—yet another sin to add to the list of things she must confess one day.

"How much farther?"

"The steward said Hokenall lies a league south of Newstead Abbey." Steinarr had stopped at a small hall on the outskirts of Mansfield to ask the way to Torcard. He'd been told the name belonged not to a place but to a family, the noble lords of a village called Hokenall, and there they were bound.

"But where is Newstead?"

"Over that way." He gestured vaguely east, then slashed at another bush to make the path wide enough for the rouncey's pack. "I could take you there. The monks could offer you a roof and a warm fire so you can dry out."

"You, too."

"I will stay warm enough wherever I land, but I worry for you tonight." He broke a smaller branch by hand and urged the stallion forward. "I wish I knew this part of the woods better. There could be a woodward's hut a stone's throw away, and we could not see it for these trees."

"I am fine until Hokenall," she repeated. "I am not so frail as you seem to think."

"You have shown me your strength time and again. To Hokenall, then."

They pushed on, resting when they could find a dry spot under a broad tree, but stopping made Matilda feel the chill and she insisted on moving on. The afternoon stretched out and the dim light began to grow dimmer. She prepared herself for a cold, wet night.

And then the forest ended and they were at the edge of a broad pasture, with fields beyond and a village beyond that. Even the horses seemed to feel the excitement, and they hurried toward the village and the possibility of a warm night after all.

Steinarr rode straight to the manor, a sturdy stone building surrounded by a deep ditch and paling wall. A quick inquiry at the gate revealed that they had, indeed, reached Hokenall and that the hall belonged to Peter Torcard, its lord. Steinarr asked to speak with the steward.

"Inside, *monsire*. They sup. Go on, you will be wanting to get your woman out of the wet."

"My lady cousin," corrected Steinarr, giving the man a sharp look.

"Forgive me, my lord. My lady." The man stepped back to pass them through the gate with an apologetic bow.

As they neared the door, Steinarr leaned over to Matilda. "Keep behind me until we see what sort of man Peter Torcard is, and make certain he has no guests who would be a danger."

They waited just inside, behind the tapestries hung to

keep the wind from those at table, while a servant fetched the steward.

"Welcome, my lord," said the man, brushing crumbs from his beard as he came. "You wished to see me?"

"I did. I seek a pallet for my cousin for the night. We were caught by the weather and the roads."

"We always have room for travelers, though few enough stop here when we are so close to Nottingham Town."

"I would imagine there are others tonight."

"Only one, my lord, a young jongleur who has stayed with us two days."

As Steinarr negotiated their stay, Matilda stepped over to peer at the crowded, cheerful hall through the gap between tapestries. A pleasant fire blazed in the hearth, and brilliant white cloths covered the tables, which held ample food and drink though it was only supper. On the dais, a young man clad all in green and brown—not a jongleur she knew, thank the blessed saints—sat by the high table holding forth to the lord and lady. The woman had her back to the door, but her gestures seemed somehow familiar, and Matilda watched her with interest.

"She will rest with your lady's women, though?" she heard Steinarr say.

"Of course, my lord," assured the steward. "Lady Nichola sees to the chastity of all of our women and our guests, even to the poorest."

"Nichola?" The name and gestures came together. "Nichola de Markham?"

The woman turned to squint across the hall. "Do I hear my name? Who is there? Steward, bring our visitors to me."

"Yes, my lady." The steward pulled aside the curtain and started forward.

As they followed, Steinarr raised a questioning eyebrow.

"We fostered together," said Matilda. "She is short-sighted, but has the ears of a deer."

"So I do," said Lady Nichola, smiling broadly. "And now that I hear that voice clearly, I know it. Maud!"

She rose and met Matilda at the foot of the dais to

embrace her. "I cannot believe it! I thought never to see you again, and especially not here. Husband, this is Ma—"

Matilda started coughing violently, hacking and wheezing as she had when they met Baldwin.

"Oh, my. Forgive me," said Nichola. "You are sopping wet. Come let's get you out of those clothes. I should have realized. Hodde, a hot bath and dry clothes. And have some mead warmed and supper brought up. Immediately. Excuse us, husband." She put her arm around Matilda's arm and steered her toward the stairs as servants started scrambling.

"Of course, my heart. I will entertain Sir . . ."

"Steinarr." He glanced toward Matilda on the steps. "Steinarr Fitzburger. Your pardon, my lord, but I have business I must attend. I cannot stay more than a moment."

"In this weather?" said Lord Peter.

"I stopped only to find my cousin a safe place for the night. I did not know she would find a friend here, but I am glad she did. If—"

The door to the solar closed, cutting off the men's voices, and Nichola's servants surrounded Matilda, unlacing and stripping her quickly. One woman toweled her off and another wrapped her in a blanket while a third added wood to the fire and scooped coals into a brazier to warm the room more quickly. A tub was already in place near the fire, half full of water.

"Warm your hands," urged Lady Nichola. "You must be chilled through. And that cough."

"'Twas only a tickle. A bit of dust. Oh, it is so good to see someone I know." Matilda threw her arms about Nichola and pulled her close to whisper. "But you *must* call me Marian. Please. I will explain later, when we are alone."

Nichola pulled back, concern wrinkling her pretty face, but she nodded. "And it is good to see you . . . Marian."

Servants filed in and out, bringing warm mead, a change of clothing, and bucket by bucket, the hot water, fresh from the kitchen. Another pot was set to warm on the solar fire to provide fresh hot for later, and a screen pulled around to keep the heat of the fire close to the tub.

The servant, Hodde, supervised the addition of one last bucket of hot water, then stuck her arm in the tub to mix it in. "'Tis ready, my lady."

Hodde took the blanket and Matilda stepped into the tub and sank into the warm water with a sigh. "God's knees, that feels good. How is it you can have a bath ready so quickly?"

"My lord husband intended a bath tonight and the water was heating already."

"Oh, no. I do not wish to take his bath from him."

"Too late," said Nichola happily. She handed Matilda her mead. "Drink this, and we will have you warm from inside and out. And never fear, we will not waste the water. Peter can have his bath later, after we have you tucked into a warm bed. We should give that cousin of yours a bath, too. He is as wet as you."

"He is already gone, I am certain. As he said, he has business." In an odd way, it made Matilda feel a little better that he left her even here, when there were others around and he would not be expected to lie with her. It proved his nightly absences were not merely a way to avoid her. "Is your laundress to hand? I would love to have my hair washed."

"But it is not the proper weather. It will take forever to dry."

"It is already wet and dirty. I would rather have it wet and clean."

"Fine, then, but no laundress. I will wash your hair myself. Hodde, bring the hair soap and the nettle vinegar. And more towels. And the—"

"I know what to get, my lady."

Everything was brought and arranged at hand and the servants dismissed. As the door closed behind the last one, Nichola began working soap through Matilda's hair. "Remember when we used to bathe Lady Amabel?"

Matilda sighed. "Aye. She had the thickest hair."

"Not as thick as yours," said Nichola. She worked her fingers through the long strands, then abruptly twisted them around her fist and gave a yank. "But I am going to

snatch out every hair on your head, Matilda Fitzwalter, if
you don't tell me what the devil is going on."

IT STOPPED RAINING sometime during the night, and by
the time Steinarr was fully human again, the weather had
broken, leaving a sky showing as much sun as cloud. With
luck, it would continue to clear and warm up once more
and his clothes would dry before the day was out. He wasn't
counting on it, any more than he was counting on the roads
being passable, but there was at least hope for both as he
rode into the yard at Hokenall. He left the stallion in the
hands of the same stable boy who had taken the rouncey
last night.

"Saddle both horses and load my gear. We will be leaving shortly."

"Yes, my lord."

"Good morrow, *monsire*," said the steward as he entered
the hall. "Lord Peter awaits you in the solar, if you please."

Steinarr nodded to the steward and trotted upstairs. *Just
get her out of here and hope she's figured it out*, he told
himself. No mucking about. He paused in the arch of the
wide-open door.

"Good morrow, my lord. Lady Nichola." And then, to
Marian, who sat by the fire in a fresh blue gown, just having the final ribbons tied into her plaits. "Cousin. You look
well rested."

"Call her something else, *monsire*," said Lady Nichola.
"She is no more your cousin than I am."

Pillocks. "Your pardon, my lady, but she—"

"First things first." Lord Peter waved forward a servant
who had come to the door behind Steinarr. "I had the steward find some dry clothes that should fit you. They are not
fine, but they will do. Help him change, Fulk."

The servant stacked the clothes on a nearby chest and
put out his hand. "Your sword and belt, *monsire*."

Wary, Steinarr looked to Marian.

She smiled and nodded. "Go on. If you keep your wet
things, I will be soaked again within a mile."

He unfastened his belt and handed it to Fulk, then peeled off everything down to his breeks.

"Those, too, *monsire*," said Lady Nichola. "We have all that you need."

"Give me that shirt first." He pulled on the loose linen chainse and made sure it was long enough to cover his privates before he turned his back on the women and untied his laces. Moments later, he wore fresh braies, a warm woolen chainse, and a green wool gown which might not have been fine to Lord Peter, but was better than any he'd had in years. As he sat down to pull on the good, thick hose Fulk handed him, he sighed with the pleasure of being in clean, dry clothes. A shame he couldn't have a bath as well. Marian had had one; he could smell the soap and perfumes on her from here, and her hair shone like a well-polished crown. A part of him desperately wanted to make the time to enjoy all that sweetness, no matter the delay. He had to tear his eyes away and think of other things to cool his blood.

"Put his boots by the fire before you go, Fulk. They can dry a little while we talk." Peter snapped his fingers at the maids working on Matilda's braids. "You, too. Begone. And shut the door behind you."

"Yes, my lord." Fulk chased the maids out and vanished behind them, pulling the door firmly shut.

Lord Peter turned to Steinarr. "We know."

"Know what, my lord?"

"All of it. Your lady told my wife what you two are about, and then together they told *me* as I bathed last night—hoping I would be so content I would hear it more happily, I think."

Lord Peter paced back and forth in front of the fire, then stopped to give Marian a hard look before he turned back to Steinarr. "I cannot say I approve, but I do understand why you work on her brother's behalf. That fool Fitzwalter should have done his duty, fixed his mind upon an heir, and made his choice clear, not left it to young Robert to chase around the countryside. And so I said to both him and Edward when they came through setting out the riddles, but they thought it all great sport and would not hear me. And now they have gotten the lad hurt."

Steinarr's head spun as he tried to take it all in. "You know, er, knew, Lord David?"

"Only a little, but the king and I often hunt together when he passes this way. He is the one who told me what they were doing."

"Then do you know what the riddle means, my lord, or where the next one lies?"

Peter shook his head. "They shared none of it with me. But I know it must be something to do with the solar. They locked themselves in here for a full day, then came out the next morning and rode off. Headed north," he said before Steinarr could ask. "Laughing like boys off on some grand jape." He turned to Matilda, who was pinning a fresh head-rail into place. "Tell us the riddle again."

She looked at the timbers overhead and recited from memory, " 'In the Vale of the Leen, regard the lady of Tor-card at work. The way to travel will be clear.' Have you thought of anything yet, my lord?"

"No." He looked to Steinarr. "Does it mean anything to you, *monsire*?"

Steinarr shook his head. " 'Regard the lady at work' must surely mean you, Lady Nichola. Where do you do your work?"

"Most often here by the fire."

Steinarr and Lord Peter started poring over the hearth and chimney and nearby walls, looking for loose stones, markings, or any other sign that might show where Lord David or King Edward had hidden something.

Matilda crossed to her friend. "What about when you sew, Nichola?"

"By the window, of course, else I could not see a single stitch. Even so, I can only sew on the brightest days."

"Show me."

Nichola dragged her embroidery frame over before the open window, pulled a stool into position, and sat down. "Right here."

"So you sit here even in winter?" asked Matilda.

"Aye. Peter bought me a real glass window. He tired of gowns with missing stitches. You must see it." She stood up and pulled the shutter closed. At first glance, Steinarr couldn't see why she was so proud, but then she swung open a smaller shutter within the shutter, revealing a rose of glass about as wide as her forearm was long. The outside edges consisted of many pieces of glass, leaded together like a church window, but the center was a single round of plain, water-like glass.

"Clear," breath Matilda. She nudged Nichola out of the way to peer through the window. "The way will be *clear.*"

"Oh, my," said Nichola. "My lords!" But Steinarr and Lord Peter were already there.

"I had just put that in when Edward and Fitzwalter were here," said Peter.

"I remember," said Lady Nichola. "The king commented on what a pleasant thing it must be for me to have such a well-lit place to work, even in winter."

"Do I see a tower?" asked Marian. "What lies on that hill, my lord?"

"I set the glass where it would light my wife's spirit as much as her stitchery, even though she cannot make it out at such a distance," said Lord Peter. He closed the smaller shutter and opened the larger one, then pointed to the tip of a bell tower just rising above the swirl of low clouds. "There lies the abbey at Newstead—and that is the way I last saw Edward and Fitzwalter riding."

"Then we go to Newstead," said Matilda, excited, but her smile faded in the next instant. "But without a new riddle, how we will know what to look for when we get there?"

"You might ask the abbot," said Nichola. "Edward kept repeating the abbot's name that morning: Abbot Talebot. He had turned it into a sort of song. *Abbot Talebot. Abbot Talebot.* I was at the window watching as they left, and heard them sing it as they went up the road. At the time, I thought he found the rhyme of it amusing, but now I would wager my best needle they were trying to draw my attention. I think they went to the abbot with the next of your riddles."

"And I think you are right. You have done it, Nichola." Matilda threw her arms around her friend. "You and your windowglass and your deer's ears."

Laughing, Nichola kissed Matilda's cheek. "I am so glad you came to us, even calling yourself Marian. It has been too long since I was told I have deer's ears. Now, let us break our fast and get you two on the road." Arms linked, the two women headed downstairs.

Steinarr looked to Lord Peter. "Are we of any use here at all, my lord?"

Grinning, Peter shook his head. "They will think of something for us to do. You'll want your boots." As Steinarr sat to pull on his still-damp boots, Peter leaned back against the doorframe. "When next I see you, I expect to hear that you have married Marian. Maud. Whatever her name is."

"Marian," said Steinarr without thinking, even as the young lord's words sliced through his gut like a hot blade. He yanked on the second boot and rose. "I am only her escort, my lord. When this quest is done, I return her to her brother's charge and am released."

He started to leave, but Peter put an arm across the doorway to block him. "Balls. You care for her. 'Tis clear in your eyes whenever you look at her. And in hers when she looks at you, or even merely speaks of you."

In *hers*? "Is it?"

"Aye, even half-blind, my wife sees it. Or perhaps she hears it in your voices with those deer's ears." He chuckled. "Marian has it right, you know. Nichola hears things most do not. But whether she saw or heard, she knows you care for each other, and she said I should warn you that if her friend turns up with child and you do not wed her, I will have your balls. And I will, *monsire*, for I both trust my lady's counsel and have a taste for her smiles." He straightened and gave Steinarr a friendly cuff on the shoulder. "As you do Marian's, I think. Now, let us join our ladies before they decide to set off for the abbey on their own."

Steinarr followed him downstairs, where Marian and Nichola were holding court at the high table. The green-clad young man sat at the next table down, staring at Marian as she nibbled at a slice of cheese. Steinarr took a stool beside her and took some pottage and a thick slice of cold beef. The taste of beef after so long nearly took his mind off what Lord Peter had said.

But not quite. A child was a possibility; he'd known that from the start. He recalled with shame his intention to pass his get off as another man's. But if she turned up breeding, what would he do? He knew what he wanted to do—precisely what Lord Peter urged—but he also knew what was possible and what was not. Then again, a fortnight ago, he would have sworn it was not possible for this aggravating woman to own his heart. He glared at the green man until the fellow stopped staring at Marian.

They finished the simple meal and, after a brief Mass in the chapel, said their farewells, which consisted of many hugs and promises for visits between the two women as both men looked on, smiling. Lord Peter directed them toward an old track that ran directly between Hokenall and Newstead, and they headed out with his assurances it would not be as muddy as the road.

It wasn't. The track was used little enough that grass covered much of it, keeping the mud down, but often enough that the bushes were held back. It made for easy riding. But what should have been a pleasant morning was caught up in thoughts of Lord Peter's half-joking threat, not in fear of Peter, but in fear for Marian and the impossibility of doing anything that would be right by her.

She rubbed her palm over his chest, bringing him back. "You are quiet this morning, *monsire*. What occupies your thoughts?"

"You. How sweet you smell. It is like riding with a rose-bush behind me."

"You should have stayed for a bath last evening. Nichola and I would have scrubbed you, as well, and I could have shaved you." She ruffled her fingers along the growth of whiskers on his chin. "You, too, could smell of roses."

"Thank you, no. You helped bathe Lord Peter?"

"Of course. Nichola and I washed many a visiting noble-man together when we were fostering with Lady Amabel. He is a well-favored man," she mused, as though he cared to hear this. "I think Nichola much enjoys the marriage bed."

She laughed as he spluttered. "I would not think I could shock you more, my lord."

"An unmarried woman should not be bathing strange men."

"An unmarried woman should not be tupping strange men either, but you made no complaint of that."

"That is different."

"Aye, it is." She gave him a squeeze. "Ladies in waiting bathe men all the time. Have you never been offered a bath when you visit a noble house?"

"No." In truth, he had so seldom visited a noble house that there had been no time for bathing. "And it is not our custom at home. Men and women bathe apart." Or they had, last he knew.

"Well, here, all the ladies help, married or not. 'Tis a way of honoring guests and, I think, of getting husbands for an excess of daughters, by the amount of bathing that took place at one of our neighbors."

"Why?"

She chuckled. "They had eight daughters."

"Eight!" He grinned, remembering another gaggle of girls. "I had a friend who had six, all with red hair like their mother. I saw them once when he brought them through on the way to London to the Curia Regis. I doubt he let them bathe anyone."

"I wager he did. Father always said red-haired women bring bad luck."

"These brought nothing but good to my friend. Espe-cially his lady wife. Her name was Alaida. I only ever saw her the once, but even graying and gone plump from bear-ing all those daughters, it was clear why Ivar treasured her so deeply." To this day, she was the woman whose image Steinarr clung to for hope, the way the Christians clung to their Virgin. He had long ago stuffed that hope down deep, where it could not torture him, but now it welled up again, this time wearing a face with strawberry lips and a crown of glorious golden hair.

"He loved her very much," said the owner of that face in a soft voice. "I can tell it from the sound of your voice."

"He did indeed."

"Then she was as fortunate as he."

They settled into a silence that had lasted only a few dozen yards when the stallion suddenly pricked up his ears and swiveled them to the rear. The rouncey nickered and did likewise, and Steinarr sat up straighter. "We are being followed."

"We are?" She started to twist around to look, but Steinarr gave her arm a squeeze.

"Be still," he said as he unhooked his bow from where it hung by his knee and pulled an arrow from the quiver next to it. "Hold tightly and be prepared for anything."

He had just nocked arrow to string and was calculating how quickly they could reach the abbey when hoofbeats sounded, coming up behind. Marian squeaked and grabbed on, and Steinarr whipped the stallion around and drew his bow.

The young jongleur from Hokenall came into his sights, aboard the ugliest dun horse Steinarr had ever seen. The fellow spotted the bow in Steinarr's hand and pulled up short. "Pray, do not kill me, my lord. I only come to ride with you."

"God's knees, man." Steinarr eased off the string and started putting the bow away. "You do not ride up on a man so in a forest where there are outlaws."

"There are outlaws in every forest, my lord."

"Sherwood is worse than most."

"As well I know, my lord."

"What are you doing here, Jongleur?" demanded Marian.

"Coming with you, I do hope, my lady, to be your guard."

"She already has a guard," said Steinarr.

"Of course, my lord. But such a treasure surely needs more than one man protecting her."

"A trusted soldier, not a stranger and jongleur."

"I may sing a bit, but I have a sharp sword and a willingness to use it. Let me earn your trust, my lord."

"Earn Lord Peter's trust. He can use a good man."

"He offered me a place, but I cannot stay with him, my lord. I am outlaw like you."

"I am not outlaw. Why does everyone think I am outlaw? I probably should be, but I am not. Why are you outlaw . . . What is your name?"

"William, my lord, William Scathelocke of Crigglestone. I killed a man."

"And I am supposed to trust you because you have done murder?"

"'Twas one of the sheriff's men. He forced himself on a woman in our village, and I pulled him off. We fought and I killed him, and now I am the wanted man, and outlaw. If the sheriff catches me, I will hang."

"A good reason to avoid him," admitted Steinarr. "But why come with us?"

"Because of who you are, my lord," he said, as if it should be evident even to a fool.

"And who do you think we are, William Scathelocke?" asked Marian.

The fellow smiled. "'Tis who I *know* you are, my lady. I heard of you in Retford, and saw you there, too, talking to the man who told the tale. You are the Maid Marian. And your good knight, here, is Robin Hood."

CHAPTER 16

"I AM GOING to kill him this time," said Steinarr.

"Will?"

"No, Ari. Will cannot help that he's a fool. Ari should know better."

They'd argued the nonexistence of Robin Hood with Will Scathelocke all the way to Newstead Abbey without success. The notion that Robin Hood was real, that Steinarr was he, and that Marian was Robin Hood's Marian, was so solidly fixed in the fellow's head that their arguments left it undented. Of course, it would have helped if they could have told him the truth, but Steinarr didn't trust him enough for that. In the end, he'd left Will to watch the main road for Guy—a somewhat useful duty that kept him out of mischief—while he and Marian rode the last way into the abbey, threading their way between the ponds where the canons raised fish for the abbey table.

"First I will kill Guy. Then Baldwin. Then Ari," Steinarr went on. "By then my blade will be dull and it will hurt more."

"He cannot help it that someone believes his tale so completely."

"He should never have told it—not with real names. He did this to me once in Vass. Made up some story about a fellow named Steinarr who had been tupping the *jarl*'s daughter. It was a humorous tale and we all laughed—until the *jarl* came through and heard it. It nearly got me flayed."

"So you had not been tupping the earl's daughter?" she asked, shifting the title to something more familiar.

"Only the daughter of a merchant-trader," said Steinarr. He felt Marian stiffen and added, "'Twas long before you were even born, so do not make that face. I can feel how sour it is without even looking."

"My face is not sour. And you are not so old you would have been tupping anyone's daughter before I was born. Unless boys of five and six years are familiar with women in your land."

"We actually start earlier than that," he said and laughed as she huffed at him. "I have told you, I am older than you think."

"But you—"

"I am older, Marian. Much older. 'Tis time you believed me. Now hush. The gatehouse is just ahead."

As they reached the little hut, a sturdy monk dressed in the simple gray robe of a Franciscan friar stepped out, a long staff in his hand. "How may I help you, my lord. My lady."

"We would speak with Abbot Talebot."

"He is just finishing his prayers, my lord. I will show you where you may wait." He had them tie the horses by the gate, then led them into a chamber that stood tucked up hard against the wall. "The lady may go no farther. I will send word you are here."

Steinarr folded his arms and stood silently. Marian, on the other hand, fidgeted, toying with the ends of her girdle, with the flap on her scrip, with the end of her plaits beneath her headrail, until finally, Steinarr crossed to where she was pacing and enfolded her hands in his just to still them. "Why are you so nervous?"

"It seems wrong to be here without a riddle or clue of any sort. What if we missed something at Hokenall?"

"Then we will go back and you will have another visit with Lady Nichola while we search once more. But let us see what the abbot has to say before we look for trouble."

"Wise knight." She feathered kisses across his knuckles. "What would I do without you?"

Steinarr had asked himself the same question at dawn.

What would he do without her? How could he go on without her when this was done?

They were still standing like that when the light shifted. "Do you come to marry, my children?"

They pulled apart hurriedly, and Marian knelt to kiss the abbot's ring. "No, Lord Abbot. We come to ask a question."

Unlike the monk at the gate, the abbot wore white, with a short, dark fur cape around his shoulders, the mark of the Augustinian canons who resided within Newstead's walls. "What question would that be?"

"About my father, Lord David Fitzwalter, and a certain riddle I think he left with you."

"Ah, you must be Matilda. And you have been to Hoke-nall. Well done, my lady, but where is your half-brother, young Robert? I know him only a little, but enough to know this knight is not him."

"No, my lord Abbot. Sir Steinarr is here to help me follow Father's trail."

"It is Robert's task to follow it, not yours, my lady."

"True enough, Lord Abbot. But Father's quest has left Robert with a broken leg. I come to help him, and this knight to help me. Do you know where the next part of the puzzle lies?"

The abbot's face pinched as he looked from Steinarr to Marian. "A question I fear I cannot answer. I pledged to Lord David and, more importantly, to the king, that I would only reveal the next portion of the riddle to Robert. They feared he would find someone to do the work for him."

"But he would be here if not for his leg, which Father and King Edward caused," protested Marian.

The abbot held out his empty hands to show his helplessness. "Send him back here when his leg is healed and I will gladly give him the next riddle."

"It is here, then?"

"Aye, most assuredly."

"Please, my lord. We have less than a fortnight before Robert must present the prize to the king, and we do not even know how many more clues there are or where the king may be found."

The abbot's concerned face cleared. "That I may help with. This riddle that I possess is the last one. Once Robert presents himself, he has only to follow it to the treasure, and thence carry it to the king."

"If you will not tell us where the treasure is, will you at least tell us what it is?"

The abbot's lips thinned. "No. But I will say it is something you and Robert know very well. Bring him here, my lady, and all will be revealed."

"All right. We can do this," said Steinarr, taking Marian's hand. "Robin can surely ride by now. I will get him back here and then find the king and get Robin to him. I promise you."

"It will not be difficult, *monsire*." The abbot smiled broadly. "I received a message only yesterday. The king lies in Leicestershire even now and—"

"So near?" Marian's face lit up. "Then we *can* reach him!"

"If you would let me finish . . ."

Marian flushed. "Forgive me, Lord Abbot."

"What I started to say is, the king is in Leicestershire, but the message was to say that he comes here to Newstead in the next days. We are to prepare for a royal—"

Abbot Talebot stopped, for there was no point in going on: the receiving hall was empty. A moment later he heard hoofbeats drumming away down the road. Smiling, he turned to retire to his chamber. For once, it might actually be worthwhile hosting the king. The next week should prove interesting, indeed.

"I WOULD LIKE to see the prioress," said Ari once more.

The servant, a bent old man who had been peeling rushes by the fire when Ari entered, held up his hands helplessly. "Gone to Tuxford, my lord. She said to give her regards and say that the boy is much better and you may see him when she returns."

Ari glanced toward the solar. This mysterious prioress had banned him from it for five days now, supposedly to assure Robin's rest after his quinsy had taken a turn for the worse. With each day, his unease had grown deeper and his attempts to call a vision more urgent. Just this morning he had stopped by the pool to try once more to persuade the gods to talk to him, spilling so much blood that he was still light-headed. For naught, again. And to add to the uselessness of it, if he hadn't stopped at the pool, he might have caught the prioress before she left.

Ari grumbled his thanks and turned to go. But as his hand touched the door, his sight clouded over, just for an instant. He reached for the vision and it faded, leaving only a sense of warning, even deeper than before.

"I already knew that," he muttered.

"What was that, my lord?" asked the old man.

"Nothing. I will just be a moment." Ari turned and pounded up the stairs as the old man called after him.

Robin lay on the cot, limp and colorless, so pale he might have been a cloud on the linens, except for the bloodstained bandage on each arm. Ari quickly barred the door and went to the boy. "Robin. Robin. Rouse yourself."

Slowly, his eyes opened. "*Monsire*? You have come at last."

"What has she been doing to you?" Ari pulled aside the bandage on one arm to see three sets of parallel cuts, one still oozing blood.

"Bleeding me." Robin struggled to raise his head. "I told her to stop, but she says my blood is poisoned."

"Pillocks. You had the quinsy, is all. This is too much. I need to get you out of here before the old fool kills you."

He threw aside the bed coverings and checked Robin's leg. All the swelling was gone, and the bone looked to have set fairly straight. "This looks like it will hold you. Have you tried walking yet?"

Robin shook his head. "I think I could, if I had my strength."

"You are going to have to. Come, let's get you up. First just sit."

As Robin sat, wobbly as an infant, on the edge of the bed, someone pounded on the door. "Hey. What are you about in there? The boy is ill, leave him be."

"A moment," called Ari. He knelt in front of Robin. "Listen to me. I can carry you out if I must, but the fool nun has told her men you are ill and must be kept here. They will want to stop us on her behalf, unless you can convince every last one of them that you are fit to leave."

"I will do what I must, *monsire*. I know I cannot stay here longer. Help me up."

"Let's get you dressed first." As the man outside pounded on the door again, Ari jerked open cupboards and chests, tossing clothes toward Robin as he found them, then helped him dress. Finally, Ari checked the splints once more. "Are you ready?"

Robin nodded, put his hand on Ari's shoulder, and pushed up onto his good leg. He swayed precariously, and his face got paler, if that was possible, but after a moment, he steadied.

"Good lad. Put your foot down."

Hesitantly, Robin shifted weight onto his injured leg. A wan smile showed his pleasure. "I can stand."

"Try a step or two."

Hand still on Ari's shoulder, Robin hobbled toward the door. "It does not hurt, but 'tis weak. And my head spins so."

"From all the bleeding. 'Tis only a few steps down, and then out to the horse. Can you do it?"

"I can. I will, just . . . stay nearby." Robin positioned himself before the door and drew a deep breath. "Open it."

'Twas remarkable to watch. As the door opened, Robin appeared to grow a good two inches, straightening and setting himself with that same determined grit he'd shown on the way to the colliers' camp.

"Is there some problem?" Robin asked the burly fellow who led the men blocking the way.

"Um, er, that is, you are ill. Prioress Celestria said you were."

"Clearly, she was mistaken," said Ari, stepping up to Robin's shoulder. "He is well, and he wishes to go."

"But the prioress said not to—"

"Am I a prisoner?" asked Robin.

"No, but—"

"Then I may go at my will," said Robin. "And it is my will to go."

"We are most grateful for your lady's charity," said Ari, "but it is time for Robin here to be gone. Give the prioress our thanks. We leave."

Robin started forward, but the man didn't give way. Ari stepped around to confront him. "I said, we leave. Stand aside."

For a heartbeat, the big fellow stood there glowering, but then his gaze drifted down to where Ari's fingers touched his sword. "I, er, suppose the boy can go. It is his choice, healthy or not. But if he dies, it is on you, *monsire*."

"Agreed. Now move."

The fellow turned to the others. "Out of the way, so he can manage the stairs."

The rumble of heavy feet signaled that the stairs were being cleared. Robin stepped forward onto the landing, and Ari took a position at his side, prepared to catch him if he gave out.

But it wasn't necessary. Robin took one look at the men and women watching below, squared his shoulders once more, and marched down the stairs and across the hall. Only the extreme paleness of his face and the stiffness of his splinted leg gave any sign he was hurting. Outside, Ari quickly brought the horse around to the mounting block, helped Robin into the saddle, and swung up behind him, reaching around to support him as he took the reins.

"You are hurt, too, *monsire*."

Ari glanced at his bandaged hand. "'Tis nothing. I cut myself, is all. Come. Let us leave this place."

The Headon men followed them clear out to the road, watching and muttering among themselves. A few notes of admiration caught Ari's ear.

"Well done, lad," murmured Ari as he turned toward the colliers' camp. He felt Robin sway in the saddle and tightened his grip to steady him. "Hold on a little longer."

They had reached the far edge of the fields when Robin asked. "Are we away, *monsire*?"

"Aye."

"Good. Catch me," said Robin, and fainted dead away.

CWEN WATCHED THE raven and the sleeping boy ride past from the shadows of a big oak. It was difficult, letting them go when young Robin was so close to death, but she had found something so much more valuable than the boy's lifeblood.

The raven's. This was why she had been brought here.

She'd discovered his vision pool on a quiet walk just the day before, drawn to it by the raven himself as he'd called to the gods. She'd stood, watching him spill his blood into the water and ride away afterward having failed, and she had rejoiced in his failure. She'd known he would be back, spilling more of his magic into the water with his blood, just as she had known that once he had the boy, he would stay away.

So she'd let him have Robin, and now the pool was hers. Finally it was all in place: the pool, its waters, the raven's blood, and tonight, the full moon.

She passed the day in the woods nearby, preparing, watching, waiting, until the moon rose late that afternoon. As the sky slowly darkened around it, she laid out her tools on the water's edge and began her spell-spinning. Hours passed, the moon climbed higher, and Cwen continued her ceaseless chant. The power stirred to life around her, ruffling the trees and frightening the beasts away. One frightened rabbit bolted straight into her arms, and she accepted its sacrifice with a quick slash of the knife. She spilled the first of the warm, rich blood to the gods and drank the rest to strengthen herself for what was to come.

In the last moment before the moon broke above the trees, she stripped away her garments, baring herself to the gods' power, and stepped to the edge of the pool.

"Blood and water, man and beast, light and dark, earth and sky," she said, arms spread wide to the heavens. "I am here, Great Ones. Make me your instrument again, and they will all know your power and revel in your glory."

The moon shone above the treetops, its perfect roundness reflected in the center of the pool. Cwen's breath caught in her throat. "So beautiful, my lords. I give myself to it and you."

She waded into the pool, gasping as the cold and the power closed around her waist. The waters began to swirl, to glow, to pulse, around her. Unflinching, she stepped to the center and sank to the bottom, letting the consecrated water, fecund with the seer's vision-blood, close over her head. Water flowed into her mouth and she drank, taking the power in, but her lungs fought, aching, burning, her frail human body fighting what must be done.

And then it could fight no longer. With a sense of triumph, she breathed in the water, and in the moment of her drowning, once more knew the true power of the gods.

"BEWARE," SAID STEINARR as they rode down the forest path east of Headon. "Osbert will come rolling out of the woods shortly, full of hope once more."

"Is Osbert one of your men?" asked Will Scathelocke from the place in the rear where Steinarr had made him ride most of the way.

"I have no men," growled Steinarr over his shoulder for the hundredth time. "Osbert is a collier. A very round collier, who courts Marian for wife."

"Do not mock poor Osbert," said Matilda. "He only wants a mother for his children."

"Aye, and to get a dozen more on her. I pity the woman he marries next. Her life will be all children and charcoal."

"I considered him," she said.

"You *what*?"

Unprepared for his sudden outrage, she flinched. "'Twas only a moment's thought, when I feared we would never complete the quest."

"But why Osbert?"

"He is not so fat as Baldwin, and he has a far better

spirit. I also considered taking the veil." That made him angry, too, but not so angry as the idea of Osbert.

"They both seem poor choices for a fair lady," mused Will. "To work yourself to death as the wife of a fat collier or wither away as a nun."

"At least I had the choice. Some women have none. Most women, perhaps." She traced a line just above Steinarr's belt with one fingertip and murmured, "And I did have one other idea that proved worthwhile."

This time, she kept her defenses down on purpose, the better to savor the desire that lurched off him. They had not spoken of lovemaking since Will had attached himself, much less found time to actually enjoy any—although perhaps it wasn't fair to blame Will when the race back to Headon had eaten every hour between dawn and dusk. Throughout, Steinarr had struggled to keep his good humor, but his mind had begun to seethe with that wild darkness again, desire overlaid with anger and that other thing she still didn't understand but had begun to recognize as a part of what made him himself. She wanted him, and she liked that the sharpness of his need matched and heightened her own. She yearned to drown in all that wildness again.

As if he understood, he lifted her hand to his lips, pressing kisses to each finger before he drew the tip of one into his mouth and sucked. Suddenly she was back in that moment in the elf house, waiting for his mouth to close on her. If Will were not there . . .

"Riders! Riders!" A call went up, jerking them both out of the moment. A moment later, Much's cracking voice called, "'Tis Sir Steinarr and Marian and a stranger."

"It seems we are arrived." Steinarr pressed a last, tender kiss to her fingertips and released her to murmur, "If it is of any account, I am glad you chose the last."

"As am I," she whispered.

Children came bounding around the end of the charcoal pit like so many hares, followed by the men who began to straggle out of the woods in pairs, calling greetings. Goda reached the horses and took hold of Marian's ankle, the only thing she could reach. "I knew you would be back today."

"She 'knew' you would be back every day since you left," said her brother.

Ari's long legs carried him more quickly than the other men's, and he reached them just after the children. "God's knees, I am glad you two are back."

"You will not be for long," promised Steinarr. He slid off and reached up for Matilda. "Ari, *that* is Will. He will tell you why he has been following us since Hokenall, and then I will tell you what I am going to do to you because of it. Where is Robin? He should be up and about by now."

"Still abed. There was a bit of a problem. This nun—"

Matilda didn't bother to hear the rest, hurrying off toward where her brother lay just outside one of the huts. His paleness shocked her to a standstill. "Oh, Rob . . ."

His smile was warm, but wan. "Do I look so bad?"

"Aye." She knelt by the cot and put a hand to his forehead. "What happened?"

"Well, it started with the quinsy."

Matilda listened with growing anger as he told of the prioress, of being carried off to Headon, of too many bleedings. She pulled aside the bandages on his arm, saw all the cuts, and rounded on Ari in a fury. "You were supposed to keep him safe!"

"Sir Ari is not to blame," said Edith. "The prioress came upon us when he was gone to Retford and carted Robin away before we could say aught."

"Robin!" came a voice from the back. "*He* is Robin? But he—"

"Shut up, Will," said Steinarr and Matilda together.

"No, Marian is right," said Ari. "It is all on me. I should have brought him back here as soon as I found out. But when I went to see him the first day, he was well and happy."

"I was," Robin confirmed. "I asked him to leave me there, thinking to give Edith and Ivetta some respite. Then she said my throat was worse."

"I did not realize she was bleeding him," said Ari. "She kept me away, saying he was too ill."

"But he came anyway and rescued me, and I am safe here now and getting stronger already, thanks to Edith's herbs and Ivetta's good food. I will be ready to ride in a day or two. Have you found the . . ." He glanced at the colliers who had gathered around. "Is that why you are here?"

"We will speak of that later," said Steinarr. "Right now, you rest. Ari, a word." He started to walk off, then came back and grabbed Will by the collar to haul him along. "You, too."

'Twas more than a word, and they were all said loudly and at length at the far side of the clearing. Chuckling, Hamo and his men watched a little, then drifted back to their work. As Steinarr gradually calmed down, Matilda sat on the ground beside Robin, holding his hand and talking with the children and the women, sharing what she could about her journey without giving away too much before the others. Eventually, Osbert called the older boys back to work and Ivetta set the girls and the little ones to various chores; Matilda found herself alone with Robin.

He glanced around to be sure no one was near enough to hear. "What about the rest of it?"

She gave him a brief accounting of the riddles. When she got to Tuxford and the egg, he shook his head glumly.

"I would never have been able to do it."

"You would, Rob. You would have needed help—not me, or at least more than me—but you could have done it. You still must do some." She explained about Hokenall and Newstead and the abbot and the final riddle. "He would not say what it is, but finding the riddle itself was so simple, I fear that solving it may be more difficult than all the rest."

"That would be like him," said Robin, and the sadness beneath his words tore at Matilda's heart. "Even when I was a child, he would offer a toy or sweet, set me some task to earn it, then snatch it away at the last instant by making the final part of the task more difficult than I could manage."

"But this time, he meant for you to succeed. Steinarr says he could have made it much more difficult, and he could, truly, Rob. But he didn't. You will be able to do this final thing, whatever it is, just as you could have found a way to do the rest. And at least we know where the king is, or where he will be. 'Tis only a matter of getting you and it and him all together at one place."

"Do we know yet what it is we seek?"

"The abbot would not say, but I have had these last days as we rode back to think of nothing else. I think I may know. Do you remember the box where Father kept his rings and cloak pins?"

"The one of copper, with the figures on it?"

"Aye. That was what was in Sudwell. Do you remember what else he kept in it?"

Robin stared at the sky, thinking, but in the end, shook his head. "I was never allowed to play in it the way you were."

"Even I did not recall, at first." She reached into her scrip and pulled out the scrap of parchment from Blidworth. She turned it over to show him the fragment of knotwork on the back. "Does this remind you?"

"Should it?"

"Perhaps this." She pulled out the cylinder from the Lady Well. "We discovered the Seven Sins at Harworth— that is, Steinarr discovered them, but—"

"Steinarr?"

"Aye, he—"

"That is the second time you have called him just Steinarr and not *Sir* Steinarr."

Her cheeks heated. "Sir Steinarr, then. We spent so much time on a horse together that we grew less proper."

"How much less proper?" asked Robin, frowning. "Did he keep to his vow?"

"Yes." *The one he'd made to her anyway.*

"Maud . . ."

"He kept to his vow," she repeated more firmly, unwilling to have Robert's trust in Steinarr fail just when he so needed it. There would be time later for truth and apologies. "As I said, he discovered the Sins, which we needed to find the riddle in Harworth. But it was only later I noticed this."

She flipped the cylinder over and showed Robin the three tiny figures on the bottom. "More of the tarnish rubbed away inside the scrip and revealed it."

"The king's lions. Oh." Robin picked up the scrap of parchment from Blidworth again. "Now I know this knot-work. 'Tis from the covenant piece. That was the other thing he kept in the box."

"Aye. And there was more knotwork like it on the egg at Tuxford. It took so long to come to mind because I have not seen the piece for so long because—I think—that is what Father has hidden."

"Surely not. He would not have let it out of his keeping."

"Let what out of his keeping?"

Matilda started at Steinarr's voice, but Robert was already smiling up at him. "A lion, *monsire*."

Steinarr got the strangest look. "What lion?"

"My lord father's sign."

"Your sign, Robin, once we find it," said Matilda. "It may be what my father hid, *monsire*—a piece given by King Richard Lionheart to an ancestor who saved his life in the Holy Land. Perhaps to that very Robert whose grave we found."

"The grave in Sudwell?" Excitement vibrated off Stein-arr, unlike any Matilda had felt off him before.

"Lord David showed me that very grave when we were on the Gate," said Robin. "He said King Richard gave the lion to that Lord Robert as pledge that the Crown would be as careful of Huntingdon as he had been of the king."

Ari leaned forward, his face nearly as intense as his friend's. "What does this lion look like?"

"Matilda knows it far better than I," said Robert.

"'Tis a planchet of gold, perhaps as big as my palm." She held up her hand and traced a circle on it to show.

Steinarr abruptly turned and stalked away, leaving a wake of bitter disappointment that made Matilda reel. He went straight to the ale barrel, filled the first jar he could find and drained it, then refilled it and carried it off, headed into the forest. Tears that weren't entirely her own pricked at Matilda's eyes.

Ari watched after him, shaking his head. "He is, um . . .
I had better go after him."

"No." Matilda pushed to her feet. "I will go."

Robin grabbed at her hand. "Marian . . ."

"I have ridden with the man better than a fortnight. I
have learned to deal with his moods." She looked to Sir
Ari. "Do I have your leave, *monsire*?"

He nodded. "He will not have gone far."

"I know how to find him," she said. She filled another
jar with ale and set out to find her knight.

STEINARR HID HIMSELF in the shadow of a great silver birch,
far beyond the last trace of the colliers' axes, but it wasn't
far enough. He'd barely gotten himself settled, back against
the trunk, when he heard footsteps.

" 'Twill take more than that to get you drunk, my lord, if
that is your intent."

Ah, pillocks. It would be her. He'd been hoping for Ari.
He could start a fight and see if beating the shite out of him
might ease the ache. All this time searching, then to learn
the prize was a lion, and then a moment later . . . Fool that
he was, for that one moment, he had dared hope beyond
hope. "Go back. I am not fit company."

"I know. I brought you this anyway." Marian stepped
beneath the branches and held out a full jar of ale.

He ignored it, nursing the last of the one he already had.
She hesitated, then took a sip herself. "Did I say something
wrong, *monsire*? About the covenant piece?"

He closed his eyes and sighed. "No."

"I do not believe you."

"Believe what you want. I need some time alone, is all,
without Will Scathelocke and Ari and—"

"And me?"

"Yes." Steinarr drained the rest of his ale and set aside
the jar, then reached for the one she held. His fingers
brushed hers. "No."

She came with the jar, moving to kneel between his legs
as though she belonged there. She leaned forward to kiss

him, her tongue sweeping into his mouth, and he groaned as his senses filled with her. Her answering chuckle was low and wise, and the ale jar hit the ground as the need for her took away everything else. He scooped her breasts into his hands and found the crests, already hardened beneath the cloth.

"Mmm." She groaned into his mouth. "I thought we would never find time to ourselves again."

"It is not right, how much I want you," he whispered, even as he lifted her to straddle his legs.

"No more than I want you." She tossed her headrail aside.

"But I can offer you nothing in return." He pulled at her skirts, hauling the cloth out of the way. "I keep thinking, hoping, that I can find some way, but I cannot. You have to know that, Marian. I cannot give you anything, not even my nights."

"Then I will take your days." She pressed him back against the tree and pulled his gown up, tugged at the knot of his braies, freed him. Her fingers curled around him, and she smiled. "You do want me."

"I do." He found bare thighs and slid his hands up to where the soft hair curled at their juncture, then into the slickness that waited for him, and he smiled, too. He tugged her forward and showed her how he wanted her to move.

"Steel to flint," she whispered against his mouth, telling him she understood. Eyes closed, she glided over him, using him and pleasing him at the same time, her languid motions suiting them both. Slowly, slowly, the heat built, caught, burned. Fire danced between them, and she arched back, hard, there.

And then he was in her, not sure how he'd gotten there, but knowing he wanted to be nowhere else as she peaked, that every spasm of her body over his was a gift that he could never repay. The need to join her in pleasure dragged at him, but he fought it for the sake of watching her, the way her throat vibrated with her moan, the flush on her skin, the beads of sweat across her brow. He slipped his hand between them to feel where they fit together, how she fluttered and pulsed around him, how her release came in slow waves, amazing waves, deep and rolling as the open ocean, stronger than he knew was possible, going on and on and on until at last she spent herself and collapsed against his chest.

Pleased beyond imagining, he gathered her close and held her, sprinkling kisses over her brow between endearments in Norse and French and English because he didn't know enough words in any one tongue to tell her how sweet and warm and wonderful and necessary she was.

Slowly she came back into herself, and, without him telling her, understood once more. She began to move on him, tentatively at first, then more surely. She leaned forward to kiss him, drawing his tongue into her mouth in the same way she took him into her body. He matched his rhythm to the pace of her body over his, and the two meshed into one. Unprepared for the intensity, he felt himself begin to go up in flames.

She stilled, and he skidded back from the edge with a jolt and a groan. Her hands soothed over the bare skin of his belly. "Shh. Shh."

She hung there, still, until his heart slowed and his body relaxed, then began to move again, pushing him toward the end. His fingers dug into her hips, preparing.

She stopped again. His groan rose to a snarl, but he understood now what she was doing, though how she knew what to do, when to do it, he didn't know. Every motion, every stillness, was perfection. He held himself, waiting for her to move again.

She did, finally, dancing around him, over him, luring him higher. She pushed his gown up, her hands cool over the heated flesh she bared. He prepared himself for another stop, anticipating.

She didn't stop. Her fingers flicked over his nipples and she bore down and he came, bucking up into her, pulling her down, shattering. She was heat and light, so brilliant she burned away everything else until there was only her. Only her.

Only her, and he wrapped his arms around her and held her, determined he would never let her go. Somehow, she was going to be his. Whatever he had to do, she was going to be his.

CHAPTER 17

THE NEXT MORNING, Steinarr carried a haunch of lion-killed venison into camp and tossed it down next to the fire.

Ivetta and Edith both paled. "We cannot, my lord."

Matilda raised her head from the gown she was mending for Goda. "What are you thinking, *monsire*? Every person here could be fined and whipped for killing the manor's deer."

"Wolves killed it, and the meat was going to waste. If anyone complains, I will show them the carcass. It is on me."

"They may not believe you," said Matilda.

"I will take the risk. We must have Robin fit to ride, and he needs the meat to build his strength." He gave Edith a wink. "Go on. The sooner you cook it, the sooner we eat the evidence of the crime. The wolf's *and* mine."

Ivetta eyed the haunch doubtfully. "I have never cooked venison. I never *had* any to cook."

"Roast it as you would a cow," said Steinarr.

"I have never had a cow to roast either, my lord." Her lips worked in and out as she considered. "But I have roasted a half a sheep. It cannot be so different."

Steinarr grinned at her. "There, see?"

"We could make broth from the bones, too, after you break them for the marrow," suggested Matilda.

"Aye, and that would be good for Robin's blood as well, both the marrow and the broth." Decided, Ivetta and Edith turned their full attention to readying the venison for the fire, and Matilda went back to her mending.

Steinarr saw to his horse, then came back to break his

fast. He brought his bread and ale to sit near Matilda—close enough that his presence set her blood humming, but not so close that Robin or anyone else should notice, and they made pleasant conversation for a little while before he summoned Will Scathelocke and went off with him to work with the other men.

Matilda quickly fell back into the rhythm of the camp, doing the simple chores Edith gave her, then going off with Ivetta that afternoon to pick the last of the brambleberries. The patch Ivetta chose lay in the same direction as the birch, and as they picked, the tree's soaring crown held Matilda's attention. She wandered a bit, and before long she found herself standing beneath its branches, staring at the place she'd given herself to Steinarr the day before, aching to do it again.

What was it about this man that made her surrender so utterly and happily to lust, with so little regard to past or future? She'd given up everything she'd ever been taught, by her mother, by her father, by the Church, for a few hours with a man who told her outright he would never give her more, a man who refused to pass so much as a single night with her.

And she wasn't sorry.

They would leave in another day or so, racing with Robin back to Newstead, and there would be no more time for each other on the return than there had been coming here. Then they would find the token and the king and it would be over, just like that. Steinarr would not be bound to her any longer, and whether they succeeded or not, she would have to go to wife—if not to Baldwin, then to someone else—and that man would learn, even if no one else ever did, what she had done.

And still she wasn't sorry.

Her only regret came from the knowledge that the time was coming when he would ride away, when she would never be able to touch him again, mind or body. That alone made a lump form behind her breastbone, solid and heavy as stone, a lump not of regret but of loneliness, as deep as she'd ever felt within him. Only this loneliness would be hers, and she would carry it for the rest of her life.

"He's a strange one."

Matilda turned to find Ivetta standing in the sun just beyond, her basket of berries on her hip. "What?"

"That Sir Steinarr. I was saying, he and Sir Ari are strange ones. The way they go off each night and turn up again in the morning."

"I suppose." Matilda came back out in the sun and they started toward camp.

"Did Sir Steinarr do that while you were on your journey?"

Matilda nodded.

"And left you alone in the woods each night?"

"He found good shelter for me each night. And a friend traveled with us to stand watch against wolves and outlaws."

"That is a comfort, at the least. I worried for you, going off with him like that, and Robin was in a state, too." Ivetta spotted a cluster of fat berries on a nearby bush and veered off the path to pick them. "What is it you sought? I mean, I overheard—not of a purpose, but I heard, still. I know you seek something for Robin."

"'Tis a token he needs to claim his father's land, a small gold piece that was hidden away. We must find it in time for Robin to prove the land is his to inherit."

"Gold, eh? Lucky lad," said Ivetta, but her interest seemed to flag. They picked a little longer before she asked, "Why do you suppose they go? At night, I mean."

"Sir Steinarr has bad dreams. Violent ones. He does not wish to harm anyone, so he sleeps far from people."

"I have never heard of such a thing."

"Nor I. But I have seen many things since Robin and I left our home that I had not heard of before."

"Still . . . are you certain he tells the truth?"

"He has no reason to lie."

"If I were you, I would want to know," mused Ivetta. "He could be doing anything at night. He could be off wenching, as Sir Ari does in Retford. You would want to know if he goes off wenching, would you not?"

"I . . . It is not my business."

"Of course it is. You care for him. Perhaps you have even been lying with him . . . Ah. Ah! Look at that blush. You have, haven't you?" Ivetta laughed, delighted. "Maid no more, you are. Maid no more."

Matilda ducked her head, trying to hide her blazing cheeks.

"Do not be ashamed. Many of us are not maids the night we go to bride, though more often than not it is the groom who has done the job." Ivetta's hearty laugh took away some of the embarrassment. "Do you hope to marry Sir Steinarr?"

The question, so bluntly and unexpectedly asked, made Matilda catch her breath. She shook her head. "It is not possible."

"All sorts of things are possible. The question is, do you *want* to? Do you choose him? Do you love him?"

Whatever her arguments to Will, choice in love was for peasants, not noblewomen. Her lot, her duty, was to marry where she was told, to seal alliances and meld fortunes and produce heirs. Taking the veil, marrying Osbert, those were choices, not of love but of avoidance. But choose love? She hadn't considered it. She had not allowed her mind turn to Steinarr beyond the moment. But now that Ivetta pressed, there was no doubt. "Yes, I have come to love him."

"And he loves you?"

Matilda reached back into her memory for what she'd felt yesterday as they joined, and she nodded. "I think so. Yes."

"Then something must be done." Ivetta's face set in determination, and there was a strange, dark glint in her eyes that Matilda had never noticed before. "The first thing is to see for certain what he is about each night. Whether 'tis really nightmares that keep him from you or something else."

"And if it is foul dreams?"

"He cannot hide from them—the *mæres* find you, wherever you lay your head. But *you* can keep them away. They do not dare lie upon a man when he is held in the arms of a beloved."

Perhaps especially if that beloved—was she his beloved?—held the ability to join with his mind and soothe him. "But how, when he will not stay?"

"You must go after him. Follow him into the woods and spy to see what it is he does. If it truly is the *mæres*, you can go to lie with him, and show him that your love is strong enough to keep their evil at bay. Aye, you must go after him and pass the night at his side."

"But everyone will . . . Robin will . . . They will know."

"Aye, they will. That is the price. You must decide if it is worth the shame. If *he* is worth the shame." Ivetta peered at her basket and picked off a few leaves and stems that had mixed in, then checked Matilda's. "I think we have enough. 'Tis time to return."

They once more started back, heading toward the ring of axes and the scrape of saw blades which marked where the men were working bare-chested in the warm afternoon sun. Steinarr worked among them, handling one end of a long saw, at the other end of which stood Osbert. They were sectioning out the yard-thick trunk of a downed tree, each man's muscles straining in turn as they hauled the blade back and forth. The collier glanced up, saw Matilda, and smiled in that hopeful way of his, and that caught Steinarr's attention. He turned, grinning, his chest slick with sweat, his hair plastered to his head, and sawdust clinging to every inch of him. He was filthy. And he took her breath away.

"Aye, a hard decision, that," muttered Ivetta, and Matilda knew that there was no decision at all.

Tonight, one way or the other, she would know the truth about him.

And, she resolved, so would he know the truth about her.

HANDS ON HIPS, Ivetta stood turning circles by the fire. "Now where is it? Marian, have you seen the dipper?"

"No."

"I wonder if Goda took it. Would you mind looking? She was playing behind the far hut. See if she left it there."

"Of course." Marian set aside the basket of nuts she was shelling and went off to hunt down Goda and the ladle. She'd barely reached the corner of the first hut when a strong hand grabbed her by the wrist and pulled her between the huts. Steinarr's lips came down over hers in a searing kiss as his free hand swept over her hip and up to cup her breast.

With a groan, she pulled away. "Someone will see."

He dragged her around to the back, where Goda was supposed to have left the dipper, then backed her against the wall and kissed her again, more gently but just as thoroughly. "Better?"

"Yes." She ran her fingers into his hair and pulled him down to kiss him back. "How are you so clean? The others came back still covered with sawdust."

"Bathed." *Kiss.* "Stream." *Another*, deeper, as his hands wandered unhampered by the need to restrain her. "All I had to do was see you this afternoon, and I wanted you—though unlike you, I did not seek my own pleasure while washing."

Her cheeks flamed. "You will not let me forget."

"Why should you forget when *I* cannot?" He put his lips by her ear. "I want to watch you take yourself all the way."

"Nnn." Desire sparked through her and settled between her legs. If he were to make her do it now, she would be crying out in moments. "You are the very devil."

"That will be only the beginning. Next I will use my mouth to pleasure you again. And only then will I take you, but you must tell me how. Something else you saw in that loft that you want to try."

"Ah, God's knees." She gripped him by the ears and pulled his head back. "Stop it lest you have me looking to Osbert for relief."

He pulled his head back to look at her quite seriously. "I would have to kill him."

"'Twould hardly be fair when 'tis your fault for filling my head with such thoughts. I must go. Ivetta—"

"Ivetta sent you back here to me. The dipper was in her hand, hidden in her skirts." He pushed her headrail aside, found a favorite spot just below her ear, and ran his tongue over it until she shivered.

"Nnn. Even so, I cannot stay."

"Then just a kiss. Or two. Or three." He took them as he counted them out, then stole another before he released her. "Now tame that too-broad smile and go. I will come anon, and none will be the wiser but Ivetta."

Matilda rubbed the corners of her mouth to erase the foolish smile, straightened her headrail, and went back, trying to look innocent. "I am sorry, Ivetta. I could not find it or Goda."

"I know. Foolish me, 'twas right here before my eyes." Ivetta waved the dipper and shot her a wink and a smile.

A few moments later, Steinarr strode into camp from the opposite side of the clearing, from the same direction the other men had come a little earlier. As he passed a group of the youngest children playing, Goda popped up—she'd been there all along, no doubt—to demand something of him. To Matilda's surprise, he squatted, let Goda clamber up on his shoulders, and pickabacked her over toward the huts at a trot. His face was neutral, except for his eyes, which sparkled with mischief as he passed Matilda. "Good day, Maid Marian."

"Good day, my lord," she answered, ignoring Will Scathelocke's suddenly avid attention. She made a pretty courtesy to Goda. "And good day to you, my lady Godiva. Have you enjoyed a pleasant ride? I see you chose to wear your clothes today."

"Ladies do not ride naked," said Goda, giggling. "More, Sir Horse. And faster now."

Steinarr did two circuits of the huts at a gallop, then dropped her off near Ivetta, who sent her to fetch two bowls. "Hurry now, Sir Steinarr and Sir Ari must leave soon." She gave Matilda a significant look.

Steinarr didn't notice. "How is our young Robin today?"

"Much better, my lord," piped up Robin. "I sat up most of the day, and I walked the whole circle of the glade."

"With or without the splint?" asked Ari as he came over, tailed by Will.

"With. But I went to the privy without it. And see?" He carefully bent his knee back and forth. "I am already less stiff. I will be good to ride tomorrow."

"You have the leg," agreed Steinarr. "But do you have the strength? 'Tis one thing to sit a stool, another to sit a horse."

"He is a good rider, my lord," said Matilda.

"That is not the question. He's been overbled. Will you last out the day?"

"I will. And I will keep up with you, especially if you carry Marian behind."

"Marian is not going."

"What! Of course I am going."

Steinarr shook his head. "It will be too dangerous. By now Guy has figured out I am not bringing you back. He may even suspect I have changed my allegiance."

"If I were he, I would be set on keeping Robin from reaching the king," said Ari.

"He will surely have his own men on the roads by now," said Steinarr. "Baldwin may even be involved, searching for you. It is far too dangerous."

"I am going," she said stubbornly.

"What if I need her to solve a riddle?" asked Robin. "I am a poor reader in French or English, and my Latin is little better. And I cannot cipher at all."

"Ari reads."

"Not Latin," said Ari.

"You see?" said Robin. "I need her."

Steinarr glared at Robin. "You would put her at risk for the sake of your fortune?"

"Of course not but—"

"I am at greater risk if he fails, and you know it," interrupted Matilda. "Or do you wish to see me in Baldwin's bed? I *must* go to help."

"No," said Steinarr. "We will fare fine without you."

"And how will I fare? When you all ride off, who is to

keep Baldwin or Guy from finding this camp and carrying me away?"

"Will Scathelocke."

"One man, whom we barely know?"

"One man you barely knew is all you had for the last month," said Steinarr.

"But it was *you*, not Will," she protested.

"Hey!" said Will, offended. "I *fought* for King Edward in Wales."

"Your pardon, Will, but I have not seen you fight. I want a sword I know to defend me. Besides, if I go, I will have *all* of you to guard me."

"And you would need every man, because you would be riding into the midst of trouble. Here no one knows where you are. Here you are safe." Steinarr folded his arms across his chest. "And here you are staying."

"Sir Ari, tell him . . ."

Ari shook his head. "He is right. You are better off here."

"Bah."

"I will guard you with my very life, fair Maid Marian," vowed Will. "Even from the sheriff himself."

"Oh, shut up, Will," she said, and turned and stalked away to the fire, where she picked up the never-missing dipper and started stirring the pottage.

"Gently. You will turn it to mash," said Ivetta.

"I would turn *him* to mash."

Shaking her head, Ivetta took away the ladle and dipped out two bowls. She sliced off thick pieces of venison to lay across each bowl, then handed both to Goda. "Do you have the spoons? There's a girl. Now take it to them and be careful."

"Yes, Ivetta."

Ivetta watched her go, then turned to Matilda. "I could hear you argue, but I could not hear the words."

"He will not let me go to help my own bro—" Matilda stopped, realizing she was about to give too much away. "My own cousin. He says 'tis too dangerous."

" 'Tis only proof he cares for you," said Ivetta, smiling happily.

"Aye, he cares. He cares so much that he would leave me behind." Matilda watched Steinarr and Ari set into the food, hurrying in preparation for going off for the night. " 'Twould be better for Robin if he cared less."

"That token could be anywhere," said Ivetta. "Why do you think you can find it when the others cannot?"

"I have no such conceit. But if they do need me and I am not there, Robin may lose all."

"Ah, well." Ivetta used a pothook to lift the lid on the big pot where a berry tart baked among the coals. "This is doing well." She dropped the lid back and raked the coals back into place. "Perhaps you can convince him tonight, when you go to him."

"I am not going."

"But you must. They ride tomorrow and you will lose your chance."

"I am too angry. I am much inclined to let the *mæres* have him and laugh while they do."

"That would not be good. That would not be good at all." Ivetta shook her head, clucking disapproval at Marian. "The *mæres* are not to be mocked. They can lie so hard on a man that they press the breath out of him and leave him dead. Or they can steal his mind and make him mad as a hare. Clearly, they bedevil Sir Steinarr worse than most. Angry or not, if you care for him, you will go."

"I will think on it," she said peevishly.

"Think quickly, girl, for they take their leave." Ivetta tipped her head toward the pair, who were already handing their bowls to Goda. Ari whistled to Goda's brother, Much, who led their horses out from the pen, and with a few quick farewells, they were gone.

Matilda stood for barely a heartbeat, then dashed for the pen. She grabbed the mare's bridle, slipped the bit in her mouth, quickly fastened the buckles, and led her out.

"Help me mount," she told Much, and the snap of command in her voice made him do so without question.

"Where are you going?" hollered Robin. "Maud?"

"Ask Ivetta," she shouted and turned the mare down the path.

"IVETTA?" ROBIN TURNED toward the fire, his face a mask of concern and anger. "Do you know where she goes?"

"She goes to find out where he vanishes to each night," she told him honestly.

"Why?"

"Because she must. I told her she must."

"You, but—"

"Calm yourself, boy. There is nothing you can do now. By morning, all will be settled, and you will know, too."

"Know what?"

"Why he leaves." Ivetta smiled. "Are you hungry? Of course you are. Someone get the lad a big slice of that meat. I need a moment to myself."

She left as if going to the privy, but as soon as she was out of sight, she veered away, heading into the deep woods.

She found her body still where she'd left it, well hidden in the center of the bramble patch near where the woman and Marian had been picking earlier. It had been so easy, slipping out of one body into another. The lion's woman hadn't even noticed the difference between the simple collier's wife and her.

And yet to Cwen the difference was immense. This body felt fresh and alive and aware, as her own had not for years. It pulsated with life and desire, tempting Cwen to stay in it, to pass the night beneath the woman's husband just for the pleasure of enjoying a man once more. But she had places to be that were not a collier's camp, and she wasn't certain yet how long she could remain in another's form. She did not want to stay too long and be trapped.

This was the gift the Old Ones had given her in the bottom of the pool: the ability to borrow another's body. She'd discovered it as soon as she'd woken by the pool's edge, coughed up by the waters after they were done with her to live once more. The barest thought of the little green frog hopping by and she had been in its body, looking through its round eyes at her own form, lying immense among the reeds. Fright had pushed her back into herself, and the frog had hopped away, unharmed.

It had taken courage to try again—a bird this time, its wings strange, but not so strange as its ability to look down on her own empty body from the sky.

She'd returned after a brief flight, then practiced a few more times with other creatures, slipping back and forth more easily each time. She had tried her other powers as well, the ones she used to have, but they were still missing. The gods had not seen fit to return the lightning to her hands, or the ability to turn to mist, or to have clear knowledge of what was to come. But this new skill, this was good and useful right now, and she was well pleased. She would offer them a fitting sacrifice as soon as she found one.

She dragged her limp body out into the open and lay the borrowed one down beside it. With a simple wish, she slipped back and sat up to compose herself before the collier's woman came back to herself.

"What?" The woman looked around, confusion glazing her eyes. "Who?"

"Prioress Celestria, child. Surely you remember. We were talking, and you swooned dead away."

"Swooned. Did I? Why is it so dark?"

"'Tis late. Almost supper."

"But it . . . it was midday. I was picking berries with Marian."

"Your swoon has left you confused, my child. You were with the others and you came out here to piss, you did, just moments ago. You took a wrong turn and ended here. Let me help you rise."

"My thanks, Lady Mother." The woman shook away the cobwebs and pushed heavily to her feet with Cwen's help. "I . . . I must get back."

"Aye. You must. But you must not tell them what happened. It will only worry your husband and the others. 'Twas nothing. You do not want to worry them."

"No. No, James would only worry. Thank you, Lady

Mother. Thank you." She stumbled away, slowly at first, then more hurriedly, running back toward camp and her husband, frightened of the darkening forest.

Cwen watched her go. If she had her choice, she would linger, just to see how much the woman remembered: that would be a useful thing to know. But it would have to wait.

Just now, she wanted to find the perfect place to watch the dawn tomorrow.

The perfect place to watch as the man awoke and saw what the lion had done to the woman he loved.

IT WAS HARDER tracking Steinarr than Matilda had thought. She had to stay far enough back that neither he nor Ari nor their horses would notice—simple enough on the road, but much harder once they turned into the forest. She managed to find the marks of their passing among the leaves, though, and follow them. She had just drawn within sight when Steinarr left his stallion and set off on foot in one direction while his friend rode the other way, leading the stallion. She waited while Ari vanished into the woods, then she turned to follow Steinarr north and east, moving farther and farther from the colliers' camp and safety.

Even on foot, he moved quickly. Whether he ran away from something or toward it, she had no idea, but she urged the mare to follow as fast as she dared in the growing gloom. Still, he got away from her. A lifetime's fear of the night forest, gone for weeks now, breathed back to life as she imagined herself lost without even Sir Torvald as guard. And then she felt a tremor of something, that wild thing inside Steinarr, and she realized she could use that to find him.

She reached out, seeking, and found him just at the edge of consciousness . . . that way. She turned the mare toward it and him, anxious to find him and learn how terrible these dreams must be, that they could drive him so.

He grew stronger in her mind, and she knew she was getting close. She dismounted and tied the mare's reins to a slim rowan so she could proceed on foot, moving as carefully as possible to avoid breaking twigs. She didn't want him to know she was there, not yet, not until she saw for herself. At last she came to the edge of a clearing where she could spy him ahead. As a magpie laughed and chattered overhead, she crouched down behind a bush and peered between the leaves.

So sad, he seemed, standing there alone. And then he started pulling off his clothes. Confused, she watched him strip and stuff his things into the hollow beneath a fallen log. He moved to the center of the clearing and stood there, staring at the sky, glorious in his nakedness, the last rays of sun filtering through the trees to touch his golden skin and set it aglow. She had touched his skin that way, and the remembered heat of his body made her palms tingle. Lust rose up in her, just the way she'd felt it rise in him when he saw her in the stream, and she pressed her hands together.

"Marian." He turned, his eyes going straight to her. "Marian. No. No. You cannot be here. Go."

She rose to face him. "I am not afraid of a dream, no matter how bad it is. You will not hurt me."

"Odin, no," he begged. "It isn't a dream, Marian. Go. Run. Run away!"

The words tore from his throat in a snarl that rose into a scream. He started to turn, to run, but pain crumpled him to the ground. The scream shifted, turned animal.

Horror rooted her to the ground as his body twisted and deformed before her. His face drew into a muzzle full of teeth. A great mane of hair sprouted around his neck and shoulders, growing dark and rank. A tail sprang from his hips. His feet and hands clubbed into paws that grew long raking claws. Fur covered his body. And through it all, the creature roared its agony and she felt every tearing pain and stood frozen, screaming with him as the magpie cackled overhead.

Suddenly the pain was gone. She and the beast both dropped silent. The lion rolled to its feet, stretched and yawned, as though awaking from sleep, and then threw its head back, sniffing at the air. The great head swung toward her, the yellow eyes narrowed.

Only when he dropped into a crouch did it occur to her terrified body to move, and by then it was too late.

She was being hunted.

CHAPTER 18

RUN AND DIE.

The thought slammed into Matilda's mind, driving out the sheer panic in the last instant before she twisted to run. She froze again, trembling, forcing her body to stillness, knowing it was truth.

It wanted her to run. It wanted the chase before the kill.

"No," she whispered to herself. To it. The lion hunkered lower, legs and feet flexing, great body quivering in anticipation of the killing leap. Everything in her shrieked to be away. "No. I will not run."

She stayed there, the blood pounding in her ears so loudly she was sure the beast could hear.

No, not a beast. *Steinarr.*

She latched on to that certainty. It was Steinarr. That's why she was still alive. He existed within this creature, just the way its wildness—for she knew it now—existed within him. If she could find him . . .

She reached out.

The lion snarled as she touched its mind, its ferocity nearly knocking her to the ground. Pure force of will kept her on her feet, kept her facing it, kept her breathing. Her muscles cramped with the desire to run, she so wanted to run, but she made herself stay.

For him. For Steinarr. He was there, someplace.

Once again, she opened her mind, more slowly this time. Raw savagery inundated her senses. *Hunt. Kill. Mate. Hunger. Mine. Pain.* It all mixed together, frightening, horrible, agonizing. She whimpered under the weight of it, and the lion quivered again, ready to pounce, cat on prey.

Where are you? She probed deeper, searching for something familiar, hoping for even a fleeting touch.

Kill. Mine. Then, faintly, *Alone.*

Yes. That was he, that loneliness. It matched the stone in her own chest, and she embraced it.

"'Tis all right," she whispered. "I am here."

The great cat shifted uneasily, and then settled back on its haunches, head back, tongue out and curled, huffing at the air. She'd seen cats do that, hadn't realized they actually tasted scent. The lion was tasting for her. She breathed, sending more of her scent wafting into the air, and waited.

Food. Mine. Mate.

Yes, yours. Yours. Mate. She centered on that. *Here. I am here. Yours. Your mate.* She raised her eyes to meet the lion's golden gaze.

You. Recognition jolted through her, then spread as their minds mingled, like molten gold and molten silver flowing together. Sensations recalled, hazy and undefined, swirled through her: his, hers, the lion's. The shared release of that first blind joining. Visions of her asleep. The scrape of whiskers on her cheek as he kissed her. The invitation of her body spread before him. Rage at the man who guarded her in the night mixed with the shameful horror of having attacked him. Her taste flooding his mouth. His hardness invading her body. Whispered words. The smell of food linked inextricably with the smell of her. The loneliness, both eased and made more bitter. All of it, all at once.

The last sunlight faded, and with the descending darkness, the deep connection available through the lion's eyes dwindled away. A rumbling growl frightened her back into herself as the beast fixed on her again as prey. Dark or not, he could see her.

"You do not want this," she whispered into the blackness as she forced herself to reach out again. Ah, God, he'd nearly killed Torvald and he would kill her. The beast's hunger, its consuming wish to pounce, set her quaking with terror, but she opened her mind more. *Mine. Mate. You.* The recognition came again as she found him, deep within.

But not so deep as before. He was fighting upward. She wrapped her mind around his essence the way she'd wrapped her arms around his body for the past weeks, now offering steadiness instead of taking it, and she felt him fight to grow stronger. Slowly, the moon rose over the trees to show the lion still there; it reflected in the beast's eyes, turning them to bronze flames in the night. She met their unearthly beauty and once more permitted that strange merging. The cat's mind lay open to her, waiting, now, wary, and beneath it, Steinarr, stronger.

Him. Her mate.

You. Want you. The memories rushed forward again, clearer, keener, his desire and recollection so fierce that her body began to respond, to soften, to grow slick and wet with longing. She let it happen, knowing this was the root of the bond between them, the way they'd first touched so deeply.

And so she stayed with him, offering him a calm human center within the feral chaos of the lion's mind, until her body ached with need and with exhaustion. The night spun out around them. Stars swept the arc of the sky; the moon traveled its path. Smaller creatures of the forest skittered at the edge of Matilda's awareness, fearful of both lion and human. And still she stood, one with him.

Slowly the hours passed, evening into midnight into dawn. The sky lightened from obsidian to the almost-black of tarnished pewter then lighter still to ashen gray touched with rose and scarlet that set the birds twittering overhead. The lion's eyes turned first more ghostly as the moonlight faded into dawn, then grew substantial again as light painted his body.

There was a shift inside the beast, too, the need for mating rising up, every bit as powerful as the need to kill. Steinarr's need, turned to desperation. *Mine. Need. Mate. You. Want you. Need you. Have. Now. Naked. Now. You. Only you. Must have.*

The depth of his need crystallized hers, making it far too great to resist. *Naked. Now. Must have.* Her hands went to her laces. As the sky lightened in a wide band behind the trees, she yanked at them. Gown. Chainse. Shoes. Hose. Each garment shed called Steinarr forward more, made him stronger.

The lion, agitated, rose and paced back and forth before her, snarling, but she was no longer afraid. She could feel Steinarr clearly now, not deep at all but right behind those eyes, watching her, waiting for that instant he could have her. Ready, understanding what he needed her to give, she stripped away her linen kirtle, the last thing between them. The lion threw back his head and huffed delicately, tasting her scent, clearer now. Muskier. *Female*.

The first ray of sun split the sky, stabbing through a cleft in the eastern clouds like a fiery sword. The lion roared in agony, and its pain, Steinarr's torment, crushed her to the ground as the creature began to pulse and change. Unable to bear it, she pulled in and the remaining contact fell away. Alone, all she could see was lion, terrifying even as it shifted toward human.

The beast turned toward her and crouched to gather itself. Its roar, half-human and full of rage and pain, shook the air. Panicked, Matilda turned her back on it and scrabbled away, and then it was on her, teeth closing on her shoulder, bearing her to the ground. Only it wasn't the lion but him, or nearly him, a measure of beast clinging even as he covered her mind and body. Snarling as the last of the lion possessed her as well, she arched down and lifted her hips, cat-wise, opening to him, and he was in, a simple taking. Pure animal need.

"Mine," he growled into her ear as his weight pressed her down. "You are mine."

His hands gripped her hips, positioning her as he drove into her hard, hard, then gradually less so, less frantic, more slowly. His touch changed, the madness eased. He pulled away and rolled her over onto her back and moved between her legs. His eyes burned with such blazing hunger, she could hardly bear to look at him. And then there finally came the instant when he saw her. *Her.* "Marian, I . . ."

"Shh. I know." She reached for him, pulled him down,

sighed as he fell into her and lost himself in her body. She wrapped her legs and arms around him, squeezing a groan from him as she pulled him to her as tightly as she could. "Take me, my lord lion. I know, and I am yours."

Overhead, Cwen glared down through the magpie's bead-like eyes, watching them join as anger grew within her. If she had her rightful powers . . . But she did not, and even if she did, her body lay elsewhere, too far away to strike.

Why do you show me this? she silently questioned the gods. *Why do you give me this power, if I may not watch him kill her and know the sweetness of his grief? Do you merely taunt me to prove how bootless I am? Or is there more I do not ken?*

She took to the skies, circling once overhead to watch them swive before heading back to where her body lay safe by the sacred pool, praying with each beat of the magpie's wings that, in their wisdom, the Old Ones planned for more.

"OUR *JARL* SENT us to take a village. There were rumors of great treasure."

"I thought everyone could do it, until my father beat me for devilry."

"We killed her son, and she cursed us."

"I learned to hide it, to lie. I convinced Father it had been a game. That I had outgrown it. It was the only way to stay his hand."

"There were nine of us. One broke the curse and lived out his life as a man, so we know 'tis possible."

"I could not understand why you frightened me. And enticed me."

"Brand. Ari. Torvald . . ."

"Torvald! No wonder he felt so familiar. The stallion."

Their explanations intertwined like their limbs, a tangle of thoughts that slowly sorted themselves into a coherent truth. Questions were answered, answers questioned, talk and touch and gentle kisses exchanged. It was all good, all necessary, Steinarr knew, yet none of it truly mattered. All that mattered were Marian's arms around him, that she knew and she still held him, even in the full light of day. If he never had more, it would make the years tolerable, but please, Odin, please, let there be more.

They were still there, clinging to each other, when the mare's distant whinny of greeting announced an approaching rider. With a groan, Steinarr extricated himself from those wondrous arms to sit up. He listened a moment, then whistled one of the old signals and was relieved to hear the correct answer.

"'Tis Ari." He reached for Marian's kirtle and held it out to her, then yielded to temptation and leaned over to press final kisses to those sweet breasts before she covered them. "Stay here."

He went to pull his clothes from the log, leaving her to wrestle with the garment. By the time Ari neared, Steinarr was mostly dressed and met him at the edge of the clearing.

"Why are you so late? I waited for you at . . ." Ari stopped as he caught sight of Marian, blushing as she pulled her wool chainse over the kirtle. "How did she get out here so early?"

"She didn't. You should go back. Tell them we will be there soon."

"I don't . . . She didn't come out this morning?" Ari's forehead furrowed as he tried to absorb it. "All night? And she's still alive. The lion didn't . . . ?" His eyes widened. He slid off the horse and gripped Steinarr's shoulders. "She knows?"

"She knows." Steinarr turned to watch her draw on her hose. A grin battled its way past the lump in his throat and split his face so wide his cheeks ached. "She knows."

"And you two just . . . ? She knows, and she still will have you?" Ari's grin nearly matched Steinarr's. "She loves you."

Odin, please. He lowered his voice. "She accepts me. For now, that is enough."

"But you need her to—"

"I decide what I need from her, not you. Go on. Robin will be worried about her. Say we have been talking through the night, arguing about whether she is to go."

"Is she?"

"No."

"Yes, I am," she called.

"She is not. Get out of here, Ari. Take the stallion and see he's fed and watered and ready to go. I will bring her back on the mare. We will leave as soon as I return. Make certain Robin is ready."

Ari nodded and took off, and Marian came to stand beside him.

"Will you lace me, *monsire*?" she asked after a moment. She turned her back to him and waited.

Back. A half-remembered image from those first moments returned. He pushed her clothing aside. A darkening bruise, the shape of teeth not quite human, marked her shoulder. He touched a finger to the places he'd broken the skin and she flinched.

"Ah, sweet Marian, forgive me. I hurt you."

"There is nothing to forgive."

"But I was—"

"Animal? Aye. You were. But so was I, in that moment. It excited me as it did you."

"I could have killed you. Do you not understand? The scars the horse bears are from when I attacked Torvald. *I* put those marks on him."

She turned and cupped his jaw, her thumb caressing the line of his cheek. "No. *It* did. The beast."

"But you . . ."

"It is the lion within you that drew me from the first, even as it frightened me. Do *you* not understand?"

"It has been growing stronger."

"Aye, and the fault for that lies with me. There are times when my mind opens to you and stirs the wildness of the beast." She turned back so he could continue with her laces. "Sometimes when our eyes meet. And when we tup."

"When you come."

A wash of pink colored her neck. "Aye. Especially then."

"Do you . . . open like that when you touch yourself?" He tried to control the jealousy that rose at the idea of anyone else knowing her in that way, even by accident.

"Devil," she said. "No."

"Did it ever happen when you watched the servants in the barn?"

This time she laughed, rich and deep. "Not even a little. It happens only in your arms. I feel you then as at no other time. As with no other being, man or beast."

"As I feel you." He tied the knot and pressed a kiss to the patch of skin just above it, still glowing pink. "I did not know what it was, only that you gave me ease beyond what your body offers—though your body offers much."

She leaned her head back against his shoulder. "For the first time, I am truly glad of this ability of mine. Until you, it was only a tool—at best, an amusement—but now, it is—"

"A blessing," said Steinarr firmly.

"Aye. But only because you make it so."

"I . . ." Unable to find words in the tumble of emotions that were his, he picked up the blue gown given her by Lady Nichola. "Here." Awkwardly, he gathered the yards of cloth so she could work her arms in, then helped pull it over her head and settle it down over her body. These laces went quickly in the silence between them.

When he finished, she smoothed the gown and tested the fit. "You grow skilled at this. Perhaps I should keep you about to dress me."

"I would rather undress you." He ran his hands down, shaping her waist and hips, then up and around to cup her breasts. "I could spend all day doing nothing else. But we need to be back. We should have been on the road well before now."

"Aye. *We* should."

"Marian . . ."

"Come, my bounden knight, we will discuss it on the way." She started for where the mare was tied, and he had no choice but to follow his lady. His love.

By the time they reached the road, the tenderness of the

morning had dissolved into a heated argument that lasted all the way back to camp. She dug in her heels, every bit as willful as she had been that first day outside Maltby. The worst of it, though, was that her reasoning was sound: among all of them, she was the only one who read Latin and could cipher numerals and not just peg marks. And she knew her father better even than Robin.

"It is not safe," he insisted, his sole argument but sufficient, so far as he was concerned. "Guy is dangerous."

"I know precisely how dangerous Guy is," she said. "I have dealt with him my whole life. The reason father decided against him as heir is because he grew too free with me and made it clear he wished to be freer."

"But you're his cousin."

"Aye. But it did not stop him from trying to make me his mistress. Nor, I suspect, will marriage to Baldwin."

Steinarr growled his disgust. "Another reason to kill him."

"Another reason I want to—*need* to—help Robin."

"And for me to want and need to have you safely out of Guy's reach."

"Then keep me with you. How can I be safer than in your arms?"

"And you call me devil," he grunted as his body tightened. "But you still may not go."

They veered into the forest, and as they reached the clearing, the children came running to meet them, Goda chattering as usual. "Are you fighting? Sir Ari said you were fighting. You look angry, Marian."

"Because I am," she said, jabbing Steinarr in the side to prove her point. She slid off the mare without waiting for his help.

Robin came crutching toward her, face thunderous. "You were gone all night. Alone. With *him*!"

"God's knees, Robin. I have been alone with him for the best part of a month. What is one more night among so many?"

"I should never have let you go at all. If he has ruined you . . ." Robin glared at Steinarr.

"For Baldwin? I do hope so." She stormed off toward the fire, calling over her shoulder, "And I hope you are ready. *He* wants to leave."

"You had better not . . ." he began, but Marian's obvious vexation must have convinced him he had nothing to worry about, for he fumbled to a stop midsentence. He turned and hobbled away, muttering to no one in particular, "You had better not."

By the time Steinarr put the mare away, Marian had filled a bowl with pottage and a slab of cold venison, and as he came to the fire, she held it out to him, along with a spoon. "You are starving. Eat."

He *was* starving. All times she'd ever offered him food came tumbling forward in his mind. Of course. She knew. She'd always known. He accepted the bowl, letting his fingers skim over hers. "My thanks."

She hoisted one eyebrow. There may have been a glimmer of forgiveness in her eyes, but if so, the firm line of her lips denied it. Yet, a moment later as he gobbled down the meal, he heard her whisper to Ivetta. "You were right. I needed to go after him."

Ivetta's brow wrinkled. "Pardon?"

"'Twas a good thing to go after him. I needed to know, and now I do. I am glad you said to."

"What are you talking about? I never said for you to go after him," insisted Ivetta, louder.

"But you did," said Edith. "I heard you myself. You told her to go just as Sir Ari and Sir Steinarr rode off. And you told Robin you had said for her to go."

"That cannot be," said Ivetta. "I was not even here."

"You most surely were, woman," said James. "I saw you as I came in."

"You did not." Ivetta folded her arms across her chest stubbornly. "I was in the woods. I felt ill and lay down for a time. The prioress sat with me until I woke. We were by the brambles."

"The prioress?" Ari came into the circle. "Prioress Celestria? From the manor?"

"Aye, of course, *monsire*. What other prioress would it

be? She was there, in the woods, and she sat with me until I felt myself again. She said it was only a little, but I remember it being midday, and then suddenly 'twas almost dark."

"But you walked back with me," said Marian. "We were back well before supper."

"We all saw you," said Robin. "You spoke with me about why you sent Marian after him, and then you went off toward the privy."

"I was at the brambles, I tell you, swooned away."

"Ah, balls." Ari tipped his face skyward and switched to Norse to ask the gods, "Why trouble me with them at all, if they are of so little use?"

"What?" demanded Steinarr.

Ari motion him off to the side and lowered his voice, but kept to Norse. "While Robin was at the manor. I had a glimpse of . . . I don't know. Not a vision—I could not make one come—but a sense of something awry."

A cold sense of foreboding tightened the muscles across Steinarr's shoulders. "What does this prioress look like?"

"I never saw her. She was always gone or in prayer."

"And you saw nothing suspicious in that?" Steinarr demanded angrily.

"She's a nun. What do I know of nuns and their customs?"

Steinarr switched back to English and called out. "Robin, what does your prioress look like?"

"Black eyes. Black hair, I think, from her coloring, though of course, 'tis covered by her habit. Near as tall as me. Thin as an eel." Robin scratched his wisp of beard, grown a bit thicker over the past month, then touched the right corner of his mouth. "And she has a dark mole, just here."

"Cwen," breathed Ari. He went back to Norse. "She must have taken Ivetta's form, as she did the nurse's in Alnwick."

"And then sent Marian into the woods after me." Knowledge of what the lion could have done—would have done if Marian hadn't been able to reach him—wrenched

Steinarr's gut. "She wanted me to kill her. She wanted me to know what I had done."

"Aye. She schemes to take from us what we love. To wound us as we wounded her. I should have . . ." He looked to the heavens again. "I bled for you, and you would not show me even *this*?"

"Is something wrong, my lords?" asked Marian, coming to join them.

He looked past her to Ivetta, who still frowned in confusion and argued with James that she had not been in camp, and suddenly the weapons Guy could wield seemed less terrifying compared to what Cwen might do.

"I have changed my mind," he told Marian. "You are going with us. You, too, Will Scathelocke. Get ready. Now."

And then he went to warn Hamo Collier about the evil residing in Headon Manor.

CHAPTER 19

"**THE ABBEY IS** quiet, but the road shows heavy use since the last rain. It appears the king has come and gone."

They sat in the woods not far from Newstead Abbey, having managed the trip in two and a half days despite avoiding the roads, driven as much by Cwen as by Robin's quest. Steinarr had sent Ari off to reconnoiter, and now he was back, making his report.

Robin sagged at the news. "We are too late. I slowed us too much."

"You did fine," said Steinarr. He had, too. By the end of the first day, Robin had been barely upright and looked like little more than a corpse. But he had awakened the next morning a little pinker and willing to ride again, and had clung to the mare's back that day and this with that stubborn grit he shared with his sister. Not bad at all for a man who'd been bled nearly to death within the sennight. He might make a decent lord after all. "The king cannot have gone far. We will find him."

Ari added his agreement. "A train that large moves no more than a few miles in a day. He is nearby, likely hunting. We might have crossed paths if we'd come by the road instead of overland, but it would have done us little good."

"'Tis better this way," agreed Steinarr. "Any sign of Gisburne?"

"Not on his own, but he may have fallen in with the king. 'Tis what I would do, as well as set men along the road."

Steinarr nodded. "We will worry about that later as well. For now, we keep to our course and follow the riddles to the end. Come, we have time for the abbot today."

They approached the abbey from the forested lands behind it, circling around to the front only when they must to reach the gatehouse. The same square-shouldered monk that had greeted them before stepped out.

His eyebrows shot up when he saw Steinarr and Marian. "My lord abbot said you two might be back, though he thought it would be before this. He said to pass you in, but only if you brought the boy."

"I am not a boy," said Robin.

The monk squinted at him. "No. But you are not much of a man yet either."

"Man enough to have my sword at his disposal, should he need it to deal with insolent monks," said Steinarr.

The monk glared at him, but opened the gate. "I will fetch Abbot Talebot."

"Do that." Steinarr turned to Will. "You stay here to watch the road. I do not want to be surprised. Ari will come with Robin and Marian and me."

They soon found themselves waiting in the same small chamber as before. It was not quite so long this time, however, before the abbot came in. One by one, they knelt to kiss his ring.

"Not you, my son." He lifted his hand so Robert didn't have to take a knee. "So, you truly did break your leg."

"Aye, Lord Abbot. I broke it, and Sir Ari set it."

"I thought perhaps it was a ploy by your sister to beguile the riddle from me." He paced a circle around Robin, sizing him up. "Do you remember me, Robert?"

"You were at the Gate when my lord father and I were on pilgrimage. You shared some good wine with us, as I recall."

The abbot laughed. "Indeed. What use is there being an abbot if you cannot have good wine? That was a long time ago and you were young. I am surprised you remember."

"'Twas very good wine, Lord Abbot."

"I wonder what else you remember of Sudwell. Your father gave me a gift. Do you remember that?"

Robin's lips pursed as he considered. "Aye. 'Twas a girdle book." Robin pointed at the little book at the abbot's waist, hanging from a long tail of leather that looped through his cincture. "Not that one, but much like it."

"Very much like it, though that one was a breviary while this is a book of Proverbs." Smiling, the abbot carefully pulled the book off his belt, wrapped the long tail around the book, and held it out to Robin. "He did not think you would remember, and truth be told, neither did I. You were carving a little—what was it?—ah, yes, a little horse at the time, rather than paying attention."

"He thrashed me later for my rudeness to you," said Robin. "He never understood that I listen better when my hands are busy."

"The very reason I use these." Abbot Talebot patted a string of paternoster beads that also hung at his waist. "They will feel lonely now without my beautiful Proverbs at their side. Ah, well, Lord David said it was only lent for a time, but I have enjoyed it greatly these several years. 'Tis good I have the breviary to hang in its place, though it is not nearly so well wrought."

"If I am successful, I will bring this one back to you, my lord. In fact, if I am successful, I will have a matching one made for each of your canons."

"That would be a fine thing, though perhaps breviaries would be more useful. This was far simpler than either of us thought, was it not?" The abbot threw open the door. "Now be on your way, for you have little time. The king planned to go to Rufford and then to Clipstone. If you are quick at following your riddle, you will find him still there, otherwise, you may have a chase on your hands. The Lord's blessing on your search, Robert."

The door hardly shut behind him when Marian, who had been leaning forward in anticipation like a hound on a leash, pounced on Robin. "Show me."

"Not here," said Steinarr. "We will get well away and make camp before we run out of sun. You can read it later."

"Hold on." Ari went to the tiny shrine in the corner and relieved it of two slender candles. "If you are going to read tonight, you will need something to read by."

"Put those back," said Marian. "You cannot rob an abbey."

Ari tucked the candles inside his gown and pulled a penny out of his purse, which he laid on the little shelf. "There. That should pay for twice as many candles."

"'Twould be better if you asked," she said.

"Better to make apology afterward than to ask beforehand and risk being told no," said Ari, chuckling. "I am surprised Steinarr has not taught you that yet."

They went to collect their horses at the gatehouse and found Will and the gatekeeper monk in deep conversation. The monk looked at Robin and grinned. "Are you truly Robin Hood?"

"Will!"

"'Twas not me, my lord. He heard you call him Robin and asked."

"And how would a monk have heard of Robin Hood?" asked Steinarr.

"I am not a monk, my lord, nor Austin canon. I follow the rule of Saint Francis."

"Monk or friar, how did you hear of Robin Hood?" asked Marian.

"Since you were last here, I went to Nottingham Town on business for the abbot. There were players in the square, and after they did the mystery, they sat in the tavern and told of Robin Hood and how he was outlawed and of Maid Marian and Little John." He looked at Steinarr as though *he* must surely be Little John. "I thought it only a tale until I heard you call them Robin and Marian in one breath. And then young Will here confirmed it."

"Will here is an ass, and will be a skinned ass if I hear that story again," said Steinarr.

"And I may help you do it," said Marian cheerily.

Will went bright red. "All I said was that you truly are called Marian, my lady, and that Robin is Robin. Well, maybe I said a bit more than that. But he already knew all the stories."

Steinarr shook his head, disgusted. "Friar, I must ask you to keep silent about this. No one must know we were here."

"Especially not the sheriff, eh? I understand well, my lord, and I would not say a word. But you can be certain of that by taking me with you."

"What?"

"Take me with you. I am not bound to Newstead. I move from abbey to abbey, Fountain Dale to Nostell to Wakefield to the Fountains to here, as I please. They oft put me on the gate to earn my keep, as I am worldly while the monks and canons are not."

"We do not need a monk, worldly or not."

"But you do need a priest. Seldom have I seen a group of outlaws who need one more."

"I am *not* outlaw," growled Steinarr.

"You have no horse, Friar," said Ari.

"Will's dun horse will hold us both."

"And how would you know that?" demanded Steinarr, staring directly at Will.

"I was only boasting," protesting Will. "He is the ugliest beast in the Midlands, but he will carry two grown men at a gallop for ten mile."

"No. Come. We are leaving."

He headed toward the horses, with Marian and Robin on his heels. Ari followed along, speaking under his breath. "We could use him. One more man between Robin and Guy."

"A monk?"

"Aye, and more so if he knows how to use that quarterstaff. Did you see the man's arms? They're big as Gunnar's. He could be a bull himself."

Steinarr looked to Robin. It was time to start giving him some voice in this. "It is your quest, Robin, and your choice. What do you wish to do about him?"

"We could take him along, at the least, and see if he fits in. I need men, I know that, and I do not trust all of my father's. I want some loyal to me alone."

"We can send him back if he does not suit," said Marian. "Or leave him at the next abbey."

Steinarr turned and shouted to Will, "If you fall behind, we leave you. Both of you."

"I understand, my lord."

"As do I, my lord," said the friar.

"Then get your things," said Steinarr.

The friar held up his staff and the cross on his cincture. "These are all I own, my lord. Just let me tell the abbot."

He hurried off, and by the time everyone was mounted up, he was back.

"The abbot said he expects another curtal friar along with his Proverbs, whatever that means."

"It means we are saddled with you," said Steinarr, feeling himself mellow somewhat as Marian wrapped her arms around him.

"What is your name, Friar?" asked Robin.

"Turumbertus," said the monk. "But 'tis such a mouthful that most folk just call me Tuck."

I DO NOT recall Father ever owning a book like this," said Matilda as she and Robin paged through the abbot's book of Proverbs that evening. "I wish he had. 'Tis a beautiful thing."

Even by the thin light of the two stolen candles, the illuminations were like jewels, rich with color and sparkling with gold leaf. Images both sacred and secular twined among the text, illustrating the verses and covering nearly every inch of parchment that did not contain lettering. Heads together, she and Robin examined each leaf, looking for whatever Father might have hidden.

"I hope it is not buried in the text. It would take me days to sort through so much Latin."

"We do have Friar Tuck now."

"Aye, we do. Look, a windmill like the one in Tuxford. I wonder . . ." She reached for her scrip and dumped everything onto the grass at her feet, then began laying everything out in the order they'd found it. "Perhaps it all ties together and these things can be found within the figures."

Matilda started to turn back to the beginning to look for

familiar objects when she realized Robin had straightened and was staring at the book, grinning.

"What?"

Robin pointed at the first words of a verse. *"Benedictio domini."*

"I know no Latin, and even I know that," said Will, who was sitting nearby. "The blessing of the Lord."

" 'The Lord's blessing on your search,' " said Robin. "That's what the abbot said, just as he left."

" *'Benedictio Domini divites facit nec sociabitur ei adflictio,'* "read Matilda. "Something about adding no sorrow. Friar? Your aid, if you please. What does it mean?"

"The blessing of the Lord, it makes rich and he adds no sorrow with it," said Tuck.

Matilda looked to Robin, and he to her, each hoping the other recognized the verse, but no: they both shook their heads.

"Not the text, then," said Robin. "The illumination?"

Now it was Matilda's turn to smile as she recognized the subject. "David and Bathsheba. *Lord David.*"

"Wise King Solomon, who wrote the Proverbs, was the son of David and Bathsheba," said Tuck.

"And perhaps Bathsheba is meant as my mother. King David saw her in the bath and seduced her. Lord David first saw my mother when he visited at Hawkhurst and she was sent to wash his hair." Robin glanced sideways at Matilda, embarrassed. "I should not speak of her to you."

"It was Father who broke the vow of marriage, not she. At any rate, you confirm this must be the right page. And look at the knotwork between the columns of text." She found the scrap of parchment from Blidworth and held it against the book. " 'Tis the same design."

Robin squinted at the two pieces. "Not exactly. There is something . . ." He turned the book upside down, then followed the line down the center. "There are letters amongst the knots. S . . . E . . . E . . . Write them, Maud."

There was a scramble for something upon which to write, the ground being too grassy and she being unwilling to mark on the parchment for fear it might still hold some necessary secret. Torvald finally handed her a burned twig and a piece of bark. "M . . . E . . ." She started marking down the letters as Robin picked them out, one at a time.

" 'See me as at midday,' I know this. Me is David. As at midday . . ." She scrabbled through the oddments for the red carbuncle and held it up to peer at the page. "We found this at midday. I see a ghost of something in the red. Ah. 'Tis the token from King Richard. But there is something else. A few lines of text. I need more light."

Torvald brought a brand from the fire, Tuck lit a stick, and Will moved the candles closer, but even with much tilting and straining, none of them could make out more than a few letters. And when Torvald took his turn peering at it, she felt a strange disturbance in the steadiness that usually surrounded him, barely a riffle, but he must be rattled or she wouldn't feel him at all. For whatever reason, even though she could touch the stallion, Torvald the man usually stayed out of reach like everyone else.

"There is just not enough light," declared Robin at last. "We will have to wait for the morning sun."

"I do not want to wait."

"And yet you will," said Torvald. He quietly motioned her away from the others and she sidled off to the far edge of the firelight with him.

"You saw something in the image of our token, my lord."

"Aye. You must show it to Steinarr. But Ari first, I think."

"Why?"

"Just show it to them."

She looked out into the dark beyond the light. "Does he watch us now?"

"Not yet, but he will. He comes every night now." Torvald looked at the sky, and she knew he read the stars the same way Steinarr read the sun. "It is not so very long until sunrise. Rest now, Marian. Tomorrow will be a hard day for all of us."

*　　*　　*

"WHAT ARE YOU doing out here?" asked Steinarr as he spotted Marian sitting on a downed tree, basking in the first rays of sun like a turtle.

"Come to meet you, of course," she said as he slid off the stallion. "And to tell Sir Ari that Robin wishes a moment with him."

Ari raised an eyebrow. "Indeed? He acts more the young lordling every day."

"So he should," said Steinarr. "Go on, and keep him distracted so I can steal a moment with Marian."

"A moment only," said Ari as he turned his horse toward camp. "No taking her off somewhere."

"We would not be so foolish, *monsire*," said Marian. Yet as soon as Ari was out of sight, she moved into Steinarr's arms as though she never intended to leave them. "At last. I find I do not like traveling with others. Too many eyes. 'Twas much more pleasant alone with you, even when we had no time for bedding."

Steinarr tried to ignore the lurch of desire—difficult when she sensed his arousal and wriggled up against him. "Stop that. We need all those eyes to keep you and Robin safe. And he is probably happy to have them all watching us."

"Robin has convinced himself I am still virgin. He will be much disappointed when he finally admits the truth to himself."

"We should leave his belief intact, at least until we finish. It is only another day or two."

"Aye, I suppose. And then what?"

"I do not know." He knew what he wanted, but he had not yet figured out how to make it happen. "I cannot think until this is done. Be patient."

"Patience is not my strength, my lord."

"Nor mine, but we must practice it."

"We will start later. Right now, come with me. Robin has something to show you." She grabbed him by the hand and dragged him off toward camp. "I think it must be important. Sir Torvald said you must see, but that Sir Ari should see first."

"Why?"

"I do not know, but that is why I came to divert you. He has had time, and now 'tis your turn."

They entered camp to find Ari squatting beside Robert, looking at the abbot's book through the red stone from Blidworth. As Steinarr handed the stallion over to Will to be fed and watered, Ari looked up. Concern creased his brow, and he plucked the book and stone from Robin's hands and carried them away, heading out of camp. "Come. We must talk."

The tight way he held himself ruffled the hairs on the back of Steinarr's neck. "What is this about? Where are we going?"

"A ways." Ari kept going until they were well away from camp, then found a sunny spot. He flipped through the book to find a page, opened it out, and handed it to Steinarr.

"A king and his queen. So?"

"David and Bathsheba. From their Bible. David for Lord David and Bathsheba for Robin's mother. He figured out where it was, and Marian figured out how to read it." Ari held out the stone. "Turn the book upside down and look at it through this."

Humoring him, Steinarr held the stone up to his eye. The odd, red-tinged image of the king faded away, leaving the ghost of something else, a circle with some markings around the edge, and in the center, a square with . . .

"My *fylgja*." The earth shifted beneath his feet, as though the *nornir* had unraveled the weft of his life and begun to reweave it. *Marian. Freedom.* "That is my lion. My amulet."

" 'Tis Robin's lion."

"No. Marian said his is gold."

"The outside planchet is gold. I asked Robin. The center is silver, and ancient. Lionheart carried it as a luck piece, and he had it set in gold to give it more weight, to make it fit for a king to give as a gift."

"But . . ."

" 'Tis the treasure their father hid. 'Tis what Robin must return to Edward to secure his title."

"No. No. This cannot be." Hope poured through his fingers like sand. "Over four hundred years of waiting, just so the gods can steal it from me twice in one sennight? What did I do to so offend them? Why do they torture me this way? To bring me her, and this, and then . . . Where is it?"

"Edwinstowe. The writing below gives the riddle. Take it for yourself, Steinarr," Ari urged abruptly. "Take Marian and go get it and heal yourself."

Marian and freedom and nights in her arms. They could be in Edwinstowe today, and tonight could be the first of many nights. He could marry her. Love her. Grow old with her.

"I vowed to make Robin lord of Huntingdon. I swore it to her on my sword. A sword vow, Ari."

"Break it. I'll see to Robin. We'll settle him on the land at Alnwick. He will be fine. This is your one chance."

"It is no chance. If I steal the amulet, Marian will hate me. I will have it and lose her. Or I can keep her love and lose any possibility of a life with her." Bile bubbled at the rear of his throat. He swallowed hard and lifted his chin. "Tell everyone to get ready."

Ari looked as sick as Steinarr felt. "What are you going to do?"

"I do not know. Odin, help me, I do not know. But one thing I do know, is that I must be in Edwinstowe to do it."

CHAPTER 20

EVEN AVOIDING THE roads and circling wide to the west of Clipstone, Steinarr pushed them so hard that the bells were only ringing Nones as they reached Edwinstowe. A quick reconnoiter by Ari and Will showed that the village was free of visitors, royal or otherwise.

"Much of the village lies empty," said Will. "They may have been summoned to aid with the king's hunt."

"We can likely find the token without any challenge," said Ari, giving Steinarr a significant look.

Matilda frowned at the seething dismay that rumbled up from the man beside her. He had been like that all day, ever since Ari had shown him the image in the girdle book. The tumult in his mind had so disturbed her that her stomach had been aching all day, knotted by his strange agitation. She'd even asked to ride behind Will for a while, hoping for enough relief to get her balance back so that she could better block him out. Instead, it had only made Steinarr jealously angry, which in turn assailed her with more emotion. Reeling, she'd quickly gone back to her place behind him. His anger had faded, but the underlying distress had not.

Now he stood staring at the spire of Edwinstowe's church, just visible above the trees, his emotions swinging so wildly it felt as though his very soul were being torn in half.

She laid a comforting hand on his arm, felt the ungodly rigidity beneath her palm that had been her companion in the saddle all day. "We do not need to go now. It can wait until morning. There is yet time."

He turned to look down at her, his tightly schooled

expression masking the turmoil. "No. We go in now. Will, do you remember what I said?"

"If things go awry, I carry Marian back to Hokenall to the protection of Lord Peter and Lady Nichola."

"And?"

"I will protect her with my life," pledged Will, hand over his heart.

His earnestness made Steinarr's jealousy bubble up again even as he nodded. "Good. Ari?"

"I will see to Robin's well-being." That significant look again. "No matter what."

"No," said Robin, making all of them turn to him. "All of you are to protect Marian. You as well, Friar. My first duty, success or no, is to see my sister safe."

"She will be," said Steinarr. "But so will you. Success or no. Mount up. We must be in and out of Edwinstowe before dark."

He led them in cautiously, circling almost all the way around the village to look for watchers before picking up the narrow track that led into its center. As they approached the green, he asked Matilda to repeat the riddle.

" 'Saint Edwin rested here and watches over all. Look to the lord's heaven and find what you seek.' I think it means we must despoil another church."

"Robin?"

" 'Saint Edwin watches over all,' " he repeated. "There is surely a figure of him in the church. We begin there."

"As you will."

Moments later, they stood in the stone church, staring at a likeness of the ancient king of Northumbria who had become Saint Edwin. Overhead, the vault was black with the swirling marks of a smoky fire.

Matilda shook her head. "There is no Heaven here."

"Blasphemy," cried a disapproving voice. They whirled to find a priest, gaunt as a crow in his black, clambering up from prayer. "Blasphemy."

"You misunderstand, Father, I didn't . . ." By the saints, she would never survive the penances she would owe. She hurried forward and dropped to her knees at his feet, grabbing his hand to kiss. "I only meant the roof was burned. Forgive me, Father. I said it poorly."

The priest looked somewhat mollified. "It is not mine to forgive. You must ask God's mercy tonight in your prayers. And say a decade of Pater Nosters."

"Yes, Father." How long had it been since she'd said nightly prayers? A month? How many Pater Nosters would *that* cost her? "When was the fire?"

"Only this spring. We were fortunate that it was mostly smoke and that the flames were put out before the damage was too great. God willing, it will be put right soon. The king has granted us license to cut ten large oaks to pay for the repairs."

"What was it like before the fire?" asked Robin.

"Like?"

"Was it perhaps plastered or painted?"

"No. Just stone. When it is scrubbed clean once more, you will be able to see the fineness of the masons' work."

"What about the manor?" asked Robin. "We heard a tale of a fine painting of Heaven here in Edwinstowe—that is what my cousin referred to—and since we passed through, we hoped to see it. I assumed it was the church, but now I think perhaps it was . . . the hall?"

"Lord Ulmar's solar. His lady had the vault painted with a depiction of the heavens, blue like lapis stone, with stars and the moon and even a fine comet, which the king added on his last visit to please the lady.'

Matilda could barely contain herself. "The king?"

"Aye, my lord. He told her it was meant to be the great comet that portended the coming of King William from Normandy."

"That must be what we heard of," said Robin, more calmly than Matilda would have been able to manage. "Do you think the lady would show it to us?"

"She would if she were here, but she is at Rufford waiting upon Queen Eleanor, while Lord Ulmar hunts with the king. But the steward will surely let you in. Lady Joanna is quite proud of it—too proud, perhaps, for the good of her soul—and enjoys having others see it."

"A fine idea," said Robin. "Pardon us, Father. We must take our leave. We have just enough time to see this marvelous scene and reach Clipstone before dark."

Outside, Marian slipped her arm into his. "I fear I have set a poor example as sister, Rob. You lied quite well in there. And to a priest."

"I told no lie," he said. "I just did not tell the truth."

"A fine line," she said, and gave him a little squeeze. "Well done."

He rolled his eyes, but his grin said he enjoyed her teasing praise. "Sir Steinarr, I think we must all play servant to you and Sir Ari. Get us into Lady Joanna's solar."

Once more Matilda felt the upheaval in Steinarr's spirit, but he nodded.

"Will, I want you to stay in the yard with the horses as our watch. Can you whistle like this?" Steinarr blew the low but penetrating pipe of a bullfinch, and Will copied it. "Good. If there is any sign of trouble, if you think there *might* be any sign of trouble, whistle twice, then get to Marian and get her away."

The steward was as pleased to show them to the solar as the priest had said, and they followed him through the hall. Robin leaned on Tuck's sturdy arm for support as they climbed the narrow wooden stairs.

"Here, my lord," said the steward, throwing the door open. "You see it is a very fine work."

Matilda gasped as she saw it. The entire vault of the solar glowed in deepest blue, with silver-leafed stars sparkling around a clear white moon. But her eye went straight to the comet, a magnificent star of sparkling gold trailing its fairy-dust tail directly overhead. The heavy gold leaf shone so brightly that it took Matilda a moment to make out that the center of the star was a round of gold, about the size of her palm. She could not see the lion in the middle from there, but it had to be her father's planchet. She had to bite her tongue to keep it to herself.

The problem was, it was also some four or five yards off the ground, well above the thick timber beams that crossed the chamber overhead. She glanced to Robin and saw him pale. On his other side, Tuck watched him a moment, then looked to her. She glanced at the comet, and he nodded.

"Well then," said the steward, ready to lead them back out.

"It speaks to me of Heaven's greatness," said Friar Tuck. "By your leave, my lord, might we take a moment's prayer beneath this glorious roof?"

"A fine idea, Friar," said Steinarr, then to the steward, "Your lady would not mind?"

"No. No, of course not. She would take great pleasure in knowing it inspired such piety. Take your time, my lord. I will send up bread and wine for after."

"Kind, but unnecessary," said Steinarr. "We will pray and then be away. I will tell Lord Ulmar of your kindness on his behalf when next I see him."

The little group gathered around Tuck as though to prepare for prayer and the steward retreated, saying his thanks. No sooner had the door shut than they all gathered below the comet.

"Boost me up," said Ari. "I can reach it."

"No, I go."

Everyone turned to Robin at once. "Do not be foolish." "Your leg." "There is nothing to hold to for balance."

Robin set his jaw. "This quest was meant for me, yet I have done nothing in it."

"That is not your fault, Rob. Father should not have sent you up a rotten tree."

"No, but this is a sturdy beam, not a rotten tree. He meant it to challenge my fears. If I cannot do at least this much, perhaps I do not deserve to be lord." He turned to Steinarr. "I will need your aid, *monsire.*"

HIS AID? HELP Robin get what he so desperately wanted for himself? Steinarr felt his face drain of color. He nodded, unable to speak.

"Tuck, guard the door." Ari came over to stand beside Steinarr, offering some support by his presence. "We will put you up there, by the wall, Robin. You can use it to stand, then make your way to the center." He put his hands out to link arms with Steinarr to make a step.

Reaching deep for the wherewithal, Steinarr shook his head. "He can climb me, like we used to do to go over palings. It will be easier with that leg."

He turned and braced himself against the wall, arms locked and one knee bent to make a step. With a few words, Ari directed Robin where to put his feet. A stiff scramble put Robin up on Steinarr's shoulders, within reach of the beam. Steinarr straightened to give him the extra inches, and Robin wrapped his arms around the beam and swung his good leg up and over. He clung there, panting with effort, for so long it appeared he would go no farther.

Freeze, willed Steinarr. *Give up. I will get the piece and it will be mine to take by right, along with her.*

"Robin?" Marian's voice cut through the fantasy.

"I am fine." Slowly, Robin pulled himself up onto the beam, then gathered himself and sat up, pressing his back against the wall. "I can do this." He steadied himself and slowly pressed to his feet. He put his hand up and touched the vault. "'Tis not so high as it looks. I can reach it easily."

"The blue must make it seem higher," said Ari. "Keep one hand on the roof and work your way out."

Step by tentative step, Robin edged out on the beam. Steinarr watched with such intensity that all else dropped away, everything but Robin and Marian, her eyes round with worry as they flickered from Robin to him and back again. He prayed she wouldn't reach out with her mind, knowing his hold on himself was so fragile that her touch would shatter his will like the first thin ice on a pond.

Finally, Robin stood directly below the comet. He felt around the center.

"There is an edge." He reached for his knife. The motion threw him off-kilter and he swayed.

"Rob!" Marian's gasp launched Steinarr forward, arms out to catch him.

But Robin pressed both hands to the roof, just catching himself. He froze there, trembling and bloodless, for a long while before he moved again, more carefully. Pulling his knife from its sheath, he dragged the tip around the golden round. Blue plaster dust sprinkled down over Steinarr and Ari like falling sky.

And then the round came away in Robin's hand. He bobbled again and dropped to his knees, flattening on the beam to lie there, clinging, breathing hard. "I cannot deal with the token and with coming down, both. Sir Steinarr, catch it."

And as simply as that, Robin dropped the planchet into his hands.

He didn't even have to flip it over. The little lion he had not seen since the day Cwen had ripped it from his neck winked up at him, an ancient design of age-darkened silver set within a round of royal gold. *Mine.* His heart thundered in his chest. He looked up to see Marian smiling at him, reaching out. *Mine. They are both mine, and I am free.*

Ari gave Steinarr another of those looks. *Take it*, his eyes said. *Go.*

Odin, what do I do?

"Some help, if you please, *messires*."

"Make your way to the wall," said Ari. "And hurry before that steward comes back."

"I do not think that will be a problem, my lord," said Tuck by the door. "I just heard Will whistle. I think we have company."

"Down, Robin. Swing off. We will catch you." Steinarr slipped the planchet into his gown, letting the solid weight of the gold lay against his belly as he and Ari moved into position.

Robin wrapped his arms around the beam and carefully levered himself off, lowering his legs so he hung in midair. His bony arms strained with the effort. "Help."

"We have you. Let go."

Robin dropped, landing awkwardly to protect his bad leg, and Marian stepped forward to give him a quick hug. "I knew you could do it."

"Go," urged Tuck.

They pounded down the stairs and out past the bewildered

steward. A quick check showed Will still alone in the yard. He waved them forward. "Hurry. Riders come."

They dashed for their horses. Ari flung Robin up on the mare and Steinarr boosted Marian onto the stallion, but it was too late. A small band of horsemen appeared in the gate, Guy's red and yellow standing out in the center.

"Get the boy," ordered Guy. "Kill him."

The first rider swept toward Robin. Steinarr threw himself into his path, startling the horse so it reared. He dragged the man off and tossed him against the wellhouse, where he crumpled. Ari disposed of another rider in similar fashion, while Tuck stepped forward with his quarterstaff and simply swept the next off with a deadly swing.

The remaining men dismounted and charged forward with weapons drawn. Drawing their swords, Steinarr and Ari each took on two men, while Will stepped forward to put himself between Marian and a big fellow wearing Baldwin's colors. Steel rang as they flailed and parried.

Steinarr took down one man with a quick cut to the leg. The fellow screamed and bright blood sprayed across the dirt. With a roar, the other kept coming. Steinarr blocked first one blow, then another. He stepped in with a flick of the sword to disarm the man, but slipped in the blood. As he went down, the man raised his sword high to strike. Steinarr ducked under the blow, and as the fellow spun to follow, brought his sword around underhand. The tip caught the man from below, laying open the underside of his arm from armpit to elbow and sending his sword flying from nerveless fingers. He sagged to the ground in a heap next to Ari's wounded man, wailing and clutching his arm. Baldwin's man went down with a scream as Will's sword bit into his shoulder. Another skull rang under Tuck's staff.

Steinarr dealt with another man, sending him spinning into the quintain head first. "Will! Get her out of here."

"Aye, my lord." Will dashed for his mount.

Steinarr spun, searching for Guy. He spotted the rooster and barreled toward him. But Guy was headed for the stallion, and before Steinarr could reach him, he had snagged

the reins and dragged Marian off. She landed with a thump
in the dirt and Guy hauled her to her feet, locking his arm
around her waist to hold her before him as a shield.

Steinarr skidded to a stop, sword at ready. "Everyone
stay back."

"*Fils a putain.*" Cursing, Marian struggled against
Guy's arm. "Turn me loose, you dog's turd." She kicked
backward and connected with his shin.

He grunted in pain, then brought his sword up to her
neck. "Stay, cuz, lest you cut your own throat." The point
bit into her skin and she stilled. "I am going to have to train
that mouth to better suit me."

Steinarr stepped forward, shifting his sword. "You will
not live that long."

"Oh, I think I will. The sheriff is on his way. When I
heard you had ridden into Edwinstowe with the bastard, I
sent a man to him. He hunts not far from here. I do not like
betrayal, la Roche. And neither does the sheriff."

"I wonder how he feels about being lied to."

Bright pink spots formed in Gisburne's cheeks, making
him appear feverish. "There was no lie. The boy is a bastard
and not fit to be lord of a kennel, much less Huntingdon."

"And you are?" sneered Marian. She kicked at his leg
again.

"Shut up." He jerked his arm tight and she gasped for
breath.

And suddenly Robin was flying through the air,
launched from the back of the mare as she galloped past.
He hit Gisburne square on, dragging his sword arm aside.
Marian popped free and Steinarr caught her. Robin hit the
ground with an oof, but rolled up to his feet.

Guy turned on Robin with a roar, and they grappled,
barely an instant, and then there was the sound of a blade
driving into flesh and a bubbling exhalation of air.

"Robin!" Marian lurched forward. Steinarr stopped her
and shoved her behind him, and he and Ari stepped forward, swords ready.

Guy wavered and slowly folded to the ground, Robin's
knife buried to the hilt between his ribs. Robin stood over

him, shaking, his face a mask of fury. "You will never touch her again."

Friar Tuck rushed forward and dropped next to Guy. Hurriedly pulling a flacon of holy oil from his little scrip, he spilled a few drops into his palm, touched his thumb, and smeared a mark across Guy's forehead. "*Per istam sanctan unctionem . . .*"

Through the rite, Guy's eyes fixed on Robin. "Bastard," he whispered as Tuck touched oil to his eyes, his lips, his ears, his palms. "You are no lord."

Robert leaned down as the last of Guy's breath frothed the blood around the blade. "But I will be. And you can carry that knowledge with you to Hell."

He straightened, and Marian pushed between Steinarr and Ari and threw her arms around his neck, weeping. "I thought you dead."

"So did I." He gave her a rough hug, then set her away, and it was as if the last vestiges of boyhood had vanished as the light faded from Guy's eyes. "We must go. I need to get to the king before word of this does."

"I hear more riders coming," called Will.

"The sheriff," said Steinarr.

"Go," urged Ari. "I will see to him."

Steinarr looked at Marian, then at Robin, who had earned his right to lordship twice over. "Aye. You will."

He reached into his gown and fished out the planchet. He looked at his lion one last time and pressed it into Robin's hands. "Your token, my lord Robert. Carry it to Edward, and do well for your sister and your people."

He kissed Marian fast and hard, then whistled for the stallion and swung up in the saddle.

Marian grabbed his leg. "Where are you going?"

"Giving you and Robin the time you need to reach Edward." He looked to Robin. "Raise the hue and cry, as if I were the one who killed Guy. The sheriff will chase me and you can race to Clipstone and the king."

"But you—"

"They come," cried Tuck. "Ride!"

"Take care of them, Ari." Steinarr wheeled the horse out

the gate and headed north, and behind him, the cry went up. "Murderer! Murderer! Halloo. Stop the murderer!"

He slowed just long enough to be sure the sheriff's men took up the chase, then put the spurs to the stallion and hared off, racing both them and the rapidly setting sun into the forest, certain that he was a fool.

But a fool with a piece of his honor back. And perhaps a fool that Marian could love.

"WHO GOES THERE?" demanded a nervous voice.

"Only a poor traveler, robbed by a madman." Torvald stepped out of the darkness of the forest night into the circle of firelight.

"You are naked, man," exclaimed one of the soldiers.

"Aye. He stole everything. My horse. My purse. My clothes. Even my breeks."

"Send that fellow over here to me," commanded a voice from the far side of the fire.

"Yes, my lord." Torvald made his way around the circle, then bowed to the well-dressed man lounging beneath a tree. "Would there be a spare cloak among your men, my lord? 'Tis a cold night."

"Find him some clothes. Do you know who I am?"

"Aye, I have seen you. You are the lord sheriff." Someone tossed him a cloak and Torvald pulled it around his shoulders.

"Good. Who robbed you?"

"A big fellow, gold hair, dressed in green."

"Was he riding a horse?"

"Aye, a fine white stallion. And yet he took my poor brown mare." A short gown was produced and Torvald pulled it on and replaced the cloak. "I do not know why he'd want either my clothes or my horse, my lord. Neither were as fine as his."

"He is a murderer, running from the gallows. He likely looks to disguise himself."

"A murderer. Then I will count myself lucky to be freezing, for it means I am still alive." A pair of chausses were passed across the circle, and Torvald sat down to pull them on. "I suppose no one has extra breeks or shoes? No. Well, I am grateful for what I have."

"Which way did he go?"

Torvald looked around, then scratched his head as though working it out. "That way, my lord. North by west. And if he wears my clothes, he will be in blue and yellow."

The sheriff nodded, his beliefs confirmed. "What are you doing so deep in the woods alone?"

"I did not start alone. I am headed to work the hunt at Clipstone, but I became separated from my companions. And then that madman robbed me. I have been walking a long while, trying to stay warm."

"Mmm." The sheriff considered him. "You may have a place by our fire. We will be on our way before dawn, but you will be safe for a few hours." He snapped his fingers at one of the men. "Give the poor devil some food."

"You are most kind, my lord. I will say a prayer for you when I reach Clipstone."

Torvald took a place by the fire, enjoying the bit of bread and ale that the men shared. As they settled down to catch a few hours of sleep, he wrapped his borrowed cloak around his shoulders and eased back. A long while later, he heard some creature moving through the brush, far beyond the fire, headed south, and hoped it was the lion. He wasn't sure Steinarr had enough control over the beast, but perhaps so.

Sometime before dawn he would head south as well, and leave these new clothes in an obvious place in the hope Steinarr would find them. A mile or two north and west, the sheriff's men would find another, more obvious pile of clothing, the abandoned green garb belonging to the supposed murderer of Sir Guy of Gisburne. The white horse would be gone, of course, but they would follow a false trail north until it got lost among the tracks on the Mansfield road.

And by sundown tomorrow, or perhaps the day after, they would give up the chase, certain the outlaw had escaped into Yorkshire, never to be found.

*   *   *

"THAT I WILL hold only to thee, my lord and king, and to thy successors against all others . . ."

Matilda stood in the church at Edwinstowe, listening to Robert recite the vow of fealty to the king. He had already made his pledge of homage, and now, hands pressed to the Gospel, was confirming the duties he owed the Crown in exchange for the lands at Huntingdon and Loxley.

As the lengthy vows stretched out, she glanced around the chapel. The presence of so many great barons of England at the ceremony—all those hunting with the King—assured that no one would challenge Robert's right to hold the title. He even had men of his own in attendance, or *two* men, at least: Will stood by, calling himself Will Scarlet to avoid arrest, but ready to do homage, and Tuck had agreed to serve as chaplain to Huntingdon.

But the face she most wanted to see was not there. Three full days had passed, and still neither he nor Ari, who had ridden off after seeing her and Robert to Clipstone, had turned up.

Robert finished his vows, received the king's acceptance, and rose to be presented to the waiting barons. She stood off to the side between Will and Tuck, watching her brother, now Lord Robert, make his way between the rows of powerful men.

And that's when she felt it: the tremor that she'd been waiting for all these days. She searched the chapel and spied two white-hooded monks slipping into place at the back of the crowd. How had she never noticed the smooth way his limbs flowed when he walked? Like a cat. She tried to stay calm, but she couldn't help the grin that spread across her face as relief flooded her body. Relief and desire and longing, not all hers. He raised his head, just enough to meet her eyes from beneath the hood.

And then suddenly an arrow of black and white feathers shrieked through the open door and struck at Steinarr's head, raking the hood back just as every man turned toward the noise.

"You!" said Gervase de Clifton. "Block the door. Arrest that man."

Steinarr and Ari threw aside the monks' robes and reached for their swords, but the screaming bird skimmed past Steinarr's head again, then veered toward Ari's face, claws out. Ari threw his hand up just in time, and the bird tore into his palm, beating and tearing at him as though possessed by a demon. With a shout, he snatched the bird out of midair and flung it aside.

In the heartbeat they were distracted, the sheriff's men acted. The door slammed shut and a dozen men encircled them, weapons raised. The bird circled over their heads, cackling like a mad thing.

"Hold!" shouted Edward over the tumult. "You arrest men in a Holy Church and during a royal ceremony? Explain yourself, my lord Sheriff."

"My apologies, Your Grace, but one of these men killed Sir Guy de Gisburne." The sheriff strode toward the front of the church, signaling his men. As the magpie sailed up into the vault of the church to perch, four sturdy men dragged Steinarr and Ari forward and forced them to their knees at the king's feet. Matilda started forward, but Robert stopped her with a warning look.

The sheriff grabbed Steinarr by the hair to force his head back. "This is the man known as la Roche. He killed Sir Guy, then escaped us through the woods."

"Alas, I did not, Your Grace," said Steinarr. "That is, I did lead the sheriff and his men on a merry chase, but I did not kill Gisburne, as often as I planned to."

"Planning murder may be a sin, but 'tis no crime," said the king. "No more than planning a marriage is the same as tupping your wife."

The priest flushed, but Friar Tuck laughed aloud, along with most of the rest of the watching crowd.

"And it happens," said Edward, "that I know who did kill Gisburne, for he has already confessed to me."

De Clifton's face darkened. "And who is that, Your Grace?"

"Me," said Robin clearly. "I killed him."

"Then seize *him*," ordered the sheriff once more, and his men surged forward.

The king held up a finger, and everyone froze once more. "Hear his story first, before you act."

Robert stepped forward, his limp still obvious, but his head high. "My cousin, Guy, was intent on stopping me from completing the task the king and my lord father set me. He attacked, and when my companions beat back his men, he took my sister as hostage. So I fought him and, in the fight, killed him."

"But you brought the hue and cry against La Roche!" said the sheriff.

"To make you ride past, so I could reach the king."

"I told him to do it, my lord," said Steinarr. "Since you were the one who set me to help Sir Guy to stop Robin, er, Lord Robert, I feared you were also working to keep him from the king."

"Eh? I had not heard this part of the tale." Edward frowned at the sheriff, who paled. "I will have your explanation of this later, de Clifton, and it had better be satisfactory if you wish to stay sheriff. Can any man here speak to the truth of Lord Robert's story?"

"I am no man, Your Grace," said Matilda, "but it is the truth." Will and Tuck spoke up to agree.

"She is his sister," protested the sheriff. "And they are his men. They would support him, truth or not."

"I am neither his sister nor his man, and 'tis still truth." The steward from the manor stepped forward. "Your pardon, Your Grace. I saw the other knight launch the attack and then wield the lady as shield in his cowardice. The boy . . . his lordship, that is, attacked in her defense, and the other knight died in a fair fight. But these same knights did damage to my lord's house here in Edwinstowe. They hacked away the golden comet you gave my lady, Your Grace. I would seek recompense on my lord's behalf."

"Um." Edward flushed slightly. "That would be ours to repair. I fear we helped set our new young lord on that path and left him little choice in it. Repairs will be made at our expense. So, where were we?" He rubbed his hands together, savoring the moment. "Lord Robert, I pardon you in the death of Sir Guy and declare it due to Guy's own misadventure. Sir Stee—"

"Steinarr."

"Sir Steinarr." Edward pronounced it carefully, then frowned. "Are you one of our knights?"

"No, Your Grace. A knight, but not yet of England."

"Are you willing to become one?"

"'Twould be my honor, Your Grace."

"Well, then, you are also pardoned, though I am not certain of what. Leave him be, de Clifton."

The sheriff glared down at Steinarr, but nodded and released his hair. "Yes, Your Grace."

"What about you?" Edward asked Ari. "Who are you?"

"Sir Ari, Your Grace." Also freed, he wrapped his hand in the hem of his chainse to staunch the bleeding where the bird had torn his hand open.

"And what have you done?"

"Helped raise the false hue and cry. And helped Steinarr elude the sheriff."

"Pardoned. Is someone recording all this?"

"Yes, Your Grace," said a scribe, glancing up from the wax tablet where he was scratching madly. "I will have the proper documents drawn up for your seal."

"Good. I am feeling most generous this morning. Is there anything else?"

Matilda, who had been watching with a mix of concern and bemusement, saw her chance. She took a deep breath and stepped forward. "I have a boon to ask, Your Grace."

Edward turned, smiling. "And what would that be, fair Matilda of Huntingdon."

"I would like you to order that knight"—she pointed at Steinarr—"to marry me."

"Marian, no!" Steinarr shot to his feet. "You know I cannot."

She ignored him and spoke directly to the king. "He seduced me to lie with him with false promises, and then he rode away. I am ruined, and I wish justice."

"As do I, her brother," said Robin.

Steinarr gaped at them, stunned. By the gods, she had Robin in on this, and he didn't even know about the curse. "Marian, do not do this."

"Who is this Marian?" Edward looked from her to Steinarr.

"He called me that as we lay together, Your Grace. 'Tis a sort of eke name."

The church echoed with laughter. Gossip would fly for years, and she didn't care. She didn't care, and she wanted to marry him, and Steinarr stood there with his blood racing so loudly it sounded in his ears like the lion's roar.

"Is this true, *monsire*?" asked the king.

Steinarr slowly nodded. "Aye. It is, Your Grace."

"So you admit you seduced her?"

"Aye, but I cannot marry her, Your Grace, much as I do care for her."

"Why not? Are you already married?"

Steinarr hesitated, knowing he could lie and say yes and end this. And yet Marian's eyes begged him not to. He felt himself sliding into the green, into the solace of her mind's touch. "No."

"Are you sworn to the Church as monk or priest?"

"No, Your Grace, but I—"

"Are you kin to her, within the sixth degree?"

"No, Your Grace."

"Then there is no impediment. You *will* say vows to her. Now. Before us all. That is my command as king."

Marian stepped forward and held out her hand. "'Tis all right," she whispered. "All will be well."

And so Steinarr found himself standing before the king of England, stumbling over the words to take Matilda Fitzwalter for wife. A dream. It was a dream and a nightmare and a prayer all mixed up together. He would not let his eyes leave hers, for fear that it would all turn to smoke and ash.

Then it was her turn. "I, Matilda, do take you, Steinarr Fitzburger, as my husband and my lord, to have and hold, in sickness or health, for as long as we both shall live."

"A ring, *monsire*?" said the priest.

"I . . . I have none. I have nothing. Marian, are you certain of this?"

"'Tis too late." Her smile brimmed with confidence and mischief. "You have already taken me. They all heard you."

Laughing, King Edward twisted a ring off his little finger and handed it to Steinarr. "This will do. A gift to you, for which I expect you to do homage to the crown of England."

"Yes, Your Grace." Still holding her eyes, he slipped the heavy band on her finger. "With this ring I do wed thee and make thee mine." *Mine. My mate. Now.* The lion stirred, and Marian's eyes widened in recognition.

"So, it is done. Lord Robert, I trust that you will see this knight is well situated to care for your lady sister."

"Of course, Your Grace. I have lands in mind already."

"As do I. Gisburne has no heir and his estates need a new lord. But I will deal with that later as well. Now, we hunt. I have heard of a great beast seen to the north, toward the crags. Some sort of cat, I am told. I wish to seek it out."

Steinarr looked up, startled. Him. The king was hunting him and didn't even know it. A laugh rose up from his belly, and he had to bite his tongue to hold it back. At his side, the corner of Marian's eyes twinkled, and she pressed her lips together tightly and squeezed his hand.

The buzz of gossip and excitement carried the barons toward the door, Edward with them. "Are you coming, Lord Robert?"

"Anon, Your Grace. I would have a word with Sir Steinarr in private."

"As you wish. You, too, Father. Let them speak."

It took a few moments for the church to clear. The last two out were Friar Tuck and Will, who pulled the door firmly shut behind them, clearly following orders from Robert.

"You are mad," said Steinarr to Marian. "You know what I am."

"Aye. I do. And so does Robert."

"I told him," said Ari. "He needed to know."

"You were willing to give up your one chance to be healed of this terrible curse for my sake," said Robert.

Steinarr's eyes locked on Marian's fingers, curled into his, a king's ring on her finger marking her as his. "I told her I would. It was yours, Robin. My lord."

"No. I only borrowed it for a little." Robert opened a purse at his waist and pulled out a round planchet of gold. "In truth, it is yours."

A furious screech overhead made them look up just as the magpie swooped past one last time before it vanished out the open arch of the bell tower.

"Crazy bird," said Robert and turned back to Steinarr.

IMPOTENT TO STOP what was about to happen and unwilling to watch it, Cwen sailed out into the sun.

I am a fool, she thought as she flew back toward the cave where her body lay waiting. The mention of gold had made her dismiss too easily the possibility that the token was the lion's amulet, and now one more of them had the chance to slip through her grasp without the satisfaction of vengeance.

And yet she felt strangely well as she soared over the forest, stronger than she had in years, even in this delicate creature's body. She skimmed the treetops, reveling in the freedom of flight, hers in this strange gift from the gods.

It wasn't until she reached the cave and slipped back into her own body that she understood why she felt so strong.

Blood.

In her rage, the bird must have torn the seer's hand open, for his undiluted blood, rich with his life force and magic, streaked the creature's breast, thick over the same place her own wound was.

"You have brought me a gift, magpie." She put her hand out and the bird willingly hopped up onto her finger. Cwen stroked the fine feathers, gathering the clotting blood onto her finger. "My thanks, little one."

She let the bird flutter away, then opened her gown and spread the blood over her wound. Warmth slowly spread out from the place that had been cold so long. She drew in a sharp breath and let it out on a sigh.

Yes. She threw her head back as power flowed back into her, sweet and rich, and she felt herself begin to heal at last. The raven had no idea what he possessed, what power the gods would grant him if he only had the courage to ask. No, he was too frightened of it.

She was not frightened. She was Cwen. If he wouldn't use the power, she would.

There were, after all, seven of them left. They would all pay, especially the bear. And now that she shared this blood link with the raven, she could use him to help.

With a smile, she turned toward the little magpie, sitting on a nearby stone. Chortling softly, the bird met her black eyes with its own. Cwen tapped her shoulder, and the bird flew up to take its place as her familiar.

"Come, my pet." She stepped out into the sun and drew in the clean forest air. "We must find ourselves a new home. I tire of being a nun."

STEINARR STARED AT the gold-encrusted lion in Robert's hand, not comprehending. "You had to give that to the king."

"I had only to present it to him. Not give it. He handed it back in nearly the same moment."

"But I thought . . ."

"I know. I thought he would keep it, too, but he said it is Huntington's. And now it is yours." Robert pressed the planchet into Steinarr's hand and curled Marian's fingers around both. "As is my sister's heart."

Odin, please. "Is it?" he asked Marian, uncertain of anything beyond his own fear of the answer. "Do I have your heart, even knowing what I am?"

"Even knowing what you are." She lifted the planchet and pressed the lion to the center of his chest. "I do love you."

Pain ripped through Steinarr, like the changing but

worse, a thousand times worse, and he felt the lion claw its way up. "Run."

But they stayed, Ari and Robert and, most of all, Marian. He arched back and forward, fell to his knees, screamed his pain, and she stayed with him. Fury, hunger, the need to kill, mate, hunt, it all spun out of him in ropes of black smoke that looped around his chest, squeezed the air from his lungs, strangled him.

"I love you," she repeated, tears choking her voice. More pain hammered him to the ground. A scream tore from his throat and rose into a roar.

And then it was gone, silent, and he was alone in his body. He shook, terrible wracking spasms, like tertian fever. Marian wrapped her arms around him, those wondrous arms that would be his forevermore, except not forever, but just for one glorious lifetime full of nights.

"'Tis all right," she whispered a long time later as the shaking finally stopped. "'Tis all right."

And thank the gods, it finally, truly was.

Epilogue

"**AND SO ROBIN** Hood took Maid Marian by the hand and asked her to be his wife. And with the king's leave, they were wed that very day on the step of Saint Mary's Church in fair Edwinstowe before Will Scarlet and Friar Tuck. And they lived happily ever after as man and wife in the Greenwood, amongst their merry men."

"I still think it strange you used Uncle's name instead of Father's," said Ranulf.

"Steinarr Hood does not have the same ring," said Ari, closing the small book of tales he'd been working on for these last years. He'd carried it with him from Sussex, where he and Brand searched once more for Cwen.

"I like the story, Sir Ari," said little Susanna, standing up to nestle a too-small daisy crown into his curls. "I like all the stories you tell."

"You are a wise woman."

"But it seems so . . . *wrong*," said Ranulf. "In truth, Robin and Marian are brother and sister."

"But only we know that," said Ari. "For everyone else, the names *Robin* and *Marian* are just names. Well-loved names," he added with a bit of pride. And destined to be even more well loved in a century or two, if he had anything to say about it.

"Father doesn't love them," said Emma. She was eight, and always quite certain of what Steinarr did and didn't like. "He says we shouldn't use real names when we tell stories. It gets people in trouble. He says you got him in lots of trouble using his name in made-up stories."

"Well, a little," Ari admitted. "But we always laughed afterward."

"Do you think they're ever going to finish their nap?" asked Susanna.

Ari glanced back toward the clearing where the elf house stood a few hundred paces away. "Soon. But we must not bother them. Come, we shall take a walk."

He got up, holding his head carefully so his crown didn't slip. Emma skipped up beside him to grab his hand and he flinched. His palm never had healed properly, in all these dozen years since the bird had torn it open. But that wasn't what had made him take to wearing thin leather gloves when he was around others. It was the scars. They'd taken on a strange look, the marks of the bird's claws making them look like runes, and he did not like what they spelled:

ᚲ ᚹ ᛖ ᚾ

Cwen.

She was out there, somewhere, waiting for the next man to have his chance at happiness, so she could try to ruin it again. They all knew it, but they didn't need to know she'd marked one of them. He would bear that burden alone. Even Brand didn't know.

"Where will you take us, Sir Ari?" asked Emma, drawing him back to the present.

He considered a moment. "I know where there is a spring with water so clear it almost isn't there."

"How can water not be there?" demanded Ranulf, ever the doubter. "If it isn't there, it isn't water. It is air."

"Then we will visit the air spring, and you can explain to me why you get wet when I push you in."

"You can't push me in, I am almost as big as you."

"I wager he can," said Emma.

"I wager he cannot," said Susanna.

"Beh," said Alexander, barely a year old.

Ari reached down to chuck the babe under the chin.

"Well said, lad. Come, Goda. Bring that wet dumpling along. The rest of you, too." He waved over the cook and groom and lady's maid who lingered near the wagon and tents. "We will give his parents more privacy. Perhaps they will sleep more soundly and end their *nap* sooner."

The collier girl, now grown and married and serving as nurse, chuckled knowingly. "I always liked midday naps myself."

"Midday, midmorning, midnight. They seem to enjoy naps at any and every hour." He said it loudly, hoping they'd hear, then led his procession off toward the spring. "Not that I blame them."

In the depth of the elf house, Steinarr and Marian— she'd finally given up on getting him to call her otherwise and decided to take the name *Marian* in all things—lay twined together on a bed of thick furs. They had brought the family out here on a whim, a diversion on the way to Huntingdon to see Robert, with no purpose for the stop other than the rekindling of pleasant memories. But now they must move on, and tonight, their last night here, all the children would be allowed to crawl into the elf house together. Only Alexander and Goda would be banished to the family tent on the far side of the clearing, next to the tent full of servants.

"I am glad you thought of coming here," she whispered. "I am even glad we brought the children, though it is more difficult to, um, let go with them and Ari chattering just outside."

"They are clear over by the stream," he said. "And I thought you, um, let go just fine." He slipped his hands up, filling them with the richness of her breasts, fuller now that she'd born four children. "However, if you would like to try again . . . ?" He rolled her nipples between his thumbs and fingers and she groaned.

"Devil." She pushed his hands down. "We should get dressed. I heard them wondering about our nap."

"Let them wonder. Can I not keep you here for a year, naked as those birds above?"

"They are not naked. They have feathers for clothes. I

cannot be naked if we are going to have the whole clan in here tonight."

"I should never have let Emma convince me I wanted them all in here with us."

"We had two nights of the magic ourselves. It is time to share."

"I am not certain they will appreciate the magic."

"They will," she said with certainty. "The elf magic is not about tupping. 'Tis about love. This is where I first began to love you. Did you know?"

"No, but I knew it was where I first began to love these." He curled down to taste her breast. "And this." He curled farther, to press a kiss into the curls between her thighs. "And this." He tipped her onto her back and pressed her knees apart and settled himself into her with a sigh.

"Devil," she whispered.

"And most especially you," he whispered, and he kissed her, long and slow, as he began to move.

ACKNOWLEDGMENTS

The Robin Hood story in its many incarnations has been a constant source of delight in my life since Richard Greene first made me want to be Maid Marian. It was inevitable that I would write a Robin Hood story myself, heavy on the romance that was largely missing from those old black-and-white reruns. Imagine my surprise when I discovered that there was even less of Marian in the original tales. Silly men.

You can find out more about those tales, movies old and new, TV shows, and the real life Robin at my favorite Robin Hood website, "Robin Hood, Bold Outlaw of Barnsdale and Sherwood," http://boldoutlaw.com.

Thanks to my own band of Merry Men and Women, who helped make this book a reality: my husband and two children; my editor, Kate Seaver; my agent, Helen Breitwieser; my whip, the inimitable R. Scott Shanks, Jr. (who has, since the last book in which I wished him praise and contracts, sold two stories. More! More!); and my good pal Sheila Roberts, who sets a good example, then kicks my butt just often enough to keep me honest.

A final acknowledgment (not thanks) goes to the plumbers who provided much financial motivation. To quote young Alexander, "Beh."